NATURE'S WARNINGS

NATURE'S WARNINGS

Classic Stories of Eco-Science Fiction

edited by

MIKE ASHLEY

BRITISH LIBRARY

This collection first published in 2020 by
The British Library
96 Euston Road
London NW1 2DB

Cataloguing in Publication Data
A catalogue record for this publication is available from the British Library

ISBN 978 0 7123 5357 1
e-ISBN 978 0 7123 6712 7

The cover and frontispiece illustrations are composite images combining multiple illustrations from the British Library collections, arranged and recoloured by Jonny Davidson. Cover design by Jason Anscomb.

Text design and typesetting by Tetragon, London
Printed in England by TJ International, Padstow, Cornwall, UK

CONTENTS

INTRODUCTION

Total Dependency

> *"Today we understand that the future of humanity very much depends on our planet, and that the future of the planet very much depends on humanity."*
>
> THE DALAI LAMA (*My Tibet*, 1990)

The ecological movement is stronger now than it has ever been and the harm that is happening to the planet, primarily because of human intervention, is at last being fully understood. It has even been suggested that we have moved into a new geological epoch, the Anthropocene, which recognizes the human impact upon the planet's ecosystems. Just when this began is still the subject of discussion, but dates range from twelve thousand years ago, with the start of agriculture, to as recent as 1945 and the dawn of the Atomic Age.

Whatever we call it, and whenever it began, no one can deny that the growth of human civilization has had an enormous impact on the planet, in many ways. The obvious one is pollution which began to have a significant impact with the Industrial Revolution and its effect upon our weather with the emission of carbon dioxide through burning fossil fuels. Another is our plundering of resources, exhausting the planet of vital minerals. Humans have also played their part in the extinction of animals over the last few centuries. The flightless moa bird which had lived in New Zealand for millennia was hunted to extinction following the arrival of humans in 1280 and had died out within two hundred years. Another flightless bird, the dodo was first recorded in 1598 and was last seen in 1662—its very name has become synonymous with extinction.

It's not just birds. The large wild cattle, the aurochs, were hunted to extinction by 1627. We all know how the American bison was hunted by settlers in North America, their numbers declining from the tens of millions to just a few hundred. How much longer will we be privileged to see a living black rhinoceros or a tiger?

We continue to have a severe impact upon wildlife by not understanding the relationship between animals and their environment. A well-known example is the introduction of the grey squirrel into Britain in the 1870s with a devastating effect upon the red squirrel population. Perhaps the most severe was the introduction of the European rabbit to Australia in the 1780s with its impact on vegetation and soil erosion.

Then there is the problem of invasive plants, such as Japanese knotweed, or the clearance of vast areas of forest or jungle, or the pollution of seas and oceans with plastic, which in turn leads to the destruction of sea life and coral. It was eventually realized that our attempts to control one form of pest with pesticides such as DDT had a detrimental effect on other organisms, including our own health. Indeed it was the problem of pesticides that encouraged Rachel Carson to produce her ground-breaking book *Silent Spring* in 1962 which effectively kick-started the environmental and ecological movement.

It's a depressing catalogue of disaster, and every one of these problems was caused by mankind initiating changes with no understanding or consideration of how they might affect the local ecosystem.

You might think that science fiction, with its eye on the future and its delight in exploring the alien, might have considered ecology much earlier than others. The word itself was only coined in 1873 by Ernst Haeckel, but prior to that writers did take note of pollution, plagues and other catastrophes though initially little of it was seen as a result of human intervention.

Little by little, however, writers did consider how humans were impacting upon the planet and how this might have a noticeable effect in the future or, indeed, on other planets. This anthology brings together early examples, almost all written before *Silent Spring*, where science fiction considered environmentalism or the long-term damage to our ecosystems, both on Earth and beyond. Some of these stories date back to the 1920s and even earlier, and though individually they did not have the impact that *Silent Spring* had, they do show an awareness of potential disaster. A remarkable early example, included here, is by Laurence Manning, a horticulturalist by trade, who in "The Man Who Awoke", from 1933, has a future environmentalist bemoan to a man from the present day how that generation has plundered all of Earth's natural resources. Nathan Schachner took his lead from Manning and depicted an Earth utterly devoid of almost everything in "The Sterile Planet" (1937).

Writers also considered the ramifications of humans exploring other worlds creating ecological puzzles that needed to be understood if the humans themselves were going to survive elsewhere in the universe. Two examples included here are "Drop Dead" by Clifford Simak and "A Matter of Protocol" by Jack Sharkey whilst, in "Hunter, Come Home", Richard McKenna shows how the determination to plunder other planets and change their ecosystems needs to be controlled.

These stories show that in the world of science fiction at least some awareness was made about the environment long before the rest of the world sat up and took notice. To show the full depth of this, the following explores how science fiction came to recognize environmentalism and the need to save the planet.

SAVING THE PLANET

It should not come as too much of a surprise that for centuries mankind gave little thought to the ecology of the planet and the role that humankind played. After all, the Bible stated that God commanded Adam and Eve to "have dominion… over every living thing."

That mantra continued for centuries. The British philosopher Francis Bacon declared in the 1620s that "The world was made for man, not man for the world…" In his utopia, *The New Atlantis*, written around 1623, Bacon explored man's control over nature. His world of Bensalem is "free from all pollution or foulness". It has tall towers which are used for "insolation, refrigeration and conservation" and from which they observe the weather.

For British writers the weather was always of concern. Weather control became a frequent theme in science fiction, starting, I believe, in Samuel Johnson's *Rasselas* (1759), though here the claim by the Astronomer that he can control the weather by power of his will seems somewhat dubious. More believable was the claim in *The Mummy* (1827) by Jane Webb that weather could be controlled locally by means of an "electrical machine". *The Mummy* also considered the problem of pollution, and in its future setting of the year 2126 the air in London is pure thanks to the abolition of coal and wood fires. Jane Webb, who became Jane Loudon after her marriage in 1831, was a leading horticulturalist of the day and her interest in plants and their environment encouraged her interest in pollution and the climate.

The pioneer of understanding nature was the Prussian polymath Alexander von Humboldt whose *Views of Nature* (1807) was one of the bestsellers of the day. It is impossible to overestimate the influence and significance of Humboldt's research and publications. He created weather maps with isotherms which allowed for a study and comparison of climatic conditions across the globe. He became aware how deforestation was affecting the weather. As Andrea Wulf reveals in her study of Humboldt, *The Invention of Nature* (2015), he believed that the intervention of humans upon the planet was "incalculable" and that if it continued it would be "catastrophic". Humboldt is the true godfather of ecology.

One of Humboldt's devotees was Jules Verne, who used Humboldt's books as research for his famous *voyages extraordinaire*. In *20,000 Leagues Under the Sea* (1870) Captain Nemo boasts that he has the complete works of Humboldt in his library aboard the *Nautilus*. Verne was also one of the first to consider the impact upon the climate of human intervention, albeit somewhat drastically. In *Sans dessus dessous* (1889), usually translated as *The Purchase of the North Pole*, the Baltimore Gun Club buy an island at the North Pole which they believe has rich coal deposits and to access it, they must first melt the ice. They plan to set off a series of huge explosions which will shift the Earth on its axis and remove the present tilt. They believe that by having the Earth rotate upright it will improve the planet's climate though they also recognize that melting the ice will raise sea levels, submerge some countries, elevate others, and possibly kill millions, none of which deters them!

Verne highlighted a problem which few writers at the time sought to resolve. A magnificent super-scientific idea with potentially marvellous results might well help some people but would almost certainly destroy the lives or livelihood of others. Writers needed to explore the interconnectivity between schemes and ideas to assess their overall benefits. Yet that was almost anathema to most proto-sf writers at the time. The preference was to write warning stories of impending catastrophes—pollution, plagues or storms—rather than seek solutions.

Whilst plagues and storms were implied to be of natural origin, pollution was another matter. The pollution of industrialized Britain was only too evident and writers concentrated on the effects and consequences rather than the solution. A potent example was *The Doom of the Great City* (1880) by William Delisle Hay, where smog suffocates London leaving many dead. However, the short story reprinted here, "The Dust of Death" (1903) by Fred M. White, did consider the cause and solution.

A rebellion against pollution and industrialization was inevitable. At one level it took the form of societies such as the National Trust, founded in 1895, to preserve and protect our environment and heritage. At another level, writers such as William Morris and Lord Dunsany created pre-industrial fantasies which considered a lost world of beauty and romance. Morris had already founded the Society for the Protection of Ancient Buildings as early as 1877 and through such books as *The Earthly Paradise* (1870), *News from Nowhere* (1890) and *The Story of the Glittering Plain* (1891) he began to invent worlds that recast life as it could be.

There was yet a third level, which was those books that considered the catastrophe imagined by Humboldt and explored a post-apocalyptic world. In *After London* (1885), Richard Jefferies depicts Britain after some unknown catastrophe where within a generation or two, "It became green everywhere…". Jefferies' future is not all sunshine and roses for the population of Britain has reverted to barbarism and tribalism, but his description of the aftermath of the catastrophe and the remains of what was London are powerful. At its heart, the book looks to mankind reverting to a simpler life, existing alongside nature, not trying to dominate it. A similar book was *A Crystal Age* (1887) by William Henry Hudson, which explores a future society long after civilization has collapsed and is barely remembered. The book's powerful message is of a society living in harmony with nature which is reflected in the beauty of the soul.

Alongside these books were others that explored the consequences of human activity. One that was especially topical was *The Decline and Fall of the British Empire* (1890) by the Australian Henry Marriott

Watson. He drew upon the vast engineering project then underway in central America—the construction of the Panama Canal. This had been started in 1881 by France but the project was beset by so many problems that it was halted until the United States took it over in 1904, and completed it in 1914. Watson was thus writing when the project was in hiatus but he believed that the completion of the canal would severely affect the Gulf Stream in the Atlantic, changing course into the Pacific. As a consequence, the British Isles, which benefitted from the warmth brought by the Gulf Stream, froze and the British Empire collapsed.

Interfering with the Gulf Stream became quite a theme during the construction of the Panama Canal. The American naturalist Louis P. Gratacap also had the Gulf Stream diverted when, in *The Evacuation of England* (1908), the completion of the Panama Canal caused the central American isthmus to collapse and the Atlantic flowed into the Pacific. Earlier, in *The Recovered Continent* (1898), the pseudonymous Oto Mundo has the aptly named Meddlers' Club acquire Greenland, melt the ice-cap by heat ray and turn the island over to forest and agriculture, its heat sustained by diverting the Gulf Stream.

In his short story "Within an Ace of the End of the World" (1900)*, Robert Barr showed how science and industry could destroy the planet without thinking. The growing world population and the demand for bread meant that the production of wheat needed to improve and that needed sodium nitrate as a fertilizer. Industrial plants were built to extract nitrogen from the atmosphere but this resulted in an oxygen-rich environment. Such was not only toxic for humans but a fire risk and the inevitable happened.

* This story is available in *The End of the World and Other Catastrophes*, also published by the British Library.

The outbreak of the First World War and the horrors of the devastation and slaughter on the battlefields caused further concern about mankind's role. In *The Terror* (serial, 1916) Arthur Machen saw nature, and in particular animals, turn against mankind as being unsuitable to run the planet. Violet Murray developed that idea in *The Rule of the Beasts* (1925) where, in the future, mankind succumbs to a devastating plague with only a few survivors. When they try to rebuild society, they discover that animals with increased intelligence have the upper hand and control any human development.

Man's control over the environment became the key for several stories featuring deranged master scientists who can influence the climate. The doyen of this type of story at the time was Murray Leinster. In "A Thousand Degrees Below Zero" (1919) his mad scientist creates a cold projector which freezes the oceans. In "The Silver Menace" (1919) it is the creation of a jelly-like creature that clogs the oceans. Whilst "The Storm That Had to be Stopped" (1930) has his scientist create a method to stop the circulation of heat resulting in gigantic storms. Leinster also gave detailed consideration to mankind's effect upon the environment. At the start of "The Mad Planet" (1920) he looks back over the millennia to the end of the twentieth century when the amount of carbon dioxide in the atmosphere, mostly due to the burning of coal and petroleum, had reached a critical stage, and when further CO_2 emerges through fissures in the Earth, the climate changes rapidly. The planet grows warmer. Storms increase. Plants can no longer exhale carbon dioxide and begin to die. Humans cannot breathe other than at high levels and before long the population declines. Humans do gradually adapt, their growth stunted. It takes thousands of years by which time the Earth's ecosystems have also changed significantly with a world of fungi, grasses, giant insects and intolerable heat. Humans have not seen the Sun for generations.

Leinster's stories were written on the grand scale, but the more detailed exploration of ecological balance came in small doses. Edgar Wallace occasionally dabbled with science fiction and in one of his lesser known stories of the Four Just Men, "The Man Who Hated Earthworms" (1921) he showed in miniature how one individual could devastate the Earth. A scientist has a morbid loathing of earthworms and has created a poison that would rapidly infect the planet and destroy the worms. Thankfully one of the Four Just Men gets to him first. As the story ends he explains the importance of the worm, saying: "There isn't a scientist in the world who does not agree that if the earthworm was destroyed the world would become sterile and the people of this world would be starving in seven years."

Taking his lead from Wallace, J. D. Beresford took matters much further in "The Man Who Hated Flies" (1929), which is reprinted here. At this same time Alfred Stewart, a professor of chemistry who wrote under the alias J. J. Connington, produced *Nordenholt's Million* (1923) which effectively launched the eco-catastrophe sub-genre. It tells of a dabbler in science who has been experimenting with strains of bacteria for affecting plant growth, one group being a denitrifying bacteria which halts plant development. During a storm the incubators with the bacteria are destroyed and it spreads rapidly round the world, carried by air currents. Before long plants die, food shortages begin and much of the world's population dies.

It was also in the 1920s that several studies appeared revealing the impact of humans upon animal and plant life. In *The Population Problem* (1922), Alexander Carr-Saunders demonstrated how the growing density of human population was influencing the environment. Charles Elton built upon this in *Animal Ecology* (1927) which explored the niche different animals had in the overall ecosystem, including the food chain.

Interestingly the food chain was picked up by pulp writer Edmond Hamilton, though I have no idea if he had read Elton's book. In "The Plant Revolt" (1930) he has a mad scientist fill the atmosphere with nutrients to encourage plants to grow, but it also makes them mobile! Hamilton was amongst the first to consider environmentalism on other worlds. In "A Conquest of Two Worlds" (1932) he depicts humans plundering the resources of Mars and Jupiter and causing genocide amongst the natives. P. Schuyler Miller built upon this in "The Forgotten Man of Space"* (1933) where a prospector abandoned on Mars takes it upon himself to protect the local fauna from destruction.

Back on Earth, John Beynon Harris (better known as John Wyndham) showed how plants could be used in biological warfare. In "Spheres of Hell" (1933) the leader of an imaginary Asian nation, which is in conflict with Britain, sends the spores of an invasive plant to Britain which multiplies rapidly and swamps the countryside.

In his short novel "The Metal Doom" (1932), which is spoiled by the author's racist and other prejudicial views, David H. Keller implies that mankind has become too detached from nature which now seeks its revenge, resulting in a disease which rots all metals and rapidly brings an end to civilization.

In the 1930s, the pulp writer who best expressed mankind's relationship with nature was the Canadian gardener and nurseryman Laurence Manning. In his series, "The Man Who Awoke" (1933) we follow the banker Norman Winters who, by suspended animation, sleeps his way into the future, awaking at certain times and exploring the locality. We thus have an episodic future history. In the first story, which is reprinted here, he encounters a society in the year 5000, which has reverted to nature and which views our own period as the Age of Waste. It asks the sobering question, "...for what should we thank the humans of

* This story is available in *Lost Mars*, also published by the British Library.

three thousand years ago?" Fellow pulpster Nathan Schachner took his lead from this story with "Sterile Planet" (1937), also reprinted here, and which shows the ultimate fate of the Earth if no thought is given to how we treat the planet and its resources.

This same dichotomy is multiplied in manifold ways when trying to understand the ecology of another world. Stanley G. Weinbaum had much fun with creating strange creatures ideally suited to their world in several stories starting with "A Martian Odyssey"* (1934) and including "The Lotus Eaters" (1935) and "Flight on Titan" (1935). Pulp writers, especially those writing for John W. Campbell, Jr's *Astounding* (later *Analog*) and Horace Gold's *Galaxy*, enjoyed developing ecological puzzles that human explorers had to resolve if they wanted to survive. Eric Frank Russell produced a complex and almost unresolvable problem in "Symbiotica" (1943) where it only gradually becomes evident how reliant and supportive one plant or animal species is upon another including possible higher life-forms of which the humans are unaware.

The master of these puzzle worlds was Clifford D. Simak. He started in a small way with "Tools" (1942) in which explorers on Venus unwittingly allow an intelligent gaseous life-form access to their tools, which the beings did not hitherto have, and once equipped they soon take control. In "Ogre" (1944) those seeking to plunder the resources of a world in which there are strange forms of plant-life find themselves in peril. In "You'll Never Go Home Again" (1951) it's a microbe that attacks their spaceship that makes explorers realize they are trapped. Arguably his best exploration of the theme is "Drop Dead" (1956), which is included here.

In "The Lonely Planet" (1949) Murray Leinster introduced the idea of a planet covered by a single, sentient being—the oldest creature in the universe. The concept was later considered by James Lovelock in

* This story is also available in *Lost Mars*, published by the British Library.

his ground-breaking book *Gaia: A New Look at Life on Earth*, published in 1979. It was not new to science fiction or fantasy writers. Elements of it had been propounded by the German philosopher Gustav Fechner in *Zend-Avesta* (1851) and was developed by perhaps Fechner's greatest literary disciple Algernon Blackwood in *The Centaur* (1911) and various short stories. Blackwood believed that the Earth had a consciousness of its own, a literal Mother Earth, and that some of our mythical visions such as centaurs and fairies, were manifestations of the Earth spirit. The idea was further explored by Sir Arthur Conan Doyle in "When the World Screamed" (1928) in which the planet reacts violently to deep drilling through its crust. Edmond Hamilton suggests a specific being in "The Earth-Brain" (1932) which is housed in a mountain near the North Pole and is generally oblivious to the flora and fauna on the planet's surface until humans interfere. Of more recent vintage the idea of a sentient world was developed powerfully by the Polish writer Stanisław Lem in *Solaris* (1961).

In the decade or so after World War II, particularly in Britain, there was a deluge of eco-catastrophe novels. These included *Death of a World* (1948) by J. Jefferson Farjeon in which a host of possible weapons, including bacteriological and weather control, rapidly cause the destruction of life on Earth; *Not in Our Stars* (1949) by Edward Hyams where a fungus for plant control is used in biological warfare; *The Day of the Triffids* (1951) by John Wyndham, in which mobile plants developed experimentally, possibly in the Soviet Union, break free and wreak havoc on a world struck blind; *The Death of Grass* (1956) by John Christopher where a virus destroys all grass-related crops; *A Scent of New-Mown Hay* (1958) by John Blackburn, where a plague virus is released in northern Russia and spreads rapidly with a horrible effect upon humans; and *The Furies* (1966) by Keith Roberts in which experiments result in a huge strain of wasps. The pinnacle of these post-war catastrophes were those written by J. G. Ballard which began with *The Wind from Nowhere* (1961) where an unaccountable storm-wind ravages the planet. *The Drowned World* (1962) is the most ecologically sensitive for, although the rise in Earth's temperature is due to solar activity and has led to the melting of the ice-caps, the change in the planet's flora (in particular) results in a seeming regression to a prehistoric age.

It was in 1962 that Rachel Carson published the results of her studies about the adverse effect of pesticides upon the Earth in *Silent Spring* and this ushered in a new age of environmentalism, further encouraged by the remarkable "Earthrise" photo taken from lunar orbit on Christmas Eve 1968 by William Anders. Clifford Simak responded to the book with "Unsilent Spring" (1976), written with his son, Richard, which considers the ongoing effects upon humans of the impact of pesticides.

There have been many science-fiction novels and stories developing ecological themes since Carson's book, perhaps the best-known being *Ecotopia* (1978) by Ernest Callenbach. Ecotopia is a new country on the west coast of America which has isolated itself from the United States and endeavours to live by an ecological code of conduct. The book is attributed with kickstarting the "green" movement though, as I hope this anthology demonstrates, science fiction had been exposing environmental issues for generations.

MIKE ASHLEY

SURVEY TEAM

Philip K. Dick

Philip K. Dick (1928–1982) has become one of the best known and influential of all science-fiction writers, despite a relatively short career—barely thirty years—and an all-too short life—he was only 53 when he died. Most of his short fiction was published in the 1950s, produced at an astonishingly intense rate as if he were desperate to let the world understand his worries and concerns. Despite his creativity and diversity there is a central theme to so much of his work—that we should be wary of our surroundings and dealings with the world, as all is not how it seems. His creation of worlds of paranoia or alternate possibilities and probabilities are evident from his earliest stories, such as the classic "Impostor" (1953), with its devastating final line, through such novels as The Cosmic Puppets *(1957) and his best known* The Man in the High Castle *(1962). Perhaps Dick's ultimate paranoia is evident in his most popular book* Do Androids Dream of Electric Sheep? *(1968), successfully filmed as* Blade Runner *(1982), where, as in "Impostor", it becomes vital to distinguish humans from simulacra.*

The following story, first published in 1954, takes his paranoia beyond Earth.

HALLOWAY CAME UP THROUGH SIX MILES OF ASH TO SEE HOW the rocket looked in landing. He emerged from the lead-shielded bore and joined Young, crouching down with a small knot of surface troops.

The surface of the planet was dark and silent. The air stung his nose. It smelled foul. Halloway shivered uneasily. "Where the hell are we?"

A soldier pointed into the blackness. "The mountains are over there. See them? The Rockies, and this is Colorado."

Colorado... The old name awakened vague emotion in Halloway. He fingered his blast rifle. "When will it get here?" he asked. Far off, against the horizon, he could see the Enemy's green and yellow signal flares. And an occasional flash of fission white.

"Any time now. It's mechanically controlled all the way, piloted by robot. When it comes it really comes."

An Enemy mine burst a few dozen miles away. For a brief instant the landscape was outlined in jagged lightning. Halloway and the troops dropped to the ground automatically. He caught the dead burned smell of the surface of Earth as it was now, thirty years after the war began.

It was a lot different from the way he remembered it when he was a kid in California. He could remember the valley country, grape orchards and walnuts and lemons. Smudge pots under the orange trees. Green mountains and sky the colour of a woman's eyes. And the fresh smell of the soil...

That was all gone now. Nothing remained but grey ash pulverized with the white stones of buildings. Once a city had been in this spot. He could see the yawning cavities of cellars, filled now with slag, dried rivers of rust that had once been buildings. Rubble strewn everywhere, aimlessly...

The mine flare faded out and the blackness settled back. They got cautiously to their feet. "Quite a sight," a soldier murmured.

"It was a lot different before," Halloway said.

"Was it? I was born undersurface."

"In those days we grew our food right in the ground, on the surface. In the soil. Not in underground tanks. We—"

Halloway broke off. A great rushing sound filled the air suddenly, cutting off his words. An immense shape roared past them in the blackness, struck someplace close, and shook the earth.

"The rocket!" a soldier shouted. They all began running, Halloway lumbering awkwardly along.

"Good news, I hope," Young said, close by him.

"I hope, too," Halloway gasped. "Mars is our last chance. If this doesn't work we're finished. The report on Venus was negative; nothing there but lava and steam."

Later they examined the rocket from Mars.

"It'll do," Young murmured.

"You're sure?" Director Davidson asked tensely. "Once we get there we can't come running back."

"We're sure." Halloway tossed the spools across the desk to Davidson. "Examine them yourself. The air on Mars will be thin, and dry. The gravity is much weaker than ours. But we'll be able to live there, which is more than you can say for this God-forsaken Earth."

Davidson picked up the spools. The unblinking recessed lights gleamed down on the metal desk, the metal walls and floor of the office. Hidden machinery wheezed in the walls, maintaining the air and temperature. "I'll have to rely on you experts, of course. If some vital factor is not taken into account—"

"Naturally, it's a gamble," Young said. "We can't be sure of all factors at this distance." He tapped the spools. "Mechanical samples and photos. Robots creeping around, doing the best they can. We're lucky to have *anything* to go on."

"There's no radiation at least," Halloway said. "We can count on that. But Mars will be dry and dusty and cold. It's a long way out. Weak sun. Deserts and wrinkled hills."

"Mars is old," Young agreed.

"It was cooled a long time ago. Look at it this way: We have eight planets, excluding Earth. Pluto to Jupiter is *out*. No chance of survival there. Mercury is nothing but liquid metal. Venus is still volcano and steam—pre-Cambrian. That's seven of the eight. Mars is the only possibility *a priori*."

"In other words," Davidson said slowly, "Mars *has* to be okay because there's nothing else for us to try."

"We could stay here. Live on here in the undersurface systems like gophers."

"We could not last more than another year. You've seen the recent psych graphs."

They had. The tension index was up. Men weren't made to live in metal tunnels, living on tank-grown food, working and sleeping and dying without seeing the sun.

It was the children they were really thinking about. Kids that had never been up to the surface. Wan-faced pseudo mutants with eyes like blind fish. A generation born in the subterranean world. The tension index was up because men were seeing their children alter and meld in with a world of tunnels and slimy darkness and dripping luminous rocks.

"Then it's agreed?" Young said.

Davidson searched the faces of the two technicians. "Maybe we could reclaim the surface, revive Earth again, renew its soil. It hasn't really gone that far, has it?"

"No chance," Young said flatly. "Even if we could work an arrangement with the Enemy there'll be particles in suspension for another fifty years. Earth will be too hot for life the rest of this century. *And we can't wait.*"

"All right," Davidson said. "I'll authorize the survey team. We'll risk that, at least. You want to go? Be the first humans to land on Mars?"

"You bet," Halloway said grimly. "It's in our contract that I go."

The red globe that was Mars grew steadily larger. In the control room Young and van Ecker, the navigator, watched it intently.

"We'll have to bail," van Ecker said. "No chance of landing at this velocity."

Young was nervous. "That's all right for us, but how about the first load of settlers? We can't expect women and children to jump."

"By then we'll know more." Van Ecker nodded and Captain Mason sounded the emergency alarm. Throughout the ship relay bells clanged ominously. The ship throbbed with scampering feet as crew members grabbed their jump-suits and hurried to the hatches.

"Mars," Captain Mason murmured, still at the viewscreen. "Not like Luna. This is the real thing."

Young and Halloway moved toward the hatch. "We better get going."

Mars was swelling rapidly. An ugly bleak globe, dull red. Halloway fitted on his jump helmet. Van Ecker came behind him.

Mason remained in the control cabin. "I'll follow," he said, "after the crew's out."

The hatch slid back and they moved out onto the jump shelf. The crew were already beginning to leap.

"Too bad to waste a ship," Young said.

"Can't be helped." Van Ecker clamped his helmet on and jumped. His brake-units sent him spinning upward, rising like a balloon into the blackness above them. Young and Halloway followed. Below them the ship plunged on, downward toward the surface of Mars. In the sky tiny luminous dots drifted—the crew members.

"I've been thinking," Halloway said into his helmet speaker.

"What about?" Young's voice came in his earphones.

"Davidson was talking about overlooking some vital factor. There is one we haven't considered."

"What's that?"

"The Martians."

"Good God!" van Ecker chimed in. Halloway could see him drifting off to his right, settling slowly toward the planet below. "You think there *are* Martians?"

"It's possible. Mars will sustain life. If we can live there other complex forms could exist, too."

"We'll know soon enough," Young said.

Van Ecker laughed. "Maybe they trapped one of our robot rockets. Maybe they're expecting us."

Halloway was silent. It was too close to be funny. The red planet was growing rapidly. He could see white spots at the poles. A few hazy blue-green ribbons that had once been called *canals*. Was there a civilization down there, an organized culture waiting for them, as they drifted slowly down? He groped at his pack until his fingers closed over the butt of his pistol.

"Better get your guns out," he said.

"If there's a Martian defence system waiting for us we won't have a chance," Young said. "Mars cooled millions of years ahead of Earth. It's a cinch they'll be so advanced we won't even be—"

"Too late now," Mason's voice came faintly. "You experts should have thought of that before."

"Where are you?" Halloway demanded.

"Drifting below you. The ship is empty. Should strike any moment. I got all the equipment out, attached it to automatic jump units."

A faint flash of light exploded briefly below, winked out. The ship, striking the surface…

"I'm almost down," Mason said nervously. "I'll be the first…"

Mars had ceased to be a globe. Now it was a great red dish, a vast plain of dull rust spread out beneath them. They fell slowly, silently, toward it. Mountains became visible. Narrow trickles of water that were rivers. A vague checker-board pattern that might have been fields and pastures…

Halloway gripped his pistol tightly. His brake-units shrieked as the air thickened. He was almost down. A muffled *crunch* sounded abruptly in his earphones.

"Mason!" Young shouted.

"I'm down," Mason's voice came faintly.

"You all right?"

"Knocked the wind out of me. But I'm all right."

"How does it look?" Halloway demanded.

For a moment there was silence. Then: "Good God!" Mason gasped. "A *city!*"

"A city?" Young yelled. "What kind? What's it like?"

"Can you see them?" van Ecker shouted. "What are they like? Are there a lot of them?"

They could hear Mason breathing. His breath rasped hoarsely in their phones. "No," he gasped at last. "No sign of life. No activity. The city is—it looks deserted."

"*Deserted?*"

"Ruins. Nothing but ruins. Miles of wrecked columns and walls and rusting scaffolding."

"Thank God," Young breathed. "They must have died out. We're safe. They must have evolved and finished their cycle a long time ago."

"Did they leave us anything?" Fear clutched at Halloway. "Is there anything left for *us?*" He clawed wildly at his brake-units, struggling frantically to hurry his descent. "Is it all gone?"

"You think they used up everything?" Young said. "You think they exhausted all the—"

"I can't tell." Mason's weak voice came, tinged with uneasiness. "It looks bad. Big pits. Mining pits. I can't tell, but it looks bad..."

Halloway struggled desperately with his brake-units.

The planet was a shambles.

"Good God," Young mumbled. He sat down on a broken column and wiped his face. "Not a damn thing left. Nothing."

Around them the crew were setting up emergency defence units. The communications team was assembling a battery-driven transmitter. A bore team was drilling for water. Other teams were scouting around, looking for food.

"There won't be any signs of life," Halloway said. He waved at the endless expanse of debris and rust. "They're gone, finished a long time ago."

"I don't understand," Mason muttered. "How could they wreck a whole planet?"

"We wrecked Earth in thirty years."

"Not this way. They've *used* Mars up. Used up everything. Nothing left. Nothing at all. It's one vast scrap-heap."

Shakily Halloway tried to light a cigarette. The match burned feebly, then sputtered out. He felt light and dopey. His heart throbbed heavily. The distant sun beat down, pale and small. Mars was a cold, a lonely dead world.

Halloway said, "They must have had a hell of a time, watching their cities rot away. No water or minerals, finally no soil." He picked up a handful of dry sand, let it trickle through his fingers.

"Transmitter working," a crew member said.

Mason got to his feet and lumbered awkwardly over to the transmitter. "I'll tell Davidson what we've found." He bent over thc microphone.

Young looked across at Halloway. "Well, I guess we're stuck. How long will our supplies carry us?"

"Couple of months."

"And then—" Young snapped his fingers. "Like the Martians." He squinted at the long corroded wall of a ruined house. "I wonder what they were like."

"A semantics team is probing the ruins. Maybe they'll turn up something."

Beyond the ruined city stretched out what had once been an industrial area. Fields of twisted installations, towers and pipes and machinery. Sand-covered and partly rusted. The surface of the land was pocked with great gaping sores. Yawning pits where scoops had once dredged. Entrances of underground mines. Mars was honeycombed. Termite-ridden. A whole race had burrowed and dug in trying to stay alive. The Martians had sucked Mars dry, then fled it.

"A graveyard," Young said. "Well, they got what they deserved."

"You blame them? What should they have done? Perished a few thousand years sooner and left their planet in better shape?"

"They could have left us *something*," Young said stubbornly. "Maybe we can dig up their bones and boil them. I'd like to get my hands on one of them long enough to—"

A pair of crewmen came hurrying across the sand. "Look at these!" They carried armloads of metal tubes, glittering cylinders heaped up in piles. "Look what we found buried!"

Halloway roused himself. "What is it?"

"Records. Written documents. Get these to the semantics team!" Carmichael spilled his armload at Halloway's feet. "And this isn't all. We found something else—installations."

"Installations? What kind?"

"Rocket launchers. Old towers, rusty as hell. There are fields of them on the other side of the town." Carmichael wiped perspiration from his red face. "They didn't die, Halloway. They took off. They used up this place, then left."

Doctor Judde and Young pored over the gleaming tubes. "It's coming," Judde murmured, absorbed in the shifting pattern undulating across the scanner.

"Can you make anything out?" Halloway asked tensely.

"They left, all right. Took off. The whole lot of them."

Young turned to Halloway. "What do you think of that? So they didn't die out."

"Can't you tell where they went?"

Judde shook his head. "Some planet their scout ships located. Ideal climate and temperature." He pushed the scanner aside. "In their last period the whole Martian civilization was oriented around this escape planet. Big project, moving a society lock, stock and barrel. It took them three or four hundred years to get everything of value off Mars and on its way to the other planet."

"How did the operation come out?"

"Not so good. The planet was beautiful. But they had to adapt. Apparently they didn't anticipate all the problems arising from colonization on a strange planet." Judde indicated a cylinder. "The colonies deteriorated rapidly. Couldn't keep the traditions and techniques going. The society broke apart. Then came war, barbarism."

"Then their migration was a failure." Halloway pondered. "Maybe it can't be done. Maybe it's impossible."

"Not a failure," Judde corrected. "They lived, at least. This place was no good any more. Better to live as savages on a strange world than stay here and die. So they say, on these cylinders."

"Come along," Young said to Halloway. The two men stepped outside the semantics hut. It was night. The sky was littered with glowing stars. The two moons had risen. They glimmered coldly, two dead eyes in the chilly sky.

"This place won't do," Young stated. "We can't migrate here. That's settled."

Halloway eyed him. "What's on your mind?"

"This was the last of the nine planets. We tested every one of them." Young's face was alive with emotion. "None of them will support life. All of them are lethal or useless, like this rubbish heap. The whole damn solar system is out."

"So?"

"We'll have to leave the solar system."

"And go where? *How?*"

Young pointed toward the Martian ruins, to the city and the rusted, bent rows of towers. "Where *they* went. They found a place to go. An untouched world outside the solar system. And they developed some kind of outer-space drive to get them there."

"You mean—"

"Follow them. This solar system is dead. But outside, someplace in some other system, they found an escape world. And they were able to get there."

"We'd have to fight with them if we land on their planet. They won't want to share it."

Young spat angrily on the sand. "Their colonies deteriorated. Remember? Broke down into barbarism. We can handle them. We've got everything in the way of war weapons—weapons that can wipe a planet clean."

"We don't want to do that."

"What *do* we want to do? Tell Davidson we're stuck on Terra? Let the human race turn into underground moles? Blind crawling things..."

"If we follow the Martians we'll be competing for their world. They found it; the damn thing belongs to them, not us. And maybe we can't work out their drive. Maybe the schematics are lost."

Judde emerged from the semantics hut. "I've some more information. The whole story is here. Details on the escape planet. Fauna and flora. Studies of its gravity, air density, mineral possessions, soil layer, climate, temperature—everything."

"How about their drive?"

"Breakdown on that, too. Everything." Judde was shaking with excitement. "I have an idea. Let's get the designs team on these drive schematics and see if they can duplicate it. If they can, we could follow the Martians. We could sort of *share* their planet with them."

"See?" Young said to Halloway. "Davidson will say the same thing. It's obvious."

Halloway turned and walked off.

"What's wrong with him?" Judde asked.

"Nothing. He'll get over it." Young scratched out a quick message on a piece of paper. "Have this transmitted to Davidson back on Terra."

Judde peered at the message. He whistled. "You're telling him about the Martian migration. And about the escape planet."

"We want to get started. It'll take a long time to get things under way."

"Will Halloway come around?"

"He'll come around," Young said. "Don't worry about him."

Halloway gazed up at the towers. The leaning, sagging towers from which the Martian transports had been launched thousands of years before.

Nothing stirred. No sign of life. The whole dried-up planet was dead.

Halloway wandered among the towers. The beam from his helmet cut a white path in front of him. Ruins, heaps of rusting metal. Bales of wire and building material. Parts of uncompleted equipment. Half-buried construction sections sticking up from the sand.

He came to a raised platform and mounted the ladder cautiously. He found himself in an observation mount, surrounded by the remains of dials and meters. A telescopic sight stuck up, rusted in place, frozen tight.

"Hey," a voice came from below. "Who's up there?"

"Halloway."

"God, you scared me." Carmichael slid his blast rifle away and climbed the ladder. "What are you doing?"

"Looking around."

Carmichael appeared beside him, puffing and red-faced. "Interesting, these towers. This was an automatic sighting station. Fixed the take-off for supply transports. The population was already gone." Carmichael slapped at the ruined control board. "These supply ships continued to take-off, loaded by machines and dispatched by machines, after all the Martians were gone."

"Lucky for them they had a place to go."

"Sure was. The minerals team says there's not a damn thing left here. Nothing but dead sand and rock and debris. Even the water's no good. They took everything of value."

"Judde says their escape world is pretty nice."

"Virgin." Carmichael smacked his fat lips. "Never touched. Trees and meadows and blue oceans. He showed me a scanner translation of a cylinder."

"Too bad we don't have a place like that to go. A virgin world for ourselves."

Carmichael was bent over the telescope. "This here sighted for them. When the escape planet swam into view a relay delivered a trigger charge to the control tower. The tower launched the ships. When the ships were gone a new flock came up into position." Carmichael began to polish the encrusted lenses of the telescope, wiping the accumulated rust and debris away. "Maybe we'll see their planet."

In the ancient lenses a vague luminous globe was swimming. Halloway could make it out, obscured by the filth of centuries, hidden behind a curtain of metallic particles and dirt.

Carmichael was down on his hands and knees, working with the focus mechanism. "See anything?" he demanded.

Halloway nodded. "Yeah."

Carmichael pushed him away. "Let me look." He squinted into the lens. "Aw, for God's sake!"

"What's wrong? Can't you see it?"

"I see it," Carmichael said, getting down on his hands and knees again. "The thing must have slipped. Or the time shift is too great. But this is supposed to adjust automatically. Of course, the gear box has been frozen for—"

"What's wrong?" Halloway demanded.

"That's Earth. Don't you recognize it?"

"Earth!"

Carmichael sneered with disgust. "This fool thing must be busted. I wanted to get a look at their dream planet. That's just old Terra, where we came from. All my work trying to fix this wreck up, and what do we see?"

"*Earth!*" Halloway murmured. He had just finished telling Young about the telescope.

"I can't believe it," Young said. "But the description fitted Earth thousands of years ago…"

"How long ago did they take off?" Halloway asked.

"About six hundred thousand years ago," Judde said.

"And their colonies descended into barbarism on the new planet."

The four men were silent. They looked at each other, tight-lipped.

"We've destroyed two worlds," Halloway said at last. "Not one. Mars first. We finished up here, then we moved to Terra. And we destroyed Terra as systematically as we did Mars."

"A closed circle," Mason said. "We're back where we started. Back to reap the crop our ancestors sowed. They left Mars this way. Useless. And now we're back here poking around the ruins like ghouls."

"Shut up," Young snapped. He paced angrily back and forth. "I can't believe it."

"We're Martians. Descendants of the original stock that left here. We're back from the colonies. Back home." Mason's voice rose hysterically. "We're home again, where we belong!"

Judde pushed aside the scanner and got to his feet. "No doubt about it. I checked their analysis with our own archaeological records. It fits. Their escape world was Terra, six thousand years ago."

"What'll we tell Davidson?" Mason demanded. He giggled wildly. "We've found a perfect place. A world untouched by human hands. Still in the original cellophane wrapper."

Halloway moved to the door of the hut, stood gazing silently out. Judde joined him. "This is catastrophic. We're really stuck. What the hell are you looking at?"

Above them, the cold sky glittered. In the bleak light the barren plains of Mars stretched out, mile after mile of empty, wasted ruin.

"At that," Halloway said. "You know what it reminds me of?"

"A picnic site."

"Broken bottles and tin cans and wadded up plates. After the picnickers have left. Only, the picnickers are back. They're back—and they have to live in the mess they made."

"What'll we tell Davidson?" Mason demanded.

"I've already called him," Young said wearily. "I told him there was a planet, out of the solar system. Someplace we could go. The Martians had a drive."

"A drive." Judde pondered. "Those towers." His lips twisted. "Maybe they did have an outer space drive. Maybe it's worth going on with the translation."

They looked at each other.

"Tell Davidson we're going on," Halloway ordered. "We'll keep on until we find it. We're not staying on this God-forsaken junkyard." His grey eyes glowed. "We'll find it, yet. A virgin world. A world that's unspoiled."

"*Unspoiled.*" Young echoed. "Nobody there ahead of us."

"We'll be the first," Judde muttered avidly.

"It's wrong!" Mason shouted. "Two are enough! Let's not destroy a third world!"

Nobody listened to him. Judde and Young and Halloway gazed up, faces eager, hands clenching and unclenching. As if they were already there. As if they were already holding onto the new world, clutching it with all their strength. Tearing it apart, atom by atom...

THE DUST OF DEATH

Fred M. White

Fred Merrick White (1859–1935) was a prolific contributor to the popular magazines at the start of the twentieth century. He wrote in all genres, mostly mystery, spy and historical, but also enjoyed exploring the potential danger of advancing science. His earliest work in the field was "The Island of Shadows", serialized in 1892, a rousing boys' adventure of an undersea island which is an entrance to a lost world. In The White Battalions *(1900) a scientist invents a super-explosive with which he blows up the Nicaraguan isthmus and allows the Pacific to pour into the Atlantic and disrupt the Gulf Stream. The result is that western Europe is frozen. His best known work is the series "The Doom of London" serialized in* Pearson's Magazine *during 1903. Each story subjects London to a new and devastating threat including fire, plague, snow and smog. The following threat is still with us today—pollution and what to do with our waste.*

THE FRONT DOOR BELL TINKLED IMPATIENTLY; EVIDENTLY somebody was in a hurry. Alan Hubert answered the call, a thing that even a distinguished physician might do, seeing that it was on the stroke of midnight. The tall, graceful figure of a woman in evening dress stumbled into the hall. The diamonds in her hair shimmered and trembled, her face was full of terror.

"You are Dr Hubert," she gasped. "I am Mrs Fillingham, the artist's wife, you know. Will you come with me at once… My husband… I had been dining out. In the studio… Oh, please come!"

Hubert asked no unnecessary questions. He knew Fillingham, the great portrait painter, well enough by repute and by sight also, for Fillingham's house and studio were close by. There were many artists in the Devonshire Park district—that pretty suburb which was one of the triumphs of the builder's and landscape gardener's art. Ten years ago it had been no more than a swamp; today people spoke complacently of the fact that they lived in Devonshire Park.

Hubert walked up the drive and past the trim lawns with Mrs Fillingham hanging on his arm, and in at the front door. Mrs Fillingham pointed to a door on the right. She was too exhausted to speak. There were shaded lights gleaming everywhere, on old oak and armour and on a large portrait of a military-looking man propped up on an easel. On a lay figure was a magnificent foreign military uniform.

Hubert caught all this in a quick mental flash. But the vital interest to him was a human figure lying on his back before the fireplace. The clean-shaven, sensitive face of the artist had a ghastly, purple-black tinge, there was a large swelling in the throat.

"He—he is not dead?" Mrs Fillingham asked in a frozen whisper.

Hubert was able to satisfy the distracted wife on that head. Fillingham was still breathing. Hubert stripped the shade from a reading lamp and held the electric bulb at the end of its long flex above the sufferer's mouth, contriving to throw the flood of light upon the back of the throat.

"Diphtheria!" he exclaimed. "Label's type unless I am greatly mistaken. Some authorities are disposed to scoff at Dr Label's discovery. I was an assistant of his for four years and I know better. Fortunately I happen to know what the treatment—successful in two cases—was."

He hurried from the house and returned a few minutes later breathlessly. He had some strange-looking, needle-like instruments in his hands. He took an electric lamp from its socket and substituted a plug on a flex instead. Then he cleared a table without ceremony and managed to hoist his patient upon it.

"Now please hold that lamp steadily thus," he said. "Bravo, you are a born nurse! I am going to apply these electric needles to the throat."

Hubert talked on more for the sake of his companion's nerves than anything else. The still figure on the table quivered under his touch, his lungs expanded in a long, shuddering sigh. The heart was beating more or less regularly now. Fillingham opened his eyes and muttered something.

"Ice," Hubert snapped, "have you got any ice in the house?"

It was a well-regulated establishment and there was plenty of ice in the refrigerator. Not until the patient was safe in bed did Hubert's features relax.

"We'll pull him through yet," he said. "I'll send you a competent nurse round in half-an-hour. I'll call first thing in the morning and bring Dr Label with me. He must not miss this on any account."

Half-an-hour later Hubert was spinning along in a hansom towards Harley Street. It was past one when he reached the house of the great

German savant. A dim light was burning in the hall. A big man with an enormous shaggy head and a huge frame attired in the seediest of dress coats welcomed Hubert with a smile.

"So, my young friend," Label said, "your face promises excitement."

"Case of Label's diphtheria," Hubert said crisply. "Fillingham, the artist, who lives close by me. Fortunately they called me in. I have arranged for you to see my patient the first thing in the morning."

The big German's jocular manner vanished. He led Hubert gravely to a chair in his consulting-room and curtly demanded details. He smiled approvingly as Hubert enlarged upon his treatment of the case.

"Undoubtedly your diagnosis was correct," he said, puffing furiously at a long china pipe. "You have not forgotten what I told you of it. The swelling—which is caused by violent blood poisoning—yielded to the electric treatment. I took the virus from the cases in the north and I tried them on scores of animals. And they all died.

"I find it is the virus of what is practically a new disease, one of the worst in the wide world. I say it recurs again, and it does. So I practise, and practise to find a cure. And electricity is the cure. I inoculate five dogs with the virus and I save two by the electric current. You follow my plans and you go the first stage of the way to cure Fillingham. Did you bring any of that mucous here?"

Hubert produced it in a tiny glass tube. For a little time Label examined it under his microscope. He wanted to make assurance doubly sure.

"It is the same thing," he said presently. "I knew that it was bound to recur again. Why, it is planted all over our big cities. And electricity is the only way to get rid of it. It was the best method of dealing with sewage, only corporations found it too expensive. Wires in the earth charged to say 10,000 volts. Apply this and you destroy the virus that lies buried under hundreds of houses in London. They laughed at me when I suggested it years ago."

"Underground," Hubert asked vaguely.

"Ach, underground, yes. Don't you recollect that in certain parts of England cancer is more common than in other places? The germs have been turned up in fields. I, myself, have proved their existence. In a little time, perhaps, I shall open the eyes of your complacent Londoners. You live in a paradise, ach Gott! And what was that paradise like ten years ago? Dreary pools and deserted brickfields. And how do you fill it up and level it to build houses upon?"

"By the carting of hundreds of thousands of loads of refuse, of course."

"Ach, I will presently show you what that refuse was and is. Now go home to bed."

Mrs Fillingham remained in the studio with Hubert whilst Label was making his examination overhead. The patient had had a bad night; his symptoms were very grave indeed. Hubert listened more or less vaguely; his mind had gone beyond the solitary case. He was dreading what might happen in the future.

"Your husband has a fine constitution," he said soothingly.

"He has overtried it lately," Mrs Fillingham replied. "At present he is painting a portrait of the Emperor of Asturia. His Majesty was to have sat today; he spent the morning here yesterday."

But Hubert was paying no attention.

The heavy tread of Label was heard as he floundered down the stairs. His big voice was booming. What mattered all the portraits in the world so long as the verdict hung on the German doctor's lips!

"Oh, there is a chance," Label exclaimed. "Just a chance. Everything possible is being done. This is not so much diphtheria as a new disease. Diphtheria family, no doubt, but the blood poisoning makes a difficult thing of it."

Label presently dragged Hubert away after parting with Mrs Fillingham. He wanted to find a spot where building or draining was going on.

They found some men presently engaged in connecting a new house with the main drainage—a deep cutting some forty yards long by seven or eight feet deep. There was the usual crust of asphalt on the road, followed by broken bricks and the like, and a more or less regular stratum of blue-black rubbish, soft, wet, and clinging, and emitting an odour that caused Hubert to throw up his head.

"You must have broken into a drain somewhere here," he said.

"We ain't, sir," the foreman of the gang replied. "It's nout but rubbidge as they made up the road with here ten years ago. Lord knows where it came from, but it do smell fearful in weather like this."

The odour indeed was stifling. All imaginable kinds of rubbish and refuse lay under the external beauties of Devonshire Park in strata ranging from five to forty feet deep. It was little wonder that trees and flowers flourished here. And here—wet, and dark, and festering—was a veritable hotbed of disease. Contaminated rags, torn paper, road siftings, decayed vegetable matter, diseased food, fish and bones all were represented here.

"Every ounce of this ought to have gone through the destructor," Label snorted. "But no, it is used for the foundations of a suburban paradise. My word, we shall see what your paradise will be like presently. Come along."

Label picked up a square slab of the blue stratum, put it in a tin, and the tin in his pocket. He was snorting and puffing with contempt.

"Now come to Harley Street with me and I will show you things," he said.

He was as good as his word. Placed under a microscope, a minute portion of the subsoil from Devonshire Park proved to be a mass of living matter. There were at least four kinds of bacillus here that

Hubert had never seen before. With his superior knowledge Label pointed out the fact that they all existed in the mucous taken from Fillingham on the previous evening.

"There you are!" he cried excitedly. "You get all that wet sodden 'efuse of London and you dump it down here in a heap. You mix with it a heap of vegetable matter so that fermentation shall have every chance. Then you cover it over with some soil, and you let it boil, boil, boil. Then, when millions upon millions of death-dealing microbes are bred and bred till their virility is beyond the scope of science, you build good houses on the top of it. For years I have been prophesying an outbreak of some new disease—or some awful form of an old one—and here it comes. They called me a crank because I asked for high electric voltage to kill the plague—to destroy it by lightning. A couple of high tension wires run into the earth and there you are. See here."

He took his cube of the reeking earth and applied the battery to it. The mass showed no outward change. But once under the microscope a fragment of it demonstrated that there was not the slightest trace of organic life.

"There!" Label cried. "Behold the remedy. I don't claim that it will cure in every case, because we hardly touch the diphtheretic side of the trouble. When there has been a large loss of life we shall learn the perfect remedy by experience. But this thing is coming, and your London is going to get a pretty bad scare. You have laid it down like port wine, and now that the thing is ripe you are going to suffer from the consequence. I have written articles in the *Lancet*, I have warned people, but they take not the slightest heed."

Hubert went back home thoughtfully. He found the nurse who had Fillingham's case in hand waiting for him in his consulting-room.

"I am just back from my walk," she said. "I wish you would call at Dr Walker's at Elm Crescent. He has two cases exactly like Mr Fillingham's, and he is utterly puzzled."

Hubert snatched his hat and his electric needles, and hurried away at once. He found his colleague impatiently waiting for him. There were two children this time in one of the best appointed houses in Devonshire Park, suffering precisely as Fillingham had done. In each instance the electric treatment gave the desired result. Hubert hastily explained the whole matter to Walker.

"It's an awful business," the latter said, "Personally, I have a great respect for Label, and I feel convinced that he is right. If this thing spreads, property in Devonshire Park won't be worth the price of slum lodgings." By mid-day nineteen cases of the so-called diphtheria had been notified within the three miles area known as Devonshire Park. Evidently some recent excavations had liberated the deadly microbe. But there was no scare as yet. Label came down again hotfoot with as many assistants as he could get, and took up his quarters with Hubert. They were going to have a busy time.

It was after two before Hubert managed to run across to Fillingham's again. He stood in the studio waiting for Mrs Fillingham. His mind was preoccupied and uneasy, yet he seemed to miss something from the studio. It was strange, considering that he had only been in the room twice before.

"Are you looking for anything?" Mrs Fillingham asked.

"I don't know," Hubert exclaimed. "I seem to miss something. I've got it—the absence of the uniform."

"They sent for it," Mrs Fillingham said vaguely. She was dazed for want of sleep. "The Emperor had to go to some function, and that was the only uniform of the kind he happened to have. He was to have gone away in it after his sitting today. My husband persuaded him to leave it when it was here yesterday, and—"

Hubert had cried out suddenly as if in pain.

"He was here yesterday—here, with your husband, and your husband with the diphtheria on him?"

Then the weary wife understood.

"Good heavens—"

But Hubert was already out of the room. He blundered on until he came to a hansom cab creeping along in the sunshine.

"Buckingham Palace," he gasped. "Drive like mad. A five-pound note for you if you get me there by three o'clock!"

Already Devonshire Park was beginning to be talked about. It was wonderful how the daily press got to the root of things. Hubert caught sight of more than one contents bill as he drove home that alluded to the strange epidemic.

Dr Label joined Hubert presently in Mrs Fillingham's home, rubbing his huge hands together. He knew nothing of the new dramatic developments. He asked where Hubert had been spending his time.

"Trying to save the life of your friend, the Emperor of Asturia," Hubert said. "He was here yesterday with Fillingham, and, though he seems well enough at present, he may have the disease on him now. What do you think of that?"

Hubert waited to see the great man stagger before the blow. Label smiled and nodded as he proceeded to light a cigarette.

"Good job too," he said. "I am honorary physician to the Court of Asturia. I go back, there, as you know, when I finish my great work here. The Emperor I have brought through four or five illnesses, and if anything is wrong he always sends for me."

"But he might get the awful form of diphtheria!"

"Very likely," Label said coolly. "All these things are in the hands of Providence. I know that man's constitution to a hair, and if he gets the disease I shall pull him through for certain. I should like him to have it."

"In the name of all that is practical, why?"

"To startle the public," Label cried. He was mounted on his hobby now. He paced up and down the room in a whirl of tobacco smoke. "It would bring the matter home to everybody. Then perhaps something will be done. I preach and preach in vain. Only the *Lancet* backs me up at all. Many times I have asked for a quarter of a million of money, so that I can found a school for the electrical treatment of germ diseases. I want to destroy all malaria. All dirt in bulk, every bit of refuse that is likely to breed fever and the like, should be treated by electricity. I would take huge masses of deadly scourge and mountains of garbage, and render them innocent by the electric current. But no; that costs money, and your poverty-stricken Government cannot afford it. Given a current of 10,000 volts a year or two ago, and I could have rendered this one of the healthiest places in England. You only wanted to run those high voltage wires into the earth here and there, and behold the millions are slain, wiped out, gone for ever. Perhaps I will get it *now*."

London was beginning to get uneasy. There had been outbreaks before, but they were of the normal type. People, for instance, are not so frightened of smallpox as they used to be. Modern science has learnt to grapple with the fell disease and rob it of half its terrors. But this new and virulent form of diphtheria was another matter.

Hubert sat over his dinner that night, making mental calculations. There were nearly a thousand houses of varying sizes in Devonshire Park. Would it be necessary to abandon these? He took down a large scale map of London, and hastily marked in blue pencil those areas which had developed rapidly of recent years. In nearly all of these a vast amount of artificial ground had been necessary. Hubert was appalled as he calculated the number of jerry-built erections in these districts.

A servant came in and laid *The Evening Wire* upon the table. Hubert glanced at it. Nothing had been lost in the way of sensation. The story of the Emperor's visit to the district had been given great prominence. An inquiry at Buckingham Palace had elicited the fact that the story was true.

Well, perhaps no harm would come of it. Hubert finished a cigar and prepared to go out. As he flung the paper aside a paragraph in the stop press column—a solitary paragraph like an inky island in a sea of white—caught his eye.

"No alarm need be experienced as to the danger encountered by the Emperor of Asturia, but we are informed that His Majesty is prevented from dining at Marlborough House tonight owing to a slight cold and sore throat caught, it is stated, in the draughts at Charing Cross Station. The Emperor will go down to Cowes as arranged tomorrow."

Hubert shook his head doubtfully. The slight cold and sore throat were ominous. His mind dwelt upon the shadow of trouble as he made his way to the hospital. There had been two fresh cases during the evening and the medical staff were looking anxious and worried. They wanted assistance badly, and Hubert gave his to the full.

It was nearly eleven before Hubert staggered home. In the main business street of the suburb a news-shop was still open.

A flaming placard attracted the doctor's attention. It struck him like a blow.

"Alarming illness of the Asturian Emperor. His Majesty stricken down by the new disease. Latest bulletin from Buckingham Palace."

Almost mechanically Hubert bought a paper. There was not much beyond the curt information that the Emperor was dangerously ill.

Arrived home Hubert found a telegram awaiting him. He tore it open. The message was brief but to the point.

"Have been called in to Buckingham Palace, Label's diphtheria certain. Shall try and see you tomorrow morning. Label."

London was touched deeply and sincerely. A great sovereign had come over here in the most friendly fashion to show his good feeling for a kindred race. On the very start of a round of pleasure he had been stricken down like this.

The public knew all the details from the progress of that fateful uniform to the thrilling eight o'clock bulletin when the life of Rudolph III was declared to be in great danger. They knew that Dr Label had been sent for post haste. The big German was no longer looked upon as a clever crank, but the one man who might be able to save London from a terrible scourge. And from lip to lip went the news that over two hundred cases of the new disease had now broken out in Devonshire Park.

People knew pretty well what it was and what was the cause now. Label's warning had come home with a force that nobody had expected. He had stolen away quite late for half-an-hour to his own house and there had been quite free with the pressmen. He extenuated nothing. The thing was bad, and it was going to be worse. So far as he could see, something of this kind was inevitable. If Londoners were so blind as to build houses on teeming heaps of filth, why, London must be prepared to take the consequences.

Hubert knew nothing of this. He had fallen back utterly exhausted in his chair with the idea of taking a short rest—for nearly three hours he had been fast asleep. Somebody was shaking him roughly. He struggled back to the consciousness that Label was bending over him.

"Well, you are a nice fellow," the German grumbled.

"I was dead beat and worn out," Hubert said apologetically. "How is the Emperor?"

"His Majesty is doing as well as I can expect. It is a very bad case, however. I have left him in competent hands, so that I could run down here. They were asking for you at the hospital, presuming that you were busy somewhere. The place is full, and so are four houses in the nearest terrace."

"Spreading like that?" Hubert exclaimed.

"Spreading like that! By this time tomorrow we shall have a thousand cases on our hands. The authorities are doing everything they can to help us, fresh doctors and nurses and stores are coming in all the time."

"You turn people out of their houses to make way then?"

Label smiled grimly. He laid his hand on Hubert's shoulder, and piloted him into the roadway. The place seemed to be alive with cabs and vehicles of all kinds. It was as if all the inhabitants of Devonshire Park were going away for their summer holidays simultaneously. The electric arcs shone down on white and frightened faces where joyous gaiety should have been. Here and there a child slept peacefully, but on the whole it was a sorry exodus.

"There you are," Label said grimly. "It is a night flight from the plague. It has been going on for hours. It would have been finished now but for the difficulty in getting conveyances. Most of the cabmen are avoiding the place as if it were accursed. But money can command everything, hence the scene that you see before you."

Hubert stood silently watching the procession. There was very little luggage on any of the cabs or conveyances. Families were going wholesale. Devonshire Park for the most part was an exceedingly prosperous district, so that the difficulties of emigration were not great. In their panic the people were abandoning everything in the wild flight for life and safety.

Then he went in again to rest before the unknown labours of tomorrow. Next morning he anxiously opened his morning paper.

It was not particularly pleasant reading beyond the information that the health of the Emperor of Asturia was mentioned, and that he had passed a satisfactory night. As to the rest, the plague was spreading. There were two hundred and fifty cases in Devonshire Park. Label's sayings had come true at last; it was a fearful vindication of his prophecy. And the worst of it was that no man could possibly say where it was going to end.

Strange as it may seem, London's anxiety as to the welfare of one man blinded all to the great common danger. For the moment Devonshire

Park was forgotten. The one centre of vivid interest was Buckingham Palace.

For three days crowds collected there until at length Label and his colleagues were in a position to issue a bulletin that gave something more than hope. The Emperor of Asturia was going to recover. Label was not the kind of man to say so unless he was pretty sure of his ground.

It was not till this fact had soaked itself into the public mind that attention was fully turned to the danger that threatened London. Devonshire Park was practically in quarantine. All those who could get away had done so, and those who had remained were confined to their own particular district, and provisioned on a system. The new plague was spreading fast.

In more than one quarter the suggestion was made that all houses in certain localities should be destroyed, and the ground thoroughly cleansed and disinfected. It would mean a loss of millions of money, but in the scare of the moment London cared nothing for that.

At the end of a week there were seven thousand cases of the new form of diphtheria under treatment. Over one thousand cases a day came in. Devonshire Park was practically deserted save for the poorer quarters, whence the victims came. It seemed strange to see fine houses abandoned to the first comer who had the hardihood to enter. Devonshire Park was a stricken kingdom within itself, and the Commune of terror reigned.

Enterprising journalists penetrated the barred area and wrote articles about it. One of the fraternity bolder than the rest passed a day and night in one of these deserted palatial residences, and gave his sensations to the Press. Within a few hours most of the villas were inhabited again! There were scores of men and women in the slums who have not the slightest fear of disease—they are too familiar with it for that—and they came creeping westward in search of shelter.

The smiling paradise had become a kind of Tom Tiddler's ground, a huge estate in Chancery.

Nobody had troubled, the tenants were busy finding pure quarters elsewhere, the owners of the property were fighting public opinion to save what in many cases was their sole source of income. If Devonshire Park had to be razed to the ground many a wealthy man would be ruined.

It was nearly the end of the first week before this abnormal state of affairs was fully brought home to Hubert. He had been harassed and worried and worn by want of sleep, but tired as he was he did not fail to notice the number of poorer patients who dribbled regularly into the terrace of houses that now formed the hospital. There was something about them that suggested any district rather than Devonshire Park.

"What does it mean, Walker?" he asked one of his doctors.

Walker had just come in from his hour's exercise, heated and excited.

"It's a perfect scandal," he cried. "The police are fighting shy of us altogether. I've just been up to the station and they tell me it is a difficult matter to keep competent officers in the district. All along Frinton Hill and Eversley Gardens the houses are crowded with outcasts. They have drifted here from the East End and are making some of those splendid residences impossible."

Hubert struggled into his hat and coat, and went out. It was exactly as Walker had said. Here was a fine residence with stables and greenhouses and the like, actually occupied by Whitechapel at its worst. A group of dingy children played on the lawn, and a woman with the accumulated grime of weeks on her face was hanging something that passed for washing out of an upper window. The flower beds were trampled down, a couple of attenuated donkeys browsed on the lawn.

Hubert strolled up to the house fuming. Two men were sprawling on a couple of morocco chairs smoking filthy pipes. They looked up at the newcomer with languid curiosity. They appeared quite to appreciate the fact that they were absolutely masters of the situation.

"What are you doing here?" Hubert demanded.

"If you're the owner well and good," was the reply. "If not, you take an' 'ook it. We know which side our bread's buttered."

There was nothing for it but to accept this philosophical suggestion. Hubert swallowed his rising indignation and departed. There were other evidences of the ragged invasion as he went down the road. Here and there a house was closed and the blinds down; but it was an exception rather than the rule.

Hubert walked away till he could find a cab, and was driven off to Scotland Yard in a state of indignation. The view of the matter rather startled the officials there.

"We have been so busy," the Chief Inspector said; "but the matter shall be attended to. Dr Label was here yesterday, and at his suggestion we are having the whole force electrically treated—a kind of electrical hardening of the throat. The doctor claims that his recent treatment is as efficacious against the diphtheria as vaccination is against smallpox. It is in all the papers today. All London will be going mad over the new remedy tomorrow."

Hubert nodded thoughtfully. The electric treatment seemed the right thing. Label had shown him what an effect the application of the current had had on the teeming mass of matter taken from the road cutting. He thought it over until he fell asleep in his cab on the way back to his weary labours.

London raged for the new remedy. The electric treatment for throat troubles is no new thing. In this case it was simple and painless, and it had been guaranteed by one of the popular heroes of the hour. A week before Label had been regarded as a crank and a faddist; now people were ready to swear by him. Had he not prophesied this vile disease for years, and was he not the only man who had a remedy? And the Emperor of Asturia was mending rapidly.

Had Label bidden the people to stand on their heads for an hour a day as a sovereign specific they would have done so gladly. Every private doctor and every public institution was worked to death. At the end of ten days practically all London had been treated. There was nothing for it now but to wait patiently for the result.

Another week passed and then suddenly the inrush of cases began to drop. The average at the end of the second week was down to eighty per day. On the seventeenth and eighteenth days there were only four cases altogether and in each instance they proved to be patients who had not submitted themselves to the treatment.

The scourge was over. Two days elapsed and there were no fresh cases whatever. Some time before a strong posse of police had swamped down upon Devonshire Park and cleared all the slum people out of their luxurious quarters. One or two of the bolder dwellers in that once favoured locality began to creep back. Now that they were inoculated there seemed little to fear.

But Label had something to say about that. He felt that he was free to act now, he had his royal patient practically off his hands. A strong Royal Commission had been appointed by Parliament to go at once thoroughly into the matter.

"And I am the first witness called," he chuckled to Hubert as the latter sat with the great German smoking a well-earned cigar. "I shall be able to tell a few things."

He shook his big head and smiled. The exertion of the last few weeks did not seem to have told upon him in the slightest.

"I also have been summoned," Hubert said. "But you don't suggest that those fine houses should be destroyed?"

"I don't suggest anything. I am going to confine myself to facts. One of your patent medicine advertisements says that electricity is life. Never was a truer word spoken. What has saved London from a great scourge? Electricity. What kills this new disease and renders it powerless? Electricity. And what is the great agent to fight dirt and filth with whenever it exists in great quantities? Always electricity. It has not been done before on the ground of expense, and look at the consequences! In one way and another it will cost London £2,000,000 to settle this matter. It was only a little over a third of that I asked for. Wait till you hear me talk!"

Naturally the greatest interest was taken in the early sittings of the Commission. A somewhat pompous chairman was prepared to exploit Label for his own gratification and self-glory. But the big German would have none of it. From the very first he dominated the Committee, he would give his evidence in his own way, he would speak of facts as he found them. And, after all, he was the only man there who had any practical knowledge of the subject of the inquiry.

"You would destroy the houses?" an interested member asked.

"Nothing of the kind," Label growled. "Not so much as a single pig-sty. If you ask me what electricity is I cannot tell you. It is a force in nature that as yet we don't understand. Originally it was employed as a destroyer of sewage, but it was abandoned as too expensive. You are the richest country in the world, and one of the most densely populated. Yet you are covering the land with jerry-built houses, the drainages of which will frequently want looking to. And your only way of discovering this is when a bad epidemic breaks out. Everything is too expensive. You will be a jerry-built people in a jerry-built empire. And your local authorities adopt some cheap system and then smile at the ratepayers and call for applause. Electricity will save all danger. It is dear at first, but it is far cheaper in the long run."

"If you will be so good as to get to the point," the chairman suggested.

Label smiled pityingly. He was like a schoolmaster addressing a form of little boys.

"The remedy is simple," he said. "I propose to have a couple of 10,000 volts wires discharging their current into the ground here and there over the affected area. Inoculation against the trouble is all very well, but it is not permanent and there is always danger whilst the source of it remains. I propose to remove the evil. Don't ask me what the process is, don't ask me what wonderful action takes place. All I know is that some marvellous agency gets to work and that a huge mound of live disease is rendered safe and innocent as pure water. And I want these things *now*, I don't want long sittings and reports and discussions. Let me work the cure and you can have all the talking and sittings you like afterwards."

Label got his own way, he would have got anything he liked at that moment. London was quiet and humble and in a mood to be generous.

Label stood over the cutting whence he had procured the original specimen of all the mischief. He was a little quiet and subdued, but his eyes shone and his hand was a trifle unsteady. His fingers trembled as he took up a fragment of the blue grey stratum and broke it up.

"Marvellous mystery," he cried. "We placed the wires in the earth and that great, silent, powerful servant has done the rest. Underground the current radiates, and, as it radiates, the source of the disease grows less and less until it ceases to be altogether. Only try this in the tainted areas of all towns and in a short time disease of all kinds would cease for ever."

"You are sure that stuff is wholesome, now?" Hubert asked.

"My future on it," Label cried. "Wait till we get it under the microscope. I am absolutely confident that I am correct."

And he was.

THE MAN WHO HATED FLIES

J. D. Beresford

John Davys Beresford (1873–1947) is best remembered for The Hampdenshire Wonder *(1911), regarded as the first important novel about the next step in evolution in terms of human intelligence. As a child, Beresford suffered from polio and was confined to bed, spending long hours reading. He rebelled against his clergyman father's strict religious views and, for many years, was an avowed agnostic. His vision was always towards a better world but recognized that hurdles could not be overcome without some cataclysm. In* Goslings *(1913) a plague wipes out most men in Europe and Asia and humanity has to rediscover the basics to rebuild the world. In* Revolution *(1921) the social and political upheaval in a post-war England leads to famine and a breakdown in society. In* A Common Enemy *(1942) a series of earthquakes puts an end to the Second World War and eventually brings mankind to its senses. Beresford's literary spirit continued through his children, notably Elisabeth, the creator of the environmentally friendly Wombles.*

HIS WIFE LAUGHED AT THAT ONE WEAKNESS OF HIS; AND ALL his scientific explanations of the harm flies may do as germ-carriers, spreaders of disease, failed to convince her that his detestation of them was not an amusing eccentricity. She was one of those women who have a quiet contempt for science, although her husband was a scientist, and would almost certainly be famous in a few years' time, because he had the rare gift of becoming entirely absorbed by his work. There was no need for him to work. He had ample private means. But he always worked twelve hours a day.

"Ah! You want to improve the world too much," Madame Aumonier would say to her husband. "I am satisfied with it as it is. As for the flies you make so much fuss about, you may be sure Providence gave them to us for some good reason. Why don't you forget them?"

"I can't," Professor Aumonier would reply. "They worry me."

In his laboratory he was free from them, since they were strictly, scientifically excluded. But his brief hours of rest were spoiled for him seven or eight months out of the year; and he complained that the annoyance was telling upon his health, spoiling his work.

When he came in for his mid-day meal, still absent-mindedly intent upon his research, he would suddenly become aware of his tormenters. So often the skullcap he wore in the house, had been mislaid (he had been bald for ten years, although he was only thirty-seven); and the attractions of that smooth shining head, appeared to offer an irresistible attraction to the flies. Even when it was covered, he found little relief. The brutes would settle upon his face and hands; or engage one another with a maddening buzz close to his ear. They were so exasperatingly foolish, so completely careless of the wild waving of his handkerchief, so disdainful of his dignity, so impudent, so apparently unconscious of his rage.

He had had gauze blinds made for the windows, but they were always being taken down by Mme. Aumonier to air the rooms. They lived near Avignon, and it was very hot there in the summer months. Also, it was a great place for flies—all kinds of flies.

Their only child, Bertrand, a steady, intelligent little boy of seven who was doing very well at school, used to watch his father's impatient battles, with a quiet shrewd stare. And it was he who one day started the brilliant mind of Professor Albert Aumonier on that investigation which was to have such a vast and unanticipated influence on the future of the world.

"If you think flies do so much harm, father," the child thoughtfully remarked one day, after listening attentively to one of the Professor's fiercest lectures to his exasperatingly careless wife, who had had all the gauze blinds removed that morning on some absurd theory of giving the place a good clean: "Why don't you invent something to kill them all?"

In his uninstructed mind, he had no doubt some romantic idea of a super-trap, but the childish remark set the able mind of the Professor thinking in a new direction.

At the moment he merely shrugged his shoulders and replied: "If only I could, my little one"; following that up by a dissertation on the lassitude and indifference of the world at large. For if, as he said—he had said the same thing so often before, that his wife never even pretended to listen—if you could stimulate people to concerted action, the thing could be done. Scrupulous attention for a few years to the destruction of all waste and putrefying matter; the avoidance or treatment of all stagnant water; a little care and forethought exhibited by the many; and the pest of flies and mosquitoes could be greatly alleviated, and perhaps, finally, eliminated. "But the mass of the people are careless, indifferent, even to their own welfare," he concluded with a glance at his wife.

Nevertheless, that casual suggestion of his little son's returned to him that afternoon; got between him and his work, bothered him almost as much as the flies themselves.

And it so happened that that year they had a particularly trying summer. There was a very plague of insect life in early June; and the weather, the flies, and the consequent stimulus to solve the essential problem his son had set him, began to get on Aumonier's nerves.

It was no better when they went to Normandy in August; worse, in fact, for he had then neither the refuge of his laboratory nor the distraction of his work. He tried to forget the problem because it was obviously outside his proper sphere. He was an experimental chemist and was conducting some very important investigations in the realm of molecular physics. And although he would have been willing to admit that summer, that the achievement of ridding the world of flies would be one of far greater value to the community than any discovery he was likely to make relative to the constitution of matter, he felt that it was not his job.

On their way back to Avignon at the beginning of September, however, he stayed a night in Paris in order to call on a brother scientist, who was making a name as a biologist. This friend listened with interest to Aumonier's statement, but smilingly declined to undertake the proposed investigation. Nevertheless, he let fall one or two comments that were to have a decisive effect upon the future of the world.

"The thing to discover," he said, "would be some kind of highly infectious disease to which flies were subject, and—well, intensify it. As a matter of fact, it is known that flies do suffer from some disease that gets hold of them in wet summers—a sort of fungus. You'll find them wasted by it; almost transparent. Sometimes, too, as you've probably noticed, they get affected with a peculiar giddiness. It is at least, a theoretical possibility. But—" he smiled again, "it's not my job, Aumonier."

And Aumonier realized after this conversation, that it would never be anybody's job unless he made it his own.

He did not succumb immediately. That autumn, he still worked intermittently at his own research; but he began two new lines of reading, entomology and bacteriology. He had a wonderful memory; he could read all the principal European languages; and he learned very fast.

His wife only laughed when he told her what he proposed to do. It would not affect their income. "Ah! You want to improve the world too much"; she said. "No doubt, Providence sent the flies for some good purpose."

It took Professor Aumonier twenty years of arduous labour and experiment to solve his problem, and the great clue came at last almost by accident. The scientific reader will be able to follow in full detail the line of the research in Aumonier's tremendous monograph, modestly entitled "Musca Vulgaris". His Memoirs also provide much interesting material in this connection. It will be sufficient to recall, in this place, the broad lines upon which the experiments were conducted, noting more particularly what he, himself, never alludes to, the heroism of the researcher—typical as it is of so many of our inspired workers in the field of science.

For Aumonier began by making the immense sacrifice of all those peaceful hours of immunity he had hitherto spent in his laboratory. That refuge from which every fly had been strictly excluded, now became their very home and breeding-place; to which they were invited, nay, compelled, to come by every ingenious bait that could be devised. In short, Aumonier's laboratory now so swarmed with flies *all the year round*, that even his wife found it unendurable.

And there the devoted man studied every habit of the species, contributing incidentally a store of knowledge relative to insect life, such as Henri Fabre had never dreamed of. To quote but one instance, he discovered that within certain limits, individuals of the species could be educated, trained to come at a given signal for food, and tamed so far as to suffer a light touch.

But the core of the study was the observation of insect diseases and ailments; no less than nineteen of which he has convincingly diagnosed and described. No weakness in the world of flies escaped him, and the sufferers were caught, marked, isolated in gauze cages, kept under rigorous observation, and a "culture" made of their inferentially affected fluids. Other healthy flies were then brought into contact with the sufferers, or inoculated with the culture, until it may truly be said that Aumonier knew more of the diseases of the common house-fly than the most skilled physician knows of the diseases of humanity. Is there, indeed, any door to knowledge that cannot be opened by the life-work of such a mind as this?

Before proceeding to the Professor's supreme triumph, however, one curious side-issue must be noted: Aumonier, all unwittingly, cured himself. He who had been driven to fury and desperation by the torment of flies, became within twelve months, utterly indifferent to them, in this aspect. They had ceased to be an intrusion, becoming instead the single object of his interest. Indeed, in the later years of his research, he came, so one infers from his Memoirs, almost to love them. In the winter, at which season he tells us flies become more amenable to human influence, he had what can be described only as "pet" flies, which came to greet him when he entered the laboratory, would eat sugar from his finger, and stayed with him while he worked.

We find in his Memoirs, in fact, something like a note of regret when he announces that the long-sought culture had at last been found—the faint suggestion of a brief hesitation before he gave his discovery to the world. It may be that that note is due only to the regret of one who, having worked twenty years for a particular end, finds with its attainment a too sudden cessation of the familiar stimulus; but a passage here and there, unquestionably conveys the feeling that he suffered a qualm or two before promulgating the sentence that condemned every fly in the world to death.

For it was nothing less than that. The bacillus he had, as he admits, almost accidentally stumbled upon at last, was death to flies. None was immune. Moreover, the disease was almost incredibly infectious. The period of incubation was forty-eight hours, and during that time the infected fly which remained active and to all appearances healthy, could carry the germ far and wide.

The efficacy of the "A-A" germ, as it was called from the initials of its brilliant discoverer, was proved beyond all question within three months from its first trial. It was a hot summer again in the South of France that year, but in July there was never a fly or a blue-bottle to be found in the Rhone Valley from Lyons to Marseilles.

And Mme. Aumonier, grown stouter now, but not less placid, was one of the first to contribute to that meed of praise which was so soon to flow in upon her household from every corner of the habitable globe.

"Well, I will admit, Albert," she said complacently, "that it is rather a comfort to be rid of them. The meat keeps better."

Professor Aumonier absently stroked his fly-free bald head and looked wistfully about the room. "I am glad to have succeeded, Anastasie," he replied. "But for myself, I confess that I miss something."

In his son's "Life" of the Professor, we find a casual note that in his later years, he had a taste for having his head tickled with a feather.

If it were his work alone that he missed, he must have found some compensation in the invitations to lecture that now poured in upon him. The work of producing and intensifying the "A-A" culture was out of his hands. In every civilized country, laboratories had been established to carry on those operations, and he was free to go whither he would. He went. He had no other occupation, and the thought of foreign travel appealed to him.

He was in Chicago when the first disturbing suggestion of trouble reached him from Europe. It was no more than a paragraph in the London *Times*, relative to the new disease among bees, which had lately made its appearance in France and England. But the symptoms were described, and Aumonier guessed instantly that bees were not immune to some form of the "A-A" infection.

He paused thoughtfully for a few minutes on that inference, and then shrugged his shoulders. After all, every great discovery carried with it some minor disadvantage. And he made no mention of this new development in his lecture that evening. He was enjoying the magnificent reception America was giving him, a reception that was, if possible, heightened when it became known that mosquitoes had also proved susceptible to Aumonier's disease. In the Southern States, said the *New York Herald*, all the women were busy transforming mosquito-curtains to other household uses.

He was in Japan when, nearly a year later, he read of the strange failure of the fruit and vegetable crops in the West. There had been abundant blossom and the season had been favourable, but the fruit had not set on the trees or formed in the pods. One account, probably exaggerated, declared that there would not be a kilo of peas, that year, to be found in the whole of France.

And then, almost at once, everyone seemed to understand what was happening; to realize that the Aumonier disease was performing far more than it had promised; and that ten thousand forms of insect life, irrespective of species, were being rapidly eliminated. Nothing seemed to be exempt: butterflies, moths, beetles, ants, spiders, and (thank goodness!) fleas were vanishing from the economy of nature. And although no one except the entomologists would greatly regret any of them, humanity at large was suddenly brought face to face with facts that had been common knowledge since the days of Charles Darwin, namely, that the majority of fruits, vegetables and flowers are dependent for their existence upon the pleasant labour of the swarming world of insects.

Fortunately there are some notable exceptions to this dependence of vegetable upon insect life. Wheat, other cereals, and most grasses are fertilized by the action of wind current. Potatoes, forming tubers underground, are not influenced by the failure of the flowers to fruit. But such things as peas and beans failed at once; the whole cabbage tribe could no longer be propagated by seed; and the majority of fruits were so scarce that apples, pears, peaches and plums were fetching anything from ten to twenty dollars a pound in New York, three years after Aumonier's great discovery had been given to humanity. If the disease had affected house-flies only, it would not have mattered. They perform little or no work as pollen-carriers. But no one could have foreseen that every form of insect life would be involved.

There could be no question, now, that the world was faced with an unprecedented calamity. A form of scrofula was becoming endemic among the poorer classes; and a wasting anaemia; both due to the lack of the vitamines provided by fresh fruit and vegetables. Something was being done in the creation of a new industry, and a few years later it became a common sight to see men, women and children armed with long-handled camel-hair brushes, industriously carrying pollen from flower to flower of fruit trees and vegetable plants. But immense labour was required to do in a week what the myriads of busy little winged creatures had unconsciously performed in an hour. And fruit and vegetables from being the natural food of the many, had become a luxury for the few.

It was, indeed, a strangely altered world in those days! Gone were the majority of the sweet wild-flowers that had made beautiful the Northern Spring; and gone, too, were many forms of bird-life dependent for their food either upon flying insects or their grubs. And with the loss of insects and birds, something of music had gone from the Earth. The world was stiller than of old, less beautiful, noticeably moribund. There was less colour, less variety, less vitality.

Professor Aumonier had taken to living in retirement in his old age. Honours and degrees had been showered upon him; he had increased his already ample income; but he was not, he knew it all too well, any longer a popular figure.

There were active A.A. (Anti-Aumonier) Societies in most civilized countries; and their aims beside the apparently hopeless task of re-establishing insect-life, included forms of virulent propaganda designed to asperse the fame of the best-known scientist of the century.

So Aumonier kept apart from the world. In his thoughts it seemed to him as if the activities of the A.A. Societies was a form of persecution very like that he had once endured from flies. He was getting old, and his mind was apt to return to memories of his youth, skipping all the period that had intervened. He was little stirred when one day his son Bertrand came to see him after an absence of over three years.

Bertrand Aumonier, whose name now rivals that of his father, was not then famous, although he, too, had been for twenty years a patient, devoted student of science. But that day when he called upon his old father, he had the great announcement to make which soon put him on a level with the other celebrities of his time.

Aumonier, half dozing in his chair, with his wife incredibly stout now, but still placid as ever beside him, was sitting in the garden when Bertrand found him.

"I have made the great discovery," he announced quietly when he had greeted his parents. "I have discovered a rare fly on the upper Amazon, that although it stings human beings, is a honey-eater and a pollen-carrier. And it is, almost certainly, immune to the Aumonier disease. In a few years I hope to acclimatize it all over the world. It breeds rapidly, and I have every hope that it will soon become as numerous and as widely distributed as the old house-fly!"

Professor Aumonier roused himself a little, shook his head, and with a half-mechanical movement began to flap about him with his handkerchief.

His wife chuckled complacently. "Ah! you little Bertrand," she said. "You want to improve the world too much. No doubt, Providence had some good purpose in letting all the flies be killed. And we have all the vegetables we want here."

THE MAN WHO AWOKE

Laurence Manning

Laurence Manning (1899–1972) was a Canadian-born writer and nurseryman who later became a US citizen. He was also one of the founders of the American Interplanetary Society. Almost all of his best work appeared in the 1930s and was amongst the more thoughtful material appearing in the pulp magazines, rather than brash adventure. His first appearance was in collaboration with Fletcher Pratt with "The City of the Living Dead" (1930) where people have retreated into a world of virtual reality. Besides "The Voyage of the Asteroid*" and its sequel "The Wreck of the* Asteroid*" (both 1932), which showed the hazards of attempting to travel to first Venus and then Mars, most of Manning's work fell into two series. In "The Man Who Awoke", the first episode of which is reprinted here, a man of the year 2000 re-awakes at different periods in the future following the rise, fall, rise and deeper quest of humanity. The "Stranger Club" series are tales told by different adventurers as they explore unknown parts of the Earth.*

IT WAS IN ALL THE NEWSPAPERS FOR THE ENTIRE MONTH OF September. Reports came in from such out-of-the-way places as Venezuela and Monte Carlo: "MISSING BANKER FOUND." But such reports always proved false. The disappearance of Norman Winters was at last given up as one of those mysteries that can only be solved by the great detectives Time and Chance. His description was broadcast from one end of the civilized world to the other: Five feet eleven inches tall; brown hair; greyish dark eyes; aquiline nose; fair complexion; age forty-six; hobbies: history and biology; distinguishing marks: a small mole set at the corner of the right nostril.

His son could spare little time for search, for just a month before his disappearance Winters had practically retired from active affairs and left their direction to his son's capable hands. There was no clue as to motive, for he had absolutely no enemies and possessed a great deal of money with which to indulge his dilettante scientific hobbies.

By October only the highly paid detective bureau that his son employed gave the vanished man any further thought. Snow came early that year in the Westchester suburb where the Winters estate lay and it covered the ground with a blanket of white. In the hills across the Hudson the bears had hibernated and lay sleeping under their earthen and icy blanket.

In the pond on the estate the frogs had vanished from sight and lay hidden in the mud at the bottom—a very miracle in suspended animation for biologists to puzzle over. The world went on about its winter business and gave up the vanished banker for lost. The frogs might have given them a clue—or the bears.

But even stranger than these was the real hiding place of Norman Winters. Fifty feet beneath the frozen earth he lay in a hollow chamber a dozen feet across. He was curled up on soft eiderdown piled five feet deep and his eyes were shut in the darkness of absolute night and in utter quiet. During October his heart beat slowly and gently and his breast, had there been light to see by, might have been observed to rise and fall very slightly. By November these signs of life no longer existed in the motionless figure.

The weeks sped by and the snow melted. The bears came hungrily out of winter quarters and set about restoring their wasted tissues. The frogs made the first warm nights of spring melodious to nature-lovers and hideous to light sleepers.

But Norman Winters did not rise from his sleep with these vernal harbingers. Still—deathly still—lay his body and the features were waxy white. There was no decay and the flesh was clean and fresh. No frost penetrated to this great depth; but the chamber was much warmer than this mere statement would indicate. Definite warmth came from a closed box in one corner and had come from it all the winter. From the top of the chamber wall a heavy leaden pipe came through the wall from the living rock beyond and led down to this closed box. Another similar pipe led out from it and down through the floor. Above the box was a dial like a clock-face in appearance. Figures on it read in thousands from one to one hundred and a hand pointed to slightly below the two thousand mark.

Two platinum wires ran from the box over to the still figure on its piled couch and ended in golden bands—one around one wrist and one circling the opposite ankle. By his side stood a cabinet of carved stone—shut and mysterious as anything in that chamber. But no light was here to see by, only darkness; the black of eternal night; the groping stifling darkness of the tomb. Here was no cheering life-giving radiation of any kind. The unchanging leaden metal sealed in the air from which the dust had settled completely, as it never does on the surface of our world, and had left it as pure and motionless as crystal—and as lifeless. For without change and motion there can be no life. A faint odour remained in the atmosphere of some disinfectant, as though not even bacteria had been permitted to exist in this place of death.

At the end of a month Vincent Winters (the son of the missing man) made a thorough examination of all the facts and possible clues that the detectives had brought to light bearing upon his father's disappearance. They amounted to very little. On a Friday, September 8th, his father had spent the day on his estate; he had dinner alone, read awhile in the library, had written a letter or two and retired to his bedroom early. The next morning he had failed to put in an appearance for breakfast and Dibbs the butler, after investigating, reported that his bed had not been slept in. The servants had, of course, all been minutely questioned even though their characters were such as almost to preclude suspicion. One only—and he the oldest and most loyal of them all—had acted and spoken in answer to questions in a fashion that aroused the curiosity of Vincent Winters. This man was Carstairs, the gardener—a tall ungainly Englishman with a long sad-looking face. He had been for twelve years in the employ of Mr Winters.

On Friday night, about midnight, he had been seen entering his cottage with two shovels over his shoulder—itself, perhaps, not an incriminating circumstance, but his explanation lacked credibility: he had, he said, been digging in the garden.

"But why *two* shovels, Carstairs?" asked Vincent for the hundredth time and received the same unvarying answer: "I'd mislaid one shovel earlier in the day and went and got another. Then I found the first as I started home."

Vincent rose to his feet restlessly.

"Come," he said, "show me the place you were digging."

And Carstairs paled slightly and shook his head.

"What, man! You refuse?"

"I'm sorry, Mr Vincent. Yes, I must refuse to show you… *that*."

There were a few moments of silence in the room. Vincent sighed.

"Well, Carstairs, you leave me no choice. You are almost an institution on this place; my boyhood memories of the estate are full of pictures of you. But I shall have to turn you over to the police just the same," and he stared with hardening eyes at the old servitor.

The man started visibly and opened his mouth as if to speak, but closed it again with true British obstinacy. Not until Vincent had turned and picked up the telephone did he speak.

"Stop, Mr Vincent."

Vincent turned in his chair to look at him, the receiver in his hand.

"I cannot show you the place I was digging, for Mr Winters ordered me not to show it to anyone."

"You surely don't expect me to believe that!"

"You will still insist?"

"Most assuredly!"

"Then I have no choice. In case it were absolutely necessary to do so, I was to tell you these words. 'Steubenaur on Metabolism.'"

"What on earth does that mean?"

"I was not informed, sir."

"You mean my father told you to say that if you were suspected of his… er… of being connected with his disappearance?"

The gardener nodded without speaking.

"H'm… sounds like the name of a book…" and Vincent went into the library and consulted the neatly arranged card catalogue. There was the book, right enough, an old brown leather volume in the biological section. As Vincent opened it wonderingly an envelope fell out and onto the floor. He pounced upon this and found it addressed to himself in his father's handwriting. With trembling anxious fingers he opened and read:

"My dear son:

"It would be better, perhaps, if you were never to read this. But it is a necessary precaution. Carstairs *may* in some unforseen way be connected with my disappearance. I anticipate this possibility because it is true. He has in very fact helped me disappear and at my own orders. He obeyed these orders with tears and expostulation and was to the very end just what he has always been—a good and devoted servant. Please see that he is never in want.

"The discovery and investigation of the so-called 'cosmic' rays was of the greatest interest to us biologists, my son. Life is a chemical reaction consisting fundamentally in the constant, tireless breaking up of organic molecules and their continual replacement by fresh structures formed from the substance of the food we eat. Lifeless matter is comparatively changeless. A diamond crystal, for instance, is composed of molecules which do not break up readily. There is no change—no life—going on in it. Organic molecules and cells are termed 'unstable,' but why they should be so was neither properly understood nor explained until cosmic rays were discovered. Then we suspected the truth: The bombardment of living tissue by these minute high-speed particles caused that constant changing of detail which we term 'life.'

"Can you guess now the nature of my experiment? For three years I worked on my idea. Herkimer of Johns Hopkins helped me with the drug I shall use and Mortimer of Harvard worked out my ray-screen requirements. But neither one knew what my purpose might be in the investigations. Radiation cannot penetrate six feet of lead buried far beneath the ground. During the past year I have constructed, with Carstairs' help, just such a shielded chamber on my estate. Tonight I shall descend into it and Carstairs shall fill in the earth over the tunnel entrance and plant sod over the earth so that it can never be found.

"Down in my lead-walled room I shall drink my special drug and fall into a coma which would on the surface of the earth last (at most) a few hours. But down there, shielded from all change, I shall never wake until I am again subjected to radiation. A powerful X-ray bulb is connected and set in the wall and upon the elapse of my allotted time this will light, operated by the power generated from a subterranean stream I have piped through my chamber.

"The X-ray radiation will, I hope, awaken me from my long sleep and I shall arise and climb up through the tunnel to the world above. And I shall see with these two eyes the glory of the world that is to be when Mankind has risen on the stepping-stones of science to its great destiny.

"Do not try to find me! You will marry and forget me in your new interests. As you know, I have turned over to you my entire wealth. You wondered why at the time. Now you know. By all means marry. Have healthy children. I shall see your descendants in the future, I hope, although I travel very far in time: One hundred and twenty generations will have lived and died when I awaken and the Winters blood will have had time to spread throughout the entire world.

"Oh my son, I can hardly wait! It is nine o'clock now and I must get started upon my adventure! The call is stronger than the ties of blood. When I awaken you will have been dead three thousand years, Vincent. I shall never see you again. Farewell, my son! Farewell!"

And so the disappearance of Norman Winters passed into minor history. The detective agency made its final report and received its last check with regret. Vincent Winters married the next year and took up his residence upon his father's estate. Carstairs aged rapidly and was provided with strong young assistants to carry on the work of the place. He approached Vincent one day, years later, and made the request that he might be buried on the estate at the foot of the mound covered with hemlock and rhododendrons. Vincent laughed at the suggestion and assured him that he would live many a year yet, but the old gardener was dead within a year and Vincent had the tomb dug rather deeper than is usual, peering often over the shoulder of the labourer into the depth of the grave. But he saw nothing there except earth and stones. He erected a heavy flat slab of reinforced concrete on the spot.

"Most peculiar, if you ask me," said old Dibbs to the housekeeper. "It's almost as if Mr Vincent wanted Carstairs' stone to last a thousand years. Why, they cut the letters six inches deep in it!"

In due time Vincent Winters himself died and was buried beside the gardener at his earnest request. There remained no one on the earth who remembered Norman Winters.

CHAPTER II

AWAKENING—IN WHAT YEAR?

It was night and great blue sheets of flame lit the sky with a ghastly glare. Suddenly a blinding flash enveloped him—he felt a million shooting pains in every limb—he was lying on the ground helpless and suffering—he fell into a brief unconsciousness.

A dozen times he awakened and each time he shrieked with the pain in his whole body and opened his eyes upon a small room lit by a penetrating blue electric bulb. Numberless times he tried to move his right hand to shield his eyes but found he could not force his muscles to obey his will. Days must have passed, as he lay there, with sweat dotting his brow with the effort, and finally one day his hand moved up slowly. He lay a full minute recovering. He did not know where he was. Then from the depths of infinity a little memory came into his dulled brain; a memory with a nameless joy in it. And slowly his surroundings struck new meaning and a vast thrill coursed through him. He was awake! Had he succeeded? Was he really alive in the distant future?

He lay quiet a moment letting the great fact of his awakening sink in. His eyes turned to the stone cabinet beside his couch. Slowly his hand reached out and pulled softly at the handle and a compartment on the level of his face revealed two bottles of yellowish liquor. With gasping effort he reached one and dragged it over to him, succeeding in spilling a little of its contents but also in getting a mouthful which he swallowed. Then he lay quietly a full half hour, eyes purposefully shut and lips tightly pressed together in the agony of awakened animation, while the medicine he had taken coursed through his veins like fire and set nerves a-tingling in arms and legs and (finally) in very fingertips and toes.

When he again opened his eyes he was weak but otherwise normal. The stone cabinet now yielded concentrated meat lozenges from a metal box and he partook very sparingly from the second bottle of liquid. Then he swung his legs down from the eiderdown couch, now tight-compressed from its original five feet to a bare two feet of depth by his age-long weight, and crossed the chamber to the clock.

"Five thousand!" he read breathlessly, clasping his thin hands together in delight. But could it be true? He must get outside! He reached down to a valve in the leaden piping and filled a glass tumbler with cold water which he drank greedily and refilled and drank again. He looked about curiously to note the changes time had produced on his chamber, but he had planned well and little or nothing had deteriorated.

The lead pipe was coated with a few tiny cracks in its surface and particles of white dust lay in them, where the cold water had gathered the moisture of the air by condensation. But this could not have been helped, for the stream of water through this pipe was all that kept the tiny generator turning—that made possible the heated chamber and the final blaze of the specially constructed X-ray lamp that now filled his whole being with its life-restoring radiations.

Winters removed the cover from the power box and examined the motor and generator with great care. The chromium metal parts and the jewelled bearings showed no slightest sign of wear. Did that mean that only a few years had elapsed? He doubted his clock's accuracy. He replaced the covering and brushed off his hands, for everything was coated with dusty sediment. Next, Winters examined the heat elements and placed a glass container of water upon them to heat. With more of his meat concentrate he made a hot soup and drank it thankfully.

Now he went eagerly to the door in the lead wall and pulled at the locking lever. It resisted and he pulled harder, finally exerting all the strength he had in the effort. It was useless. The door was immovable! He leaned against it a moment, panting, then stooped and scrutinized the door-jamb. With a chill of dread he observed that the leaden chamber-wall had become coated at the crack with a fine white dust. It had rusted the door into place! Had he awakened only to die here like a rat in a trap?

In his weakened condition he felt despair creep over his body and mind helplessly. He again sank back on his couch and stared desperately at the door. It was hours before the simple solution to his difficulties occurred to him. The locking lever—of course! It was of stainless steel and held to the door only by one bolt. A matter of a dozen turns loosened the nut on this bolt and the lever came away freely in his hands.

With this bar of stout metal as a crowbar he easily pried into the soft lead wall beside the door-jamb and, obtaining a fulcrum, put his frail weight on the end of the lever. The door gave inward an inch! In a few minutes his efforts were rewarded. The door groaned protestingly as it swung open and Winters looked up the ancient stone steps, half-lit by the room's illumination. But in the open doorway a chill draught blew on his ragged and time-tattered garments and he went back to the chamber and commenced unscrewing a circular cover set into the wall.

It came away heavily with a hiss of air, for it had enclosed a near-vacuum, and Winters pulled out clothes neatly folded. He was relieved to find a leather jacket still strong and perfect. It had been well oiled and was as supple as new. Some woollen things had not fared so well, but stout corduroy breeches of linen fibre seemed well preserved and he put these on. A tightly covered crock of glass filled with oil yielded up a pistol designed to shoot lead bullets under compressed air and a neat roll of simple tools: a small saw, a file, a knife and a hand-axe. These he thrust into the waist-band of his breeches, which had been slit around the belt to accommodate them.

Now with a last look around, Norman Winters started up the steps, guided only by the light from the chamber behind. He stumbled over fallen stones and drifted earth as he climbed and at the top came to a mat of tree-roots sealing him in. And now the axe was wielded delicately by those enfeebled arms and many minutes passed in severing one small piece at a time. The cap-stone which had originally covered the tunnel had been split and pressed to one side by the force of the growing tree and after the third large root had been severed a small cascade of earth and pebbles let down on him a blazing flood of sunlight.

He paused and forced himself to return to his chamber; filled a glass bottle with water and slung it to his belt; put a handful of concentrated food in his pocket, and left the chamber for good, closing the door behind him and turning off the light.

It took a few minutes only to squeeze his head and shoulders through the opening between the roots and he looked about him with pounding heart.

But what was this? He was in the middle of a forest!

Upon all sides stretched the trees—great sky-thrusting boles with here and there a clump of lesser growth, but set so evenly and spaced so regularly as to betray human oversight. The ground was softly deep in dead leaves and over them trailed a motley of vine-like plants. Winters recognized a cranberry vine and the bright wintergreen berries among many others he did not know. A pleasant sort of forest, he decided, and he set off rather hesitantly through the trees to see what he could find, his mind full of speculations as to how long it must have taken these trees to grow. To judge from the warmth it must be about noon of a midsummer's day but what year? Certainly many of the trees were over 100 years old!

He had not progressed more than a hundred yards before he came upon a clearing ahead and, passing beyond a fringe of shrubs he came into full view of a great highway. North and south it stretched and he stamped his feet upon the strange hard surface of green glass-like material. It was smooth in texture and extraordinary straight and level. For miles he could look in both directions but, gaze as he might, no slightest sign of buildings could he detect.

Here was a poser indeed, where had the suburbs of New York gone? Had even New York itself joined the lost legion in limbo? Winters stood in indecision and finally started tramping northward along the road. About a mile further along had once been the town of White Plains. It was nearby and, even if no longer in existence, would make as good a starting point as any. His pace was slow, but the fresh air and bright sunshine set the blood coursing through his veins and he went faster as he felt his strength returning with each step. He had gone half an hour and seen no sign of human habitation when a man came out upon the glass roadway a hundred yards ahead of him. He was dressed in red and russet and held one hand over his eyes, peering at Winters, who hesitated and then continued to approach with a wild thrill surging through his veins.

The man seemed in some vague way different. His skin was dark and tanned; features full and rounded; and eyes (Winters observed as he got nearer) a soft brown. The supple body seemed alert and exuded the very breath of health, yet it was indefinably sensuous and indolent—graceful in movement. He could not for the life of him decide even what race this man of the future represented perhaps he was a mixture of many. Then the man made a curious gesture with his left hand—a sort of circle waved in the air. Winters was puzzled, but believing it was meant for greeting imitated it awkwardly.

"Wassum! You have chosen a slow way to travel!"

"I am in no hurry," replied Winters, determined to learn all he could before saying anything himself. He had to repress his natural emotions of excitement and joy. He felt an urge to shout aloud and hug this stranger in his arms.

"Have you come far?"

"I have been travelling for years."

"Come with me and I will take you to our orig. No doubt you will want food and drink and walling." The words were drawled and his walk was slow: so much so that Winters felt a slight impatience. He was to feel this constantly among these people of the future.

The surprising thing, when he came to think about it, was that the man's speech was plain English, for which he was thankful. There were new words, of course, and the accent was strange in his ears—a tang of European broad As and positively continental Rs. He was wondering if radio and recorded speech had been the causes of this persistence of the old tongue when they came to a pleasant clearing lined with two-storey houses of shiny brown. The walls were smooth as if welded whole from some composition plastic. But when he entered a house behind his guide he perceived that the entire wall admitted light translucently from outside and tiny windows were placed here and there purely for observation and air. He had little time to look around, for a huge dark man was eyeing him beneath bushy grey eyebrows.

"A stranger who came on foot," said his guide and (to Winters) "Our chief Forester." Then he turned abruptly and left them together, without the slightest indication of curiosity.

"Wassum, stranger! Where is your orig?" asked the Forester.

"My orig? I don't understand."

"Why, your village of course!"

"I have none."

"What! A trogling?"

"I don't understand."

"A wild man—a herman—don't you understand human speech?"

"Where I come from there were several forms of human speech, sir."

"What is this? Since the dawn of civilization two thousand years ago there has been one common speech throughout the world!"

Winters made an excited mental note of the date. Two thousand years then, at the least, had elapsed since he entered his sleeping chamber!

"I have come to learn, sir. I should like to spend several days in your village observing your life in… er… an elementary sort of way. For instance, how do you obtain your food here in the middle of a forest. I saw no farms or fields nearby."

"You are wassum to the walling, but farms—what are they? And fields! You will travel many a mile before you find a field near here, thanks to our ancestors! We are well planted in fine forests."

"But your food?"

The Forester raised his eyebrows. "Food—I have just said we have fine forests, a hundred square kilos of them—food and to spare! Did you walk with your eyes shut?"

"Where I come from we were not used to find food in forests, exactly. What sort of food do you get from them—remember I said I wanted elementary information, sir."

"Elementary indeed! Our chestnut flour for baking, naturally, our dessert nuts and our vegetables, like the locust bean, the Keawe, the Catalpea and a dozen others—all the food a man could desire. Then the felled logs bear their crops of mushrooms—we have a famous strain of beefsteak mushroom in this orig. And of course the mast-fattened swine for bacon and winter-fats and the pitch pines for engine oils—the usual forest crops. How can it be that you are ignorant of the everyday things which even schoolboys know?"

"Mine is a strange story, sir," replied Winters. "Tell me what I ask and I will tell you later anything you want to know about myself. Tell me things as though I were—oh, from another planet, or from the distant past," and Winters forced a laugh.

"This is a strange request!"

"And my story, when I tell it to you, will be stranger still—depend upon it!"

"Ha! Ha! It should prove amusing—this game! Well then, this afternoon I will spend showing you about and answering questions. After our meal tonight you shall tell me your story—but I warn you! Make it a good one—good enough to repay me for my time!"

They went out into the sunlight together. The village proved to be a gathering of about fifty large houses stretching for half a mile around a long narrow clearing. The background consisted of the huge trunks, gnarled branches and dark green of the forest. The Forester himself was a rather brisk old fellow, but the villagers seemed to strike again that vague chord of strangeness—of indolence—which he had noticed in his first acquaintance. Groups lay gracefully stretched out here and there under trees and such occasional figures as were in motion seemed to move with dragging feet, to Winters' business-like mind. It came upon him that these people were downright *lazy*—and this he afterwards observed to be almost invariably true. They accomplished the work of the village in an hour or two a day—and this time was actually begrudged and every effort was being made to reduce it. The chief effort of world-wide science was devoted to this end, in fact.

The people were dressed in bright colours and the green grass and the rich brown of the buildings made a background to the colourful picture. Everywhere he saw the same racial characteristics of dark, swarthy faces and soft, liquid, brown eyes. There was something strange about the eyes—almost as if they were not set straight in the face, but a trifle aslant. Very little attention was paid Winters, except for occasional glances of idle curiosity aroused by his unusual attire. He thought the women unusually attractive, but the men seemed somehow effeminate and too soft; not but that they were fine specimens of humanity physically speaking, but that their faces were too smooth and their bodies too graceful to suit his twentieth-century ideas of what vigorous manhood should look like. Their bodies suggested the feline—cat-like grace and lethargy combined with supple strength.

Winters was told that a thousand people usually formed an "orig." Just now there were several hundred extra inhabitants and a "colorig" had been prepared fifty miles to the north and trees had been growing for half a century there, making ready for the new colony.

"But why should you not simply make your village large enough to keep the extra people right here?"

"The forest supports just so many in comfort—we are having trouble now as it is."

"But are there no larger villages where manufacturing is done?"

"Of course. There are factory origs near the Great Falls in the north. Our air-wheel goes there twice a week—a two-hours' flight. But there are only a few people there; just enough to tend the machines."

The people of the village seemed happy and very much contented with life, but most of the younger men and women seemed to Winters too serious. Their dark faces hardly ever showed a smile. He entered several of the houses: among others that of the guild of cloth-makers. He was greatly interested, as if seeing an old friend, to observe wood-pulp fed through a pipe into the thread-making tubes to be hardened in an acid bath. He recognized, of course, the rayon process—new in his youth, but here considered ancient beyond history.

"How many hours a day do you work here?" he asked of the elderly attendant.

"I have worked three hours every day for the past week getting cloth ready for the new colonists," he replied grumblingly. "Perhaps we shall have some peace in this orig when the youngsters are gone! At least there will be plenty of everything to go around once again!"

As he spoke, a young man, evidently his son, entered the thread room and stared at his father and the Forester with cold, supercilious eyes. "Wassum!" said the attendant, but the youth merely scowled in reply. He examined Winters silently and with distrust and went out again without speaking.

"Your son is a solemn chap!"

"Yes. So is his generation—they take life too seriously."

"But do they never enjoy themselves?"

"Oh yes! There is the hunting moon in fall. The young men track the deer on foot and race him—sometimes for days on end—then throw him with their bare hands. My son is a famous deer-chaser. He practises all year long for the Autumn season."

"But are there no... er... lighter pastimes?"

"There are the festivals. The next one is the festival of autumn leaves. At the time of the equinox the young people dress in russets and reds and gold and dance in a clearing in the woods which has been chosen for its outstanding autumn beauty of colour. The young women compete in designing costumes."

"But the younger ones—the children?"

"They are at school until they are twenty years of age. School is the time of hard work and study. They are not permitted games or pastimes except such exercise as is needed to keep them in health. When they finish school, then they enter upon the rights and pleasures of their generation—a prospect which makes them work the harder to finish their schooling as soon as may be."

As they went out into the sunlight once more Winters observed a small airship settling down in the village campus. It was the air-wheel, the Forester said, and would not leave again until dusk.

"I have never been in one," said Winters.

"You *are* a trogling," exclaimed the Forester. "Suppose we go up for a short flight, then?" and Winters eagerly agreed. They walked over to the machine which Winters examined curiously. Here, at least, three thousand years of improvements were amply noticeable. The enclosed cabin would seat about twenty persons. There were no wings at all, but three horizontal wheels (two in front and one in the rear) above the level of the cabin. A propeller projected from the nose and this was still idling when they arrived. The Forester explained his wishes to the pilot who asked which direction they should prefer to take.

"South to the water and back!" put in Winters, with visions of the thriving New York metropolitan area of his day running through his memory. They took their places and the air-wheel rose gently and with only a faintly audible hum—it was practically silent flight and made at enormous speed.

In ten minutes the sea was in sight and Winters gazed breathless through the crystal windows upon several islands of varying sizes—clothed in the green blanket of dense forest. Slowly he pieced out the puzzle: there was Long Island, evidently, and over there showed Staten Island. Beneath him then lay the narrow strip of Manhattan and the forest towered over everything alike.

"There are ruins beneath the trees," said the Forester, noting his interest. "I have been there several times. Our historians believe the people of ancient times who lived here must have been afraid of the open air, for they either lived beneath the ground or raised stone buildings which could be entered without going out-of-doors: There are tunnels, which they used for roadways, running all beneath the ground in every direction."

CHAPTER III

"HE HAS AN APPENDIX!"

And now the airship turned about and as it did so Winters caught sight of one grey pile of masonry—a tower-tip—showing above the forest. Surely it must have taken thousands of years to accomplish this oblivion of New York! And yet, he thought to himself, even one century makes buildings old.

He scarcely looked out of the window on the way back, but sat engrossed in sad thoughts and mournful memories. They landed once more in the village clearing and he continued his tour under the Forester's guidance, but a recounting of this would be tedious. When the afternoon was over he had gathered a confusing mass of general information about life in the new age. Metals were carefully conserved and when a new colony was started its supply of metal utensils and tools was the final great gift of the parent villages. Farming was entirely unknown, and grain—which the Forester did not know except as "plant-seed"—was not used for food, although primitive races had once so used it, he said. Everything came from trees now, food, houses, clothing—even the fuel for their airships, which was wood alcohol.

The life of a villager was leisurely and pleasant, Winters decided. Hours of labour were short and the greater part of the day was devoted to social pleasures and scientific or artistic hobbies. There were artists in the village, mostly of some new faddist school whose work Winters could not in the least understand. (They painted trees and attempted to express emotions thereby.) But many beautiful pieces of sculpture were set about in some of the houses. Electric power was received through the air from the great Falls, where it was generated, and each socket received its current without wiring of any sort. The village produced its own food and made its own clothes and building materials, paper, wood-alcohol, turpentine and oils. And as this village lived so, apparently, did the rest of the world.

As Winters pictured this civilization, it consisted of a great number of isolated villages, each practically self-sufficient, except for metals. By taking the air-wheel from one village to the next and there changing for another ship, a man could make a quick trip across the continents and oceans of the globe. But science and art were pursued by isolated individuals, the exchange of ideas being rendered easy by the marvellously realistic television and radio instruments.

At dusk they returned to the Chief Forester's house for dinner.

"I must apologize to you for the food," said he. "We are on slightly curtailed supplies, due to our population having grown faster than our new plantings. Oh, you will have a good meal—I do not mean to starve you,—but merely that you will be expected not to ask for a second service of anything and excuse the absence of luxuries from my table." His great body dropped into an upholstered chair.

"Is there no way to arrange things except by rationing yourselves while you wait for the new forests to bear crops?"

The Forester laughed a trifle bitterly. "Of course—but at a price. We could easily fell some trees for mushroom growing (they grow on dead logs) and also we could cut into the crop of edible pith-trees a little before maturity—and so all along the line. It would set us back in our plans a few years at the most, but there is no use talking about it. The Council of Youth has claimed the Rights of its Generation. The future is theirs, of course, and they object to our spending any of their resources now. We older people are a little more liberal in our views—not selfishly, but on a principle of common-sense. There have been some bitter words, I'm afraid, and the matter is by no means settled yet—for their attitude is almost fanatical and lacks all reason. But there is no need to bother you with our local affairs," and he turned the conversation into other channels.

He was forever using the expression "thanks to our ancestors," a point which Winters noted with surprise. So far one thing had eluded Winters completely: that was the history of the past ages during which all these drastic changes had come about. When the time came that he was bade tell his story, at the conclusion of the meal, he thought a moment as to how he might best obtain this information.

"I have travelled far," he said. "But in time—not in distance."

The Forester held a forkful of food poised in the air, eyebrows raised.

"What nonsense is this?" he demanded.

"No nonsense… your mushrooms *are* delicious… I have succeeded in controlling the duration of a state of suspended animation. I went to sleep many years ago; woke up this morning."

The Forester was incredulous.

"How long do you pretend to have slept?"

"I don't know for sure," replied Winters. "My instruments showed a certain figure, but to be at all certain I should prefer that you tell me the history of the world. No need of anything but the rough outlines."

"Ha, Ha! You promised me a story and you are most ingenious in fulfilling your promise, stranger!"

"I am, on the contrary, absolutely serious!"

"I cannot believe it—but it may be an amusing game. Let me see… Last year the first breadfruit trees bore in the lower temperate zones of the earth (that is a piece of it in your plate). It has greatly changed our mode of life and it may soon be unnecessary to grind chestnut flour for baking."

"Interesting," replied Winters. "But go back a thousand years more."

The Forester's eyes opened wide. Then he laughed delightedly. "Good! It is no lowly boaster, eh! A thousand years… That would be about the time of the great aluminium process. As you know, prior to that time the world was badly in need of metals. When Koenig perfected his method for producing aluminium from clay the economics of the world was turned topsy-turvy and… what! Farther back than a thousand years!"

"I think you might try two thousand."

The Forester exploded with laughter and then sobered at a sudden thought. He glanced shrewdly at his companion a moment, and a slight coldness appeared in his eyes.

"You are not by any slightest chance serious?" he asked.

"I am."

"It is absurd! In those days the human body still had an appendix—that was just after the Great Revolution when the Wasters were finally overthrown and True Economics lifted her torch to guide the world on its upward path. Two thousand years ago! Thence dates all civilized history! Such archaic customs as organized superstitions, money and ownership by private people of land and a division of humanity into groups speaking different languages—all ended at that time. That was a stirring period!"

"Well then, go back another five hundred years."

"The height of the false civilization of Waste! Fossil plants were ruthlessly burned in furnaces to provide heat, petroleum was consumed by the million barrels, cheap metal cars were built and thrown away to rust after a few years' use, men crowded into ill-ventilated villages of a million inhabitants—some historians say several million. That was the age of race-fights where whole countrysides raised mobs and gave them explosives and poisons and sent them to destroy other mobs. Do you pretend to come from that shameful scene?"

"That is precisely the sort of thing we used to do," replied Winters, "although we did not call it by the same set of names." He could barely repress his elation. There could no longer be the slightest doubt of it—he was alive in the year 5000! His clock had been accurate!

The Forester's face was growing red. "Timberfall! You have been amusing long enough—now tell me the truth: Where is your orig?"

"I don't understand. I have told you the truth."

"Stupid nonsense, I tell you! What can you possibly hope to gain from telling such a story? Even if people were such fools as to believe you, you could hardly expect to be very popular!"

"Why," said Winters in surprise, "I thought you were so thankful for all your ancestors had done for you? I am one of your ancestors!"

The Forester stared in astonishment. "You act well," he remarked drily. "But you are, I am sure, perfectly aware that those ancestors whom we thank were the planners for our forests and the very enemies of Waste. But for what should we thank the humans of three thousand years ago? For exhausting the coal supplies of the world? For leaving us no petroleum for our chemical factories? For destroying the forests on whole mountain ranges and letting the soil erode into the valleys? Shall we thank them, perhaps, for the Sahara or the Gobi deserts?"

"But the Sahara and the Gobi were deserts five thousand years before my time."

"I do not know what you mean by 'your' time. But if so, all the more reason you should have learned a lesson from such deserts. But come! You have made me angry with your nonsense. I must have some pleasant sort of revenge! Do you still claim to be a living human from the Age of Waste?"

Winters' caution bade him be silent. The Forester laughed mischievously: "Never mind! You *have already* claimed to be that! Well then, the matter is readily proved. You would in that case have an appendix and... yes... hair on your chest! These two characteristics have not appeared in the last two thousand years. You will be examined and, should you prove to have lied to me, a fitting punishment will be devised! I shall try to think of a reward as amusing as your wild lies have proved."

His eyes twinkled as he pressed a button hidden in his chair arm and a minute later two young men entered. Winters was in no physical condition to resist and was soon stripped of his clothing. He was not particularly hairy of chest, as men of his age went, but hair there was unquestionably and the Forester stepped forward with an incredulous exclamation. Then he hurriedly seized the discarded clothing and felt the material carefully—examining the linen closely in the light of the electric lamp concealed in the wall.

"To the health room with him!" he cried.

Poor Winters was carried helplessly down a corridor and into a room lined with smooth white glass and set about with apparatus of an evident surgical nature. The place was odoriferous with germicide. He was held against a black screen and the Forester snapped on an X-ray tube and peered at his nude body through a mask of bluish glass. After a minute he left the room and returned again almost instantly with a book in his hands. He opened to a page of photographs and studied them carefully, once more peering at Winters through the mask. Finally he grunted in stupefaction and with close-pressed lips and puzzled eyes turned to the two attendants.

"He has an appendix—there can be no doubt of it! This is the most amazing thing I have ever imagined! The stranger you see before you claims to have survived from the ancient days—from the age of waste! And he has an appendix, young comrades! I must talk to the biologists all over the country—the historians as well! The whole world will be interested. Take him along with you and see that he is provided with walling for the night."

He turned to the door and Winters heard him in the next room talking excitedly over the radio-telephone. The two young attendants led him along the hall and as he passed he could observe that the Forester was speaking to a fat red-headed, red-faced man, whose features showed in the televisor—and who evidently was proving difficult to convince. Winters stared a minute for this was the first man he had seen whose face was anything except swarthy and slender.

Winters was led down the hall and permitted to resume his clothing. He was in an exalted mood. So his arrival in this new world was creating a stir after all! In the morning the air-wheel would perhaps bring dozens of scientists to examine into his case. He was beginning to feel weak and fatigued after his exciting day, but this latest thrill gave a last flip to his nerves and gave him strength just long enough to prove his own undoing.

One of the attendants hurried out of sight as they left the house. The other guided him along the edge of the village.

"We young members of the village have a gathering tonight, sir. It is called the Council of Youth and at it we discuss matters of importance to our generation. Would it be too much to ask that you address our meeting and tell us something of your experiences?"

His vanity was stirred and he weakly agreed, tired and sleepy though he was. The meeting place was just a little distance away, explained his guide.

In the meantime the youth who had hastened on ahead had entered a small room off the assembly hall. The room contained only three persons and they looked up as the newcomer entered.

"It is as we thought, comrades, the Oldsters have brought him here for some purpose of their own. He pretends to have slept for three thousand years and to be a human relic of the Age of Waste!"

The others laughed. "What will they try on us next?" drawled one lazily.

"Stronghold is bringing him here," continued the latest arrival, "and will persuade him to speak to us in the meeting, if he can. You understand the intent?"

There was a wise nodding of heads. "Does he know the law of the Council?"

"Probably, but even so it is worth the attempt—you know I'm not certain myself but that he may be from the old days—at least he is a startling good imitation. The man has hair on his body!"

There was a chorus of shocked disbelief, finally silenced by a sober and emphatic assurance. Then a moment of silence.

"Comrades, it is some trick of the Oldsters, depend upon it! Let the man speak to the Council. If he makes a slip, even a slight one, we may be able to work on the meeting and arouse it to a sense of our danger. Any means is fair if we can only prevent our inheritance being spent! I hear that the order to fell the half-matured pith-trees will go out tomorrow unless we can stop it. We must see what we can do tonight—make every effort."

When Winters arrived at the hall the three young men stood on the platform to welcome him. The room was low-raftered and about fifty feet square. It was filled with swarthy young men and women. The thing that most impressed Winters was the luxury of the seating arrangements. Each person sat in a roomy upholstered arm-chair! He thought of the contrast that a similar meeting-hall in his own times would have afforded—with its small stiff seats uncomfortably crowded together and its stuffy hot atmosphere.

The lighting was by electricity concealed in the walls and gave at the moment a rosy tint to the room, though this colour changed continually to others—now red or purple or blue—and was strangely soothing. There was a lull in the general conversation. One of the young leaders stepped forward.

"Comrades! This stranger is of another generation than ours. He is come especially to tell us of conditions in the ancient days—he speaks from personal experience of the Age of Waste, comrades, from which times he has survived in artificial sleep! The Forester of our orig, who is *old* enough to know the truth, has so informed us!" Winters missed the sarcasm. He was tired now and regretting that he had consented to come.

There was a stir of astonishment in the audience and a low growling laughter which should have been a warning, but Winters, full of fatigue, was thinking only of what he should say to these young people. He cleared his throat.

"I am not sure that I have anything to say that would interest you: Historians or doctors would make me a better audience. Still, you might wish to know how the changes of three thousand years impress me. Your life is an altogether simpler thing than in my day. Men starved then for lack of food and youth had no assurance of even a bare living—but had to fight for it." (Here there were a few angry cheers, much to Winters' puzzlement.) "This comfortable assurance that you will never lack food or clothing is, to my mind, the most striking change the years have brought."

He paused a moment uncertainly and one of the young leaders asked him something about "if we were perhaps trying to accomplish this assurance too quickly."

"I am not sure that I know what you mean. Your Chief Forester mentioned something today of a question of economics. I am not familiar with the facts. However, I understand you have a very poor opinion of my own times, due to its possibly unwise consumption of natural resources. We had even then men who warned us against our course of action, but we acted upon the belief that when oil and coal were gone mankind would produce some new fuel to take their place. I observe that in this we were correct, for you now use wood alcohol—an excellent substitute."

A young man leaped to his feet excitedly. "For that reason, comrades," he said in a loud voice, "this stranger of course believes his age was justified in using up all the oil and fuel in the world!"

There was a slow growling which ended in a few full-throated cries and an uneasy stirring about in the audience. Winters was growing dazed with his need for rest and could not understand what was going on here.

"What you say interests us very much," said another of the men on the platform beside him. "Was it very common to burn coal for its mere heat?"

"Yes. It burned in every man's house—in my house as well."

There was an ugly moving about in audience, as though the audience was being transformed into a mob. The mob, like some slow lumbering beast, was becoming finally aroused by these continual pin-pricks from the sharp tongues of its leaders.

"And did you also use petroleum for fuel?"

"Of course. We all used it in our automobiles."

"And was it usual to cut down trees just for the sake of having the ground clear of them?"

"Well... yes. On my own land I planted trees, but I must say I had a large stretch of open lawn as well."

Here Winters felt faint and giddy. He spoke quietly to the young man who had brought him. "I must lie down, I'm afraid. I feel ill."

"Just one more question will be all," was the whispered reply. Then aloud: "Do you think we of the Youth Council should permit our inheritance to be used up—even in part—for the sake of present comfort?"

"If it is not done to excess I can see nothing wrong in principle—you can always plant more trees... but I must say good night for I am..."

CHAPTER IV

REVOLT OF THE YOUTH

He never finished his sentence. A very fury of sound arose from the hall of the Council. One of the leaders shouted for silence.

"You have heard, comrades! You observe what sort of man has been sent to address us! We of Youth have a lesson to learn from the Age of Waste, it appears! At least the Oldsters think so! The crisis that has arisen is a small matter, but if we should once give in when will the thing stop? What must they think of our intelligence if they expect us to believe this three thousand-year sleep story? To send him here was sheer effrontery! And to send him here with *that* piece of advice passes beyond all bounds of toleration. Timberfall! There can be only one answer" (here he turned to glare at poor dazed Winters, stupefied by the effect of his long emaciation). "We must make such an example of this person as shall forever stamp our principles deep in the minds of the whole world!"

There were loud shouts and several young people rushed up on the platform and seized Winters.

"He has confessed to breaking the very basic laws of Economics!" shouted the leader. "What is the punishment?"

There were cries of "Kill him! Exile! Send him to the plains for life!" and over and over one group was chanting savagely "Kill him! Kill him!"

"I hear the sentence of death proposed by many of you," cried the leader. "It is true that to kill is to waste a life—but what could be more fitting for one who has wasted things all his life?" (Loud cries of furious approval) "To your houses, every one of you! We will confine this creature who claims to be three thousand years old in the cellar of this hall. In the morning we will gather here again and give these Oldsters our public answer! And comrades! A piece of news for your ears alone—Comrade Stronghold has heard that in the morning the Oldsters will issue a felling order on the immature pith-trees!"

And now was such a scene of rage and violence that the walls shook and Winters was dragged away with dizzy brain and failing feet and thrust upon a couch in a stonewalled room beneath the hall. He fell instantly in utter exhaustion and did not hear the tramp of departing feet overhead. His horror and fright had combined with his fatigue to render him incapable of further emotion. He lay unconscious, rather than asleep.

Above in the small room off the now empty hall three young men congratulated each other, their soft brown eyes shining exultantly, and chatted a few minutes in great joy that they had protected the rights of their generation, regardless of the means which had been used to this desirable end. They parted for the night with that peculiar circling movement of the hand that seemed to have taken the place of the ancient hand-shaking.

But while they talked (so swift does Treason run) a young man crouched in the shadows back of the Forester's house and fumbled with the latch of a small door on the forest side. As the young men were bidding each other good night, a voice was whispering swiftly in the ear of the Chief Forester, whose rugged face and bristling eyebrows betrayed in turn astonishment, indignation, anger and fierce determination.

Winters woke to watch a shaft of dawn-light lying upon the stone floor. His body was bruised from the rough handling he had received and his wasted muscles felt dull and deadened. But his brain was clear once again and he recalled the events of the meeting. What a fool he had been! How he had been led on to his own undoing! His eyes followed the shaft of light up to a grating set in the stone wall above his couch and he could see a little piece of sky softly blue there with a plump little cloud sailing in it, like a duck in a pond. There came upon him a wave of nostalgia. Oh to see a friendly face—or one homely thing, even a torn piece of newspaper lying on the cellar floor! But there was no use in such wishes. Thirty centuries lay between those things and himself—lay like an ocean between a shipwrecked sailor and his homeland.

And then came other thoughts, his natural fund of curiosity arising in him once again. After all, this age was a reaction against his own. There had been two extremes, that was all history would say of it. Truth lay in neither, but in some middle gentler path. Mankind would find the road in time—say another thousand years or more. But what difference to him now? In a few more hours he would be dead. Presently the young men would come for him and he would be their sacrifice for some fancied wrong. In his weakened condition the whole thing struck him as unutterably pathetic and tears welled into his eyes until they were brushed away as the bitter bracing humour of the situation dawned upon his mind. As he mused he was startled to notice a shadow pass across the window grating and he thought he heard low voices.

Now in an instant he was full of lively fears. He would not be taken to his death so tamely as this! He turned over on the couch to get upon his feet and felt a hard object beneath him. He felt and brought forth his revolver which he fell at once to examining—ears and senses attuned to hints of danger, though nothing further came. The weapon was an air-pistol firing.22 calibre lead slugs. It was deadly only at very close ranges—thirty feet or less, perhaps—and the extending lever compressed enough air for ten shots. It was something, at all events. Hastily he worked the lever, loaded and pulled the trigger to hear a satisfying "smack" of the lead against the stone wall.

Now his mind was working full tilt and he brought the file from his belt and turned to the grating above his couch. If he could sever the bars he could manage to squeeze through the window! To his amazement these bars proved to be of wood—and his heart lifted in hope. The saw was out of his belt and he was at work in an instant. By dint of much arm-ache he severed four of the bars in as many minutes. Day was now dawning apace and a panic of haste seized him; he brought the hand-axe into play and with three blows had smashed the remaining wood in the window. As he did so a shadow approached and a face was thrust forward, blocking out the light. Winters crouched below with pistol pointed, finger on trigger.

"Here he is!" said the face in shadow and Winters recognized the voice of the Chief Forester and held his fire.

"Take my hand, stranger, and climb up out of there. We have been looking for you half an hour. Oh, have no fear, we will not permit you to come to harm!"

But Winters was cautious. "Who will protect me?"

"Hurry, stranger! You have fallen afoul of our young hot-heads in the orig—I blame myself for not taking greater thought—but there are a hundred Oldsters here with me. You will be safe with us."

And now Winters permitted himself to be helped through the window and up into the full light of morning. He was surrounded by men who gazed at him with interest and respect. Their attitude calmed his last suspicions.

"We must hurry," said the Forester. "The younger men will resist us, I am afraid. Let us reach my own house as soon as possible."

The party started across the clearing and two young men appeared almost at once in the doorway of a building near by. At sight of Winters in the midst of the Oldsters they turned and raced off in separate directions, shouting some indistinguishable cry as they ran.

"We must go faster than this!"

A short fat man with a red face and reddish hair put his arm beneath Winters' shoulders and half carried him along. His face was familiar and Winters remembered the man he had seen in the televisor the day before. His strength was enormous and his energy indefatigable—a tie that drew Winters to him in this age of indolence. "I am Stalvyn of History at the next orig," he boomed at Winters as they hurried along. "You are so valuable to me that I hope you do not mind if I take a personal interest in your protection!"

They had a quarter of a mile to go and had half accomplished the distance when a mob of shouting youths burst from behind a house just ahead of them. There was a pause as though their natural disinclination to physical exertion might even yet prevent the clash. But their leaders were evidently urging them on and suddenly they charged down amid a shower of stones and waving of clubs. In an instant the shock was felt and a furious mêlée commenced—a primitive angry fight without science or direction.

Here two youths beat an elderly man senseless with clubs and sprang in unison upon the next victim. There some mature, full-muscled bull of a man ran berserk among striplings, crushing them in his great arms or flailing fists like hams at their onrushing faces. As they fought, they kept moving toward their objective and had gone almost another hundred yards before the youths retreated. The superior numbers of the older ones had swung the balance.

Fifty men, however, were all that remained around the Chief Forester. The others had either deserted the fight or been injured—perhaps killed, thought Winters, looking back at a score of still figures lying on the earth. The youths had retired only a hundred feet and still kept pace with the fugitives. Fresh bands of young men were hurrying from every direction and it would be a matter of minutes before the attack would recommence with the odds on the other side this time.

Winters and Stalvyn, his self-appointed bodyguard, had not taken part in the struggle, for they had been in the centre of the rescue party. Now they worked to the front of the party where the Forester strode along determinedly. Winters showed his pistol. "With this thing I can kill them as they run there. Shall I use it, sir?"

The Forester grunted. "Kill them, then. They are coming now to kill you!"

As he spoke the mob of youths rushed upon them in a murderous fury. The elder men closed together in a compact mass and Winters shot into the front rank of the attackers, to see three of them topple over and thereby lessen the shock of the charge, for those who followed tripped over the fallen. And now Stalvyn and the Forester stepped forward and around these immovable figures the fight raged. Winters crouched behind them, swiftly pulled back his lever, loaded bullets and pulled the trigger like an automaton in a nightmare. Cries of passion and pain mingled with the thud of blows and the panting gasps of the fighters. It was a savage scene, the more shocking because of the unfitness of these quiet people for such work.

Suddenly the attackers withdrew sullenly, bearing injured with them. Two dozen remaining Oldsters looked dazedly around—free now to proceed to shelter. Fifty or more figures lay about on the ground and the Forester called out to the watchers in the windows to come and give first aid to friend and foe alike. This work was commenced at once, but with characteristic slowness, and he led his little band to the door of his house and inside.

"Give the stranger some food and drink, Stalvyn," drawled a tall thin man with ungainly limbs, who proved to be the biologist from an orig nearly a thousand miles away. "If I know our Youth they would never have wasted sustenance on a man who was so soon to die!" and he smiled a lazy sardonic smile at Winters as he placed in his hands a tumbler full of brown liquid. "Drink it without fear. It will both stimulate and nourish."

Winters was in a state of collapse now and Stalvyn had to help him drink and then carried him over to a couch. The biologist spent a few minutes examining him. "He must rest," he announced. "There will be no questions asked him today. I will prepare some medicine for him." Whereupon everyone left the room and Winters swallowed more drink and dropped fathoms deep in slumber. A man was set to guard the door of his room and the biologist tended him day and night. For a full week he was not permitted to wake. He had vague impressions as he slept of being rolled over, bathed, fed, massaged and watched over—impressions that were as dreams in an ordinary sleep. Under such expert ministration the thin cheeks filled out and the wasted flesh became plump and smooth.

When Winters awoke it was late afternoon. His blood pulsed strongly through his body and he was wide awake the instant his eyes opened. There on a stool were set out his clothes, and he got to his feet and dressed. His belt still contained the pistol and hatchet as well as the smaller tools. Feeling like a new man he strode to the door and opened it, to be surrounded presently in another room by a swarthy group of a dozen of the greatest scientists in the world—for the news had by this time spread everywhere and there had been time for travel from the most distant points. And now there followed a long period of questions and examinations. Stalvyn and the historians plied him with posers as to the life and habits of his world; the biologists demanded the secret of his sleeping potion and control of the period of suspended animation; he was put before the fluoroscope and his appendix photographed; his measurements were taken and plaster moulds of his hand, foot and head were cast for a permanent record.

Through it all Winters had a feeling of consummation—this was one of the things he had planned when he set off on his voyage into the future. Here was sane intelligence taking advantage of his work and respecting him for his exploit. But one thing was lacking completely. He had no sense of belonging to these people. He had hoped to find gods in human form living in Utopia. Instead, here were men with everyday human passions and weaknesses. True, they had progressed since his day—but his insatiable curiosity itched to learn what the future might produce.

After an evening meal which all partook together, Winters retired to his room with the Chief Forester, the biologist and Stalvyn and the four men sat talking lazily.

"What do you plan to do now?" drawled the biologist.

Winters sighed. "I don't know exactly."

"I would ask you to settle down in my orig here," remarked the Forester, "but most of our young people and many of the Oldsters who should know better hold you to blame for the recent troubles. I am helpless before them."

"Hold *me* to blame!" exclaimed Winters bitterly. "What had I to do with it?"

"Nothing, perhaps. But the principle of the rights of the new Generation is still unsettled. The Council of Youth is obstinate and must be brought to see the sensible side of the matter. Their leaders pretend you, in some way, have been brought here to persuade them to cut down trees right and left at the whim of the nearest Oldster. Where it will end, I cannot say."

★

Stalvyn laid a friendly hand on his shoulder. "Human nature is seldom reasonable. Of course there is no logic in their attitude. Forget it! We will get you quietly into an airship and you shall come away from here and live with me. Together we will review and rewrite the history of your times as it has never been done!"

"Stop a moment! Do you mean that I shall have to escape secretly from this village?"

The others looked sheepish and the Forester nodded his head. "I am helpless in the matter. I could get perhaps twenty or thirty men to do my bidding—but you see, most of the villagers will not concern themselves with your fate. It is too much trouble to bother about it at all."

"Are they afraid of the youngsters?"

"No, of course not! They greatly outnumber the youths. They merely are not willing to work beyond the village figure of one hour and fifty minutes a day so they say. I'm afraid you will not find any men to take your side except the four of us and a handful of my oldest men. That's the way the world is made, you know!" and he shrugged his shoulders expressively.

"It is a simple matter to escape from this house," suggested the biologist. "Why not tour quietly around the globe and see our world entire before you decide upon your future plans?"

Winters shook his head wearily. "I thank you for your kindness, gentlemen. I would never find a place for myself in this age. I gave up my own age for the sake of an ideal. I am searching for the secret of happiness. I tried to find it here, but you do not know it any more than we did three thousand years ago. Therefore I shall say goodbye and—go on to some future period. In perhaps five thousand years I shall awaken in a time more to my liking."

"Can your body support another long period of emaciation?" drawled the biologist. "To judge from your appearance you have hardly aged at all during your last sleep—but... five thousand years!"

"I feel as if I were a little older than when I left my own times—perhaps a year or two. Thanks to your attention I am again in excellent health. Yes, I should be able to survive the ordeal once again."

"Man! Oh man!" groaned the red-headed Stalvyn. "I would give my right hand to take a place with you! But I have my duty to my own times."

"Is your hiding-place near here?" asked the Forester.

"Yes. But I prefer to tell no one where it is—not even you three. It is well hidden and you cannot help me."

"I can!" put in the biologist. "I studied your metabolism as you lay unconscious all this week and I have prepared a formula. From it I shall make a drink for you to take with you. When—or *if*—you wake from your long sleep you must swallow it. It will restore your vitality enormously in a few hours."

"Thank you," said Winters. "That might make all the difference between success and failure."

"How are you going to reach your hiding place? Suppose some youth sees you and follows—remembering old grudges as youth can?"

"I must leave here secretly just before dawn," said Winters thoughtfully. "I know in a general way where to go. By daylight I shall be close by and shall have hidden myself forever long before anyone in the village is awake."

"Well—let us hope so! When will you start?"

"Tomorrow morning!"

They parted for the night with many a last word of caution and advice. Winters lay down to sleep and it seemed only a few seconds before the Forester stood over him shaking him awake. He arose and made sure of such things as he was to take with him, Stalvyn and the biologist were on hand in the darkness (they did not dare show a light) and Winters took a light breakfast and said his goodbyes. The three friends watched his body show shadowy against the trees and vanish into the dark night.

Winters walked with great care along the hard-surfaced roadway for almost an hour. He was sure he had made no slightest sound. He felt he must be almost at the right spot and left the road for the woods where he waited impatiently for the greying east to brighten. He spent half an hour in the shrubbery beside the road before he could see clearly enough to proceed. Just before he turned away he glanced from his leafy hiding back along the stretch of highway. In the distance, to his horror, he observed two figures hurrying toward him!

With panting fear he slipped back into the woods and cruised over the ground looking for his one particular tree-trunk out of all those thousands. Seconds seemed like hours and his ears were strained back for some sign of his pursuers. Sweating, panting, heart pounding, he ran back and forwards in an agony of directionless movement.

Then he became frantic and hurried faster and faster until his foot caught over some piece of stone and sent him sprawling. He rose to his knees and stopped there, frozen, for he heard voices! They were still distant, but he dared not rise. His eyes fell upon the stone over which he had stumbled. It was flat and thick and rather square in outline. Some marks appeared on the top—badly worn by weather. He brushed aside a few dead leaves listlessly, hopelessly and before his startled eyes there leaped the following:

> "Carstairs, a gardener lies here—faithful servant to the end—he was buried at this spot upon his own request."

Buried here at his own request—poor old Carstairs! Could it be? If this grave were directly above his underground chamber then there, only fifty feet to the south, must lie the entrance! He crawled with desperate hope over the soft ground and there, sure enough, was a familiar tree and a leaf-filled depression at its base! The voices were approaching now and he slithered desperately into the hole, pushing the drifted leaves before him with his feet. Then he gathered a great armful of leaves scraped from each side and sank out of sight, holding his screen in place with one hand. With the other hand he reached for some pieces of cut roots and commenced to weave a support for the leaves. He was half done when his heart stood still at the sound of voices close by. He could not make out the words and waited breathlessly second after second. Then he heard the voices again—receding!

Winter came and the frogs found their sleeping places beneath the mud of the little pond that lay where once was the lake. And with the next spring the great tree had commenced spreading a new mat of roots to choke forever the entrance to that lead-lined chamber where, in utter blackness, a still figure lay on a couch. The sleeper's last hazy thoughts had taken him back in his dreams to his own youth and the wax-white face wore a faint smile, as if Winters had at last found the secret of human happiness.

THE STERILE PLANET

Nathan Schachner

Nathaniel Schachner (1895–1955) was an American lawyer who became a prolific writer for the pulp magazines and later a noted historian and biographer with studies of Alexander Hamilton and Aaron Burr. Amongst his early work was the short series "The Revolt of the Scientists" (1933) where scientists in the form of Technocrats fight back against organized crime and corrupt politicians. Many of his stories from this period have political elements but he also enjoyed playing with science and the realities and in a couple of stories, "The Living Equation" (1934) and "The Orb of Probability" (1935), we get a glimpse of the real world of which ours is but a shadow. Unfortunately Schachner found he could earn more money writing for the weird-menace and horror magazines and by the early 1940s had moved away from science fiction. The following story, though, gives some idea of the bold ideas Schachner enjoyed in his fiction.

I

THE DEEPS WERE ALIVE WITH MOVEMENT. VAGUE SHAPES SHIFTED stealthily through the water-scoured gorges, climbed with feral certainty up the Continental shelf. The sun had long since set over the dun plateau of the interminable desert beyond, but the oasis of New York, set on its eerie perch, glowed in the darkness like a jewel of many colours.

Inclosed within its gigantic bubble of force, shimmering with a thousand hues, its central tower surging upward almost to the limits of the shielding screen, its lesser structures spaced at regular intervals over the fifty-mile radius of lush, green fields and close-cultivated crops, New York slumbered peacefully, unwitting of the threat that was gathering in the Deeps.

Earth was a dying planet. Yet the year was only 4260 A. D., not, as might have been imagined, a hundred million centuries thence. The sun rode as high in the heavens as ever, resplendent in all its pristine brilliance. But it shone on scenes of unimaginable desolation. Where once dense forests had swayed to kindly breezes, where once ripe, golden grain had interspersed with the green of many grasses, where once limpid streams had tapped the snows of mountain flanks and poured their life-giving floods to limitless oceans, where once populous cities, sprawling villages and isolated farms had dotted the planet's surface with the busy hum of activity, now there was lifelessness, death, drought, the fierce aridity of sun-baked wilderness.

Man, the favoured and latest offspring of evolution, had done this—even as had been prophesied in the early twentieth century. Deaf to all warnings, heedless of the future, he had denuded the forests, ploughed up the soil, meddled recklessly with the delicate balances of nature. This, in his vanity, he had called the march of civilization; and an outraged earth struck back. As civilization marched, so did the deserts.

The matted roots of the trees, the tangled bottoms of the prairie grasses, no longer held the rain in their intertwined fingers, to soak slowly and gently into fertile loam. Instead, the falling waters ran off in quick, scouring torrents, digging huge gullies in the land, bearing countless millions of tons of crop-bearing soil into the oceans. Then drought came, and heat, and dust storms, that lifted the dried and powdered remnants to the heavens, scattered them afar, leaving naked to the parching sun the sterile sands beneath.

The process widened and deepened, even while man fought back blindly, unwilling to sink his selfish, immediate purposes in the larger, remoter good. The streams became torrents, the rivers floods that inundated, vast watersheds, scouring more and more of the fertile mulch away, dumping it into the recipient oceans, choking them, filling them up with residual silt.

Then the waters retreated, and the rains ceased. For the exposed, porous earth drank thirstily and deep of the lakes, the streams and the rivers. These sank out of sight. The falling rain made chemical combination with the elemental rawness of the underground; the oceans evaporated and were not replenished; the skies became cloudless, burning glasses to continue and hasten the process. The deserts were on the march!

Men fell back before their resistless sweep, huddled in the remaining well-favoured places, fought one another for a foothold, harried and maimed and slew for the too-scanty food. The strong drove out the weak; the cunning evicted the simple; the ruthless slaughtered the mild, and gained for themselves temporary possession of the few oases that were left on all the earth.

But they had learned their lesson. Unless drastic measures were taken, even these still fertile spots must yield to the inevitable onslaught of the deserts, must lay forever exposed to the hatred of the dispossessed. Wherefore a certain number of scientists, men of the requisite knowledge and attainments, were graciously permitted to remain and employ their talents for the common weal.

They laboured well and mightily, fighting a desperate battle against time. The oases were located in places where certain peculiar underground formations, vast, cupping strata of impermeable rock, had caught and held the ancient waters and made of them tremendous reservoirs. New York, lower Westchester and adjoining Connecticut, had such a rocky basin, a thousand feet beneath. San Francisco and its hills had another; so had Capetown; a few square miles in the Crimea; the overhang of Cornwall; Lake Tahoe; the easternmost end of the Caspian— In all, there were not over a dozen small segments of earth where man could still find the precious fluid in underground basins.

Here the scientists reared huge bubbles of force, screens of close-knit electromagnetic vibrations, shimmering with a ceaseless play of iridescence, intangible, yet more solid and repellent than the hardest rock or steel; permitting, in regulated, tempered form, the sun's light and heat to enter, but interposing an insuperable barrier to all other vibration lengths, to the coarser molecules of tangible things.

Within these shelters the scientists evolved miniature worlds of a more primitive time. The precious waters were raised to the surface by powerful pumps, spread with careful anxiety over the hoarded topsoil.

Crops were grown in the most scientific manner, from pedigreed seeds and roots, bathed in the forcing rays of ultraviolet generators. The soil's virility was renewed with alternate fields of leguminous, nitrogen-fixing plants, with fertilizers extracted directly from the atmosphere. Meat and dairy products were obtained from strictly regulated herds, pastured on the fallow, clover-bearing lands.

Air was renewed by cautious filtering through the screens, keeping within, by special absorbents, every molecule of the precious water vapour. The plants exhaled oxygen and moisture, which latter was condensed, at proper intervals, within the orbed round of the impalpable domes by ionizing discharges of frictional electricity, and dropped back to earth in gentle showers of rain. At stated periods, when the coast seemed cleared, strongly armed expeditions took off in rocket-firing planes for the vast desert regions, where iron and copper and coal and oil still discoloured the otherwise featureless terrain. They mined these essential materials in frantic haste, while wary guards stood watch with death-dealing weapons.

All in all, it was a circumscribed, precarious existence. New York housed barely a hundred thousand beings, the other oases even less. All told, not a million members of earth's once teeming, magnificent civilizations were crowded into these shelters, where life could still go on and man evolve.

But, though the people of the oases made hasty, desperate trips into the limitless deserts for the supplies they needed, there were other vast areas of earth's surface where they dared not penetrate, which they avoided with shuddering horror and the instinctive repulsion of long-imbrued tradition.

These were the Deeps!

The oceans had dried up, their waters lifted to the heavens by the burning rays of the sun, precipitated on the hungry deserts, and there absorbed beyond all recovery. But the mingled salts had remained behind, and now, as the seas retreated and laid bare their ancient, hidden beds, their tremendous concavities and sunken valleys and mountain ranges, the dried mineral salts formed dazzling coatings of bleached white, fifty to a hundred feet thick, forming a crust in which all life suffocated and died.

In the deeper reaches, however, those countersunk gorges and sinks known earlier as the Deeps, some water still lingered and festered. So thick it was with brine, so fully saturated, so remote and shaded from the absorbent sun, that no further evaporation could ensue. In these stagnant marshes coarse sea grasses grew, and certain fishes and molluscs, adapted by long centuries of slow change to such repellent quarters, moved sluggishly.

Always a miasmatic mist hovered over the surfaces of the sinks, shrouding them, hiding the struggle that went on interminably beneath. Yet the Deeps were not devoid of human kind. The hordes of the weaker, who, long eras before, had been thrust out from the ever-narrowing oases, sought shelter on the fringes of the receding seas, followed the briny waters as they shrank farther and farther into the remoter depths, found final resting place on the shores of the quiescent sinks in the very bowels of the ancient ocean beds.

There they spawned and reverted early to a primitive savagery. The coarse grasses made their cereals, the fish and molluscs their animal food. But the greatest delicacy of all was the newly evolved protoplasmic blobs of amorphous matter that put out pseudopods in the tideless sinks. Somehow, such is the inherent vitality of human kind, the population of the Deeps had grown by the year 4260 A. D. to a hundred million—a hundred million, in whose fumbling brains lingered the tradition of their ancestral expulsion from the oases, in whose savage breasts burned an ineradicable hatred for the fortunate inhabitants of those segregated Paradises, an inextinguishable longing for their possessions.

Woe to the oasis dweller who ventured from the protection of the screen, and fell into the hands of the ever-lurking denizens of the Deeps. Woe to the luckless rocket plane, winging its way high over the sunken salt beds in infrequent intercourse with the other far-flung oases, whose power failed and was compelled to seek forced landing near the mist-shrouded Deeps.

And now, unknown to slumbering New York, the coastal depths were swarming with countless thousands of skulking creatures. Great, hairy, feral men they were, unkempt, shaggy, nostrils flaring with the hunt, swift of foot and nimble of step, armed with primitive weapons formed from the bones of long-wrecked vessels, with the precious freight of tumbled rocket planes.

A million wild men climbed up the steep Continental shelf and crouched in salt-incrusted valleys, panting for the signal that would precipitate them upon the looming play of colours that was their goal. For strange things had been happening in the wide-scattered Deeps. Like beasts, they had spawned and bred beyond all the primitive sources of food supply. Hunger and gaunt want stalked their ranks, drove savage bands from their lurking abodes upon the hitherto tabooed areas sacred to other tribes. Internecine war flared and died and flared again. The precious food supplies were ravaged and destroyed. Famine devoured its own.

Then a miracle occurred: a god appeared, or so he seemed to the awestruck millions. And with him came a subsidiary god. Out of the most sacred of the Deeps of old Atlantic—the Nares Deep, north of ancient Porto Rico, and descending to the incredible depth of over 27,000 feet beneath the once universal level of forgotten oceans—came the two gods, attended by a small but haughty band of attendants and warrior deities.

There had been legends about them—this secret tribe who ages before had found a home in the horrifying depths where the concentrated sun beat mercilessly upon thick, gummy air and pressures of many atmospheres. Tales of an impenetrable veil thrust over the sacred chasms, through which unwary prowlers had gone and never returned, of rumblings and tremblings that emanated from the pall and the clankings of metals on metals. A strange place, to be avoided on peril of fearsome consequences.

But now the gods had emerged. In their hands were curious weapons, similar neither to the primitive arms of the dwellers of the Deeps, nor like unto those wrested intermittently from the denizens of the oases. Their slender bodies were swathed in glittering, flexible garments and their faces hidden with terrible, godlike masks. In low, swift planes of an elder day, their messengers sped from Deep to Deep, exhorting the startled tribes in archaic language, preaching the message of revolt against the selfish masters of the oases, preaching the senselessness of communal slaughter.

The message spread like fire through stubble grass. The hungry hordes drifted stealthily by night from the farthest deeps, toiled up and down great mountain ranges, skulked by day within the shadowed gorges to avoid the scouting planes of the oasis men, gathered for the final assault on New York—a million brawny savages, driven by famine, animated by ancient injustice, led by a small, compact group that stood apart, dominated by a masked god and his subsidiary deity.

The night was dark, breathless. A faint moon gilded the sunken mountaintops, failed to penetrate the fantastic deeper valleys. The salt ridges of the Continental shelf, pitted and scarred by a myriad gullies and holes, showed motionless and dim, disclosing no wit of the clinging hordes, alert for the ultimate signal.

The leader raised himself warily, stared at the beautiful hemisphere of tenuous fires that housed the faerie towers of New York, started to lift his arm. The slighter, slenderer figure at his side caught it with restraining fingers, pressed silver mask close to his, and whispered inaudible words.

He hesitated a moment, shook his head in denial, raised his arm again. Blue sparks flew upward into the darkness from the wand in his hand. At once, like insubstantial wraiths, the waiting hordes moved forward, wave on wave, toward the city of selfish plenty. The god had given the signal!

II

High in the topmost observatory of the central tower, Brad Cameron kept watch. He was obviously angry. His grey eyes snapped as he checked the detector screens, made certain that the power flowed evenly through the electromagnetic mesh. His jaw was good, his nose straight, his mouth as sensitive as an artist's, but the smooth rippling of flat-banded muscles beneath his garments as he walked, the set of his shoulders, belied all possibility of effeminacy. His companion, an older, dark-visaged man, watched his irritation with a certain gloomy understanding.

"Another night wasted with this silly watching," Brad snapped, as his pacing round brought him to the screens which gave on the Deeps. Any untoward movement in those down-plunging abysses, any unusual vibration, must register on the sensitive surfaces of the plates. But they were darkly blank. "Those poor devils out there haven't the courage, the organization, to attack our defences. Would to Heaven they had!"

Jex Bartol paled, lifted warning finger. "You're talking treason, Brad," he whispered in frightened accents. "If Doron Welles, our leader, should hear you—"

Brad's lean face hardened. "I've already told him," he answered more quietly. "We're pretty damn selfish, locking ourselves up, a limited number of aristocrats, within impenetrable walls of force, partaking of all the good things of life, while out there millions of our fellow creatures are starving and dying."

"But they're savages, worse than beasts," Jex protested in shocked accents. "Remember what they did to the passengers of the Caspian plane that fell in their clutches only last week."

"I know," Brad retorted gloomily. "Tore them to pieces and ate them raw. But whose fault is that? They're ravenous, desperate, and we made them so. Our ancestors drove them out centuries ago, to live or die—*we* didn't care which, as long as we were safe and snug with water and food."

"That's all ancient history," Jex said reasonably. "Earth's story from earliest times is but a repetition of old injustices. It can't affect the present. Talk sense, Brad. What would you have us do? Open our screens and let the hordes of the Deep in? Even if they didn't slaughter us at once, even if by some miracle they acted like human beings—which I seriously doubt—how long could the resources of all the oases take care of them? You know the answer. We'd all starve and die of thirst in a month—and that would be the end of life on this planet. Would you wish that?"

"N-no!" Brad admitted unwillingly. He recognized the force of his friend's arguments, had wrestled them out with himself in the stillnesses of the night. Yet they had not lessened the suffocating feeling of impotence he had always felt when thinking of the swarming savages who inhabited the Deeps. He could not, from earliest childhood, accustom himself to the hard, defensive mechanism of the others.

To them the Deeps men were foul degradations, monstrosities spawned by the fetid swamps of the ocean bed, creatures to be killed mercilessly on sight, beings without a spark of human intelligence or human emotion. Nor could Brad accustom himself to the smug self-satisfaction of the oases, to their contentment with a limited, circumscribed life, their awareness that the scanty supplies of water must inevitably disappear by slow evaporation, by absorption into the surrounding terrain. That—they shrugged—must take some thousands of years. Why should they—whose life span was but a hundred years—bother about the remote future? The adventurous spirit, the feeling of pity, of upward striving, that, in part, had actuated earlier civilizations, had died. And with it had died the true reason for man's existence.

Yet Brad retained this last precious instinct: thought of life as something more than a settled, prescribed path. He longed with an ineradicable longing for something more than the limited terrain of New York, or the occasional flying visits to other oases as self-contained as his own. The illimitable vastness of the deserts, the precipitous drops of the vanished oceans, arid as they were, cruel as they must be, tugged at his errant feet with a sense of freedom, of glorious adventure.

"No," he repeated. "But there's another possibility."

"What is that?"

"To recreate life in the deserts, to bring back the oceans, to make this planet once more habitable, as we know it was in the past."

"Why should we bother?" Jex asked in some amazement. "Even if it were possible, and we know that it is not. It would mean endless toil, endless sacrifices on our part, and to what end? We are comfortable as we are; *we* don't need more territory, more food, more amusements than we have."

Brad looked at him sadly. "Jex Bartol," he said, "you're as bad as the rest of them—almost as bad as Doron Welles himself. Don't you understand? We might as well be dead as live the selfish, petty lives we do. Our civilization is stagnant; we've hardened in a mould." He laughed harshly. "Perhaps you are right. We're beyond all hope; it is better to let the human race die out in another thousand years or so, to let earth become a sterile orb, an empty planet revolving around a blind sun, rid at last of the disease called life. But there were moments, Jex, when I thought you understood, when I thought you might help—"

Pain showed in his friend's sombre eyes. "What help could I give," he answered gloomily, "even if I were insane enough to agree? Doron has decreed that—"

Brad was swiftly at his side, his face aglow. "Blast Doron!" he cried joyfully. "I knew I could count on you."

"Are you mad?" Jex whispered feverishly. "Don't you know Doron has eyes and ears in every cranny of New York? Do you wish to be cast out into the Deeps, and left to the tender mercies of those very savages you're so much concerned about?"

"Don't get scared, old man." Brad grinned. "Long ago I made it my business to spy out all Doron's little gadgets for snooping on his most loyal and submissive compatriots." His grin widened.

"It's a funny thing, but an accident happened about five minutes ago. Every one of them in the observation tower has gone strangely blank. Now listen to me. I've been working in secret for the last year—ever since Doron ordered me to stop my pernicious experiments. With your help I could—"

He stopped abruptly. His eyes widened past his friend's shoulder, fixed on the detector screen that gave on the Continental shelf. A shower of blue sparks sprayed upward over the sensitized surface, died down almost at once to unrelieved blankness.

"Hey!" Jex grunted. "What's wrong?"

But Brad had already sprung to the controls, thrust every ounce of power humming into the secondary coils. The shimmering of the outer field increased in intensity, wrapped itself round with pulsing vibrations of shattering force. It was death to stumble into their invisible path.

"I don't know," he answered finally. A puzzled frown wrinkled his forehead; his eyes were narrowed on the screen. It was still blank. "I saw something—blue sparks that flared up out there in the Deeps, died down at once. It looked like a signal."

Jex stared at the moveless plate, smiled darkly. "You must have imagined it. The detector would have picked up even the faintest vibration."

"I tell you I saw it."

Jex cast him a queer look. "Think the Deeps men are going to attack, eh? Suppose they do. Isn't that what you were hoping for only a minute ago?"

Brad shifted his feet, did not relax his intense watchfulness. "Don't rub it in. I'm sorry for the poor devils, but they wouldn't know it. I'd go with the rest of you."

"At least you're frank," Jex murmured.

But Brad wasn't listening. "Suppose," he broke in abruptly, "they have a screen, like our own, to blank all vibrations. Our detectors would be useless. Suppose even now—"

"Don't," remarked Jex reasonably, "be an ass. Your imagination is running altogether wild tonight. Those hairy, brainless beasts fashioning a screen?"

Brad turned on him fiercely. His eyes burned. "Suppose," he retorted, "they've received help. Suppose some one else from another oasis has been dreaming the dreams I dreamed. Suppose he slipped out into the Deeps, organized them—"

"Stuff and nonsense!" Jex said impatiently. "No oasis man would be a traitor to his own kind. Would you be a party to the slaughter of every one you knew, to the end of the oases?"

Brad's jaw was a hard rigidity. "Of course not," he growled. "That's why I'm giving the alarm."

His hand reached for the button that would fling a brazen clamour throughout the wide circumference of New York, that would bring the sleeping thousands tumbling out of their beds, and send the guards in swift aero-cars to the flame guns and Dongan blasters. Within generations such an alarm had not been sounded.

"Stay your hand, Brad Cameron!"

The cold, passionless accents seemed to come out of thin air. They brought Brad and Jex whirling on the balls of their feet like pirouetting dancers.

They had not heard the smooth rolling back of the entrance panel, the cat-like emergence of the speaker.

"Doron Welles!" croaked Jex.

The leader surveyed them both with unblinking eyes. He was a small man, smaller than either of them, but he held himself with an arrogant poise that gave the illusion of height. His lips were thin and set in a straight line, his nose pinched and bloodless, and he never smiled. For twenty years he had ruled New York, as his father had done before him, and his ancestors for five hundred years previous.

For the oasis people were an easygoing race, shorn of all initiative, of all the sterner qualities that had been bred out of their soft-lapped, limited environment. They submitted willingly, nay, gladly, to orders, to a shifting of responsibility. Brad Cameron was an exception, an alien sport. Even Jex, subjected for long hours to the fiery tirades of his friend, had not quite lost that fatalistic shrug.

Doron fixed Brad with his pale, expressionless eyes. "You have been ever a source of trouble, Brad Cameron," he said evenly. "First it was forbidden experiments—experiments that would, if successful, have inevitably disrupted the even tenor of our existence, have thrown us open to certain disaster. Then you set yourself up as an advocate of the degraded creatures of the Deeps; and even, to our face, dared question our authority.

"Worse still, wherever you have been of late, strange accidents have taken place—always accidents, so you assure me—whereby your activities are withdrawn from the necessary and lawful scrutiny of your leader. For some time I have pondered your case. You are a spot of contagion which may spread and do evil. Therefore—"

Brad grinned wryly. He had been expecting this for some time. But first—"Spare your breath, Doron," he said tightly. "You may never get around to it. The Deeps men are attacking."

Doron Welles swung swiftly, yet without haste, to the banked screens. The secondary current raced through the outer shells, but the plates themselves were still quiescent.

"If you are trying to delay your sentence—" he commenced.

But even as he spoke, the detectors sprang into turbulent life. Signal after signal blazed into being, shouted ominous warnings to the three men in the room.

The first wave of attack had rolled up to the shell of force, was hammering with flaming weapons and twitching bodies against the impalpable fields.

III

Brad leaped to the alarm button, jabbed it with stiff fingers.

At once the oasis of New York burst into a jangle of great sound. In every sleeping cell, in every nook and corner, in every tower and laboratory, in the depths of the pump rooms, the long-disused alarm sent the echoes scurrying and clamouring.

The city awoke, stumbled blindly out into night, fearful, soft, unused to war and violence, trying vainly to remember dim instructions, positions to be assumed in such an event.

Doron was a brave man, and swift in his decisions. "Get to your allotted posts at once," he said calmly. "I'll deal with you later." Then he was gone, back to his aero-car, hastening to take command of the defences.

Jex stared at his friend and groaned. "What will you do now?" he asked.

"Do?" Brad echoed cheerfully, swiftly buckling a flame gun to his belt. "Fight, of course." His face was transfigured; his eyes glowed. Here was balm for his restless spirit, adventure, the shock of untoward events. In a trice he had forgotten his former qualms, his brooding sense of injustice.

"I don't mean that," Jex countered impatiently. "We're safe enough against any primitive weapons the Deeps men can bring to bear. I mean Doron's sentence. He never changes a decision once made."

Brad paused in his outward flight, looked strangely at his anxious friend. "Jex," he answered soberly, "I'm afraid there's more to this assault than you think. The Deeps men never dared make a frontal attack before; they never massed the hordes that our screens indicate. Perhaps Doron will never have a chance to execute his sentence."

"You mean the Deeps men may win?" Jex demanded incredulously.

Brad did not answer. Instead, his hand went forward in an ancient gesture. They shook hands. Jex was speechless. Then Brad was gone, out of the observatory, into his parked aero-car on the landing space outside. His last glimpse of his friend was one of open-mouthed amazement—an awkward, undramatic picture with which to feed the memory. He never saw Jex Bartol again.

At the rim of the abyss Brad found wild turmoil and confusion. The men of the oasis, roused from sleep, blind with fear, scurried wailing and helpless from post to post, wasting their flame discharges on their own wall of force, missing completely the synchronized slits that formed and reformed with scientific precision for their benefit.

The great Dongan blasters were better manned; here a trained band of guards took command, sent infernos of destruction hurtling out into the night. Brad took his station quietly, calmly, before a synchronized slit, pressed the trigger of his flame gun as fast as fingers could twitch.

There was no question about it—the Deeps were in motion. Before him stretched the transparent, multicoloured thinness of the defending mesh of electromagnetic vibrations. So tenuous, so impalpable, a mere racing whirl of shimmering rainbow, that it seemed incredible it could hold more than an instant against the incalculable hordes who washed up against it in surge on surge.

Star shells sent up from the oasis burned bright day into the Deeps—a swift slant of a hundred feet from the outer rim of New York, crusted with salt; then, far out, where the old Continental shelf ended, a great drop into depths unfathomed, into the very bowels of the earth.

Yet from those dreadful depths spewed out, in ceaseless billows, an endless spawn of men, hairy, semi-naked, snarling with savage hate, brandishing weapons of modern make and ancient resurrection alike. On they came, thousands, hundreds of thousands, millions!

The great Dongan blasters caught their crowded, swarming ranks, tore wide gaps of destruction; the flame guns, in the hands of those like Brad who kept their head, spurted liquid fire on screaming, writhing bodies. But still they came, billowing, interminably inexhaustible.

Their weapons blazed futilely against the mesh of force, splashed huge blobs of flame along its curving surface; they threw themselves in desperate madness against the thin transparency that held them from their enemies, and piled up in smoking heaps on the secondary screen that Brad had established. Yet, with a reckless bravery that Brad could only admire, they clambered up and over the dead, seeking somehow to break through by sheer weight of numbers.

And ever and anon, the synchronized slits did not close fast enough, and a thin sheath of destruction seared through screeching defenders, crisped far off buildings, to powdered ash.

Brad squinted at his weapon, found it empty, recharged its catalysts from a placement tank, sighted coolly through the slit as it opened, squeezed. Flame caught furious faces, carried them howling into char and liquefaction.

"You are doing very well, Brad Cameron," a calm voice said in his ear.

Brad flung a hasty look to one side, saw Doron Welles, slight, erect, imperturbable, thin lips compressed, carefully waiting for his breach to flash wide. Then he took aim, fired. Strapped to his chest was a tiny microphone, into which, between shots, he spoke in level accents, sending orders to all the harried fronts, receiving information from his panicky lieutenants.

"Thank you," Brad retorted with a grin. "You're not doing so bad yourself."

The leader frowned. "You need not think," he said precisely, "by disrespectful adulation to swerve me from the sentence I shall impose on you."

Brad grinned mockingly. "Far from it. Only—I don't think you'll get the chance."

Doron swung half around, weapon covering Brad. "Just what," he rasped, "do you mean by that?"

But Brad disregarded the threatening flame gun. "Look for yourself," he said soberly. "Something's happening—at Station 15."

Doron's eyes followed his gesture suspiciously. His small eyes narrowed; in one swift movement he was on his feet, racing toward the beleaguered station, purring swift orders into his microphone even as he ran. Brad was at his side, running easily. In spite of himself, he confessed a certain admiration for Doron Welles. He was a man.

"I suspected something like this from the beginning," Brad jerked out as they raced along, side by side. "I knew the Deeps men couldn't have planned such a terrific attack by themselves. They've been organized—and skilfully—by some one intellectually our equal—or superior. Their massed assault has been a blind; the real siege was concentrated on Station 15."

Station 15 was the portal through the defence screen which gave on a narrow, subterranean plain where the Rockaways had once shelved off gradually into the depths. On this plain stood a group of a hundred men or so, clad in jet-black, flexible garments, their faces hidden behind black, anonymous masks. But two of them were differently attired—in shining, glittering garments, and masks of silver splendour. One, seemingly the leader of the band, was heavy of body and broad of shoulder; the other was slight and slender and springy of carriage.

Before them, on a rolling platform, a disk whirled around and around on a cradled axis, and, as it spun at incredible speed, a shining wall of transparent force built up in front. As the platform steadily advanced, the frontier of energy moved along until it made contact with the defending vibration mesh. There was a blinding flash of incandescent energy, a sizzling, roaring sound that blasted all the other noise of battle into quietude, a flame that leaped high into the night toward the tingling stars—and the impregnable bubble that surrounded New York sagged and pressed inward.

Already the guards who manned the Dongan blasters whirled from their weapons, fled screeching and howling toward the interior city. Already the first thin gash showed ominously black in the multihued screen.

Brad ripped out an oath, flung himself upon the nearest abandoned blaster. Without a word, Doron stationed himself at the second.

Outside, the strange invaders pushed forward in triumph, the two shining figures in the lead. The tear was getting wider. The howling Deeps men swerved from their assault, pelted madly toward Station 15. The Continental shelf was a tossing, heaving bedlam of racing savages.

"Shoot as you've never shot before," Brad shouted. "They'll be upon us in a minute."

Doron turned prim face upon the man he intended to punish. It bespoke stern disapproval. Even in the face of swift annihilation Doron Welles could not forget matters of punctilio.

But his Dongan blaster spoke, and spoke again. There was no need to wait for slits to widen and close. The rip was wide enough for ten men to plunge through abreast. Brad's mighty weapon belched forth its cargo of destruction in quick, staccato phrases. Wherever the hurtling disruption met the lunging, unprotected savages of the Deeps, it cut wide swathes of frightful death in the close-packed ranks. But it battered harmlessly at the countervailing screen, making no slightest dent in its shining surface, and diffused into flashes of impotent energy.

On and on pressed the field of force; behind it rolled the generating disk; and on and on sped the little band of masked invaders, sheltered from all harm.

Even in the face of inevitable defeat, of sudden annihilation, Doron Welles did not, by so much as a twitching muscle, reveal concern. The Dongan blaster smoked and roared and blasted away as ever.

Brad thought quickly. The breach was growing wider. In seconds now—"Keep going, Doron!" he yelled. "Don't let up a moment." Even as he howled out his advice, he flung away from his weapon, seemed to abandon the battle in jittering flight. But he had a plan, and he wished all attention to be distracted from him.

The source of the enemy's power was the disk which built up its overwhelming shield of force. It could not be reached by frontal onslaught. But, in the swift advance, the angle of attack had shifted slightly to one side, making a thin, acute angle with the farther reaches of Station 14. There, ready at hand, on its swivel platform, rested a deserted blaster.

Crouching against observation, Brad raced for its quiescent bulk. He clawed around the edge of the platform, straightened cautiously, hidden from view. He grunted his satisfaction. It was just as he had thought. The conquering enemy screen was a thin edge toward him. By careful aiming, he could sheer along its inner veil, barely impinge upon the rotating disk.

But he must work fast. Already the line of attack was swinging in, would pivot the impenetrable screen to a wider angle. Feverishly, yet with fingers that did not tremble, he rotated the platform through a ten-degree arc, sighted his weapon, jerked all the charges in one vast explosion from the firing chamber.

The great blaster belched its multiple swathe of flame; lightning bolts crashed out into the void. The gun vibrated with a cataclysmic roar, burst into a thousand pieces. Brad was flung sprawling from the platform. Bruised, battered, deafened by the mighty blast, he jerked groggily to his feet. A hoarse cry of joy rushed from his lips, stifled almost at inception.

His aim had been true. The whirling disk was no more; the mesh of interwoven energy it had set up was gone. But the men who had controlled it were leaping for the steadily narrowing breach in the defensive bubble. Soon the pulsing currents from the central power station, no longer rendered impotent by the counterbalancing screen, would flow into the gap and make it whole again; but before it could, the strange, masked figures would be inside the shield. And only Doron stood in their path.

Brad flung forward, jerking at his flame gun. On they came, black, terrible figures, led by two in shining silver. Doron pointed his blaster calmly. It roared. The stocky figure in gleaming metal seemed to shatter into a thousand shards. Behind him half the men in black whiffed out of existence.

Brad heard a shrill cry of anguish from the slighter, slenderer figure in flexible silver. For a moment it hesitated, swayed uncertainly; then it darted on again, toward the fast-closing breach. But it came on alone. For behind, the survivors in black milled inconclusively, aghast at the fall of their leader, at the terrible decimation of their ranks.

Doron Welles, with a slight sneer, reached bloodless fingers for the pressure trip again. But in that moment Brad had seen, and seeing, jerked forward with a terrible cry.

The mask had been ripped loose from the slender features, had revealed to his startled gaze the delicate lineaments—of a girl—a girl of aristocratic loveliness, with warm, blue eyes and rippling, golden hair, a girl of unbelievable grace and breeding!

Doron saw her, too, but no pity showed in his thin lips, his cold, expressionless eyes. His hand did not waver from the trip. Brad could have shot him down, did not. Instead, his body was an arcing catapult, his fist a slamming thunderbolt. It caught Doron, untouchable leader of New York, behind the ear. He fell in a heap, without a sound.

The girl was already within the breach. She did not know that she had no followers. Her eyes met Brad's. She knew he had saved her life. Instinctively, Brad acted.

In a single second the flowing wall would close behind her, beyond all opening. The girl was trapped; and Doron Welles was merciless. She had attacked his domain, and must suffer the consequences. Nor would he remit his proposed sentence on Brad. Further, Brad had knocked him down, had committed the unforgivable offence.

Brad swept forward in a single motion, caught the startled girl in his arms, smashed blindly on—just in time. He flung out into the shelving Deeps, rolled over and over down the long incline, the girl locked tight and warm in his arms, right into the huddled mass of the company in black. Behind him, the barrier of New York was irretrievably whole again.

He flung up his arm as a black mask bent over him. A shining weapon swung viciously down. The girl struggled in his grasp, cried out something. The weapon faltered. Then his whirling, tumbling body crashed into a jutting rock. Stars split the darkness. He lost consciousness,

IV

It was obviously all a dream, or worse. He had died and gone to—well, it did not matter. He had a distinct memory, in his semiconsciousness, of having been swiftly transported in a shining aero-car of strange construction, over subterranean mountains and fathomless gorges, over tremendous fields of crusted salt, over recessive deeps, where miasmatic mists veiled incredible crawling swamps—but always down, down, down to the uttermost bones of a skeleton planet.

Dimly, he was aware that the girl was at the controls, her hair a golden glory overtopping the silver flexibility of her garments. Near them fled other cars, piloted by men in sombre black. With a sigh, he relaxed. Obviously, the attack on New York had failed, had been abandoned. He had been responsible for that.

But where were they taking him? His brain was still a fog from the shattering blow he had received. The depth pressure grew more and more heavy, buzzed in his ears, weighed on his heart. Each inward breath was a painful effort. Then, deep beneath his swimming eyes he saw a pall, a layer of dense, unrelieved black, impenetrable to the prying rays of the moon, making a tideless sea between terrific upthrusts of baneful mountains.

The car tilted even more steeply, plunged headlong into the inky shroud. The pressure grew insupportable. But before he again passed out of the picture, Brad knew where he was being taken. He had heard strange legends from captured Deeps men of this subterranean retreat of the gods, of the invisible tribe who lurked in these terrifying depths—

She was speaking to him, and her voice was like the plangent tone of waterfalls, of silver bells striking in unison. He was seated in a great, underground cavern, carefully sealed against the terrific pressure of the Nares Deep, made breathable by ingenious generation of air currents, lighted to an even daylight by glow machines operated by the flash extinction of positrons with electrons.

All about them were evidences of a vigorous, well-advanced civilization, higher even than that of the oases. To one end of the vast cavern was a lake, its black waters sullen in a rocky rim.

Around it, spreading over fifty acres, nurtured by a battery of overhead heat and ultraviolet ray machines, were crops—wheat, rye, lettuce, asparagus, soy beans, corn, beets—sturdy, close-grown, luxuriant.

And everywhere machinery hummed and buzzed, machinery of complicated parts—some of them recognizable to Brad, others strange in design and function. Comfort was everywhere, luxury of a more Spartan mode than that of the oases. And everywhere the men and women of this underground world, strong of body, alert of visage, efficient in movement, tended the machines, harvested the crops, nursed the hurts of those who had been wounded in the assault on New York.

But Brad's gaze always came back to the face of the girl before him. She had told him her name—Ellin Garde. She was more breath-takingly beautiful than he had thought, with candid eyes in which sorrow and troubled grief still held sway. Her lips trembled as she told her story; yet her voice was steady. Her words were the words of the universal language that had ruled the earth from before the great drought; yet they were queerly archaic, liquid, polysyllabic.

"We were some of those whom your ancestors drove out from the oases to die of thirst and hunger in the Deeps, Brad Cameron," she said. "We were too civilized, too philosophical, perhaps, to fight with weapons for our homes. Weston Garde, my ancestor, went with them. He was a very great scientist."

"But why?" Brad protested. "I understand the scientists were invited to remain."

She lifted her head proudly. "The Gardes were always on the side of the oppressed," she told him coldly. "It is true they asked him to stay, to build protections for them, but he refused. He went out into exile, along with those who had been driven to a seeming certain death. At first he tried to help all of the dispersed. It soon proved impossible. There were too many; and in the ferocious struggle for a bare existence, they quickly reverted to the brute, fought and slew and drove each other from the slimy swamps that still remained.

"Sick at heart, Weston Garde gathered about him a chosen group, found this hidden cavern in the deepest part of the old Atlantic, this well of still-sweet water. Here he tried to build anew his civilization, to recreate and advance what had been his ideals on earth. To keep out the ranging tribes of savage men, he screened the entrance with a dense fog of his own contriving, skilfully scattered the legend of taboo, of godhead. Some day, he hoped, these legends might prove valuable."

A spasm of pain fled over her face. "They did; though I wish now they had never been instilled. For they have brought about the death of my brother."

Brad leaned forward remorsefully. He ached to take her in his arms, to comfort her. "He was your brother then—the figure in the silver mask?" he asked gently.

She nodded her head. Her eyes were brimming with tears, but they did not waver. "Poor Haris! It was his idea, and the memory of Weston Garde urged him on. He was an idealist. The thought of those poor, starving brutes outside kept him from sleep. The reports we received through the spies we sent out into the Deeps were horrible—of men and women and children dying by the hundreds of thousands, of food supplies, such as they were, exhausted, of cannibalism rearing its ugly head.

"And all the while you, selfishly safe within your domes of force, surfeited with food and water and all the amenities of life, paid no heed to this logical end of your ancestors' greed."

"You, also, were equally comfortable and remote from the struggle," Brad pointed out.

Ellin flashed up at that. "How dare you compare us?" she cried. "*We* had never been guilty of the foul injustice of the oases; we, too, were in exile." Then her indignation died; she nodded her bright head pathetically.

"Poor Haris thought of that as well," she said. "It made him more restless than ever. Finally, he determined to lead the dispossessed against their former homes, to compel a redivision of what rightfully belonged to all. He convinced our comrades that he was right. He was a marvellous orator. He built and perfected his screen of thrusting force—and he sent emissaries to arouse the dwellers of the Deeps. He would have succeeded, too, if it hadn't been for—for—"

"For me, you mean," Brad completed the sentence for her. He took her hand. It lay small and unresisting in his. "I know, yet I am not sorry—even though it meant your brother's life. For, like all idealists, he did not think things out very clearly. In the first place, he could never have controlled the savage hordes in the flush of their victory. They would have butchered every man, woman and child in the oases, for the remote sins of their ancestors. In the second place, even with the strictest precautions, with the most scrupulous conservation of every bit of food, of every drop of water, of every item of machinery, it would have been impossible to provide for all the teeming millions of the Deeps.

"Now almost a million are adequately housed; let us say five million, all told, could have been taken care of. There are a hundred million more. What would happen? The strong would rise and slaughter or dispossess the weak, even as in the past, and once more the cycle would start its weary round."

She looked at him, wide-eyed, startled. "We—we hadn't thought—"

He laughed, tenderly. "Of course not! Idealists never do."

She buried her head in her hands. "Then it was a mistake from the very beginning," she whispered in a still, small voice. "My brother's death, the death of so many brave comrades, of those poor, starving savages who depended on us for guidance—it was all in vain." She lifted her head; her eyes flashed. "I hate you, Brad Cameron," she cried vehemently. "You have taken away the only comfort I had: the thought that they were martyrs in a worthy cause."

He gripped her slender shoulders, said roughly: "Hold fast to that belief, Ellin. It's a fine, heart-warming belief. And I'm not so certain that it's wrong at that."

"What do you mean?" she demanded eagerly.

"Just this. For several years I've been working on the problem. Doron Welles forbade me to proceed any further. My plan, nebulous then, might, he thought, disrupt the peaceful seclusion of his domain, precipitate the oases men into a world of struggle, of sacrifice, of incalculable hardships. You, Ellin, and your brother, were not afraid; neither am I.

"Your desperate battle to gain salvation for the degraded men of the Deeps, though it cost Haris' life, and the lives of thousands of others, did this much: it released me from my bondage to the slave instincts of my community; it brought us together to pool our resources; and it forced a measure of organization, of discipline, upon the men of the Deeps." He smiled whimsically. "That latter will prove to be most necessary."

She stared at him, as if seeking to read his thoughts. The men of Nares Deep, hearing him, stopped their tasks, drew nearer to listen.

"You have a plan," she said slowly, "to—to do what?"

Brad weighed his words. "I have," he answered, "and it's nothing smaller than to rehabilitate the earth, to make it once more liveable and fertile for the outlawed denizens of the Deeps."

Now he had his sensation. They dropped their work frankly, crowded around, sceptical, serious. It was incredible what this stranger promised. For a thousand years they had lived immured in this sunless cavern; for a thousand years the few oases had been walled off from the rest of the world; for more than a thousand years the earth had been a vast, lifeless tomb.

Ellin started up, fell back in despair. "I'm sorry, Brad," she whispered, "but I can't believe it."

"Yet it's simple enough," he assured her. "The principles involved are elementary; all that is required is a vast labour power, and certain scientific equipment. The first the Deeps men shall furnish us; for the second, I shall rely on your scientists for aid."

"But—"

"I'm coming to it. The earth itself is ruined beyond all hope. The topsoil is gone forever, leaving only sterile sand and rock behind. But where did this life-breeding soil depart?"

"Why, into what once were the oceans. But—"

Brad grinned. "I know what you're going to say. It's buried beneath countless tons of salt. Well, what of it? I told you I needed tremendous man power. We'll dig the salt away, transport it to the desert plateaus of earth—not all at once, but first from the level beds, where it is not more than a few feet thick. Surely we can fashion sufficient power diggers and conveyors to release ten thousand square miles of territory within a year.

"Underneath, we shall find the most fertile, the most inexhaustible soil this planet has ever seen, even in the halcyon days of its youth. Not only does the lost topsoil of earth lie there, but also millions of years of dropped decay of plant and animal life, of dead plankton, of foraminiferous ooze.

"With this as a base, we could within the following year feed all the Deeps men on adequate rations. Meanwhile, the work will progress until all the Deeps are cleared. Actually, Ellin, since the Deeps represent about four fifths of earth's surface, there would be more habitable land than there has been since the world began."

"You forget, Brad," she protested faintly, "that there must be water before crops can be grown."

"I didn't forget. I was coming to that as the next step in our rehabilitation programme. The earth, as a matter of fact, never lost its water."

"What?" From all sides came exclamations of disbelief.

"Exactly. The water of the oceans, the streams and lakes of old, was not driven out into space; it simply sank into the arid soil and became unusable. Some part, it is true, entered into chemical combination with earth's elements, such as iron, and could only be recovered by Herculean efforts. But the most of it combined with thirsty salts and oxides and became fixed as water of crystallization. Copper sulphate and sodium carbonate are examples of such salts. But the combination is an unstable one; a mild heat will release the imprisoned water in the process known as efflorescence.

"We have the means to induct sufficient heat into the deserts abutting the Continental shelf to bring the water tumbling out of these buried salts and oxides. Place batteries of electrodes in the given areas at the desired depths, set up your disks of revolution, our solar converters, generate electromagnetic swirls of energy. The resistance of the soil between the electrodes will convert the energy into heat.

"The water will filter through the loose sand, precipitate itself by ancient gullies into the Deeps. There we can channelize the precious fluid, use it for irrigation. Year by year, the area under civilization, the water supply, will grow larger and larger, until, who knows, in some future era clouds will form and rain descend; crops will grow and forests stretch interminably, even as in forgotten ages."

A great shout burst up from his listeners at the thrilling vision he had evoked. Ellin placed her slender hand on his; her eyes looked deep into his own.

"It will not be a matter of a day or a year," Brad said somewhat unsteadily. "It means all the days of our lives, and perhaps the lives of the children who shall come after us."

"*Our* children?" she repeated softly, and flushed. But she could say no more. Her further words were oddly smothered against Brad's lips. A brave new world was to be born, and they, and those who gathered around them, were harbingers of an earth remodelled. What man had destroyed in his selfishness and greed, man could restore with sacrifice and courage. The future seemed very near to them just then.

SHADOW OF WINGS

Elizabeth Sanxay Holding

Elizabeth Sanxay (1889–1955), who took on the surname Holding when she married British diplomat George Holding in 1913, came from an upper-middle-class New York family and might well have lived happily as a society hostess. But she wanted to write, producing scores of stories for the major magazines from 1920 onward, as well as several romance novels. By 1927 she had shifted to crime and suspense fiction publishing eighteen novels from Miasma *(1929) to* Widow's Mite *(1953). She was one of Raymond Chandler's favourite writers who called her "the top suspense writer of them all." Occasionally Holding liked to experiment with fantasy and borderline science fiction. The following is the second of three stories she contributed to* The Magazine of Fantasy and Science Fiction.

IT WAS LATE IN THE AFTERNOON OF A HAPPY DAY THAT STAN Dickson first saw the shadow. He had just finished clipping the hedge, and he was sitting on the steps that led up to the veranda, looking out at the little tidal creek across the road. There was a small boat yard there, and an elderly man was using a hammer, with a clinking sound; down the street, someone was mowing a lawn. Celia was upstairs, putting the children to bed; he could hear her voice, and little Jenie's voice, loud and urgent; Jenie was four years old now, and filled with an almost desperate impatience. It no longer satisfied her to listen to a bedtime story; she wanted to compose her own, with someone to listen.

It made him smile to hear the jumbled story in that loud little voice, a bad wolf, a bad, *bad* witch, a naughty little rabbit, a good fairy, a beautiful princess. He took a pack of cigarettes out of his pocket and lit one; he smoked, well-pleased with his own life and with the tranquil Summer world. Maybe by the time little Pete grows up, there won't be any more wars.

The orange sun was swimming above the horizon, in a pale-green sky, throwing a fiery bar across the grey-green water of the creek. The old man's hammer clinked, but the lawn mower had stopped, and Jenie's voice had died away. There was another sound, somewhere in the offing; a plane, he thought, and watched for it. And then the shadow came across the face of the sun, a great flock of birds, some small, some with great wide wings beating. He heard a mewing cry, like that of a gull, he heard a fluty twitter, another unknown note; then they went sweeping past, and out of sight.

City-bred, he knew next to nothing about birds, and he frowned at the queer uneasiness that stirred in him. Damn nonsense! he told himself. Maybe this is the time of year they migrate; something of the sort, something perfectly natural.

He finished his cigarette, and went into the house. Celia was in the kitchen, beginning to dish up their early dinner. Libby was coming to sit with the babies, and they were going to the movies in the nearby town; they had made this a part of their sedate and cheerful routine. Stan did not mention the birds to Celia, but when she had gone upstairs to dress, he strolled into the kitchen where young Libby was washing the dishes. A nice girl she was, rosy and good-tempered.

"You know about these things," he said. "Do a lot of different kinds of birds often fly together in the same flock?"

"My *goodness!*" cried Libby. "Don't talk to *me* about *birds*, Mr Dickson! My uncle Joe—he's got a truck farm, you know—why, he's creating and carrying on about the birds, from morning till night."

"Mean they're eating up the crops?" Stan asked, a little uncertainly. Because what did he know about birds? Only that farmers put up scarecrows, didn't they, to keep birds away?

"Oh, it's *lots* worse than that!" said Libby. "Why, it's even in the papers, Mr Dickson, and the Government's sending people to find out about it. You see, the birds just aren't coming at all!"

"Coming where?"

"They aren't coming *anywhere,*" Libby explained. "The crops are dying, and the trees are dying, because the birds aren't killing any of the insects. Why, you wouldn't believe how bad things are getting! The flowers, and even the grass..."

"I didn't know that birds were so useful," said Stan. "Maybe that's why our garden is so—let's call it unspectacular. Why have the birds quit on the job, Libby?"

"Nobody knows," she said. "Haven't you read about it in the papers, Mr Dickson? Or heard people talking about it?"

"Well," said Stan, "the people in an advertising agency don't seem to talk much about birds."

"They'd ought to," said Libby, severely. "My father, and my Uncle Joe, and everybody, they all say there'll be a real famine in this country, in a few months, if the birds don't come back and kill the insects—worms, and beetles, and caterpillars, and goodness knows what—why, they're crawling all over the place."

"But I saw a big flock of birds, just a little while ago."

"I know," said Libby. "Everybody sees them—the biggest flocks of birds that ever came over here. Only, they don't *stop*. Not a one of them."

"But why not? They have to eat something somewhere, don't they?"

"Well..." Libby said. "Of course, I don't know if there's anything to it, but—well... some people say it's the Russians."

Stan bent his head, and flicked an ash off his sleeve, fighting back a grin.

"How would they manage that?" he asked, with polite earnestness.

"Well, I don't understand much about things like that," Libby answered. "But my father, he thinks they—" She paused, and putting her hands behind her, she leaned back against the sink. "What he calls it is '*deflecting*,'" she said. "Pop says that could be done, maybe. Something could be sort of sprinkled down from planes, something that would keep birds away."

Stan looked at her with a faint frown, a little impressed by her tone, and words. But only for a moment. Now, look here! he said to himself. These Russians "deflecting" the birds... Come, come!

He went upstairs to wash, and when he came down, Celia was waiting for him. "Hello, Perfect!" he said to her, and he thought that she was just that, a tall girl, straight and proud, in a tailored white cotton dress that well set off her olive skin, her long dark eyes, her rich dark hair. She was handsome, she was intelligent, she was good-tempered, and she was superbly capable, as a mother, a housekeeper, an organizer. He was certain of a good dinner, and served on time.

"Celia," he said, "have you heard any talk in the village about birds?"

"Not in the village," she said. "But the old man from the boat yard stopped me in the street yesterday. He's a very nice old fellow, you know, and he often stops to speak to the children. But yesterday I couldn't get away from him. He went on and on about how the fish were gettin 'out of control,' he called it. I couldn't quite follow him, but as far as I could make out, the gulls and the other sea-birds had stopped catching fish, and the inlet, he said, is teeming with them. And some species, that the birds used to eat, are getting so numerous they're crowding out the others. He was very much worried. He said the balance of nature was being upset."

"I wouldn't know..." said Stan. "Maybe nature changes its balances now and then. Think so?"

"Stan, I'm just a child of the city streets. I don't know about nature. Only, I've read that when new species are introduced into a place, they can do a lot of harm. Rabbits in Australia, for instance."

"Yes," he said. "Yes, I've heard of things like that. You think, then, that maybe some new species of bird has come here, or been brought here, that's driving out all the other kinds?"

"Stan, I'm afraid I didn't take the old man's talk very seriously. Is it serious?"

"I don't know. We might take a look in the evening paper," he said.

"Do you think it's important enough to be in the newspapers?"

"Probably not," he said.

He wanted it not to be that important; he wanted to laugh at the whole thing. But it was there, on an inside page, and he realized that the heading was one which, even this morning, he would have skipped without reading. SCIENTISTS STUDYING BIRD MYSTERY.

Scientists from the Department of Agriculture have asked the assistance of ornithologists in making a survey of the changed habits recently observed in the bird life of the New England States, and now reported to be spreading rapidly to other parts of the country.

The birds, which are an important factor in insect-control, have within recent weeks ceased to destroy various pests which formerly constituted their normal diet, and in consequence reports are pouring in to the Department of Agriculture of ruined crops, and, in some localities, of valuable timber forests succumbing to blights.

Unusually large flocks of birds, frequently composed of species hitherto regarded as inimical to one another, have been reported as flying over many areas, in a northwesterly direction. Observation planes report having occasionally seen these large flocks halting for brief periods of time in barren and inaccessible tracts, and then continuing their mysterious pilgrimages.

Scientists admit that at present they are at a loss to explain these unprecedented and increasingly serious phenomena.

BATS REPORTED JOINING BIRDS

Observers in Ohio report that vast numbers of bats have been seen flying in the wake of the great bird migrations. Mosquitoes in that region, formerly the prey of bats, are increasing to the dimensions of a plague…

There was more about grasshoppers, and worms, boll weevils, caterpillars, other insects with names unknown to Stan; he glanced through them, and handed the newspaper to Celia. She read it, frowning a little.

"Well…" she said. "The scientists will find something—some new sort of spray to control the insects."

"They'd better," said Stan.

But lying awake that night, he remembered the flock of birds he had seen that afternoon, the cries he had heard, the sweep of wide wings, the flutter of small ones, the inexorable onward rush of this multitude, and he was filled with wonder and dismay.

The next day, people were talking about birds in the office. "Too damn bad the pigeons don't go away with the rest of them," Anderson said. "We could do without them, all right, but they're still around."

"But only in parks, and places where they're fed by human beings," said Miss Zeller, the receptionist. "It said so, on the radio."

"Very good; there's the solution," said Anderson. "If people want the birds back, then feed 'em. Strew bread crumbs all over the place, and whatever else they eat."

"No, but we need them to destroy *insects!*" said Miss Zeller, indignantly.

"Well, they've gone on strike," said Anderson. "They're tired of eating insects, and worms. I don't blame them."

There were other people who took his joking tone about the matter; there were others who showed a serious, but quite academic interest. But more and more people were growing worried.

When Stan went out to lunch, in a little restaurant near the office, the waitress brought him a menu with an anxious smile.

"There's an awful lot of things crossed out," she said. "But it just seems like things didn't come in to the market this morning."

Green peas. Crossed out. Corn on the cob. Out. Strawberry shortcake. Out. Purple lines through one item after another.

"They say it's the birds," said the waitress. "They're eating up everything—or something like that. Well, I guess the scientists will fix *that* up."

The evening newspaper Stan opened in the train had an article by a scientist, an ornithologist. It was, he said, erroneous to speak of the present phenomenon as a "migration."

> Our birds have not, in any area under observation, deserted their natural habitat, nor are they anywhere less numerous than usual. Nidification is normal. The remarkably large flocks of birds, comprising species never before observed in association, make from one to two flights daily, leaving their customary areas at fairly definite times, and returning after a fairly definite interval, ranging from three to eight or nine hours.
>
> The disturbing factor in these hitherto unexplained movements is that the birds are no longer feeding upon the insects and grubs which normally constitute their diet, and, in consequence, the Insecta are menacing crops, orchards, and all forms of plant life.
>
> It has been suggested that our birds are now being fed by what in marine life is known as "plankton." In the ocean, this consists of a continual rain of more or less invisible matter, drifting down from the surface through various strata of the sea, and providing nourishment for an amazing variety of marine life. It is suggested that some cosmic disturbance is causing a similar condition in the atmosphere, so that in certain regions the birds are now receiving sustenance from the air, ample and varied enough to satisfy their needs.

The man sitting beside Stan in the smoker had a different newspaper, and a different theory. "This fellow—" he said. "This scientist—he says here that experiments with the atom bomb have produced a radiation which makes insects poisonous to birds. And he says, 'Unless we can immediately find some effective method of insect extermination, this planet which we inhabit will become a desert.' The insects, he says, are going to take over."

Celia was on the veranda with the two children when he got home. "What's up?" he asked, surprised by this variation in routine; the children were always upstairs being put to bed at this hour.

"I wanted to see the birds," Celia said. "Stan, look! Here they come!"

They were visible now above the woodland across the inlet; they came sweeping on, across the face of the setting sun, casting a shadow on the calm green water; they flew over the road and past the house, mewing, twittering, honking, wide wings flapping, tiny wings spinning.

"Chickie...?" said little Pete.

"Those aren't *chickens*," said his sister, scornfully. "They're big, big, *big* owls, and they eat little bunnies and—"

"Come on, children!" said Celia.

Libby was not here this evening, but Celia, as usual, had everything organized. She came downstairs, neat and fresh and pretty. But Stan, who knew her so well, saw something new in her face.

"Was it hot in the city, Stan?" she asked.

"Hot enough," he said. "What's on your mind, Perfect?"

"Oh... Well... The dairy sent around a notice that they'll have to cut down the milk supply, starting tomorrow. 'The destruction of large areas of pasture land by insects has seriously affected the production of milk in our herds.' But you don't catch *me* napping, no, sir! I had a bright idea. Right away, as soon as the notice came in the mail, I took the children in the car, and drove down to the village to buy up some cases of canned milk. Only, other mothers had had the same idea, all the mothers in a twenty-five mile radius. It was—absolutely primitive, Stan! All of us fighting for cases of evaporated milk, telling how many children we had, and how extra-delicate they were, and then bidding against each other, offering two, three, five times the regular prices."

"But you got some," he said.

"Yes. Only, I don't like to remember how—how *fierce* I was. And the price...! Stan, I'm sorry, but I haven't got a very nice dinner for you. I couldn't get any tomatoes, or lettuce, or green vegetables—"

"Take it easy, Cecily," he said, uneasy himself to see how disturbed she was under her air of good-humoured amusement.

"And meat is getting scarce, too," she said. "And eggs. Stan, we'd better dig down into the old sock, and buy enormous stores—of everything."

"Yes..." he said.

But you can't beat the game, he thought. If it's going to be like that, we haven't that kind of money.

After dinner Cecily got a news broadcast on the radio. Experts in the nation's capital predict an early solution to the so-called "bird-mystery"... In the meantime, citizens are urged to take immediate steps to control insects by thoroughly spraying all dwellings and outbuildings. Then foreign news, domestic politics, and then a little human interest story, told in the commentator's celebrated whimsical style.

"From Vermont. A farmer, Leonard Bogardus, was arrested early today for firing a shotgun from the roof of his barn at Department of Agriculture planes. 'They came once before to spray that stuff all over my land,' Mr Bogardus told representatives of the press, 'and after they had gone, I wrote to Washington, and I saw the mayor of Stoneham, that is our township, and I warned them that I would not let them come again. I tacked signs up on the trees, and one on the chimney. Planes Keep Out. Last time they came, their dratted spray killed my heifer and my cat and her kittens, and there isn't a *leaf* left on my fruit trees. No, sir! I'll fight these plaguy insects my own way. They don't do near as much harm as them scientists and their poisons.' Well, folks, the Spirit of Seventy-six seems to be still alive in Vermont."

And later. "Stop: Over three hundred deaths have been reported throughout the country from insecticides. The great majority of the victims are children, but some adults have succumbed after eating fruit or vegetables coated with certain sprays. The public is seriously warned to take every precaution—"

"Oh, switch it off!" said Celia. "Let's get some music, something silly. It's—the whole thing is probably exaggerated. And anyhow, the scientists will cope with it."

"The scientists," Anderson said the next morning in the office, "are a damn sight more of a menace than the bugs."

"They're the *only* hope we have!" said Miss Zeller. "They're just doing everything they can think of. They're sending planes to follow the flocks of birds to find out where they go, but the birds get scared and go into the the woods. I—well, honestly, I'm *frightened*."

So was everyone else, whether frankly or secretly. The threat was developing with dreadful speed. There was something close to a panic in Wall Street as the stocks of the giant meat-packing and canning companies plummeted downward. And the lumber companies, the paper manufacturers, the publishing and textile companies were shaky.

The food situation had grown appallingly dangerous. The government issued stern warnings about hoarding; Congress was asked to rush through a bill imposing penalties for this, and authorizing a system of emergency rationing. In the meantime, prices rose and rose; Stan paid three dollars for his lunch of a ham sandwich, a cup of coffee, a piece of apple pie.

He read an evening newspaper over this lunch, read it with a cold and leaden fear. Red Cross Rushing Food Supplies to Cities. The first call had come from Pittsburgh, followed almost at once by New York, Chicago, San Francisco, Seattle. Speculators had hurried to buy up all available food supplies, dealers were charging fantastic prices, 'the low-income groups' were unable to pay for what few staples were left.

There were babies without milk, sick people without nourishment; riots were reported here and there. A meeting of scientists, including ornithologists, meteorologists—

That's it, Stan said to himself. That's the matter with us, today. We all believe there are experts around, to fix up anything and everything. Soil erosion, rivers deflected, droughts, forests destroyed, natural resources wasted away. Never mind. Scientists will make food, control soil, or water. Plagues? Let 'em come; polio, flu, anything. Scientists will cope with them. They'll also deal with crime, insanity, sex, family rows.

But we're trained to look for an expert, in any sort of trouble. Don't try to do anything for yourself, ever. Don't monkey with the buzz-saw. Don't you try to fix your own television set; you'll spoil it. Don't you try to figure out what sort of education and training your own children need. You'll ruin their lives. Call in a psychiatrist.

This is famine. Here and now. You've heard about it. You've read about it. But you thought it was something in Oriental countries, or something from the Dark Ages. Here it is. Here and now. Famine means death, and plagues, riots, insanity, and chaos. It's worse than earthquakes, volcanoes, hurricanes, tidal waves, because it's slower. But don't *you* try to do anything, little man. *You* can't do anything. Can't grow your own food, or go hunting for it, can't make your own clothes, build your own shelter. Can't even work for a living, unless someone else runs a train or a bus for you, and installs electric lights and telephones. Shut up! You're in the army now, little man. And there's no discharge in this war.

When he got to Grand Central at half past 5, it was like a dream in a fever. His train was going to be late in leaving; all the trains were late, either in leaving or arriving. Loud-speakers gave hoarse, furious announcements, as if to impertinent children who were trying to interrupt. Because of the serious food situation, it has been necessary to re-route freight and refrigeration trains in many sections… The public is requested to accept minor transportation delays with patience. Food First. They were making a slogan out of that. Food First.

There were fights, genuine hand-to-hand fights about the telephone booths. Stan gave up trying to call Celia, to tell her he would be late, and he was an hour late. The train was jammed; half or more of the commuters were carrying bags of food, anything they could get; one elderly woman had twelve cans of loganberries, a man had five pounds of cucumbers, and a gunny sack of brown sugar; a fellow Stan knew was sweating under the weight of a suitcase full of gin and rye bottles. All the liquor'll be gone in a day or two, he said.

Cigarettes were difficult to get, or cigars, or pipe mixtures. The tobacco crop was hard hit. The late editions of newspapers were strangely flimsy and small. Because of the pulp shortage, we can give our readers only the essential news at this time. And, of course, the baseball scores, the race track finals. The scientists… Hydroponics seen as possible solution… Closed-seeding successful, say Kentucky farmers. Food supply ample for present, say experts, if hoarding is stopped. Share the food. Food First.

I hope Celia's not too much worried about my being late, he thought. But probably she's heard, on the radio, or from the neighbours, that the trains are late. It's damn hard for her, all of this. The women with children have the worst of it.

When he went up the steps of the veranda, she did not come to open the door for him. He entered, and stood listening, but he did not hear her upstairs with the children. He found her in the kitchen, where it was incredibly hot; she had a white scarf tied over her forehead, like a stoker; her hair was wet, and her dark lashes; she looked pale and strange.

"I've—been baking…" she said. "Making bread. Fourteen loaves… I—never tried making bread before, but… Libby's aunt and one of her children died."

"Come out of here!" he said, sharply. "Come into the sitting room and I'll turn on the fan."

"I've got to—I've got to see..." she said, and opened the oven door. A blast of heat came out, and a sour smell.

"Two more loaves..." she said.

"I'll watch them. Come out of here!"

"Libby's aunt died, and her little boy..."

"That's too bad. Only I've never seen Libby's aunt, so I can't take it too hard."

"She bought ten pounds of rye flour. But there was something wrong with it. Something... It makes you go crazy. It kills you."

"All right. We'll cut out the rye flour."

"I bought ten pounds myself... Ten pounds... I had to throw it all away. Ten pounds... This... This is all the other kinds of flour I could get. Buckwheat, potato flour, rice flour... I—baked it quick—before it could spoil."

"Any dinner?"

"Oh, yes," she answered, with an attempt at cheerfulness. "Some nice home-made pea soup and—I've forgotten, but something else... Oh, yes! Some nice—parsley... And some delicious mint jelly I made..."

"Good!" said Stan.

I'm not a scientist, he thought. I'm not an expert, in anything. But, by God, I'm a man. I can try.

The plan came to him, then and there, before they sat down to that dinner. After they had gone to bed, he lay in the hot darkness and thought out the details. He did not feel in any way restless; he did not want to sleep.

At 4 o'clock he got up, very carefully and quietly. He dressed in the bathroom, and went down the stairs, carrying his shoes in his hand. In the hall closet which they kept locked he had a rifle and a box of ammunition. He had learned in the Army how to use a rifle; he was a pretty good shot, and when they moved out here, he had bought this rifle, with the idea of going hunting some time with some of the men he knew.

Only, I don't really want to go killing rabbits, squirrels, anything, he thought. I dare say I got an allergy in the Army toward shooting, or being shot.

He left the house by the back door. It was still dark, but he had a flashlight with him; he crossed the road, to the little ship yard, and a dog began to bark frantically. Shut up! he said to it, under his breath. You make me nervous. I don't want to have to shoot *you*. I know you, and you're a rather nice dog. Shut up!

He got into one of the rowboats tied up there; he unfastened the painter, and began to row across the inlet, and, in the hot, dark silence the noise of the oars seemed to him amazingly loud; squeak, dip, squeak, dip, a splash... Shut up! he said to the oars. I want this kept quiet.

He stopped in midstream, and waited. A cigarette is a risk, he thought. But I'll take a chance that nobody sees it, or smells it.

He was intensely wide-awake, not tired, not impatient. Just ready. And little by little the sky was growing light, a grey and secret light. There's the east, he thought, but there's no sun yet. Maybe there won't be any today. But if it rains, then what? Will they come anyhow? Or what if it's too late, and they never come again?

Ten minutes to 5. No sun; only that grey light. And no hint of that sound he was waiting for; no sounds but the queer ones that come in the dark water, a little ripple, a little splash, something that seemed to jump up, and fall back; the whisper of leaves in the woodland. Five minutes to 5.

Here they come! he said to himself. And they came with a rush, like a great wind, twittering, mewing, cawing, wide wings flailing, tiny wings humming. He set the flashlight on end, and took aim, and the shots were deafening, horrifying, as if the sky cracked open. Six shots, and he brought two of them down, tumbling into the water. He rowed after one, and picked it up, and it flapped wildly on the boards by his feet. The other bird was swimming, slowly and clumsily, and he rowed after it.

It climbed out of the water by the boat yard, and he jumped out of the boat and followed it, carrying the other wounded bird in his arm.

"Hey! *Hey!* What are you doing?" shouted the old man.

"Let me alone!" said Stan.

The dog came rushing at him, barking.

"Call off your dog, or I'll have to shoot him," said Stan. "Let me alone."

"I'll get the police on you!" cried the old man. "Shootin' off a gun and—"

"Shut up!" said Stan, casually.

The bird that had been swimming was flapping across the road now; as he came near it, it took off, with an effort, flying low. It crossed his own garden, and he followed it; across a neighbour's garden, across another road, a field, and into a little wood. There he lost track of it, could not see it or hear it. He put the other wounded bird on the ground, and it struggled forward a little, and collapsed. He stirred it with a stick, and it moved again, and again lay flat. He gave it a merciful end with a bullet, and the sound of the shot made something stir in the bushes. It was the first bird, and once more it rose into the air and began to fly, slowly and clumsily.

I'm sorry, he told it. I'm damn sorry. But I've got to try. The sun was up, a blazing sun; the bird could make only short flights now, and then collapse. He followed it, through fields and woods, along roads and lanes, up hills, down hills. There were tears on his face when he stirred the wounded creature to go on again; he was glad when at last it died. He sat down beside it, exhausted, sick with pity, and contrition;

he did not know where he was, or how far he had come, and for the moment he did not care.

Then he heard them. All through this monstrous journey, whether in the fierce sun, in the shade of trees, in gardens, in meadows, he had not once heard the sound of a bird; he had not been aware of this, but only of something strange and desolate in the summer world. And now he heard them, a multitude of them.

But we can't live without them! he cried aloud. They don't need us, but we've got to have them.

He did not know where he was; on a hilltop somewhere, overlooking a river. He listened, trying to decide the direction of the sound; then he left the dead bird lying in the sun and started down the hillside, over parched grass that was slippery underfoot. His rifle felt heavy, very heavy, but he must take it, wherever he was going. He must be ready to do whatever he might have to do.

That afternoon, a man walked into a garage in a little Connecticut township.

"I want to rent a car for twenty-four hours," he said. "Drive it myself."

He was dirty, his shirt was torn, his flannel trousers were muddy and wet up to the knees, his face was badly scratched, and he walked with a heavy limp.

"Got references?" the garage owner asked him.

"No. I don't know anyone here. But I'll give you a hundred dollar deposit."

"Got your driver's licence?"

"Yes. But—I don't want to show it just now. This is—private business. A hundred and fifty deposit."

"Sorry, man, but that's not good enough," said the owner. "My cars are all worth a lot more than that."

Some hours later, after it was dark, the man came back, and this time he had a rifle with him. He found the owner alone; he tied him up, and gagged him, and drove off in a small car, leaving two $50 bills on the desk.

The owner got himself free, and called the police, gave them a description of the car, and its licence number. A little before 11 that night, a car with those licence plates was intercepted, and the driver arrested.

But they let him go, in a hurry. He was a doctor, a well-known and respectable one. He had been sent for by a patient, and when he left the patient's house, he had got into his car and started home.

"Certainly I didn't look at my licence plates!" he shouted. "Never thought of such a thing. If you policemen were worth your salt, things like this couldn't happen. Someone must have come along while I was with my patient, and stolen my plates and tacked on his own. It's an outrage!"

He was going to sue everyone, the police Captain, the Mayor of the town, the Governor of the state; he was going to write to all the newspapers, expose everyone; he was very tired, and he was furious.

With considerable difficulty, he was persuaded to accept apologies and go home, and the police were now alerted to find the car with the doctor's licence plates. This they were not able to do at once, for it was then in a most unlikely spot. It was parked outside a police station in New Haven.

"I want to see the chief of police here—and quick!" said the young man who had driven it.

"He's home. You can tell me the tale," said the sergeant at the desk.

"I want your chief," said the young man. "This is way out of your class."

He was dirty, and muddy, with a torn shirt, a scratched face; it was obviously difficult and painful for him to walk. Nuts, that's it, thought the sergeant. And wouldn't the chief take me apart, if I called him up, this hour of the night, for some loony, or hop-head, or whatever he is.

"Listen!" said the young man. "This is the biggest thing that's ever happened."

"Sure! Sure! And you're Napoleon, aren't you?"

"Listen!" said the young man, again. "Come out and see what I've got in my car."

The sergeant went with him out into the quiet tree-lined street. He turned on the light in the car, and he saw it.

"Jeeze!" he said.

Then he went back into the station, and called his chief. The chief was with them within half an hour, and he listened to the young man's story.

"My God...!" he said to the sergeant. "*I* don't know... I don't know whether the man's insane, or not, but I'm not taking any chances. I'm calling Washington. Get McCorkle there for me."

He went back to the young man, and found him asleep, with his head on the desk. He shook him, until he opened his heavy eyes.

"Now, the best thing," he said, "is to get you right to the hospital—"

"No!" said the young man. "I'm going home."

"Be reasonable!" said the chief. "You've hurt your leg, and you've got some bad scratches on your face. You need treatment, and a good night's rest."

And a bath, he thought. You need a bath worse than anyone I ever came across before in my life.

"No. I'm going home," said the young man.

"Now, look!" said the chief. "You come driving up here, with—with *that* in your car, and a story which—well, which hasn't yet been substantiated in any way. If you refuse to go to the hospital voluntarily, there's nothing for it but to put you under arrest. But if you'll be reasonable... There are a couple of men flying here from Washington to see you tomorrow—"

"All right!" said the young man, after a moment. "Maybe these men from Washington will have enough sense to see the importance of this. I'll have to call my wife, though."

"We'll attend to that," said the chief.

"Don't tell her I'm in a hospital," said the other. "Say I'm detained in New York, on business."

So Stan went off, to a nice little private room in a hospital. There was a policeman sitting just outside his door all night, but he didn't know that. He was given a bath, his injuries were dressed, and he got an injection that sent him to sleep for over ten hours.

When he waked, a doctor came to look him over, and a nice young nurse brought him a pot of hot coffee, and orange juice, and fried eggs, and bacon, and toast, and he ate and drank all of it. Then the nurse lit a cigarette for him, and in a moment the men from Washington came into his room.

There were four of them. He was never to learn their names, or their functions, but they had, all of them, an air of authority. And a certain hostility. He felt that, at once, and it gave him a cold, queer feeling.

"This isn't an easy story to tell," he said. "In a way, I wish I—couldn't remember it."

"Take your time," said one of the older men.

"I went out early in the morning—yesterday, was it? Seems longer... I took my rifle, and I rowed out into the middle of the inlet, and waited for the birds to come over. Then I shot down a couple of them."

"Why?" asked another of the men.

"I thought that if I could manage just to injure one of them, I might be able to follow it. But I... They both died. I kept them going, as long as I could... Drove them. Forced them on, until they both died. They were—I don't know what kind of birds, but they were pretty. One was grey. One had blue wings, and a white breast. I drove them on..."

"Yes," said the second man.

"But the last one brought me to where I could hear the whole flock. And I found them. Down on the bank of the river. A very lonely place. There was a sort of pit dug there, in the mud. The birds were just leaving, after their morning feed, but there was still quite a lot of... It's pretty nearly impossible to—describe it. Insects, worms, a mass of crawling, creeping things moving at the bottom of the pit. Phosphorescent. Green, blue, yellow... And a stench like nothing you can imagine. I—feel as if I could never wash it off..."

"Yes," said the second man.

"I was sitting down for a moment. Tired. I suppose I was pretty well hidden by the rocks, because the three men didn't see me. If they can be called men. They came down with parachutes. So small... But you saw the one in my car."

"Go on," said a third man. "You wish to assert that you saw three men descend by parachute? Descend from what? Did you see or hear a plane overhead at any time?"

"No."

"A balloon?"

"No. Nothing. They came down—very slowly. Their shoes—the things they had on their feet—were tremendously heavy... They were not more than—say—three feet high, and wrinkled. Like raisins. They came down... They had big containers full of these stinking insects—grubs—whatever they were, and they started emptying them into the pit. I got up then, and... This is the hardest part to tell... Two of them were silent, all the time, but one of them... I can't tell you, because I'm damned if I know whether he talked to me in our language, or whether... I don't know if it's possible, is it? I mean, to get what's in someone else's mind without—any common language."

"What do you think this man was saying, or trying to convey to you?" asked the fourth man.

"He said—" Stan paused. "All right," he went on. "I'm going to put it that way. I'm going to tell you he said all this. Because whether or not he spoke, I—got it. He said that the place they came from—"

"Where was this place?"

"I don't know. Either he couldn't tell me, or he didn't want me to know. Anyhow, he said that their population had increased, and the place where they lived was too small and too poor to support them comfortably. They want to live here, on Earth. But they don't want us around. But they want everything else unchanged, the animals, the birds, the fish. The oceans, the mountains, the rivers. The trees, the flowers... He made it sound like Paradise. And he thought it could be like that. Without us."

"What was so objectionable in us?"

"He must have been here often, or heard a lot, or studied a lot. He said we ruined everything we touched. He said we've wiped out whole species of beautiful and valuable animals and birds. He said we use an incredible amount of our time, and energy, and ingenuity to finding new ways for destroying one another. He said we were too dangerous to keep around. So they've decided to get rid of us, and then take over."

"By warfare?"

"No. They don't go in for that. He said it seemed plain idiocy to them, to risk their healthiest young men in a war. No. They think we can be destroyed by getting the birds off the job. He said they had eleven pits like this one all over the country, and that what they put into them would lure all the birds away from any other food. He said it should be obvious why they started on this country, and after they had proved the method here, and they were proving it, they could go on to the rest of the planet. I asked him where the other pits were, and... He didn't want to answer that one, but he did. I mean, it was all there, like a map—"

"All where?"

"Well, in his mind, I suppose," said Stan, with a growing reluctance. "I know how that must sound, but that's the way it was. He looked at me, stared at me. And somehow he knew he'd told me—let me know. And I could see—oh, hell! I can't help how it sounds. I'm giving it to you the way it was. I could see that he felt I knew entirely too much, and that this was one time when some killing had to be done. He didn't have any sort of weapon, and he was only half my size. But he was quick, and he was surprisingly strong. He jumped at me, and he brought both those metal boots, or whatever they were, down on one of my feet. Broke a couple of small bones, the doctor says. I knew what he meant to do."

"Yes? What did you think he meant to do, Mr Dickson?"

"I didn't think! I knew. He wanted to throw me into that—that foul, stinking pit. He got hold of me around the knees, but I pulled away. And I shot him."

"And the other two who were with him?"

"They... I don't know how they did it. I can just tell you what happened. They did something with their parachutes, and—they went up into the air again."

"And you allowed them to escape?"

"Yes," Stan said. "They—looked like birds. And—I didn't feel like doing any more shooting that day."

"Are you prepared to give us directions for reaching this pit, Mr Dickson?"

"Well, I can tell you where it was. But I don't think you'll find anything much left of it. After the other two were gone, I—went—a bit berserk. I dug at the bank of the river with sticks, branches, my rifle, stones, anything, until I'd made holes to let the river run in and flood it. It—you see—the smell of it was—a bit too much."

"Then this pit which you claim to have discovered is not in existence, Mr Dickson?"

"I don't think so. I hope it's completely flooded out."

"Then you have no evidence to offer, in corroboration of your story, Mr Dickson?"

"No. What about the dead man in my car?"

"There's nothing in your car, Mr Dickson."

"Look here!" cried Stan, sitting up straight in his bed. "Both the Chief and his sergeant saw that body."

"No detailed examination was made, Mr Dickson. They are not prepared to testify that what they saw in your car was a body of any sort. It might have been a puppet, a toy of some sort."

"Where is it now?"

"There is no report of anything having been found in your car, Mr Dickson," said the elderly man. "Moreover, we've received information that you had stolen the car you were driving."

"Look here! I left a hundred dollars deposit for that car."

"There is no record of that, Mr Dickson. Furthermore, you were using licence plates stolen from another car."

"Yes, I did that. I didn't want to be stopped by the police. I was in a hurry, to tell my story, and to show that body. To give someone in authority the location of the other pits. It seemed to me about as urgent as anything could be."

"Are you prepared to give us the locations of these alleged pits, Mr Dickson?"

"Not offhand. But I wrote down all I could remember, while it was fresh in my mind. I made a plan, a sort of little map, on the back of an envelope."

"Where is this envelope, Mr Dickson?"

"In my wallet."

"As a matter of routine procedure, Mr Dickson, the contents of your wallet, and all your pockets were examined and listed. There is no record of such an envelope, with a map or plan drawn on it."

"Look here!"

The fourth man spoke now, for the first time, a stout, sandy-haired man with pale-grey eyes.

"Mr Dickson," he said, "we're willing to accept this episode as a temporary aberration, caused probably by drinking."

"Provided," said the elderly man, "that we are assured it is 'temporary.' If any symptoms of a permanent obsession develop, we shall be obliged, of course, to take steps."

"What 'steps'?" Stan demanded. But he knew, by this time, what they meant.

"We can't have the public morale undermined by wild rumours," said the sandy-haired man. "The situation is bad enough, as it is. But it can be handled by the Government, and the scientists and experts employed by the Government, and it will be. Unauthenticated rumours might cause a panic to develop. And we can't allow such rumours to circulate."

"Meaning—?" said Stan. "That if I tell my story, to anyone, any time, I'll be locked up in some mental institution?"

"If a permanent obsession develops—" said the elderly man.

There was a silence.

"Any objection to my going home now?" Stan asked.

"None whatever, Mr Dickson," said the first man. "And you can rest assured that, unless you persist in some course detrimental to public morale, no charges will be brought against you."

"Damn white of you," said Stan.

⋆

He took a train home, and a taxi from the station.

I've got to have a story for Celia, he thought. But not the truth. I'll have to lie to her, and that won't be easy. It ought to be a good lie, only I don't seem very bright, just now. Could be I'm tired... She'll probably know I'm lying, and that'll hurt her. But I can't tell her the truth. She couldn't believe it. Nobody ever will. I don't want to tell anybody. I don't want to think about it, or remember it. I don't want to talk at all.

But I'll have to talk. Stan, where have you *been*? Who, me? Oh, nowhere special. I was just having a temporary aberration. Much better now, thanks.

The little house looked almost unbelievably pretty, this hot afternoon; the trees stirred in the light breeze; it was so good to get back.

Before he reached the top of the steps, Celia opened the door.

"Hello, Stan!" she said.

His heart sank, at the sight of her, so slender and straight and lovely, in her blue linen dress, smiling at him. But her nonchalance was not convincing, and she was pale; there was a look of strain about her dark eyes.

"Cecily..." he said. "I'm sorry."

And if only we could let it go at that, he thought. If I could sit down beside her, with my arm around her, or even just sit in the same room with her, and not talk, not answer questions, not make up lies...

"Stan, listen!" she cried.

He raised his head, frowning a little.

"I don't hear anything," he said.

"It's the birds, Stan! They're back again! They didn't go away this morning!"

"Good!" he said with an effort. "Fine!"

"Stan, come on in! You're just in time for the 4 o'clock news on the radio."

"Well, no, thanks, Cecily. I don't—"

"Come on!" she said, and held out her hand, and he took it and went into the house with her. A big tree outside shaded the windows here, giving a cool, greenish light to the living room that was neat almost to primness. That's how Celia wants things, he thought. Order, and decency, and peace… Only not that portentous voice on the radio.

"Turn it off, Perfect!" he said.

"But I want you to hear it, Stan," she said. "I heard the news at 3, and maybe they'll have more about it now."

"These pits filled with insects have been formed, scientists say, by unusual climatic conditions. Yesterday one of these pits was discovered in Connecticut, and two more have been found and destroyed this afternoon, one in Idaho, one in Virginia. These discoveries were made possible by a method devised by Dr Wilbur Jonas, world-famous ornithologist employed by the Government in the preservation of wild life. Dr Jonas has demonstrated that a bird's wing may be clipped in such a manner as to render its flight slow enough to be followed easily. This has led the experts—"

"Turn it off, Celia!"

"When I got up yesterday, Stan," she said, "you'd gone. And you'd taken your rifle, and all our cash. I wasn't very happy, Stan."

"Celia, I'm sorry. But—I couldn't leave a note for you. I didn't know—just where I was going, or when I'd get back."

"Birds in the vicinity of the three destroyed pits have already returned to their normal and invaluable function of controlling insect pests," said the portentous voice, "and scientists now predict that within a few days' time the food crisis will be ended—"

"The old man from the boat yard came over yesterday morning," she said. "He told me you'd been shooting birds from one of his rowboats. He said you were crazy, threatening to shoot his dog, and so on. But I thought I was beginning to understand. Only, I was worried… When the night came, and I hadn't heard… I was frightened."

"Celia... I'm sorry."

"Then this morning the head of the police here came to see me. Early, before we'd finished breakfast. He asked me where you were, and I said I didn't know, and didn't care."

"Celia!"

"He was surprised, too. He asked if that meant that you and I didn't get on together. And I said it meant just the opposite. I said we didn't need to ask each other questions, ever. I said that wherever you'd gone, it was all right with me. Then he told me he'd heard from the police in New Haven, and that you were being 'detained' there. He said you'd told them some story about having saved the earth from an invasion from another planet. I told him you didn't know how to talk that way, and he left. But he came back, in less than an hour. He said there was nothing at all in the story he'd heard, and please not to mention it to anyone; and that you weren't being 'detained,' but would be home very soon."

"And so—" boomed the portentous voice, "due to the knowledge and skill and unremitting vigilance of our Government scientists and experts, the pits are being discovered and rendered harmless, our birds are returning, and disaster has been averted. Let us all be grateful to these modest and unassuming men, whose selfless labours have—"

She turned off the radio.

"You had something to do with this, Stan," she said. "I was sure of that, as soon as the old man from the boat yard came over here. Because, you see, I know you're not crazy. And I know you're not the sportsman type who goes out to shoot birds before sunrise."

He said nothing.

"If you don't want to tell me, Stan," she said, "it's all right."

"It isn't a question of not wanting to," he said. "I don't think I *can*."

"I guess there isn't anything you can't tell me, Stan. Want to try?"

"I don't know..." he said.

He lit a cigarette, and sat down on the arm of a chair, and she sat in a corner of the sofa, and he told her. He was slow about it, at first, cautious, groping, but after the beginning it was not hard. She had asked him a few questions, but when he had finished, she was silent.

"Celia…?" he said.

"You did it," she said. "You're exhausted, and half-sick, and you've hurt your foot. You'll never get any credit for it, or any thanks. Only—*I'll* always know, Stan."

"That's good enough," he said, quietly. "Celia, are you crying?"

"It's the—birds," she said. "Maybe all the rest of my life, I'll feel like crying—when I hear the birds getting ready for bed—or early in the morning—"

"Don't cry, Celia! Please!"

"In a moment," she said, "Libby'll bring the children home—and I'll watch her feeding them—and I'll cook dinner—for you and me—and I'll be very gay and silly—so that you won't suspect—what I'm thinking. Their father, and my husband. Our man."

He crossed the room and sat down beside her; he took her hand and laid it against his cheek. "That's what I want to be," he said.

THE GARDENER

Margaret St Clair

From 1946 for nearly two decades Margaret St Clair (1911–1995) was one of the more prolific women contributors to the science-fiction pulps. She continued to appear in a variety of magazines throughout the 1950s and early 1960s, turning more to novels in later years. She wrote not only enjoyable adventure fiction but also more sophisticated stories, many under the alias Idris Seabright. Her books include The Sign of the Labrys *(1963), set underground after Earth has been devastated by a plague and* The Dancers of Noyo *(1973), a weird, post-hippie infused work where survivors of a plague in California return to a native American style culture. Only a few of her stories have been collected, in* The Best of Margaret St Clair *(1985) and, more recently,* The Hole in the Moon *(2019) compiled by Ramsey Campbell.*

TRAFFIC COPS HAVE BEEN KNOWN TO DISREGARD "NO PARKING" signs. Policemen filch apples from fruit stands under the proprietor's very eye. Even a little authority makes its possessor feel that the rules don't apply to *him*. Thus it was that Tiglath Hobbs, acting chief of the Bureau of Extra-Systemic Plant Conservation, cut down a sacred Butandra tree.

It must have been sheer bravado which impelled him to the act. Certainly the grove where the Butandra trees grow (there are only fifty trees on all Cassid, which means that there are only fifty in the universe) is well protected by signs.

Besides warnings in the principal planetary tongues, there is a full set of the realistic and expressive Cassidan pictographs. These announce, in shapes which even the dullest intellect could not misunderstand, that cutting or mutilating the trees is a crime of the gravest nature. That persons committing it will be punished. And that after punishment full atonement must be made.

All the pictographs in the announcement have a frowning look, and the one for "Atonement" in particular is a threatening thing. The pictographs are all painted in pale leaf green.

But Hobbs had the vinegary insolence of the promoted bureaucrat. He saw that he had shocked Reinald, the little Cassidan major who had been delegated his escort, by even entering the sacred grove. He felt a coldly exhibitionistic wish to shock him further.

Down the aisle of trees Hobbs stalked while the tender green leaves murmured above his head. Then he took hold of the trunk of the youngest of the Butandras, a slender white-barked thing, hardly more than a sapling.

"Too close to the others," Hobbs said sharply. "Needs thinning." While Reinald watched helplessly, he got out the little hand axe which hung suspended by his side. Chop—chop chop. With a gush of sap the little tree was severed. Hobbs held it in his hand.

"It will make me a nice walking stick," he said.

Reinald's coffee-coloured skin turned a wretched nephrite green but he said nothing at all. Rather shakily he scrambled back into the 'copter and waited while Hobbs completed his inspection of the grove. It was not until they had flown almost back to Genlis that he made a remark.

"You should not have done that, sir," he said. He ran a finger around his tunic collar uneasily.

Hobbs snorted. He looked down at the lopped-off stem of the Butandra, resting between his knees. "Why not?" he demanded. "I have full authority to order plantations thinned or pruned."

"Yes, sir. But that was a Butandra tree."

"What has that to do with it?"

"There have always been fifty Butandra trees on Cassid. Always, for all our history. We call them 'Cassid's Luck'." Reinald licked his lips. "The tree you cut down will not grow again. I do not know what will happen if there are only forty-nine.

"Besides that, what you did is dangerous. Dangerous, I mean, sir, to you."

Hobbs laughed harshly. "You're forgetting my position," he answered. "Even if they wanted to, the civil authorities couldn't do anything to me."

Reinald gave a very faint smile. "Oh, I don't mean the *civil* authorities, sir," he said in a gentle voice. "They wouldn't be the ones." He seemed, somehow, to have recovered his spirits.

He set the 'copter down neatly on the roof of the Administration Building, and he and his passenger got out. Back in the grove near the stump of the sapling Butandra something was burrowing up rapidly through the soil.

Hobbs left Cassid the next day on the first leg of the long journey back to earth. In his baggage was the piece of Butandra wood. He was taking particular care of it since one of the room maids at his hotel in Genlis had tried to throw it out. But for the first few days of his trip he was altogether too occupied with filling out forms and drafting reports to do anything with it.

About this same time, on Cassid, a conversation was going on in the Hotel Genlis dining room.

"Tell us what you thought it was when you first saw it," Berta, the room maid for the odd-numbered levels in the hotel, urged. "Go on!"

Marie, the chief room maid, selected a piece of mangosteen torte from the food belt as it went by. "Well," she said, "I was checking the rooms on that level to be sure the robot help had cleaned up properly and when I saw that big brown spot on the floor my first thought was, one of them's spilled something. Robots are such dopes.

"Then it moved, and I saw it wasn't a stain at all, but a big brown thing snuffling around on the eutex like a dog after something. Then it stood up. That was when I screamed."

"Yes, but what did it look like? Go on, Marie! You never want to tell this part."

"It was a big tall lanky thing," Marie said reluctantly, "with a rough brown skin like a potato. It had two little pink mole hands. And it had an awfully, awfully kind face."

"If it had such a kind face I don't see why you were so scared of it," Berta said. She always said that at this point.

Marie took a bite out of her mangosteen torte. She ate it slowly, considering. It was not that the emotion she had experienced at sight of the face was at all dim in her mind. It was that embodying it in words was difficult.

"Well," she said, "maybe it wasn't really kind. Or—wait now, Berta, I've got it—it was a kind face but not for people. For human beings it wasn't at all a kind face."

"Guess what room this happened in," Berta said, turning to Rose, the even-numbered room maid.

"I don't need to guess, I know," Rose drawled. "One thousand one hundred and eighty-five, the room that earthman had. The man that didn't leave any tip and gave you such a bawling-out for touching you-know-what."

Berta nodded. "If I'd *known*—" she said with a slight shudder. "If I'd *guessed*! I mean, I'd rather have touched a *snake*! Anyhow, Marie, tell Rose what you think the brown thing was."

"As Rose says, I don't need to guess, I know," Marie replied. She pushed the empty dessert plate away from her. "When a man cuts down one of our Butandra trees—that thing in the room was a Gardener."

The Gardener left the soil of Cassid with a minimum of fuss. Not for it the full thunder of rockets, the formalized pageantry of the spaceport. It gave a slight push with its feet and the soil receded. There was an almost imperceptible jetting of fire. Faster and faster the Gardener went. It left behind first the atmosphere of Cassid and then, much later, that planet's gravitational field. And still it shot on, out into the star-flecked dark.

On his fourth day in space Hobbs got out the Butandra stick. Its heavy, white, close-grained wood pleased him. It would, as he had told Reinald, make a fine walking stick. Hobbs got a knife from his pocket and began carefully to peel off the tough white bark.

The bark came off as neatly as a rabbit's skin. Hobbs pursed his lips in what, for him, was a smile. He studied the contours of the wood and then started to whittle out a knob.

The wood was hard. The work went slowly. Hobbs was almost ready to put it aside and go down to the ship's bar for a nightcap when there came a light tapping at his cabin's exterior viewing pane.

When a ship is in deep space the sense of isolation becomes almost tangible. It seeps into every pore of every passenger. The ship floats in ghostly fashion through an uncreated void in which there is nothing—can be nothing—except the tiny world enclosed by the curving beryllium hull. And now something—something *outside* the ship—was rapping on Hobbs' viewing pane.

For a moment Hobbs sat paralysed, as near to stone as a man can be and still breathe. Then he dropped the Butandra stick and turned to the viewing pane. There was nothing there, of course—nothing but the black, the black.

Hobbs bit his lips. With slightly unsteady fingers he picked up the stick from the floor and locked it away in his valise. Then he tightened his belt around his paunch, buttoned up his coat and went down to the bar.

He found the second officer there. McPherson was drinking pomelo juice and eating a bosula tongue sandwich. A plump good-natured man, he always liked a little something to eat before he hit the sack. After his own drink had been brought Hobbs got into conversation with the second officer. A possible explanation for the noise he had heard had come to him.

"Something gone wrong with the ship?" he asked. "Is that why you've got a repair crew out on the hull?"

McPherson looked surprised. "Repair crew?" he echoed. "Why no, nothing's wrong. Captain Thorwald hates making repairs in deep space—always something faulty in them—and he wouldn't order repairs here unless the situation were really emergent. There's no crew out. What makes you ask that?"

"I—thought I heard something rapping on my viewing pane."

The second officer smiled. He decided to make a joke. "Been doing something you shouldn't, sir?" he said.

Hobbs put down his glass. "I beg your pardon?" he said icily.

The second officer grew sober. Hobbs, while not coming under the heading of VIP, was fairly important all the same.

"No offence meant, sir," he said. "Just a little joke. Don't you know how, in the stories spacemen tell, the curse or doom or whatever it is always shows itself to its victim in space by tapping on his viewing pane? When a man's broken a taboo on one of the planets, I mean. That was what I was referring to. Just a little joke."

"Oh." Hobbs swallowed. He held out his glass to the barman. "Another of the same," he said in a rather hoarse voice. "Make it a double."

Tiglath Hobbs was an extremely stubborn man. This quality, in some situations, is hardly to be distinguished from courage. Next wake-period he got out the Butandra stick again. With cold, unsteady fingers he worked on the knob. He had stationed himself close to the viewing plate.

There was no rapping this time. Hobbs did not know what it was that made him look up. Look up at last he did. And there, bobbing about in the tiny spot of light which seeped out through his viewing pane, was the smiling face the room maid in Genlis had seen. Brown and rough, it was regarding Hobbs with incredible, with indescribable benignity.

Hobbs uttered a cry. He pressed the button which sent the pane shutter flying into place. And the next moment he was standing by his cabin door, as far away from the pane as he could get, his fingers pressed over his eyes. When he stopped shuddering he decided to go see Captain Thorwald.

It took him a long time to get to the point. Thorwald listened, drumming with his fingers on his desk, while Hobbs circumlocuted, hesitated, retracted and corrected himself. What came out eventually was that he wanted Captain Thorwald—just for a moment, just for a fraction of a second—to have the ship's force field turned on.

Thorwald shook his head. "I'm sorry, Mr Hobbs. It's impossible. Turning on the field would have to go into the log, you know, and there's no reason for it." Hobbs hesitated. Then he got his wallet out. "I'll make it worth your while. Five hundred I.U.'s?"

"Sorry, no."

"Six hundred? Seven hundred? Money is always useful. You could say you ran into a meteor swarm."

"I—no."

"Eight hundred? Look here, I'll give you a thousand! Surely you could fix the log."

Thorwald's face wore a faint, sour smile but still he hesitated. "Very well," he said abruptly. "Let's say you bet me a thousand I.U.'s that I can't turn the ship's force field on and off again in a sixtieth of a second. Is that it? I warn you, Mr Hobbs, you're sure to lose your bet."

Hobbs' eyelids flickered. If the captain wanted to save his pride this way—

"I don't believe it!" he said with artificial vehemence. "I don't believe a field can be turned on and off that fast. It's a bet. I'll leave the stakes on the table, captain." From his wallet he drew ten crisp yellow notes.

Thorwald nodded. "Very well," he said without touching the money. "In half an hour, Mr Hobbs, you shall have your demonstration. Will that be satisfactory?"

"Quite."

Thorwald nodded and picked up the notes with his right hand.

Hobbs went back to his cabin, raised the shutter and sat down by the viewing pane. He had keyed himself up to the pitch where it was almost a disappointment to him that the smiling face did not appear. The moments passed.

Abruptly the ship shook from stern to stern. A billion billion tiny golden needles lanced out into the dark. Then the cascade of glory was gone and the eternal black of space was back.

It had happened so quickly that, except for the pattern of light etched on his retina, Hobbs might have wondered whether he had seen it at all. Thorwald could certainly claim to have won his bet.

But Hobbs was well satisfied with what he had got for his thousand I.U.'s. In the fraction of a second that the force field had been turned on he had seen, crushed and blackened against the field's candent radiance, a dead scorched shapeless thing like a burned spider.

The myriad biting fires of the force field must have charred it instantly to the bone. What Hobbs had seen in that instant of incredible illumination was dead beyond a doubt, as dead as the moon.

By now it must be lying thousands upon thousands of kilos to the side of the ship's course, where the vast impetus of the field had sent it hurtling. Hobbs drew a deep, deep breath. Relief had made him weak.

When he and Thorwald met at the next meal they maintained a cautious cordiality toward each other. Neither of them, then or at any time thereafter, referred again to the bet.

That sleep-period Hobbs rested well. In the next few days he regained most of his usual aplomb. Leisurely he finished carving the Butandra wood into a walking stick. It made a very nice one. By the time the ship docked at Llewellyn, an earth-type planet but with a third less than earth's normal gee, he was quite himself again.

In the depths of space, uncounted millions of kilometres away, the blackened husk of the Gardener floated weightlessly. It was quite dry and dead. But did it not stir a little from time to time as though a breeze rustled it? And what were those cracks that slowly appeared in it? Were they not like the cracks in a chrysalis?

Hobbs was well pleased with the state of the plantations on Llewellyn. He told the young man in charge of the local office so and the young man was gratified. By the end of the third day Hobbs was ready to resume his interrupted voyage toward Earth.

Something he saw in a sheet of stereo-press newsprint changed his mind. "Fiend robs, mutilates liner chief!" the big red scarehead bellowed. And then, in smaller type, the paper went on, "Minus finger and 1,000 I.U.'s, captain unable to name assailant. Police make search."

Hobbs—he was at breakfast—looked at the item incuriously until, in the body of the story, his eye caught a familiar name. Then he read with avid interest.

> Eins Thorwald, captain of the luxury space liner *Rhea* (this was inaccurate—the *Rhea* was not a luxury liner but a freighter with fairly comfortable accommodation for five or six passengers) was in hospital today minus one thousand I.U.'s and the index finger of his right hand.
>
> Thorwald, found in a state of collapse in his cabin by his second officer, Joseph McPherson (see page two for pictures), was unable to give details of the attack on him. He told police he had been robbed of exactly one thousand I.U.'s. Other currency in Thorwald's wallet was untouched.
>
> Thorwald's finger, according to medical officer Dingby of the local police, appears to have been amputated with the help of a chisel or some similar instrument. No trace of the missing digit has been found.
>
> Thorwald himself, after receiving several transfusions, is in Mercy Hospital, where his condition is reported serious. Police are operating on the theory that the attack was the work of some fiend whose hobby is collecting human fingers. A thorough search is being made and they expect an arrest soon.

Hobbs put the newsprint down. His hands were trembling. His florid cheeks had turned white. What he suspected, he told himself, was sheer lunacy.

Hadn't he himself seen the—thing which had rapped at his viewing pane reduced to a blackened cinder by the ravening fires of the force field? But Thorwald had been robbed of exactly one thousand I.U.'s. And he had picked up Hobbs' bribe with his right hand.

Hobbs pushed his plate away and asked the robot for his check. In the lobby he video'd Mercy Hospital and inquired for news of Thorwald. He was told that Thorwald's condition was serious and that he could not possibly see anyone.

Hobbs sat in the lobby for an hour or so and tried to think. At the end of that time he had come to a decision. Tiglath Hobbs was a stubborn man.

He called a 'copter and had it take him to the local office of the Bureau of Extra-Systemic Plant Conservation. Scott, the young man in charge of the office, was out and Hobbs had to wait for him.

It was nearly noon when Scott came in, very brown and erect in his clothing of forest green. He had been supervising the weeding of a plantation of young Tillya trees and there was mud on the knees of his trousers from kneeling beside the seedlings. The knees of his trousers were always a little muddy. He had the green heart of the true forester.

Hobbs came to the point at once. "Scott," he said, "I want you to go to Cassid and supervise the uprooting of the plantation of Butandra trees there."

Scott looked at him for a moment incredulously. "I beg your pardon, sir?" he said at last in a neutral tone.

"I said, I want you to go to Cassid and supervise the uprooting of the plantation of Butandra trees there."

"I—sir, what is the reason for this order?"

"Because I say so."

"But, Mr Hobbs, the Butandra trees are unique. As you of course know, there is nothing like them anywhere else in the universe. Scientifically it would be criminal to destroy those trees.

"Further than that, they play a considerable role in Cassidan planetary life. To the inhabitants the trees have a large emotional significance. I must ask you, sir, to reconsider your decision."

"You have your orders. Carry them out."

"I'm sorry, sir. I decline to do so."

Hobbs' thick neck had turned red. "I'll have your job for this," he said chokingly.

Scott permitted himself a thin smile. "I have civil service tenure, sir," he said.

"You can be removed for cause. Insubordination, in this case."

Scott's smile vanished, but he did not retreat. "Very well," he said. "If it comes to a public hearing we'll see. In any case I can't carry out that order. And I very much doubt, Mr Hobbs, that you'll find anyone who will. It's not the kind of thing you can ask of a forester."

Hobbs raised his stick of Butandra wood. His expression was murderous. Then his common sense reasserted itself. He gave Scott a nod and left.

He called the travel bureau, cancelled his Earthward passage and made reservations for a cabin on the next ship back to Cassid. If he could not find anyone to carry out his orders to destroy the plantation of Butandra trees he would do it himself. Tiglath Hobbs, as has been said before, was a stubborn man.

The trip back to Cassid was unexceptional. Nothing came to rap at Hobbs' viewing pane or to peer in at him. It was so quiet, in fact, that Hobbs had fits of wondering whether he was doing the right thing.

The Butandra trees were, as Scott had said, of considerable scientific interest and Hobbs might be letting himself in for a good deal of unfavourable criticism by destroying them. And the attack on Thorwald might have been only a coincidence.

But by now Hobbs bitterly hated the Butandra trees. Guilt, anxiety and self-righteousness had coalesced in him to form an emotion of overwhelming intensity. He hated the Butandra trees. How could there be any question about destroying them?

With their repulsive staring white bark and the nasty whispering rustle their long green leaves made they deserved—yes, they positively deserved—to be killed. How could a decent-minded man let the Butandra trees live?

Usually, by the time he got to this point in his thoughts, Hobbs began to pant. He had to make a conscious effort to calm himself.

Hobbs' ship docked at Genlis spaceport late at night. Hobbs was too excited to try to sleep. He paced up and down in the waiting room until day came.

Then he rented a 'copter from a Fly-It-Yourself hangarage and flew to a supply house which specialized in compact power saws. He had decided to fell the trees first and afterwards make arrangements for having the stumps pulled up.

It was still early when he got to the sacred grove. In the tender light of morning the straight, white-barked, green-leaved trees made a pretty, peaceful sight. Hobbs hesitated, though not from any qualms about his contemplated arboricide. What was bothering him was a feeling that entering the grove to cut down the trees, even in daylight, might be dangerous.

On the other hand the best defence was always attack. What had happened to Thorwald had been almost certainly a coincidence. But if it hadn't—Hobbs swallowed—the best way of insuring himself against a similar experience was to cut down the grove.

The grove was, he had decided on Llewellyn, the—the thing's base of operations. It drew power from the grove as surely as the trees of the grove drew nourishment from the soil. Once the grove was destroyed the thing, whether or not the force field had killed it, would have no more power.

Hobbs took the portable saw from the 'copter and slung it over his shoulder. He hesitated a fraction of a second longer. A sudden gust of wind set the long leaves of the Butandras to rustling mockingly. Hobbs felt a nearly blinding surge of hate. His jaw set. He opened the gate and entered the grove.

The power saw was not heavy and he decided to begin his felling operations beside the sapling he had first cut down. He found the stump without difficulty and was pleased to see that it had not put up any shoots. But somebody had dug a deep hole in the ground beside it, and Hobbs frowned over this.

He set the saw down on the turf and knelt to adjust it. He could find out about the hole later. He touched a switch. The saw's motor began to purr.

The Gardener came out from behind a tree and smiled at him.

Hobbs gave a strangled, inarticulate shriek. He scrambled to his knees and started to run. The Gardener stretched out its lanky arms and caught him easily.

With its little pink mole hands it stripped his clothing away. His shoes came off. With ten separate chops of its strong white teeth the Gardener bit away his toes. While Hobbs struggled and shrieked and shrieked and shrieked, the Gardener peeled away the skin on the inner surfaces of his legs and thighs and bound these members together with a length of vine.

It drew scratches all over the surface of his body with its long sharp mole claws and rubbed a gritty greyish powder carefully into each gash. Then it carried Hobbs over to the hole it had made and, still smiling, planted him.

When the Gardener came back an hour or so later from its tasks of cultivation in another part of the grove, a thin crust of bark had already begun to form over Hobbs' human frame. It would not be long, the Gardener knew, before Hobbs would become a quite satisfactory Butandra tree.

The Gardener smiled benignly. It looked with approval at the graft on the trunk of the tree to the right, where what had once been Eins Thorwald's index finger was burgeoning luxuriantly.

The Gardener nodded. "A leaf for a leaf," it said.

DROP DEAD

Clifford D. Simak

Clifford D. Simak (1904–1988) was one of the greats of science fiction and a truly original writer. He is probably best remembered for City *(1952), which won him the International Fantasy Award in 1953, but this episodic novel of the future of human civilization is not typical of his work. He created his own niche in depicting strange events in rural settings or on alien worlds, and his stories often feature intelligent animals or humanistic robots. One of his best stories, "The Big Front Yard" (1958) won the Hugo Award in 1959 and he won it again in 1964 for the novel* Way Station. *Other novels include* Time and Again *(1951),* Ring Around the Sun *(1953) and* All Flesh is Grass *(1965). To my mind, though, Simak's best work was in the short story and David Wixon, on behalf of Simak's estate, has been compiling a series of collections that constitute the complete short fiction, starting with* I Am Crying All Inside *(2015). No library of science fiction should be without the works of Clifford D. Simak.*

THE CRITTERS WERE UNBELIEVABLE. THEY LOOKED LIKE SOMEthing from the maudlin pen of a well-alcoholed cartoonist.

One herd of them clustered in a semicircle in front of the ship, not jittery or belligerent—just looking at us. And that was strange. Ordinarily, when a spaceship sets down on a virgin planet, it takes a week at least for any life that might have seen or heard it to creep out of hiding and sneak a look around.

The critters were almost cow-size, but nohow as graceful as a cow. Their bodies were pushed together as if ever blessed one of them had run full-tilt into a wall. And they were just as lumpy as you'd expect from a collision like that. Their hides were splashed with large squares of pastel colour—the kind of colour one never finds on any self-respecting animal: violet, pink, orange, chartreuse, to name only a few. The overall effect was of a chequerboard done by an old lady who made crazy quilts.

And that, by far, was not the worst of it.

From their heads and other parts of their anatomy sprouted a weird sort of vegetation, so that it appeared each animal was hiding, somewhat ineffectively, behind a skimpy thicket. To compound the situation and make it completely insane, fruits and vegetables—or what *appeared* to be fruits and vegetables—grew from the vegetation.

So we stood there, the critters looking at us and us looking back at them, and finally one of them walked forward until it was no more than six feet from us. It stood there for a moment, gazing at us soulfully, then dropped dead at our feet.

The rest of the herd turned around and trotted awkwardly away, for all the world as if they had done what they had come to do and now could go about their business.

★

Julian Oliver, our botanist, put up a hand and rubbed his balding head with an absent-minded motion.

"Another whatisit coming up!" he moaned. "Why couldn't it, for once, be something plain and simple?"

"It never is," I told him. "Remember that bush out on Hamal V that spent half its life as a kind of glorified tomato and the other half as grade A poison ivy?"

"I remember it," Oliver said sadly.

Max Weber, our biologist, walked over to the critter, reached out a cautious foot and prodded it.

"Trouble is," he said, "that Hamal tomato was Julian's baby and this one here is mine."

"I wouldn't say entirely yours," Oliver retorted. "What do you call that underbrush growing out of it?"

I came in fast to head off an argument. I had listened to those two quarrelling for the past twelve years, across several hundred light-years and on a couple dozen planets. I couldn't stop it here, I knew, but at least I could postpone it until they had something vital to quarrel about.

"Cut it out," I said. "It's only a couple of hours till nightfall and we have to get the camp set up."

"But this critter," Weber said. "We can't just leave it here."

"Why not? There are millions more of them. This one will stay right here and even if it doesn't—"

"But it dropped dead!"

"So it was old and feeble."

"It wasn't. It was right in the prime of life."

"We can talk about it later," said Alfred Kemper, our bacteriologist. "I'm as interested as you two, but what Bob says is right. We have to get the camp set up."

"Another thing," I added, looking hard at all of them. "No matter how innocent this place may look, we observe planet rules. No eating anything. No drinking any water. No wandering off alone. No carelessness of any kind."

"There's nothing here," said Weber. "Just the herds of critters. Just the endless plains. No trees, no hills, no nothing."

He really didn't mean it. He knew as well as I did the reason for observing planet rules. He only wanted to argue.

"All right," I said, "which is it? Do we set up camp or do we spend the night up in the ship?"

That did it.

We had the camp set up before the sun went down and by dusk we were all settled in. Carl Parsons, our ecologist, had the stove together and the supper started before the last tent peg was driven.

I dug out my diet kit and mixed up my formula and all of them kidded me about it, the way they always did.

It didn't bother me. Their jibes were automatic and I had automatic answers. It was something that had been going on for a long, long time. Maybe it was best that way, better than if they'd disregarded my enforced eating habits.

I remember Carl was grilling steaks and I had to move away so I couldn't smell them. There's never a time when I wouldn't give my good right arm for a steak or, to tell the truth, any other kind of normal chow. This diet stuff keeps a man alive all right, but that's about the only thing that can be said of it.

I know ulcers must sound silly and archaic. Ask any medic and he'll tell you they don't happen any more. But I have a riddled stomach and the diet kit to prove they sometimes do. I guess it's what you might call an occupational ailment. There's a lot of never-ending worry playing nursemaid to planet survey gangs.

After supper, we went out and dragged the critter in and had a closer look at it.

It was even worse to look at close than from a distance.

There was no fooling about that vegetation. It was the real McCoy and it was part and parcel of the critter. But it seemed that it only grew out of certain of the colour blocks in the critter's body.

We found another thing that practically had Weber frothing at the mouth. One of the colour blocks had holes in it—it looked almost exactly like one of those peg sets that children use as toys. When Weber took out his jackknife and poked into one of the holes, he pried out an insect that looked something like a bee. He couldn't quite believe it, so he did some more probing and in another one of the holes he found another bee. Both of the bees were dead.

He and Oliver wanted to start dissection then and there, but the rest of us managed to talk them out of it.

We pulled straws to see who would stand first guard and, with my usual luck, I pulled the shortest straw. Actually there wasn't much real reason for standing guard, with the alarm system set to protect the camp, but it was regulation—there had to be a guard.

I got a gun and the others said good night and went to their tents, but I could hear them talking for a long time afterward. No matter how hardened you may get to this survey business, no matter how blasé, you hardly ever get much sleep the first night on any planet.

I sat on a chair at one side of the camp table, on which burned a lantern in lieu of the campfire we would have had on any other planet. But here we couldn't have a fire because there wasn't any wood.

I sat at one side of the table, with the dead critter lying on the other side of it and I did some worrying, although it wasn't time for me to start worrying yet. I'm an agricultural economist and I don't begin my worrying until at least the first reports are in.

But sitting just across the table from where it lay, I couldn't help but do some wondering about that mixed-up critter. I didn't get anywhere except go around in circles and I was sort of glad when Talbott Fullerton, the Double Eye, came out and sat down beside me.

Sort of, I said. No one cared too much for Fullerton. I have yet to see the Double Eye I or anybody else ever cared much about.

"Too excited to sleep?" I asked him.

He nodded vaguely, staring off into the darkness beyond the lantern's light.

"Wondering," he said. "Wondering if this could be the planet."

"It won't be," I told him. "You're chasing an El Dorado, hunting down a fable."

"They found it once before," Fullerton argued stubbornly. "It's all there in the records."

"So was the Gilded Man. And the Empire of Prester John. Atlantis and all the rest of it. So was the old Northwest Passage back on ancient Earth. So were the Seven Cities. But nobody ever found any of those places because they weren't there."

He sat with the lamplight in his face and he had that wild look in his eyes and his hands were knotting into fists, then straightening out again.

"Sutter," he said unhappily, "I don't know why you do this—this mocking of yours. Somewhere in this universe there is immortality. Somewhere, somehow, it has been accomplished. And the human race must find it. We have the space for it now—all the space there is—millions of planets and eventually other galaxies. We don't have to keep making room for new generations, the way we would if we were stuck on a single world or a single solar system. Immortality, I tell you, is the next step for humanity!"

"Forget it," I said curtly, but once a Double Eye gets going, you can't shut him up.

"Look at this planet," he said. "An almost perfect Earth-type planet. Main-sequence sun. Good soil, good climate, plenty of water—an ideal place for a colony. How many years, do you think, before Man will settle here?"

"A thousand. Five thousand. Maybe more."

"That's right. And there are countless other planets like it, planets crying to be settled. But we won't settle them, because we keep dying off. And that's not all of it..."

Patiently, I listened to all the rest—the terrible waste of dying—and I knew every bit of it by heart. Before Fullerton, we'd been saddled by one Double Eye fanatic and, before him, yet another. It was regulation. Every planet-checking team, no matter what its purpose or its destination, was required to carry as supercargo an agent of Immortality Institute.

But this kid seemed just a little worse than the usual run of them. It was his first trip out and he was all steamed up with idealism. In all of them, though, burned the same intense dedication to the proposition that Man must live forever and an equally unyielding belief that immortality could and would be found. For had not a lost spaceship found the answer centuries before—an unnamed spaceship on an unknown planet in a long-forgotten year!

It was a myth, of course. It had all the hallmarks of one and all the fierce loyalty that a myth can muster. It was kept alive by Immortality Institute, operating under a government grant and billions of bequests and gifts from hopeful rich and poor—all of whom, of course, had died or would die in spite of their generosity.

"What are you looking for?" I asked Fullerton, just a little wearily, for I was bored with it. "A plant? An animal? A people?"

And he replied, solemn as a judge: "That's something I can't tell you."

As if I gave a damn!

But I went on needling him. Maybe it was just something to while away my time. That and the fact that I disliked the fellow. Fanatics annoy me. They won't get off your ear.

"Would you know it if you found it?"

He didn't answer that one, but he turned haunted eyes on me.

I cut out the needling. Any more of it and I'd have had him bawling.

We sat around a while longer, but we did no talking.

He fished a toothpick out of his pocket and put it in his mouth and rolled it around, chewing at it moodily. I would have liked to reach out and slug him, for he chewed toothpicks all the time and it was an irritating habit that set me unreasonably on edge. I guess I was jumpy, too.

Finally he spit out the mangled toothpick and slouched off to bed.

I sat alone, looking up at the ship, and the lantern light was just bright enough for me to make out the legend lettered on it: *Caph VII—Ag Survey* 286, which was enough to identify us anywhere in the Galaxy.

For everyone knew Caph VII, the agricultural experimental planet, just as they would have known Aldebaran XII, the medical research planet, or Capella IX, the university planet, or any of the other special departmental planets.

Caph VII is a massive operation and the hundreds of survey teams like us were just a part of it. But we were the spearheads who went out to new worlds, some of them uncharted, some just barely charted, looking for plants and animals that might be developed on the experimental tracts.

Not that our team had found a great deal. We had discovered some grasses that did well on one of the Eltanian worlds, but by and large we hadn't done anything that could be called distinguished. Our luck just seemed to run bad—like that Hamal poison ivy business. We worked as hard as any of the rest of them, but a lot of good that did.

Sometimes it was tough to take—when all the other teams brought in stuff that got them written up and earned them bonuses, while we came creeping in with a few piddling grasses or maybe not a thing at all.

It's a tough life and don't let anyone tell you different. Some of the planets turn out to be a fairly rugged business. At times, the boys come back pretty much the worse for wear and there are times when they don't come back at all.

But right now it looked as though we'd hit it lucky—a peaceful planet, good climate, easy terrain, no hostile inhabitants and no dangerous fauna.

Weber took his time relieving me at guard, but finally he showed up.

I could see he still was goggle-eyed about the critter. He walked around it several times, looking it over.

"That's the most fantastic case of symbiosis I have ever seen," he said. "If it weren't lying over there, I'd say it was impossible. Usually you associate symbiosis with the lower, more simple forms of life."

"You mean that brush growing out of it?"

He nodded.

"And the bees?"

He gagged over the bees.

"How are you so sure it's symbiosis?"

He almost wrung his hands. "I *don't* know," he admitted.

I gave him the rifle and went to the tent I shared with Kemper. The bacteriologist was awake when I came in.

"That you, Bob?"

"It's me. Everything's all right."

"I've been lying here and thinking," he said. "This is a screwy place."

"The critters?"

"No, not the critters. The planet itself. Never saw one like it. It's positively naked. No trees. No flowers. Nothing. It's just a sea of grass."

"Why not?" I asked. "Where does it say you can't find a pasture planet?"

"It's too simple," he protested. "Too simplified. Too neat and packaged. Almost as if someone had said let's make a simple planet, let's cut out all the frills, let's skip all the biological experiments and get right down to basics. Just one form of life and the grass for it to eat."

"You're way out on a limb," I told him. "How do you know all this? There may be other life-forms. There may be complexities we can't suspect. Sure, all we've seen are the critters, but maybe that's because there are so many of them."

"To hell with you," he said and turned over on his cot.

Now there's a guy I liked. We'd been tent partners ever since he'd joined the team better than ten years before and we got along fine.

Often I had wished the rest could get along as well. But it was too much to expect.

The fighting started right after breakfast, when Oliver and Weber insisted on using the camp table for dissecting. Parsons, who doubled as cook, jumped straight down their throats. Why he did it, I don't know. He knew before he said a word that he was licked, hands down. The same thing had happened many times before and he knew, no matter what he did or said, they would use the table.

But he put up a good battle. "You guys go and find some other place to do your butchering! Who wants to eat on a table that's all slopped up?"

"But, Carl, where can we do it? We'll use only one end of the table."

Which was a laugh, because in half an hour they'd be sprawled all over it.

"Spread out a canvas," Parsons snapped back.

"You can't dissect on a canvas. You got to have—"

"Another thing. How long do you figure it will take? In a day or two, that critter is going to get ripe."

It went on like that for quite a while, but by the time I started up the ladder to get the animals, Oliver and Weber had flung the critter on the table and were at work on it.

Unshipping the animals is something not exactly in my line of duty, but over the years I'd taken on the job of getting them unloaded, so they'd be there and waiting when Weber or some of the others needed them to run off a batch of tests.

I went down into the compartment where we kept them in their cages. The rats started squeaking at me and the zartyls from Centauri started screeching at me and the punkins from Polaris made an unholy racket, because the punkins are hungry all the time. You just can't give them enough to eat. Turn them loose with food and they'd eat themselves to death.

It was quite a job to get them all lugged up to the port and to rig up a sling and lower them to the ground, but I finally finished it without busting a single cage. That was an accomplishment. Usually I smashed a cage or two and some of the animals escaped and then Weber would froth around for days about my carelessness.

I had the cages all set out in rows and was puttering with canvas flies to protect them from the weather when Kemper came along and stood watching me.

"I have been wandering around," he announced. From the way he said it, I could see he had the wind up.

But I didn't ask him, for then he'd never have told me. You had to wait for Kemper to make up his mind to talk.

"Peaceful place," I said and it was all of that. It was a bright, clear day and the sun was not too warm. There was a little breeze and you could see a long way off. And it was quiet. Really quiet. There wasn't any noise at all.

"It's a lonesome place," said Kemper.

"I don't get you," I answered patiently.

"Remember what I said last night? About this planet being too simplified?"

He stood watching me put up the canvas, as if he might be considering how much more to tell me. I waited.

Finally, he blurted it. "Bob, there are no insects!"

"What have insects—"

"You know what I mean," he said. "You go out on Earth or any Earthlike planet and lie down in the grass and watch. You'll see the insects. Some of them on the ground and others on the grass. There'll be all kinds of them."

"And there aren't any here?"

He shook his head. "None that I could see. I wandered around and lay down and looked in a dozen different places. Stands to reason a man should find some insects if he looked all morning. It isn't natural, Bob."

I kept on with my canvas and I don't know why it was, but I got a little chilled about there not being any insects. Not that I care a hoot for insects, but as Kemper said, it was unnatural, although you come to expect the so-called unnatural in this planet-checking business.

"There are the bees," I said.

"What bees?"

"The ones that are in the critters. Didn't you see any?"

"None," he said. "I didn't get close to any critter herds. Maybe the bees don't travel very far."

"Any birds?"

"I didn't see a one," he said. "But I was wrong about the flowers. The grass has tiny flowers."

"For the bees to work on."

Kemper's face went stony. "That's right. Don't you see the pattern of it, the planned—"

"I see it," I told him.

He helped me with the canvas and we didn't say much more. When we had it done, we walked into camp.

Parsons was cooking lunch and grumbling at Oliver and Weber, but they weren't paying much attention to him. They had the table littered with different parts they'd carved out of the critter and they were looking slightly numb.

"No brain," Weber said to us accusingly, as if we might have made off with it when he wasn't looking. "We can't find a brain and there's no nervous system."

"It's impossible," declared Oliver. "How can a highly organized, complex animal exist without a brain or nervous system?"

"Look at that butcher shop!" Parsons yelled wrathfully from the stove. "You guys will have to eat standing up!"

"Butcher shop is right," Weber agreed. "As near as we can figure out, there are at least a dozen different kinds of flesh—some fish, some fowl, some good red meat. Maybe a little lizard, even."

"An all-purpose animal," said Kemper. "Maybe we found something finally."

"If it's edible," Oliver added. "If it doesn't poison you. If it doesn't grow hair all over you."

"That's up to you," I told him. "I got the cages down and all lined up. You can start killing off the little cusses to your heart's content."

Weber looked ruefully at the mess on the table.

"We did just a rough exploratory job," he explained. "We ought to start another one from scratch. You'll have to get in on that next one, Kemper."

Kemper nodded glumly.

Weber looked at me. "Think you can get us one?"

"Sure," I said. "No trouble."

It wasn't.

Right after lunch, a lone critter came walking up, as if to visit us. It stopped about six feet from where we sat, gazed at us soulfully, then obligingly dropped dead.

During the next few days, Oliver and Weber barely took time out to eat and sleep. They sliced and probed. They couldn't believe half the things they found. They argued. They waved their scalpels in the air to emphasize their anguish. They almost broke down and wept. Kemper filled box after box with slides and sat hunched, half petrified, above his microscope.

Parsons and I wandered around while the others worked. He dug up some soil samples and tried to classify the grasses and failed, because there weren't any grasses—there was just one type of grass. He made notes on the weather and ran an analysis of the air and tried to pull together an ecological report without a lot to go on.

I looked for insects and I didn't find any except the bees and I never saw those unless I was near a critter herd. I watched for birds and there were none. I spent two days investigating a creek, lying on my belly and staring down into the water, and there were no signs of life. I hunted up a sugar sack and put a hoop in the mouth of it and spent another two days seining. I didn't catch a thing—not a fish, not even a crawdad, not a single thing.

By that time, I was ready to admit that Kemper had guessed right.

Fullerton walked around, too, but we paid no attention to him. All the Double Eyes, every one of them, always were looking for something no one else could see. After a while, you got pretty tired of them. I'd spent twenty years getting tired of them.

The last day I went seining, Fullerton stumbled onto me late in the afternoon. He stood up on the bank and watched me working in a pool. When I looked up, I had the feeling he'd been watching me for quite a little while.

"There's nothing there," he said.

The way he said it, he made it sound as if he'd known all along there was nothing there and that I was a fool for looking.

But that wasn't the only reason I got sore.

Sticking out of his face, instead of the usual toothpick, was a stem of grass and he was rolling it around in his lips and chewing it the way he chewed the toothpicks.

"Spit out that grass!" I shouted at him. "You fool, spit it out!"

His eyes grew startled and he spit out the grass.

"It's hard to remember," he mumbled. "You see, it's my first trip out and—"

"It could be your last one, too," I told him brutally. "Ask Weber sometime, when you have a moment, what happened to the guy who pulled a leaf and chewed it. Absent-minded, sure. Habit, certainly. He was just as dead as if he'd committed suicide."

Fullerton stiffened up.

"I'll keep it in mind," he said.

I stood there, looking up at him, feeling a little sorry that I'd been so tough with him.

But I had to be. There were so many absent-minded, well-intentioned ways a man could kill himself.

"You find anything?" I asked.

"I've been watching the critters," he said. "There was something funny that I couldn't quite make out at first..."

"I can list you a hundred funny things."

"That's not what I mean, Sutter. Not the patchwork colour or the bushes growing out of them. There was something else. I finally got it figured out. *There aren't any young.*"

Fullerton was right, of course. I realized it now, after he had told me. There weren't any calves or whatever you might call them. All we'd seen were adults. And yet that didn't necessarily mean there *weren't* any calves. It just meant we hadn't seen them. And the same, I knew, applied as well to insects, birds and fish. They all might be on the planet, but we just hadn't managed to find them yet.

And then, belatedly, I got it—the inference, the hope, the half-crazy fantasy behind this thing that Fullerton had found, or imagined he'd found.

"You're downright loopy," I said flatly.

He stared back at me and his eyes were shining like a kid's at Christmas.

He said: "It had to happen sometime, Sutter, somewhere."

I climbed up the bank and stood beside him. I looked at the net I still held in my hands and threw it back into the creek and watched it sink.

"Be sensible," I warned him. "You have no evidence. Immortality wouldn't work that way. It couldn't. That way, it would be nothing but a dead end. Don't mention it to anyone. They'd ride you without mercy all the way back home."

I don't know why I wasted time on him. He stared back at me stubbornly, but still with that awful light of hope and triumph on his face.

"I'll keep my mouth shut," I told him curtly. "I won't say a word."

"Thanks, Sutter," he answered. "I appreciate it a lot."

I knew from the way he said it that he could murder me with gusto.

We trudged back to camp.

The camp was all slicked up.

The dissecting mess had been cleared away and the table had been scrubbed so hard that it gleamed. Parsons was cooking supper and singing one of his obscene ditties. The other three sat around in their camp chairs and they had broken out some liquor and were human once again.

"All buttoned up?" I asked, but Oliver shook his head.

They poured a drink for Fullerton and he accepted it, a bit ungraciously, but he did take it. That was some improvement on the usual Double Eye.

They didn't offer me any. They knew I couldn't drink it.

"What have we got?" I asked.

"It could be something good," said Oliver. "It's a walking menu. It's an all-purpose animal, for sure. It lays eggs, gives milk, makes honey. It has six different kinds of red meat, two of fowl, one of fish and a couple of others we can't identify."

"Lays eggs," I said. "Gives milk. Then it reproduces."

"Certainly," said Weber. "What did you think?"

"There aren't any young."

Weber grunted. "Could be they have nursery areas. Certain places instinctively set aside in which to rear their young."

"Or they might have instinctive birth control," suggested Oliver. "That would fit in with the perfectly balanced ecology Kemper talks about."

Weber snorted. "Ridiculous!"

"Not so ridiculous," Kemper retorted. "Not half so ridiculous as some other things we found. Not one-tenth as ridiculous as no brain or nervous system. Not any more ridiculous than my bacteria."

"Your bacteria!" Weber said. He drank down half a glass of liquor in a single gulp to make his disdain emphatic.

"The critters swarm with them," Kemper went on. "You find them everywhere throughout the entire animal. Not just in the bloodstream, not in restricted areas, but in the entire organism. And all of them the same. Normally it takes a hundred different kinds of bacteria to make a metabolism work, but here there's only one. And that one, by definition, must be general purpose—it must do all the work that the hundred other species do."

He grinned at Weber. "I wouldn't doubt but right there are your brains and nervous systems—the bacteria doubling in brass for both systems."

Parsons came over from the stove and stood with his fists planted on his hips, a steak fork grasped in one hand and sticking out at a tangent from his body.

"If you ask me," he announced, "there ain't no such animal. The critters are all wrong. They can't be made that way."

"But they are," said Kemper.

"It doesn't make sense! One kind of life. One kind of grass for it to eat. I'll bet that if we could make a census, we'd find the critter population is at exact capacity—just so many of them to the acre, figured down precisely to the last mouthful of grass. Just enough for them to eat and no more. Just enough so the grass won't be overgrazed. Or undergrazed, for that matter."

"What's wrong with that?" I asked, just to needle him.

I thought for a minute he'd take the steak fork to me.

"What's *wrong* with it?" he thundered. "Nature's never static, never standing still. But here it's standing still. Where's the competition? Where's the evolution?"

"That's not the point," said Kemper quietly. "The fact is that that's the way it is. The point is *why*? How did it happen? How was it planned? *Why* was it planned?"

"Nothing's planned," Weber told him sourly. "You know better than to talk like that."

Parsons went back to his cooking. Fullerton had wandered off somewhere. Maybe he was discouraged from hearing about the eggs and milk.

For a time, the four of us just sat.

Finally Weber said: "The first night we were here, I came out to relieve Bob at guard and I said to him..."

He looked at me. "You remember, Bob?"

"Sure. You said symbiosis."

"And now?" asked Kemper.

"I don't know. It simply couldn't happen. But if it did—if it *could*—this critter would be the most beautifully logical example of symbiosis you could dream up. Symbiosis carried to its logical conclusion. Like, long ago, all the life-forms said let's quit this feuding, let's get together, let's cooperate. All the plants and animals and fish and bacteria got together—"

"It's far-fetched, of course," said Kemper. "But, by and large, it's not anything unheard of, merely carried further, that's all. Symbiosis is a recognized way of life and there's nothing—"

Parsons let out a bellow for them to come and get it, and I went to my tent and broke out my diet kit and mixed up a mess of goo. It was a relief to eat in private, without the others making cracks about the stuff I had to choke down.

I found a thin sheaf of working notes on the small wooden crate I'd set up for a desk. I thumbed through them while I ate. They were fairly sketchy and sometimes hard to read, being smeared with blood and other gook from the dissecting table. But I was used to that. I worked with notes like that all the blessed time. So I was able to decipher them.

The whole picture wasn't there, of course, but there was enough to bear out what they'd told me and a good deal more as well.

For examples, the colour squares that gave the critters their crazy-quiltish look were separate kinds of meat or fish or fowl or unknown food, whatever it might be. Almost as if each square was the present-day survivor of each ancient symbiont—if, in fact, there was any basis to this talk of symbiosis.

The egg-laying apparatus was described in some biologic detail, but there seemed to be no evidence of recent egg production. The same was true of the lactation system.

There were, the notes said in Oliver's crabbed writing, five kinds of fruit and three kinds of vegetables to be derived from the plants growing from the critters.

I shoved the notes to one side and sat back on my chair, gloating just a little.

Here was diversified farming with a vengeance! You had meat and dairy herds, fish pond, aviary, poultry yard, orchard and garden rolled into one, all in the body of a single animal that was a complete farm in itself!

I went through the notes hurriedly again and found what I was looking for. The food product seemed high in relation to the gross weight of the animal. Very little would be lost in dressing out.

That is the kind of thing an ag economist has to consider. But that isn't all of it, by any means. What if a man couldn't eat the critter? Suppose the critters couldn't be moved off the planet because they died if you took them from their range?

I recalled how they'd just walked up and died; that in itself was another headache to be filed for future worry.

What if they could only eat the grass that grew on this one planet? And if so, could the grass be grown elsewhere? What kind of tolerance would the critter show to different kinds of climate? What was the rate of reproduction? If it was slow, as was indicated, could it be stepped up? What was the rate of growth?

I got up and walked out of the tent and stood for a while, outside. The little breeze that had been blowing had died down at sunset and the place was quiet. Quiet because there was nothing but the critters to make any noise and we had yet to hear them make a single sound. The stars blazed overhead and there were so many of them that they lighted up the countryside as if there were a moon.

I walked over to where the rest of the men were sitting.

"It looks like we'll be here for a while," I said. "Tomorrow we might as well get the ship unloaded."

No one answered me, but in the silence I could sense the half-hidden satisfaction and the triumph. At last we'd hit the jackpot! We'd be going home with something that would make those other teams look pallid. *We'd* be the ones who got the notices and bonuses.

Oliver finally broke the silence. "Some of our animals aren't in good shape. I went down this afternoon to have a look at them. A couple of the pigs and several of the rats."

He looked at me accusingly.

I flared up at him. "Don't look at me! I'm not their keeper. I just take care of them until you're ready to use them."

Kemper butted in to head off an argument. "Before we do any feeding, we'll need another critter."

"I'll lay you a bet," said Weber.

Kemper didn't take him up.

It was just as well he didn't, for a critter came in, right after breakfast, and died with a *savoir faire* that was positively marvellous. They went to work on it immediately.

Parsons and I started unloading the supplies. We put in a busy day. We moved all the food except the emergency rations we left in the ship. We slung down a refrigerating unit Weber had been yelling for, to keep the critter products fresh. We unloaded a lot of equipment and some silly odds and ends that I knew we'd have no use for, but that some of the others wanted broken out. We put up tents and we lugged and pushed and hauled all day. Late in the afternoon, we had it all stacked up and under canvas and were completely bushed.

Kemper went back to his bacteria. Weber spent hours with the animals. Oliver dug up a bunch of grass and gave the grass the works. Parsons went out on field trips, mumbling and fretting.

Of all of us, Parsons had the job that was most infuriating. Ordinarily the ecology of even the simplest of planets is a complicated business and there's a lot of work to do. But here was almost nothing. There was no competition for survival. There was no dog eat dog. There were just critters cropping grass.

I started to pull my report together, knowing that it would have to be revised and rewritten again and again. But I was anxious to get going. I fairly itched to see the pieces fall together—although I knew from the very start some of them wouldn't fit. They almost never do.

Things went well. Too well, it sometimes seemed to me.

There were incidents, of course, like when the punkins somehow chewed their way out of their cage and disappeared.

Weber was almost beside himself.

"They'll come back," said Kemper. "With that appetite of theirs, they won't stay away for long."

And he was right about that part of it. The punkins were the hungriest creatures in the Galaxy. You could never feed them enough to satisfy them. And they'd eat anything. It made no difference to them, just so there was a lot of it.

And it was that very factor in their metabolism that made them invaluable as research animals.

The other animals thrived on the critter diet. The carnivorous ones ate the critter-meat and the vegetarians chomped on critter-fruit and critter-vegetables. They all grew sleek and sassy. They seemed in better health than the control animals, which continued their regular diet. Even the pigs and rats that had been sick got well again and as fat and happy as any of the others.

Kemper told us, "This critter stuff is more than just a food. It's a medicine. I can see the signs: 'Eat Critter and Keep Well!'"

Weber grunted at him. He was never one for joking and I think he was a worried man. A thorough man, he'd found too many things that violated all the tenets he'd accepted as the truth. No brain or nervous system. The ability to die at will. The lingering hint of wholesale symbiosis. And the bacteria.

The bacteria, I think, must have seemed to him the worst of all.

There was, it now appeared, only one type involved. Kemper had hunted frantically and had discovered no others. Oliver found it in the grass. Parsons found it in the soil and water. The air, strangely enough, seemed to be free of it.

But Weber wasn't the only one who worried. Kemper worried, too. He unloaded most of it just before our bedtime, sitting on the edge of his cot and trying to talk the worry out of himself while I worked on my reports.

And he'd picked the craziest point imaginable to pin his worry on.

"You can explain it all," he said, "if you are only willing to concede on certain points. You can explain the critters if you're willing to believe in a symbiotic arrangement carried out on a planetary basis. You can believe in the utter simplicity of the ecology if you're willing to assume that, given space and time enough, anything can happen within the bounds of logic.

"You can visualize how the bacteria might take the place of brains and nervous systems if you're ready to say this is a bacterial world and not a critter world. And you can even envision the bacteria—all of them, every single one of them—as forming one gigantic linked intelligence. And if you accept that theory, then the voluntary deaths become understandable, because there's no actual death involved—it's just like you or me trimming off a hangnail. And if this is true, then Fullerton has found immortality, although it's not the kind he was looking for and it won't do him or us a single bit of good.

"But the thing that worries me," he went on, his face all knotted up with worry, "is the seeming lack of anything resembling a defence mechanism. Even assuming that the critters are no more than fronting for a bacterial world, the mechanism should be there as a simple matter of precaution. Every living thing we know of has some sort of way to defend itself or to escape potential enemies. It either fights or runs and hides to preserve its life."

He was right, of course. Not only did the critters have no defence, they even saved one the trouble of going out to kill them.

"Maybe we are wrong," Kemper concluded. "Maybe life, after all, is not as valuable as we think it is. Maybe it's not a thing to cling to. Maybe it's not worth fighting for. Maybe the critters, in their dying, are closer to the truth than we."

It would go on like that, night after night, with Kemper talking around in circles and never getting anywhere. I think most of the time he wasn't talking to me, but talking to himself, trying by the very process of putting it in words to work out some final answer.

And long after we had turned out the lights and gone to bed, I'd lie on my cot and think about all that Kemper said and I thought in circles, too. I wondered why all the critters that came in and died were in the prime of life. Was the dying a privilege that was accorded only to the fit? Or were all the critters in the prime of life? Was there really some cause to believe they might be immortal?

I asked a lot of questions, but there weren't any answers.

We continued with our work. Weber killed some of his animals and examined them and there were no signs of ill effect from the critter diet. There were traces of critter bacteria in their blood, but no sickness, reaction or antibody formation. Kemper kept on with his bacterial work. Oliver started a whole series of experiments with the grass. Parsons just gave up.

The punkins didn't come back and Parsons and Fullerton went out and hunted for them, but without success.

I worked on my report and the pieces fell together better than I had hoped they would.

It began to look as though we had the situation well nailed down.

We all were feeling pretty good. We could almost taste that bonus.

But I think that, in the back of our minds, all of us were wondering if we could get away scot free. I know I had mental fingers crossed. It just didn't seem quite possible that something wouldn't happen.

And, of course, it did.

We were sitting around after supper, with the lantern lighted, when we heard the sound. I realized afterward that we had been hearing it for some time before we paid attention to it. It started so soft and so far away that it crept upon us without alarming us. At first, it sounded like a sighing, as if a gentle wind were blowing through a little tree, and then it changed into a rumble, but a far-off rumble that had no menace in it. I was just getting ready to say something about thunder and wondering if our stretch of weather was about to break when Kemper jumped up and yelled.

I don't know what he yelled. Maybe it wasn't a word at all. But the way he yelled brought us to our feet and sent us at a dead run for the safety of the ship. Even before we got there, in the few seconds it took to reach the ladder, the character of the sound had changed and there was no mistaking what it was—the drumming of hoofs heading straight for camp.

They were almost on top of us when we reached the ladder and there wasn't time or room for all of use to use it. I was the last in line and I saw I'd never make it and a dozen possible escape plans flickered through my mind. But I knew they wouldn't work fast enough. Then I saw the rope, hanging where I'd left it after the unloading job, and I made a jump for it. I'm no rope-climbing expert, but I shinnied up it with plenty of speed. And right behind me came Weber, who was no rope-climber, either, but who was doing rather well.

I thought of how lucky it had been that I hadn't found the time to take down the rig and how Weber had ridden me unmercifully about not doing it. I wanted to shout down and point it out to him, but I didn't have the breath.

We reached the port and tumbled into it. Below us, the stampeding critters went grinding through the camp. There seemed to be millions of them. One of the terrifying things about it was how silently they ran. They made no outcry of any kind; all you could hear was the sound of their hoofs pounding on the ground. It seemed almost as if they ran in some blind fury that was too deep for outcry.

They spread for miles, as far as one could see on the starlit plains, but the spaceship divided them and they flowed to either side of it and then flowed back again, and beyond the spaceship there was a little sector that they never touched. I thought how we could have been safe staying on the ground and huddling in that sector, but that's one of the things a man never can foresee.

The stampede lasted for almost an hour. When it was all over, we came down and surveyed the damage. The animals in their cages, lined up between the ship and the camp, were safe. All but one of the sleeping tents were standing. The lantern still burned brightly on the table. But everything else was gone. Our food supply was trampled in the ground. Much of the equipment was lost and wrecked. On either side of the camp, the ground was churned up like a half-ploughed field. The whole thing was a mess.

It looked as if we were licked.

The tent Kemper and I used for sleeping still stood, so our notes were safe. The animals were all right. But that was all we had—the notes and animals.

"I need three more weeks," said Weber. "Give me just three weeks to complete the tests."

"We haven't got three weeks," I answered. "All our food is gone."

"The emergency rations in the ship?"

"That's for going home."

"We can go a little hungry."

He glared at us—at each of us in turn—challenging us to do a little starving.

"I can go three weeks," he said, "without any food at all."

"We could eat critter," suggested Parsons. "We could take a chance."

Weber shook his head. "Not yet. In three weeks, when the tests are finished, then maybe we will know. Maybe we won't need those rations for going home. Maybe we can stock up on critters and eat our heads off all the way to Caph."

I looked around at the rest of them, but I knew, before I looked, the answer I would get.

"All right," I said. "We'll try it."

"It's all right for you," Fullerton retorted hastily. "You have your diet kit."

Parsons reached out and grabbed him and shook him so hard that he went cross-eyed. "We don't talk like that about those diet kits."

Then Parsons let him go.

We set up double guards, for the stampede had wrecked our warning system, but none of us got much sleep. We were too upset.

Personally, I did some worrying about why the critters had stampeded. There was nothing on the planet that could scare them. There were no other animals. There was no thunder or lightning—as a matter of fact, it appeared that the planet might have no boisterous weather ever. And there seemed to be nothing in the critter makeup, from our observation of them, that would set them off emotionally.

But there must be a reason and a purpose, I told myself. And there must be, too, in their dropping dead for us. But was the purpose intelligence or instinct?

That was what bothered me most. It kept me awake all night long.

At daybreak, a critter walked in and died for us happily.

We went without our breakfast and, when noon came, no one said anything about lunch, so we skipped that, too.

Late in the afternoon, I climbed the ladder to get some food for supper. There wasn't any. Instead, I found five of the fattest punkins you ever laid your eyes on. They had chewed holes through the packing boxes and the food was cleaned out. The sacks were limp and empty. They'd even managed to get the lid off the coffee can somehow and had eaten every bean.

The five of them sat contentedly in a corner, blinking smugly at me. They didn't make a racket, as they usually did. Maybe they knew they were in the wrong or maybe they were just too full. For once, perhaps, they'd gotten all they could eat.

I just stood there and looked at them and I knew how they'd gotten on the ship. I blamed myself, not them. If only I'd found the time to take down the unloading rig, they'd never gotten in. But then I remembered how that dangling rope had saved my life and Weber's and I couldn't decide whether I'd done right or wrong.

I went over to the corner and picked the punkins up. I stuffed three of them in my pockets and carried the other two. I climbed down from the ship and walked up to camp. I put the punkins on the table.

"Here they are," I said. "They were in the ship. That's why we couldn't find them. They climbed up the rope."

Weber took one look at them. "They look well fed. Did they leave anything?"

"Not a scrap. They cleaned us out entirely."

The punkins were quite happy. It was apparent they were glad to be back with us again. After all, they'd eaten everything in reach and there was no further reason for their staying in the ship.

Parsons picked up a knife and walked over to the critter that had died that morning.

"Tie on your bibs," he said.

He carved out big steaks and threw them on the table and then he lit his stove. I retreated to my tent as soon as he started cooking, for never in my life have I smelled anything as good as those critter steaks.

I broke out the kit and mixed me up some goo and sat there eating it, feeling sorry for myself.

Kemper came in after a while and sat down on his cot.

"Do you want to hear?" he asked me.

"Go ahead," I invited him resignedly.

"It's wonderful. It's got everything you've ever eaten backed clear off the table. We had three different kinds of red meat and a slab of fish and something that resembled lobster, only better. And there's one kind of fruit growing out of that bush in the middle of the back..."

"And tomorrow you drop dead."

"I don't think so," Kemper said. "The animals have been thriving on it. There's nothing wrong with them."

It seemed that Kemper was right. Between the animals and men, it took a critter a day. The critters didn't seem to mind. They were johnny-on-the-spot. They walked in promptly, one at a time, and keeled over every morning.

The way the men and animals ate was positively indecent. Parsons cooked great platters of different kinds of meat and fish and fowl and what-not. He prepared huge bowls of vegetables. He heaped other bowls with fruit. He racked up combs of honey and the men licked the platters clean. They sat around with belts unloosened and patted their bulging bellies and were disgustingly contented.

I waited for them to break out in a rash or to start turning green with purple spots or grow scales or something of the sort. But nothing happened. They thrived, just as the animals were thriving. They felt better than they ever had.

Then, one morning, Fullerton turned up sick. He lay on his cot flushed with fever. It looked like Centaurian virus, although we'd been inoculated against that. In fact, we'd been inoculated and immunized against almost everything. Each time, before we blasted off on another survey, they jabbed us full of booster shots.

I didn't think much of it. I was fairly well convinced, for a time at least, that all that was wrong with him was overeating.

Oliver, who knew a little about medicine, but not much, got the medicine chest out of the ship and pumped Fullerton full of some new antibiotic that came highly recommended for almost everything.

We went on with our work, expecting he'd be on his feet in a day or two.

But he wasn't. If anything, he got worse.

Oliver went through the medicine chest, reading all the labels carefully, but didn't find anything that seemed to be the proper medication. He read the first-aid booklet. It didn't tell him anything except how to set broken legs or apply artificial respiration and simple things like that.

Kemper had been doing a lot of worrying, so he had Oliver take a sample of Fullerton's blood and then prepared a slide. When he looked at the blood through the microscope, he found that it swarmed with bacteria from the critters. Oliver took some more blood samples and

Kemper prepared more slides, just to double-check, and there was no doubt about it.

By this time, all of us were standing around the table watching Kemper and waiting for the verdict. I know the same thing must have been in the mind of each of us.

It was Oliver who put it into words. "Who is next?" he asked.

Parsons stepped up and Oliver took the sample.

We waited anxiously.

Finally Kemper straightened.

"You have them, too," he said to Parsons. "Not as high a count as Fullerton."

Man after man stepped up. All of us had the bacteria, but in my case the count was low.

"It's the critter," Parsons said. "Bob hasn't been eating any."

"But cooking kills—" Oliver started to say.

"You can't be sure. These bacteria would have to be highly adaptable. They do the work of thousands of other micro-organisms. They're a sort of handyman, a jack-of-all-trades. They can acclimatize. They can meet new situations. They haven't weakened the strain by becoming specialized."

"Besides," said Parsons, "we don't cook all of it. We don't cook the fruit and most of you guys raise hell if a steak is more than singed."

"What I can't figure out is why it should be Fullerton," Weber said. "Why should his count be higher? He started on the critter the same time as the rest of us."

I remembered that day down by the creek.

"He got a head start on the rest of you," I explained. "He ran out of toothpicks and took to chewing grass stems. I caught him at it."

I know it wasn't very comforting. It meant that in another week or two, all of them would have as high a count as Fullerton. But there was no sense not telling them. It would have been criminal not to. There was no place for wishful thinking in a situation like that.

"We can't stop eating critter," said Weber. "It's all the food we have. There's nothing we can do."

"I have a hunch," Kemper replied, "it's too late anyhow."

"If we started home right now," I said, "there's my diet kit..."

They didn't let me finish making my offer. They slapped me on the back and pounded one another and laughed like mad.

It wasn't that funny. They just needed something they could laugh at.

"It wouldn't do any good," said Kemper. "We've already had it. Anyhow, your diet kit wouldn't last us all the way back home."

"We could have a try at it," I argued.

"It may be just a transitory thing," Parsons said. "Just a bit of fever. A little upset from a change of diet."

We all hoped that, of course.

But Fullerton got no better.

Weber took blood samples of the animals and they had a bacterial count almost as high as Fullerton's—much higher than when he'd taken it before.

Weber blamed himself. "I should have kept closer check. I should have taken tests every day or so."

"What difference would it have made?" demanded Parsons. "Even if you had, even if you'd found a lot of bacteria in the blood, we'd still have eaten critter. There was no other choice."

"Maybe it's not the bacteria," said Oliver. "We may be jumping at conclusions. It may be something else that Fullerton picked up."

Weber brightened up a bit. "That's right. The animals still seem to be okay."

They were bright and chipper, in the best of health.

We waited. Fullerton got neither worse nor better.

Then, one night, he disappeared.

Oliver, who had been sitting with him, had dozed off for a moment. Parsons, on guard, had heard nothing.

We hunted for him for three full days. He couldn't have gone far, we figured. He had wandered off in a delirium and he didn't have the strength to cover any distance.

But we didn't find him.

We did find one queer thing, however. It was a ball of some strange substance, white and fresh-appearing. It was about four feet in diameter. It lay at the bottom of a little gully, hidden out of sight, as if someone or something might have brought it there and hidden it away.

We did some cautious poking at it and we rolled it back and forth a little and wondered what it was, but we were hunting Fullerton and we didn't have the time to do much investigating. Later on, we agreed, we would come back and get it and find out what it was.

Then the animals came down with the fever, one after another—all except the controls, which had been eating regular food until the stampede had destroyed the supply. After that, of course, all of them ate critter.

By the end of two days, most of the animals were down.

Weber worked with them, scarcely taking time to rest. We all helped as best we could.

Blood samples showed a greater concentration of bacteria. Weber started a dissection, but never finished it. Once he got the animal open, he took a quick look at it and scraped the whole thing off the table into a pail. I saw him, but I don't think any of the others did. We were pretty busy.

I asked him about it later in the day, when we were alone for a moment. He briskly brushed me off.

I went to bed early that night because I had the second guard. It seemed I had no more than shut my eyes when I was brought upright by a racket that raised goose pimples on every inch of me.

I tumbled out of bed and scrabbled around to find my shoes and get them on. By that time, Kemper had dashed out of the tent.

There was trouble with the animals. They were fighting to break out, chewing the bars of their cages and throwing themselves against them in a blind and terrible frenzy. And all the time they were squealing and screaming. To listen to them set your teeth on edge.

Weber dashed around with a hypodermic. After what seemed hours, we had them full of sedative. A few of them broke loose and got away, but the rest were sleeping peacefully.

I got a gun and took over guard duty while the other men went back to bed.

I stayed down near the cages, walking back and forth because I was too tense to do much sitting down. It seemed to me that between the animals' frenzy to escape and Fullerton's disappearance, there was a parallel that was too similar for comfort.

I tried to review all that had happened on the planet and I got bogged down time after time as I tried to make the picture dovetail. The trail of thought I followed kept turning back to Kemper's worry about the critters' lack of a defence mechanism.

Maybe, I told myself, they had a defence mechanism, after all—the slickest, smoothest, trickiest one Man ever had encountered.

As soon as the camp awoke, I went to our tent to stretch out for a moment, perhaps to catch a catnap. Worn out, I slept for hours.

Kemper woke me.

"Get up, Bob!" he said. "For the love of God, get up!"

It was late afternoon and the last rays of the sun were streaming through the tent flap. Kemper's face was haggard. It was as if he'd suddenly grown old since I'd seen him less than twelve hours before.

"They're encysting," he gasped. "They're turning into cocoons or chrysalises or..."

I sat up quickly. "That one we found out there in the field!"

He nodded.

"Fullerton?" I asked.

"We'll go out and see, all five of us, leaving the camp and animals alone."

We had some trouble finding it because the land was so flat and featureless that there were no landmarks.

But finally we located it, just as dusk was setting in.

The ball had split in two—not in a clean break, in a jagged one. It looked like an egg after a chicken has been hatched.

And the halves lay there in the gathering darkness, in the silence underneath the sudden glitter of the stars—a last farewell and a new beginning and a terrible alien fact.

I tried to say something, but my brain was so numb that I was not entirely sure just what I should say. Anyhow, the words died in the dryness of my mouth and the thickness of my tongue before I could get them out.

For it was not only the two halves of the cocoon—it was the marks within that hollow, the impression of what had been there, blurred and distorted by the marks of what it had become.

We fled back to camp.

Someone, I think it was Oliver, got the lantern lighted.

We stood uneasily, unable to look at one another, knowing that the time was past for all dissembling, that there was no use of glossing over or denying what we'd seen in the dim light in the gully.

"Bob is the only one who has a chance," Kemper finally said, speaking more concisely than seemed possible. "I think he should leave right now. Someone must get back to Caph. Someone has to tell them."

He looked across the circle of lantern light at me.

"Well," he said sharply, "get going! What's the matter with you?"

"You were right," I said, not much more than whispering. "Remember how you wondered about a defence mechanism?"

"They have it," Weber agreed. "The best you can find. There's no beating them. They don't fight you. They absorb you. They make you into them. No wonder there are just the critters here. No wonder the planet's ecology is simple. They have you pegged and measured from the instant you set foot on the planet. Take one drink of water. Chew a single grass stem. Take one bite of critter. Do any one of these things and they have you cold."

Oliver came out of the dark and walked across the lantern-lighted circle. He stopped in front of me.

"Here are your diet kit and notes," he said.

"But I can't run out on you!"

"Forget us!" Parsons barked at me. "We aren't human any more. In a few more days..."

He grabbed the lantern and strode down the cages and held the lantern high, so that we could see.

"Look," he said.

There were no animals. There were just the cocoons and the little critters and the cocoons that had split in half.

I saw Kemper looking at me and there was, of all things, compassion on his face.

"You don't want to stay," he told me. "if you do, in a day or two, a critter will come in and drop dead for you. And you'll go crazy all the way back home—wondering which one of us it was."

*

He turned away then. They all turned away from me and suddenly it seemed I was all alone.

Weber had found an axe somewhere and he started walking down the row of cages, knocking off the bars to let the little critters out.

I walked slowly over to the ship and stood at the foot of the ladder, holding the notes and the diet kit tight against my chest.

When I got there, I turned around and looked back at them and it seemed I couldn't leave them.

I thought of all we'd been through together and when I tried to think of specific things, the only thing I could think about was how they always kidded me about the diet kit.

And I thought of the times I had to leave and go off somewhere and eat alone so that I couldn't smell the food. I thought of almost ten years of eating that damn goo and that I could never eat like a normal human because of my ulcerated stomach.

Maybe *they* were the lucky ones, I told myself. If a man got turned into a critter, he'd probably come out with a whole stomach and never have to worry about how much or what he ate. The critters never ate anything except the grass, but maybe, I thought, that grass tasted just as good to them as a steak or a pumpkin pie would taste to me.

So I stood there for a while and I thought about it. Then I took the diet kit and flung it out into the darkness as far as I could throw it and I dropped the notes to the ground.

I walked back into the camp and the first man I saw was Parsons.

"What have you got for supper?" I asked him.

A MATTER OF PROTOCOL

Jack Sharkey

Jack Sharkey (1931–1992) was a regular contributor to the fantasy and science-fiction magazines during the 1960s but when the markets changed he shifted to writing for the theatre, often light-hearted farces and bizarre murder mysteries. During his writing career he only had one book in paperback, The Secret Martians *(1960) and even then sharing the binding on an Ace Double with John Brunner, but in more recent years some of his work has been revived, notably his fantasy romp* It's Magic, You Dope!, *first serialized in 1962 and eventually released in paperback in 2009. Much of his short fiction was light-hearted but occasionally, as this story shows, he could be devastatingly grim.*

FROM SPACE, THE PLANET VIRIDIAN RESEMBLED A GREAT GREEN moss-covered tennis ball. When the spaceship had arrowed even closer to the lush jungle that was the surface of the 7000-mile sphere, there was still no visible break in the green cloak of the planet. Even when they dipped almost below their margin of safety—spaceships were poorly built for extended flight within the atmosphere—it took nearly a complete circuit of the planet before a triangle of emptiness was spotted. It was in the midst of the tangled canopy of treetops, themselves interwoven inextricably with coarse-leaved ropy vines that sprawled and coiled about the upthrust branches like underfed anacondas.

Into the centre of this triangle the ship was lowered on sputtering blue pillars of crackling energy, to come to rest on the soft loamy earth.

A bare instant after setdown, crewmen exploded from the airlock and dashed into the jungle shadows with high-pressure tanks of gushing spume. Their job was to coat, cool and throttle the hungry fires trickling in bright orange fingers through the heat-blackened grasses. Higher in the trees, a few vines smouldered fitfully where the fires had brushed them, then hissed into smoky wet ash as their own glutinous sap smothered the urgent embers. But the fire was going out.

"Under control, sir," reported a returning crewman.

Lieutenant Jerry Norcriss emerged into the green gloaming that cloaked the base of the ship with a net of harlequin diamonds. Jerry nodded abstractedly as other crewmen laid a lightweight form-fitting couch alongside the tailfins near the airlock. On this couch Jerry reclined. Remaining crew members turned their firefighting gear over to companions and stood guard in a rough semicircle with loaded rifles, their backs to the figure on the couch, facing the jungle and whatever predatory dangers it might hold.

Ensign Bob Ryder, the technician who had the much softer job of simply controlling and coordinating any information relayed by Jerry, leaned out through the open circle in the hull.

"All set, sir," said the tech. Jerry nodded and settled a heavily wired helmet onto his head, while Bob made a hookup between the helmet and the power outlet that was concealed under a flap of metal on the tailfin.

Helmet secured, Jerry lay back upon the couch and closed his eyes. "Any time you're ready, Ensign."

Bob hurried back inside, found the panel he sought among the jumble of high-powered machinery there, and placed a spool of microtape on a spindle inside it.

He shut the panel and thumbed the button that started an impulse radiating from the tape into the jungle.

The impulse had been detected and taped by a roborocket which had circled the planet for months before their arrival. It was one of the two Viridian species whose types were as yet uncatalogued by the Space Corps, in its vast files of alien life. Jerry's job, as a Space Zoologist, was to complete those files, planet by planet throughout the spreading wave of slowly colonized universe.

Bob made sure the tape was functioning. Then he clicked the switch that would stimulate the Contact centre in Jerry's brain and release his mind into that of the taped alien for an immutable forty minutes.

Outside the ship, recumbent in the warm green-gold shadows, Jerry's consciousness was dwarfed for an instant by a white lightning-flash of energy. And then his body went limp as his mind sprang with thought-speed into Contact...

*

Jerry opened his eyes to a dizzying view of the dull brown jungle floor. He blinked a moment, then looked toward his feet. He saw two sets of thin knobby Vs, extending forward and partly around the tiny limb he stood upon, their chitinous surface shiny with the wetness of the jungle air.

Slowly working his jaws, he heard the extremely gentle "click" as they came together. The endoskeleton must exist all over his host's body.

After making certain it would not disturb his balance on the limb, he attempted bringing whatever on the alien passed for hands before his face.

Sometimes aliens had no hands, nor any comparable organisms. Then Jerry would have to soft-pedal the mental nagging of being "amputated," an unavoidable carryover from his subconscious "wrong-feeling" about armlessness.

But this time the effort moved up multi-jointed limbs, spindly as a cat's whiskers, terminating in a perpetually coiling soft prehensile tip. He tried feeling along his torso to determine its size and shape. But the wormlike tips were tactilely insensitive.

Hoping to deduce his shape from his shadow, he inched sideways along the limb on those inadequate-looking two-pronged feet toward a blob of yellow sunlight nearer the trunk.

The silhouette on the branch showed him a stubby cigar-shaped torso.

"I seem to be a semi-tentacled no-hop grasshopper," he mused to himself, vainly trying to turn his head on his neck. "Head, thorax and abdomen all one piece."

He tried flexing what would be, in a man, the region of the shoulderblades. He was rewarded by the appearance of long, narrow wings—two sets of them, like a dragonfly's—from beneath two flaps of chitin on his back.

He tried an experimental flapping. The pair of wings—white and stiff like starched tissue paper, not veinous as in Earth-insects—dissolved in a buzzing blur of motion. The limb fell away from under his tiny V-shaped feet. And then he was up above the blinding green blanket of jungle treetops, his shadow pacing his forward movement along the close-packed quilt of wide leaves below.

"I'd better be careful," thought Jerry. "There may be avian life here that considers my species the *pièce de résistance* of the pteroid set..."

Slowing his rapid wingbeat, he let himself drop down toward the nearest mattress-sized leaf. He folded his out-thrust feet in midair and dropped the last few inches to a cushiony rest.

A slight shimmer of dizziness gripped his mind.

Perhaps the "skull" of this creature was ill-equipped to ward off the hot rays of the tropic sunlight. Lest his brain be fried in its own casing, Jerry scuttled along the velvet top of the leaf, and ducked quickly beneath its nearest overlapping companion. The wave of vertigo passed quickly, there in the deep shadow. Under the canopy of leaves Jerry crawled back to a limb near the top of the tree.

A few feet from where he stood, something moved.

Jerry turned that way. Another creature of the same species was balancing lightly on a green limb of wire-thickness, its gaze fixed steadily toward the jungle flooring, as Jerry's own had been on entering the alien body.

Watching out for predators? Or for victims?

He could, he knew, pull his consciousness back enough to let the creature's own consciousness carry it through its daily cycle of eating, avoiding destruction, and the manifold businesses of being an ambient creature. But he decided to keep control. It would be easier to figure out his host's ecological status in the planet's natural life-balance by observing the other one for awhile.

Jerry always felt more comfortable when he was in full control. You never knew when an alien might stupidly stumble into a fatality that any intelligent mind could easily have avoided.

Idly, as he watched his fellow creature down near the inner part of the branch, he wondered how much more time he would be in Contact. Subjectively he'd seemed to be enhosted for about ten minutes. But one of the drawbacks of Contact was the subjugation of personal time-sense to that of the host. Depending on the species he enhosted, the forty-minute Contact period could be an eternity, or the blink of an eye…

Nothing further seemed to be occurring. Jerry reluctantly withdrew some of his control from the insect-mind to see what would happen.

Immediately it inched forward until it was in the same position it had been in when Jerry made Contact: V-shaped feet forward and slightly around the narrow branch, eyes fixed upon the brownish jungle floor, body motionless with folded wings. For awhile, Jerry tried "listening" to its mind, but received no readable thoughts. Only a sense of imminence… Of patience… Of waiting…

It didn't take long for Jerry to grow bored with this near-mindless outlook. He reassumed full control. Guiding the fragile feet carefully along the branch, he made his way to his fellow watcher, and tried out the creature's communication system. His mind strove to activate something on the order of a larynx; the insect's nervous system received this impulse, changed in inter-species translation, as a broad request for getting a message to its fellow. Its body responded by lifting the multi-jointed "arms" forward. It clapped the hard inner surfaces of the "wrists" together so fast that they blurred into invisibility as the wings had done.

A thin, ratchetty sound came forth from that hardshell contact. The other insect looked up in annoyance, then returned its gaze to the ground again.

Aural conversation thus obviated, Jerry tried for physical attention-getting. He reached out a vermiform forelimb-tip and tugged urgently at the other insect's nearest hind leg. An angry movement gave out the unmistakeable pantomimic message: "For pete's sake, get off my back! I'm *busy*!" The other insect spread its thin double wings and went buzzing off a few trees away, then settled on a limb there and took up its earthward vigil once more.

"Well, they're not gregarious, that's for sure," said Jerry to himself. "I wish I knew what the hell we were waiting for!"

He decided he was sick of ground-watching, and turned his attention to his immediate vicinity. His gaze wandered along all the twists, juts and thrusts of branch and vine beneath the sunblocking leaves.

And all at once he realized he was staring at another of his kind. So still had its dull green-brown body been that he'd taken it for a ripple of bark along a branch.

Carefully, he looked further on. Beyond the small still figure he soon located another like it, and then another. Within a short space of time, he had found three dozen of the insects sitting silently around him in a spherical area barely ten feet in diameter.

Oddly disconcerted, he once more spread his stiff white wings and fluttered away through the treetops, careful to avoid coming out in direct sunlight this time.

He flew until a resurgence of giddiness told him he was overstraining the creature's stamina. He dropped onto a limb and looked about once more. Within a very short time, he had spotted dozens more of the grasshopper-things. All were the same, sitting in camouflaged silence, steadily eyeing the ground.

"Damn," thought Jerry. "They don't seem interested in eating, mating or fighting. All they want to do is sit—sit and *wait*. But what are they waiting for?"

There was, of course, the possibility that he'd caught them in an off-period. If the species were nocturnal, then he wouldn't get any action from them till after sunset. That, he realized gloomily, meant a re-Contact later on. One way or another, he would have to determine the functions, capabilities and menace—if any—of the species with regard to the influx of colonists, who would come to Viridian only if his report pronounced it safe.

Once again, he let the insect's mind take over. Again that overpowering feeling of imminence...

He was irritated. It couldn't just be looking forward to nightfall! There were too many things tied in with the imminence feeling: the necessity for quiet, for motionlessness, for careful watching.

The more he thought on it, the more he had the distinct intuition that it would sit and stare at the soft, mulch-covered jungle floor, be it bright daylight or blackest gloom, waiting, and waiting, and waiting...

Then, suddenly, the slight feel of imminence became almost unbearable apprehension.

The change in intensity was due to a soft, cautious shuffling sound from down in the green-gold twilight. Something was coming through the jungle. Something that moved on careful feet along the springy, moist brown surface below the trees.

Far below, a shadow detached itself slowly from the deeper shadows of the trees, and a form began to emerge into the wan filtered sunlight. It—

An all-encompassing lance of silent white lightning. Contact was over...

Jerry sat up on the couch, angry. He pulled the helmet off his head as Bob Ryder leaned out the airlock once more. "How'd it go, sir?"

"Lousy. I'll have to re-establish. Didn't have time to Learn it sufficiently." A slight expression of disappointment on the tech's face made him add, "Don't tell me you have the other tape in place already?"

"Sorry," Bob said. "You usually do a complete Learning in one Contact."

"Oh—" Jerry shrugged and reached for the helmet again. "Never mind, I'll take on the second alien long as it's already set up. I may just have hit the first one in an off-period. The delay in re-Contact may be just what I need to catch it in action."

Settling the helmet snugly on his head once more, he leaned back onto the couch and waited. He heard the tech's feet clanking along the metal plates inside the ship, then the soft clang of an opening door in the power room, and—

Whiteness, writhing electric whiteness and cold silence. And he was in Contact.

Darkness, and musky warmth.

Then a slot of light appeared, a thin fuzzy line of yellow striped with spiky green. Jerry had time, in the brief flicker, to observe thick bearlike forelimbs holding up a squarish trapdoor fastened with cross-twigs for support. Then the powerful forepaws let the door drop back into place, and it was dark again.

He hadn't liked those forepaws. Though thick as and pawed like a bear's, they were devoid of hair. They had skin thin as a caterpillar's, a mottled pink with sick-looking areas of deathly white.

Skin like that would be a pushover to actinic rays for any long exposure. Probably the thing lived underground here, almost permanently. His eyes had detected a rude assortment of thick wooden limbs curving in and out at regular intervals in the vertical wall of soil that was the end of this tunnel, just below the trapdoor. Tree roots. But formed, by some odd natural quirk, into a utile ladder.

But why had the thing peered out, then dropped the door to wait? Did *every* species on this planet hang around expectantly and nothing else? And what was the waiting for?

Then he felt the urge within the creature, the urge to scurry up that ladder into the light. But there was, simultaneously, a counter-urge in the thing, telling it to *please* wait a *little* longer...

Jerry recognized the urge by quick anthropomorphosis. It was the goofy urge. The crazy urge. Like one gets on the brinks of awesome heights, or on subway platforms as the train roars in: The impulsive urge to self-destruction, so swiftly frightening and so swiftly suppressed...

Yet, it had lifted and dropped that lid too briefly to have *seen* anything outside. Could it be *listening* for something? Carefully, he relinquished his control of the beast, fraction by fraction, to see what it would do.

It rose on tiptoe at once, and again lifted that earthen door.

It squinted at the profusion of green-yellow sunlight that stung its eyes. Then it rose on powerful hind limbs and clambered just high enough on that "ladder" to see over the grassy rim of the trapdoor-hole. Jerry then heard the soft shuffling sound that had re-alerted it, and saw the source.

Out on the matted brown jungle flooring, beneath the towering trees, another of the bear-things was moving forward from an open turf-door, emitting low, whimpering snorts as it inched along through the dappling yellow sunlight.

Obviously it was *following* that manic-destruction impulse that he just felt and managed to suppress. It must have been almost a hundred degrees out there. And the damned thing was *shivering.*

Here and there, Jerry noticed suddenly, other half-opened trapdoors were framing other bear-things' heads. The air was taut with electric tension, the tension of a slow trigger-squeeze that moves millimetre by millimetre toward the instant explosion...

The soft shuffling sounds of the animal's movement jogged Jerry's memory then, and he knew it for the sound he had heard when enhosted in the grasshopper-thing. Was a bear-thing what they'd been waiting in the trees so silently for? And what would be the culmination of that vigil?

Then the bear-thing he was in Contact with hitched itself up another root-rung. Jerry saw the thing toward which the quaking creature was headed, in a hunched crawl, its whimpers more anguished by the moment.

Pendant in the green gloaming, about four feet above the spongy brown jungle floor, hung a thick yellow-grey gourd at the tip of a long vine. Its sides glittered stickily with condensed moisture that mingled with the effluvium of the gourd itself. The odour was both noisome and compelling, powerful as a bushel of rotting roses. It sickened as it lured, teased the nostrils as it cloyed within the lungs.

To this dangling obscenity the bear-thing moved. Its eyes were no longer afraid, but glazed and dulled by the strength of that musky lure. Its movements were fluid and trancelike.

It arose on sturdy hind limbs and struck at the gourd with a gentle paw, sending it jouncing to one side on its long green vine. As it bobbed back, the creature struck it off in the opposite direction with a sharper blow.

Jerry watched in fascination. The gourd swung faster; the mottled pink-white alien creature swayed and wove its forelimbs and thick body in a ritual dance matching the tempo of the arcing gourd.

Then Jerry noted that the vine was unlike earth-vines which parasitically employ treetops as their unwilling trellises. It is a limp extension of the tip of a tree branch itself. So were all the other vines in that green matting overhead.

*

A ripping sound yanked his gaze back to the dazed creature and the gourd again.

A ragged tear had riven the side of the gourd. Tiny coils of green were dribbling out in batches, like watchsprings spilled from a paper bag. They struck with a bounce and wriggle on the resilient brown mulch. And then, as they straightened themselves, Jerry knew them for what they were: Miniature versions of the grasshopper-things, shaped precisely like the adults, but only a third as large.

The bear-thing's movements had gone from graceful fluidity to frenzy now. A loud whistle of fright escaped it as the last of the twitching green things flopped from its vegetable cocoon, whirred white wings to dry them and flew off.

And the lumbering creature had reason for its fright.

The instant the last coil of wiggly green life was a vanishing blur in the green shadows, a cloud of darker green descended upon the pink form of the beast from the trees.

The grasshopper-things were waiting no longer. Thousands swarmed on the writhing form, until the bear-thing was a lumpy green parody of itself.

As quickly as the cloud had plunged and clustered, it fell away. The earth was teeming with the flip-flopping forms of dying insects, white wings going dark brown and curling like cellophane in open flame. The bear-thing itself was no longer recognizable, its flesh a myriad egg-like white lumps. It swayed in agony for a moment, then toppled.

Instantly the other creatures—his host with them—were racing forward to the site of the encounter. Jerry felt his host's long gummy tongue flick out and snare one—just one—of the dead adult insects. It was ingested whole by a deft backflip of tongue to gullet. As his host turned tail and scurried for the tunnel once more, Jerry swiftly took control again, and halted it to observe any further developments.

Each of the other things, after a one-insect gulp, was just vanishing back underground. The turf-tops were dropping neatly into almost undetectable place hiding the tunnels. The sunlight nipped at his pale flesh, but Jerry held off from a return to the underground sanctuary, still watching that lump-covered corpse on the earth. Then…

The vine, its burden gone, began to drip a thick ichor from its ragged end upon the dead animal beneath it.

And as the ichor touched upon a white lump, the lump would swell, wriggle, and change colour. Jerry watched with awe as the colour became a mottled pink, and the surface of the lumps cracked and shrivelled away, and tiny forms plopped out onto the ground: miniature bear-things, tiny throats emitting eager mouse-squeaks of hunger.

They rushed upon the body in which they'd been so violently incubated and swiftly, systematically devoured it, blood, bone and sinew.

And when not even a memory of the dead beast was left upon the soil, the tiny pink-white things began to burrow downward into the ground. Soon there was nothing left in the area but a dried fragment of vine, a few loose mounds of soil and a vast silence.

"I'll be a monkey's uncle!" said Jerry… forgetting in his excitement that this phrase was nearly a concise parody of the Space Zoologists' final oath of duty, and kiddingly used as such by the older members of the group.

The whole damned planet was symbiotic! After witnessing those alien life-death rites, it didn't take him long to figure out the screwball connections between the species. Insects, once born of vine-gourds and fully grown, then propagated their species by a strange means: laying bear-eggs in a bear-thing and dying. And dying, eaten by the surviving bears, they turned to seeds which—left in the tunnels by the bear-things as droppings—in turn took root and became trees.

And the trees, under the onslaught of another bear-thing on a dangling pod, would produce new insects, then drip its ichor to fertilize the eggs in the newly dead bear-thing...

Jerry found his mind tangling as he attempted a better pinpointing of the plant-animal-insect relationship. A dead adult insect, plus a trip through a bear-thing's alimentary canal, produced a tree. A tree-pod, with the swatting stimulus of a bear-thing's paws, gave birth to new insects. And insect eggs in animal flesh, stimulated by the tree-ichor, gestated swiftly into young animals...

That meant, simply, that insect plus bear equals tree, tree plus bear equals insect, and insect plus tree equals bear. With three systems, each relied on the non-inclusive member for the breeding-ground. Insect-plus-ichor produced small animals *in* the animal flesh. Dead-insect-plus-bear produced tree *in* the tree-flesh (if one considered dead tree leaves and bark and such as the makeup of the soil.) Bear-swats-plus-tree produced insects... "Damn," said Jerry to himself, "but *not* in the insect-flesh. The thing won't round off..."

He tried again, thinking hard. In effect, the trees were parents to the insects, insects parents to the bears, and bears parents to the trees... Though in another sense, bear-flesh gave birth to new bears, digested insects gave birth (through the tree-medium) to new insects, and trees (through the insect-medium) gave birth to new trees...

Jerry's head spun pleasantly as he tried vainly to solve the confusion. Men of science, he realized, would spend decades trying to figure out which species were responsible for which. It made the ancient chicken-or-egg question beneath consideration. And a lot of diehard evolutionists were going to be bedded down with severe migraines when his report went into circulation...

A dazzle of silent lightning, and Contact was over.

*

"Ready with that first tape again," Bob Ryder said as Jerry removed the Contact helmet and brushed his snow-white hair back from his tanned, youthful face. "Or do you want a breather first?"

Jerry shook his head. "I won't need to re-Contact that other species, Ensign. I got its life-relation ships from the second Contact."

"Really, sir?" said Bob. "That's pretty unusual, isn't it?"

"The whole damned planet's unusual," said Jerry, rising from his supine position and stretching luxuriously in the warm jungle air. "You'll see what I mean when you process the second tape."

Bob decided that Jerry—running pretty true to form for a Space Zoologist—wasn't in a particularly talkative mood, so he had to satisfy himself with waiting for the transcription of the Contact to get the details.

Later that day, an hour after take-off, with Viridian already vanished behind them as the great ship ploughed through hyperspace toward Earth and home, Bob finished reading the report. Then he went down the passageway to the ward room for coffee. Jerry was seated there already. Bob, quickly filling a mug from the polished percolator, slid into a seat across the table from his superior and asked the question that had been bugging him since seeing the report.

"Sir—on that second Contact. Has it occurred to you that you'd relinquished control to the host *before* you saw that other creature move out and start swatting the gourd-thing?"

"You mean was I taking a chance on being destroyed in the host if the creature I was Contacting gave in to the urge to do the swatting?"

"Yes, sir," said Bob. "I mean, I know you can take control any time, if things get dangerous. But wasn't that cutting it kind of thin?"

Jerry shook his head and sipped his coffee. "Wrong urge, Ensign. You'll note I recognized it as the *goofy* urge, the impulse to die followed instantly by a violent surge of self-preservation. It wasn't the death-wish at all. Myself and the creatures who remained safely at the tunnel-mouths had a milder form of what was affecting the creature that *did* start swatting the gourd."

"Then what was the difference, sir? Why did that one particular creature get the full self-destruction urge and no other?"

Jerry wrinkled his face in thought. "I wish I didn't suspect the answer to that, Ensign. The only thing I hope it *isn't* is the thing I have the strongest inkling it *is*: Rotation. Something in their biology has set them up in a certain order for destruction. And that rite I saw performed was so un-animal, so formalized—"

Bob's eyes widened as he caught the inference. "You think they have an inbuilt protocol? That if one particular creature missed its cue, somehow, the designated subsequent creature would simply wait forever, never jumping its turn?"

"That's what I mean," nodded Jerry. "I hope I'm wrong."

"But the right creature made it," said Bob, blinking. "We can't have upset the ecology, can we?"

"Things develop fast on Viridian," mused Jerry. "If I figure the time-relationship between their egg-hatching rate and growth rate, those trees must mature in growth in about a month. And we managed to shrivel a half dozen vines with our rocket fires when we landed, and probably that many again when we blasted off…"

"We dropped CO_2 bombs after we cleared the trees," offered the tech, uneasily. "The fire was out in seconds."

"That wouldn't help an already-shrivelled vine, though, now would it!" sighed Jerry. "And if my hunch about protocol is correct—"

"The life-cycle would interrupt?" gasped the tech.

"We'll see," said Jerry. "It'll take us a month to get back, and there'll be another six months before the first wave of engineers is sent to begin the homesteads and industry sites. We'll see. Ensign."

★

It took two months for the engineers to go out and return.

They hadn't landed. A few orbits about the planet had shown them nothing but a vast dead ball of dust and rotted vegetation, totally unfit for human habitation. They brought back photographs taken of the dead planet that no longer deserved the name it had rated in life.

But Jerry Norcriss, Space Zoologist, made it a special point to avoid looking at any of them.

HUNTER, COME HOME

Richard McKenna

Richard McKenna (1913–1964), who died tragically young of a heart attack, is best known for his quasi-autobiographical novel The Sand Pebbles *(1962) which drew upon his experiences in the American navy serving on a gunboat in China. It was filmed in 1966. But most of McKenna's work, produced after he retired from the navy, was science fiction, starting with "Casey Agonistes" in 1958. Much of his work revolves around the idea that humans can create or somehow be absorbed into another world, perhaps the most fascinating being "The Secret Place" (1966) which went on to win the Nebula Award for that year's best short fiction. A selection of his science fiction was collected in* Casey Agonistes *(1973), which includes the following story about a planet where nature fought back.*

ON THAT PLANET THE DAMNED TREES WERE IMMORTAL, THE new guys said in disgust, so there was no wood for camp fires and they had to burn pyrolene doused on raw stem fragments. Roy Craig crouched over the fire tending a bubbling venison stew and caught himself wishing they might still use the electric galley inside their flyer. But these new guys were all red dots and they wanted flame in the open and they were right, of course.

Four of them sat across the fire from Craig, talking loudly and loading explosive pellets. They wore blue field denims and had roached hair and a red dot tattooed on their foreheads. Bork Wilde, the new field chief, stood watching them. He was tall and bold-featured, with roached black hair, and he had two red dots on his forehead. Craig's reddish hair was unroached and, except for freckles, his forehead was blank, because he had never taken the Mordin manhood test. For all his gangling young six-foot body, he felt like a boy among men. Under the new deal he caught all the menial camp jobs, and he didn't like it.

They were a six-man ringwalling crew and they were camped beside their flyer, a grey, high-sided cargo job, a safe two miles downslope from the big ringwall. All around them the bare, fluted, silvery stems speared and branched fifty feet overhead and gave a watery cast to the twilight. Normally the stems would be covered with two-lobed phytozoon leaves of all sizes and colour patterns. The men and their fire had excited the leaves and they had detached themselves, to hover in a pulsating rainbow cloud high enough to catch the sun above the silver tracery of the upper branches. They piped and twittered and shed a spicy perfume, and certain daring ones dipped low above the men. One of the pellet loaders, a rat-faced little man named Cobb, hurled a flaming chunk up through them.

"Shut up, you stupid flitterbugs!" he roared. "Let a man hear himself think!"

The men laughed. The red-and-white fibrous root tangle underfoot was slowly withdrawing, underground and to the sides, leaving bare soil around the fire. The new guys thought it was to escape the fire, but Craig remembered the roots had always done that when the old ringwall crew used to camp without fire. By morning the whole area around the flyer would be bare soil. A brown, many-legged crawler an inch long pushed out of the exposed soil and scuttled after the retreating roots. Craig smiled and stirred the stew. A small green-and-red phyto leaf dropped from the cloud and settled on his knobby wrist. He let it nuzzle at him. Its thin, velvety wings waved slowly. A much thickened midrib made a kind of body with no head or visible appendages. Craig turned his wrist over and wondered idly why the phyto didn't fall off. Then a patterned green-and-gold phyto with wings large as dinner plates settled on Wilde's shoulder. Wilde snatched it and tore its wings with thick fingers. It whimpered and fluttered. Distress shadowed Craig's gaunt, sensitive face.

"It can't hurt you, Mr Wilde," he protested. "It's just curious."

"Who pulled your trigger, Blanky?" Wilde snapped. "I wish these damn bloodsucking butterflies *could* know what I'm doing here!"

He turned and kicked one of the weak, turgor-rigid stems and brought it crumpling down across the flyer. He threw the torn phyto after it and laughed, showing big horse teeth. Craig bit his lip.

"Chow's ready," he said. "Come and get it."

After cleanup it got dark, with only one moon in the sky, and the phytos furled their wings and went to sleep on the upper branches. The fire died away and the men rolled up in blankets and snored. Craig sat up, not able to sleep. He saw Sidis come and stand looking out the lighted doorway of the flyer's main cabin. Sidis was a Belconti ecologist who had been boss of the old ringwall crew and he was along on this trip just to break Wilde in as his replacement. He insisted on eating and sleeping inside the flyer, to the scorn of the Planet Mordin red dots. His forehead was blank as Craig's, but that was little comfort. Sidis was from Planet Belconti, where they had different customs.

For Mordinmen, courage was the supreme good. They were descendants of a lost Earth-colony that had lapsed to a stone-age technology and fought its way back to gunpowder in ceaseless war against the fearsome Great Russel dinotheres that were the dominant life-form on Planet Mordin before men came. For many generations young candidates for manhood went forth in a sworn band to kill a Great Russel with spears and arrows. When rifles came, they hunted him singly. Survivors wore the red dot of manhood and fathered the next generation. Then the civilized planets discovered Mordin, knowledge flowed in, and population exploded. Suddenly there were too few Great Russels left to meet the need. Craig's family had not been able to buy him a Great Russel hunt.

I'll kill one, when I get my chance, Craig thought. Mr Wilde killed two. That don't seem fair.

Ten years before Craig's birth, the Mordin Hunt Council found the phyto planet unclaimed and set out to convert it to one great dinothere hunting range. The Earth-type Mordin biota could neither eat nor displace the alien phytos. Mordin contracted with Belconti biologists to exterminate the native life. Mordin labourers served under Belconti biotechs. All were blankies; no red dots would serve under the effete Belcontis, many of whom were women. Using the killer plant *Thanasis*, the Belcontis cleared two large islands and restocked them with a Mordin biota. They made a permanent base on one of the islands and attacked the three continents.

When I was little, they told me I'd kill my Great Russel on this planet, Craig thought. He clasped his arms around his knees. There was still only one Great Russel on the planet, on one of the cleared islands.

Because for thirty years the continents refused to die. The phytos encysted *Thanasis* areas, adapted, recovered ground. Belconti genesmiths designed ever more deadly strains of *Thanasis*, pushing it to the safe upper limit of its recombination index, and it began losing ground. The Belcontis said the attempt must be given up. But the planet had become a symbol of future hope to curb present social unrest on Mordin and the Hunt Council refused to give up. It sent red dots to study biotechnics on Belconti.

Craig had come to the planet on a two-year labour contract. He had enjoyed working with other blankies under a Belconti boss and he had almost forgotten the pain of withheld manhood. He had extended his contract for another two years. Then the Mordin relief ship a month ago landed a full crew of red dots, including biotechs to replace the Belcontis, who were all to go home in about a year, when their own relief ship came. Craig was left the only blanky on the planet, except for the Belcontis, and they didn't count.

I'm already alone, he thought. He bowed his head on his knees and wished he could sleep. Someone touched his shoulder and he looked up to see Sidis beside him.

"Come inside, will you, Roy?" he whispered. "I want to talk to you."

Craig sat down across from Sidis at the long table in the main cabin. Sidis was a slender, dark man with gentle Belconti manners and a wry smile.

"I'm worried about you for these next two years," he said. "I don't like the way they order you around, that nasty little fellow Cobb in particular. Why do you take it?"

"I have to because I'm a blanky," Craig said.

"You can't help that. If it's one of your laws, it's unfair."

"It's fair because it's natural," Craig said. "I don't like not being a man, but that's just the way things are with me."

"You are a man. You're twenty-four years old."

"I'm not a man until I feel like one," Craig said. "I can't feel like one until I kill my Great Russel."

"I'm afraid you'd still feel out of place," Sidis said. "I've watched you for two years and I think you have a certain quality your own planet has no use for. So I have a proposition for you." He glanced at the door, then back to Craig. "Declare yourself a Belconti citizen, Roy. We'll all sponsor you and I know Mil Ames will find you a job on the staff. You can go home to Belconti with us."

"Great Russel!" Craig said. "I could never do that, Mr Sidis."

"How is life on Mordin for a blanky? Could he get a wife?"

"Maybe. She'd be some woman that's gave up hope of being even number three wife to a red dot." Craig frowned and thought about his own father. "She'd hate him all her life for her bad luck."

"And you call that fair?"

"It's fair because it's natural. It's natural for a woman to want an all-the-way man instead of a boy that just grew up."

"Not Belconti women. How about it, Roy?"

Craig clasped his hands between his knees. He lowered his head and shook it slowly.

"No. No, I couldn't. My place is here, fighting for a time when no kid has to grow up cheated, like I been." He raised his head. "Besides, no Mordinman ever runs away from a fight."

Sidis smiled gently. "This fight is already lost," he said.

"Not the way Mr Wilde talks," Craig said. "Back in the labs at Base Camp they're going to use a trans-something, I hear."

"Translocator in the gene matrix," Sidis said. "I guarantee they won't do it while Mil Ames runs the labs. After we go, they'll probably kill themselves in a year." He looked doubtfully at Craig. "I hadn't meant to tell you that, but it's one reason I hope you'll leave with us."

"How kill ourselves?"

"With an outlaw free-system."

Craig shook his head and Sidis smiled.

"Look, you know how the phyto stems are all rooted together underground like one big plant," he said. "You know we design the self-duplicating enzyme systems that *Thanasis* pumps into them. You know *Thanasis* free-systems can digest a man, too, and that's what you get inoculated against each time we design a new one. Well then." He steepled his fingers. "With translocation, *Thanasis* can redesign its own free-systems in the field, in a way. It might come up with something impossible to immunize. It might change so that our specific control virus would no longer kill it. Then it would kill us and rule the planet itself."

"I don't get all that," Craig said.

"Then trust my word. It happened once, on Planet Froy."

Craig nodded. "I heard about Planet Froy."

"That's what you risk and you can't win anyway. So come to Planet Belconti with us."

Craig stood up. "I almost wish you didn't tell me that," he said. "Now I can't even think about leaving."

Sidis leaned back and spread his fingers on the table.

"Talk to Midori Blake before you say no," he said. "I know she's fond of you, Roy. I thought you rather liked her."

Craig felt his face burn. "I do like to be around her," he said. "I liked it when you used to stop at Burton Island instead of camping in the field. I wish Mr Wilde would go there."

"I'll try to persuade him. Think it over, will you?"

"I can't think," Craig said. "I don't know what I feel." He turned to the door. "I'm going out and walk and try to think."

"Good night, Roy." Sidis reached for a book.

★

The second moon was just rising. Craig walked through a jungle of ghostly silver stems. Phytos clinging to them piped sleepily, disturbed by his passage. "I'm too ignorant to be a Belconti," he said once, aloud. He neared the ringwall. Stems grew more thickly, became harder, fused at last into a sloping ninety-foot dam. Craig climbed halfway up and stopped. It was foolhardy to go higher without a protective suit. *Thanasis* was on the other side, and its free-systems diffused hundreds of feet even in still air. The phyto stems were all rooted together into one big plant and *Thanasis* ate into it like a sickness. The stems formed ringwalls around stands of *Thanasis*, to stop its spread. Craig climbed a few feet higher.

Sure I'm big enough to whip Cobb, he thought. Whip any of them, except Mr Wilde. But he knew in a quarrel his knees would turn to water and his voice squeak off to nothing, because they were men and he was not. "I'm not a coward," he said aloud. "I'll kill my Great Russel yet."

He climbed to the top. *Thanasis* stretched off in a sea of blackness beneath the moons. Just below he could see the outline of narrow leaves furred with stinging hairs and beaded with poison droplets meant to be rainwashed into the roots of downslope prey. The ringwall impounded the poisoned water and this stand of *Thanasis* was drowning in it and it was desperate. He saw the tendrils, hungry to release poison into enemy tissues and follow after to suck and absorb. (They felt his warmth and waved feebly.) This below him was the woody, climbing form, but they said even waist-high shrubs could eat a man in a week.

I'm not afraid, Craig thought. He sat down and took off his boots and let his bare feet dangle above the *Thanasis*. Midori Blake and all the Belcontis would think this was crazy. They didn't understand about courage—all they had was brains. He liked them anyway, Midori most of all. He thought about her as he gazed off across the dark *Thanasis*. The whole continent would have to be like that first. Then they'd kill off *Thanasis* with a control virus and plant grass and real trees and it would all be like Base and Russel Islands were now. Sidis was wrong—that trans-stuff would do it. He'd stay and help. He felt better, with his mind made up.

Then he felt a gentle tug at his left ankle. It stabbed with fierce and sudden pain. He jerked his leg up. The tendril broke and came with it, still squirming and stinging. Craig whistled and swore as he scraped it off with a boot heel, careful not to let it touch his hands. Then he pulled on his right boot and hurried back to camp for treatment. He carried his left boot, because he knew how fast his ankle would swell. He reached camp with his left leg one screaming ache. Sidis was still up. He neutralized the poison, gave Craig a sedative, and made him take one of the bunks inside the flyer. He didn't ask questions, just looked down at Craig with his wry smile.

"You Mordinmen," he said, and shook his head.

The Belcontis were always saying that.

In the morning Cobb sneered and Wilde was furious.

"If you're shooting for a week on the sick list, aim again," Wilde said. "I'll give you two days."

"I'll do his work," Sidis said. "He needs two weeks to recover."

"I'll work," Craig said. "It don't hurt so much I can't work."

"Take today off," Wilde said, mollified.

"I'll work today," Craig said. "I'm all right."

It was a tortured day under the hot yellow sun, with his foot wrapped in sacks and stabbing pain up his spine with every step. Craig drove his power auger deep into basal ringwall tissue and the aromatic, red-purple sap gushed out and soaked his feet. Then he pushed in the explosive pellet, shouldered his rig and paced off the next position.

Over and over he did it, like a machine, not stopping to eat his lunch, ignoring the phytos that clung to his neck and hands. He meant to finish his arc first if it killed him. But when he finished and had time to think about it, his foot felt better than it had all day. He snapped a red cloth to his auger shaft and waved it high and the flyer slanted down to pick him up. Sidis was at the controls.

"You're the first to finish," he said. "I don't see why you're even alive. Go and lie down now."

"I'll take the controls," Craig said. "I feel good."

Sidis shrugged. "I guess you're proving something," he said.

He gave Craig the controls and went aft. Driving the flyer was one of the menial jobs that Craig liked. He liked being alone in the little control cabin, with its two seats and windows all around. He lifted to a thousand feet and glanced along the ringwall, curving out of sight in both directions. The pent sea of *Thanasis* was dark green by daylight. The phyto area outside the ringwall gleamed silvery, with an overplay of shifting colours, and it was very beautiful. Far and high in the north he saw a coloured cloud among the fleecy ones. It was a mass of migratory phytos drifting in the wind with their hydrogen sacs inflated. It was beautiful, too.

"They transfer substance to grow the ringwalls," he heard Sidis telling Wilde back in the main cabin. "You'll notice the biomass downslope is less dense. When you release that poisoned water from inside the ringwall, you get a shock effect and *Thanasis* follows up fast. But a new ringwall always forms."

"Next time through I'll blow fifty-mile arcs," Wilde said.

Craig slanted down to pick up Jordan. He was a stocky, sandy-haired man about Craig's age. He scrambled aboard grinning.

"Beat us again, hey, Craig?" he said. "That took guts, boy. You're all right!"

"I got two years' practice on you guys," Craig said.

The praise made him feel good. It was the first time Jordan had called him by name instead of "Blanky". He lifted the flyer again. Jordan sat down in the spare seat.

"How's the foot?" he asked.

"Pretty good. I think I could get my boot on, unlaced," Craig said.

"I'll take camp chores tonight," Jordan said. "You rest that foot, Craig. You're too good a man to lose."

"There's Whelan's flag," Craig said.

He felt himself blushing with pleasure as he slanted down to pick up Whelan. Jordan went aft. When Rice and Cobb had been picked up, Craig hovered the flyer at two miles and Wilde pulsed off the explosive. Twenty miles of living ringwall tissue fountained in dust and flame. Phytos rising in terrified, chromatic clouds marked the rolling shock wave. Behind it the silvery plain darkened with the sheet flow of poisoned water.

"Hah! Go it, *Thanasis*!" Wilde shouted. "I swear to bullets, that's a pretty sight down there! Now where's a safe place to camp, Sidis?"

"We're only an hour from Burton Island," Sidis said. "I used to stop at the taxonomy station there every night, when we worked this area."

"Probably why you never got anywhere, too," Wilde said. "But I want a look at that island. The Huntsman's got plans for it."

He shouted orders up to Craig. Craig lifted to ten miles and headed southeast at full throttle. A purplish sea rolled above the silvery horizon. Far on the sea rim beaded islands climbed to view. It had been a good day, Craig thought. Jordan seemed to want to be friends. And now, at last, he'd see Midori Blake again.

He grounded the flyer on slagged earth near the familiar grey stone buildings on the eastern headland. The men got out and George and Helen Toyama, smiling and grey-haired in lab smocks, came to welcome them. Craig's left boot was tight and it hurt, but he could wear it unlaced. Helen told him Midori was painting in the gorge. He limped down the gorge path, past Midori's small house and the Toyama home on the cliff edge at left. Midori and the Toyamas were the only people on Burton Island. The island was a phyto research sanctuary and had never been touched by *Thanasis*. It was the only place other than Base Camp where humans lived permanently.

The gorge was Midori's special place. She painted it over and over, never satisfied. Craig knew it well, the quartz ledge, the cascading waterfall and pool, the phytos dancing in sunlight that the silvery stem forest changed to the quality of strong moonlight. Craig liked watching Midori paint, most of all when she forgot him and sang to herself. She was clean and apart and never resentful or demanding, and it was just good to be in the same world with her. Through the plash of the waterfall and the phyto piping Craig heard her singing before he came upon her, standing before her easel beside a quartz boulder. She heard him and turned and smiled warmly.

"Roy! I'm so glad to see you," she said. "I was afraid you'd gone home after all."

She was small and dainty under her grey dress, with large black eyes and delicate features. Her dark hair snugged boyishly close to her head. Her voice had a natural, birdlike quality, and she moved and gestured with the quick grace of a singing bird. Craig grinned happily.

"For a while I almost wished I did," he said. "Now I'm glad again I didn't." He limped towards her.

"Your foot!" she said. "Come over here and sit down." She tugged him to a seat on the boulder. "What happened?"

"Touch of *Thanasis*," he said. "Nothing much."

"Take off your boot! You don't want pressure on it."

She helped him take the boot off and ran cool fingertips lightly over the red, swollen ankle. Then she sat beside him.

"I know it hurts you. How did it happen?"

"I was kind of unhappy," he said. "I went and sat on a ringwall and let my bare feet hang over."

"Foolish Roy. Why were you unhappy?"

"Oh—things." Several brilliant phytos settled on his bared ankle. He let them stay. "We got to sleep in the field now, 'stead of coming here. The new boss thinks our old gang was lazy. The new guys are all red dots and I'm just a nothing again and—oh, hell!"

"You mean they think they're better than you?"

"They are better, and that's what hurts. Killing a Great Russel is a kind of spirit thing, Midori." He scuffed his right foot. "I'll see the day when this planet has enough Great Russels so no kid has to grow up cheated, like I been."

"The phytos are not going to die, Roy," she said softly. "It's very clear now. We're defeated."

"You Belcontis are. Mordinmen never give up."

"*Thanasis* is defeated. Will you shoot phytos with rifles?"

"Please don't joke about rifles," he said. "We're going to use a trans-something on *Thanasis*."

"Translocation? Oh no! It can't be controlled for field use. They wouldn't dare!"

"Red dots dare anything," he said proudly. "These guys all studied on Belconti; they know how. That's another thing—"

He scuffed his foot again. Phytos were on both their heads and shoulders now and all over his bared ankle. They twittered faintly.

"What, Roy?"

"I feel like an ignorant nothing. Here I been ringwalling for two years, and they already know more about phytos than I do. I want you to tell me something about phytos that I can use to make the guys notice me. Like, can phytos feel?"

She held her hand to her cheek, silent a moment.

"Phytos are strange and wonderful and I love them," she said softly. "They're mixed plant and animal. Life never split itself apart on this planet."

The flying phytozoons, she explained, functioned as leaves for the vegetative stems. But the stems, too, had internal temperature control. The continental networks of great conduit roots moved fluids with a reversible, valved peristalsis. A stem plus attached phytos made an organism.

"But any phyto, Roy, can live with any stem, and they're forever shifting. Everything is part of everything," she said. "Our job here on Burton Island is to classify the phytos, and we just can't do it. They vary continuously along every dimension we choose, physical or chemical, and *kind* simply has no meaning." She sighed. "That's the most wonderful thing I know about them. Will that help you?"

"I don't get all that. That's what I mean, I'm ignorant," he said. "Tell me some one simple thing I can use to make the guys take notice of me."

"All right, tell them this," she said. "Phyto colour patterns are plastid systems that synthesize different molecules. The way they can recombine parts to form new organisms gives them a humanly inconceivable biochemical range. Whatever new poison or free-system we design for *Thanasis*, somewhere by sheer chance they hit on a countersubstance. The knowledge spreads faster each time. That's why *Thanasis* is defeated."

"I couldn't say that, and don't you say it either, Midori," Craig protested. "This here translocation, now—"

"Not even that." Her voice was faintly sharp. "The phytos have unlimited translocation and any number of sexes. Collectively, I don't doubt they're the mightiest biochemical lab in the galaxy. They form a kind of biochemical intelligence, almost a mind, and it's learning faster than we are." She turned and shook his arm with both her small hands.

"Yes, tell them, make them understand," she said. "Human intelligence is defeated here. Now human ferocity—oh, Roy—"

"Say it," he said bitterly. "Mordinmen are stupid. I ought to know. You sound almost like you want us to lose, Midori."

She turned away and began cleaning her brushes. It was nearly dark and the phytos were going to rest on the stems overhead. Craig sat miserably silent, remembering the feel of her hands on his arm. Then she spoke, and her voice was soft again.

"I don't know. If you wanted homes and farms here—but you want only the ritual deaths of man and dinothere—"

"You Belcontis can't understand," Craig said. "Maybe people's souls get put together different ways on different planets. I know there's a piece missing out of mine and I know what it is." He put his hand lightly on her shoulder. "Some holidays I fly down to Russel Island just to look at the Great Russel there, and then I know. I wish I could take you to see him; he'd make you understand."

"I understand. I just don't agree."

She swished and splashed brushes, but she didn't pull her shoulder away from his hand. Craig wished he dared ask her about the phytos and that many-sex stuff; the guys'd like that. He blushed and shook his head.

"Why is it you never see a dead phyto? Why is it there ain't enough dead wood on a whole continent to make one camp fire?" he asked. "What eats 'em? What keeps 'em down?"

She laughed and turned back to him, making his arm slide across her shoulders. He barely let it touch her, and she seemed not to know.

"They eat themselves internally, resorption, we call it," she said. "They can grow themselves again in another place and form, as a ring-wall, for instance. Roy, this planet has never known death and decay. Everything is resorbed and reconstituted. We try to kill it and it suffers, but its—" her voice trembled—"yes, its *mind*—can't form the idea of death. There's no way to think death biochemically."

"Oh bullets, Midori! Phytos can't think," he said. "I wonder, can they even feel?"

She jumped up and away from his arm. "Yes, they feel! Their piping is a cry of pain," she said. "Papa Toyama can remember when the planet was almost silent. Since he's been here, twenty years, their temperature has risen twelve degrees, their metabolic rate and speed of neural impulse doubled, chronaxy halved—"

Craig stood up too and raised his hands.

"Hold your fire, Midori," he said. "You know I don't know all them words. You're mad at me." It was too dark to see her face plainly.

"I think I'm just terribly afraid," she said. "I'm afraid of what we've been doing that we don't know about."

"That piping has always made me feel sad, kind of," Craig said. "I never would hurt a phyto. But Great Russel, when you think about whole continents hurting and crying, day and night for years—you scare me too, Midori."

She began packing her painting kit. Craig pulled on his boot. It laced up easily. I ain't really scared, he thought.

"We'll go to my house and I'll make our supper," she said.

She didn't sound angry. He took the kit and walked beside her, hardly limping at all. They started up the cliff path.

"Why did you stay on here, if the work makes you sad?" she asked.

"Two more years and I'll have enough saved to buy me a Great Russel hunt," he said. He flushed and was glad it was dark. "I guess you think that's a pretty silly reason."

"Not at all. I thought you might have an even sillier one."

He fumbled for a remark, trying not to understand her sudden chill. Then Jordan's voice bawled from above.

"Craig! Ho Craig!"

"Craig aye!"

"Come arunning!" Jordan yelled. "Bork's raising hell cause you ain't loading pellets. I saved chow for you."

The rest of the field job was much better. Jordan helped on camp chores and joked Rice and Whelan into following suit. Only Wilde and Cobb still called Craig "Blanky". Craig felt good about things. Jordan sat beside him in the control cabin as Craig brought the flyer home to Base Island. Russel Island loomed blue to the south and the Main Continent coast range toothed the eastern sea rim.

"Home again. Beer and the range, eh, Craig?" Jordan said. "We'll get in some hunting, maybe."

"Hope so," Craig said.

Base Island looked good. It was four thousand square miles of savanna and rolling hills with stands of young oak and beech. It teemed with game birds and animals transplanted from Mordin. On its northern tip, buildings and fields made the rectilinear pattern of man. Sunlight gleamed on square miles of *Thanasis* greenhouses behind their ionic stockades. Base Island was a promise of the planet's future, when *Thanasis* would have killed off the phytos and been killed in its turn and the wholesome life of Planet Mordin replaced them both. Base Island was home.

They were the first ringwalling team to come in. Wilde reported twelve hundred miles of ringwall destroyed, fifty per cent better than the old Belconti average. Barim, the Chief Huntsman, congratulated them. He was a burly, deep-voiced man with roached grey hair and four red dots on his forehead. It was the first time Craig had ever shaken hands with a man who had killed four Great Russels. Barim rewarded the crew with a week on food-hunting detail. Jordan teamed up with Craig. Craig shot twenty deer and twelve pigs and scores of game birds. His bag was better than Cobb's. Jordan joked at Cobb about it, and it made the sparrowy little man very angry.

The new men had brought a roaring, jovial atmosphere to Base Camp that Craig rather liked. He picked up camp gossip. Barim had ordered immediate production of translocator pollen. Mildred Ames, the Belconti Chief Biologist, had refused. But the labs and equipment were Mordin property and Barim had ordered his own men to go to work on it. Miss Ames raised shrill hell and Barim barred all Belcontis from the labs. She counter-attacked, rapier against bludgeon, and got her staff back in the labs. They were to observe only, for science and the record.

Jealous, scared, we'll show 'em up, the Mordin lab men laughed. And so we will, by the bones of Great Russel!

Craig saw Miss Ames several times around the labs. She was a tall, slender woman and she looked pinch-mouthed and unhappy. She detached Sidis from ringwalling and made him a lab observer. Craig thought a lot about what Midori had told him. He especially liked that notion of resorption and waited for his chance to spring it at the mess table. It came one morning at breakfast. Wilde's crew shared a table with lab men in the raftered, stone-floored mess hall. It was always a clamour of voices and rattling mess gear. Craig sat between Cobb and Jordan and across from a squat, bald-headed lab man named Joe Breen. Joe brought up the subject of ringwalls and Craig saw his chance.

"Them ringwalls, how they make 'em," he said. "They eat themselves and grow themselves again; it's called resorption."

"They're resorbing sons of guns, for sure," Joe said. "How do you like the way they mate?"

"That way's not for me!" Wilde shouted from the head of the table.

"What do they mean?" Craig whispered it to Jordan, but Cobb heard him.

"Blanky wants to know the facts of life," Cobb said loudly. "Who'll tell him?"

"Who but old Papa Bork?" Wilde shouted. "Blanky, when a flitter-bug gets that funny feeling it rounds up from one to a dozen others. They clump on a stem and get resorbed into one of those pinkish swellings you're all the time seeing. After a while it splits and a mess of crawlers falls out. Get it?"

Craig blushed and shook his head.

"They crawl off and plant themselves and each one grows into a phytogenous stem," Jordan said. "For a year it buds off new phytos like mad. Then it turns into a vegetative stem."

"Hell, I seen plenty crawlers," Craig muttered. "I just didn't know they was seeds."

Cobb snickered. "Know how to tell the boy crawlers from the girl crawlers, Blanky?" he asked. Joe Breen laughed.

"You're sharp as a gunflint, ain't you, Cobb?" Jordan said. "You don't tell their sex, Craig, you count it. They got one pair of legs for each parent."

"Hey, you know, that's good!" Wilde said. "Maybe a dozen sexes, each one tearing a slow piece off all the others in one operation. That's good, all right!"

"Once in a lifetime, it better be good," Joe said. "But Great Russel, talk about polyploidy and multihybrids—wish we could breed *Thanasis* that way."

"I'll breed my own way," Wilde said. "Just you give me the chance."

"These Belconti women think Mordinmen are crude," Joe said. "You'll just have to save it up for Mordin."

"There's a pretty little target lives alone on Burton Island," Wilde said.

"Yeah! Blanky knows her," Cobb said. "Can she be had, Blanky?"

"No!" Craig clamped his big hand around his coffee cup. "She's funny, keeps to herself a lot," he said. "But she's decent and good."

"Maybe Blanky never tried," Cobb said. He winked at Joe. "Sometimes all you have to do is ask them quiet ones."

Everyone laughed. Craig scowled and clamped his teeth.

"I'm the guy that'll ask, give me the chance," Wilde shouted.

"Old Bork'll come at her with them two red dots shining and she'll fall back into loading position slick as gun oil," Joe said.

"Yeah, and he'll find out old One-dot Cobb done nipped in there ahead of him," Cobb whooped.

The work horn blared. The men stood up in a clatter of scraping feet and chairs.

"Blanky, you go on brewhouse duty till Monday," Wilde said. "Then we start a new field job."

Craig wished they were back in the field already. He felt a sudden dislike of Base Camp.

The new job was dusting translocator pollen over the many North Continent areas where, seen from the air, silver streaking into dark green signalled phyto infiltration of old-strain *Thanasis*. The flowerless killers were wind-pollinated, with the sexes on separate plants. Old ringwall scars made an overlapping pattern across half the continent, more often than not covered by silvery, iridescent strands of pure phyto growth where *Thanasis* had once ravaged. Wilde charted new ringwalls to be blown the next trip out. It was hot, sweaty work in the black protective suits and helmets. They stayed contaminated and ate canned rations and forgot about camp fires. After two weeks their pollen cargo was used up and they landed at Burton Island and spent half a day decontaminating. As soon as he could, Craig broke away and hurried down the gorge path.

He found Midori by the pool. She had been bathing and her yellow print dress moulded damply to her rounded figure and her hair still dripped. Craig couldn't help thinking, what if he'd come a few minutes earlier, and he remembered Cobb's raucous voice saying, sometimes all you have to do is ask them quiet ones. Small phytos, patterned curiously in gold and scarlet and green, clung to Midori's bare arms and shoulders. They looked natural and beautiful, and the gorge and Midori were beautiful, and Craig felt a slow ache inside him.

She was glad to see him. She shook her head sadly when he told her about the translocator pollen. A phyto settled on Craig's hand and he tried to change the subject.

"What makes 'em do that?" he asked. "The guys think they suck blood, but I know different."

"They do take body fluid samples, but so tiny you can't feel it."

"Do they so?" He shook the phyto off his hand. "Do they really?"

"Tiny, tiny samples," she said. "They're curious about us."

"Just tasting of us, huh?" he shook his head. "If they can eat us, how come us and pigs and dinotheres can't eat them?"

"Foolish Roy! They don't *eat* us!" She stamped a bare foot "They want to understand us, but the only symbols they have are atoms and groups and radicals and ions and so on." She laughed. "Sometimes I wonder what they do think of us. Maybe they think we're giant seeds. Maybe they think we're each a single, terribly complicated molecule." She brushed her lips against a small scarlet and silver phyto on her wrist and it shifted to her cheek. "This is just their way of trying to live with us," she said.

"Just the same, it's what we call eating," he said.

"They eat only water and sunshine. They can't conceive of life that preys on life." She stamped her foot again. "Eating! Oh, Roy! It's more like a kiss!"

Craig wished he were a phyto, to touch her smooth arms and shoulders and her firm cheek. He inhaled deeply.

"I know a better kind of kiss," he said.

"Do you, Roy?" She dropped her eyes.

"Yes, I do," he said unsteadily. Needles prickled his sweating hands that felt as big as baskets. "Midori, I—someday I—"

"Yes, Roy?" Her voice was soft.

"Ho the camp!" roared a voice from up the path.

It was Wilde, striding along, grinning with his horse teeth.

"Pop Toyama's throwing us a party, come along," he shouted. He looked closely at Midori and whistled. "Hey there, pretty little Midori, you look good enough to eat," he said.

"Thank you, Mr Wilde." The small voice was cold.

On the way up the path, Wilde told Midori, "I learned the *Tanko* dance on Belconti. I told Pop if he'd play, you and I'd dance it for him after we eat."

"I don't feel at all like dancing," Midori said.

Wilde and Cobb flanked Midori at the dinner table and vied in paying rough court to her afterwards in the small sitting room. Craig talked to Helen Toyama in a corner. She was a plump, placid woman and she pretended not to hear the rough hunting stories Jordan, Rice and Whelan were telling each other. Papa Toyama kept on his feet, pouring the hot wine. He looked thin and old and fragile. Craig kept watching Midori. Wilde was getting red-faced and loud, and he wouldn't keep his hands off Midori. He gulped bowl after bowl of wine. Suddenly he stood up, left hand still on Midori's shoulder.

"Hey, a toast!" he shouted. He raised his bowl. "On your feet, men! Guns up for pretty little Midori!"

They stood and drank. Wilde broke his bowl with his hands. He put one fragment in his pocket and handed another to Midori. She shook her head, refusing it. Wilde grinned.

"We'll see a lot of you folks soon," he said. "Meant to tell you, Barim's moving you in to Base Camp. Our lab men will fly over next week to pick out what they can use of your gear."

Papa Toyama's lined, gentle face paled.

"We have always understood that Burton Island would remain a sanctuary for the study of the phytozoa," he said.

"It was never a Mordin understanding, Pop."

Toyama looked helplessly from Midori to Helen.

"How much time have we to close our projects?" he asked.

Wilde shrugged. "Say a month, if you need that long."

"We do, and more." Anger touched the old man's voice. "Why can't we at least stay here until the Belconti relief ship comes?"

"This has been our home for twenty years," Helen said softly.

"I'll ask the Huntsman to give you all the time he can," Wilde said, more gently. "But as soon as he pulls a harvest of pure-line translocator seed out of the forcing chambers, he wants to seed this island. We figure to get a maximum effect in virgin territory."

Papa Toyama blinked and nodded.

"More wine?" he asked, looking around the room.

When Wilde and Midori danced, Papa Toyama's music sounded strange to Craig. It sounded as sad as the piping of phytos.

These translocator hybrids were sure deathific, the lab men chortled. Their free-systems had high thermal stability; that would get around that sneaky phyto trick of running a fever. Their recombination index was fantastic. But there'd be a time lag in gross effect, of course. The phytos were still infiltrating more and more old-strain *Thanasis* areas. Belconti bastards should've started translocation years ago, the lab men grumbled. Scared, making their jobs last, want this planet for themselves. But wait. Just wait.

Craig and Jordan became good friends. One afternoon Craig sat waiting for Jordan at a table in the cavernous, smoky beer hall. On the rifle range an hour earlier he had fired three perfect Great Russel patterns and beaten Jordan by ten points. Barim had chanced by, slapped Craig's shoulder, and called him "stout rifle". Craig glowed at the memory. He saw Jordan coming with the payoff beer, threading between crowded, noisy tables and the fire pit where the pig carcass turned. Round face beaming, Jordan set four bottles on the rough plank table.

"Drink up, hunter!" he said. "Boy, today you earned it!"

Craig grinned back at him and took a long drink.

"My brain was ice," he said. "It wasn't like me doing it."

Jordan drank and wiped his mouth on the back of his hand.

"That's how it takes you when it's for real," he said. "You turn into one big rifle."

"What's it like, Jordan? What's it really like, then?"

"Nobody can ever say." Jordan looked upward into the smoke. "You don't eat for two days, they take you through the hunt ceremonies, you get to feeling light-headed and funny, like you don't have a name or a family any more. Then—" His nostrils flared and he clenched his fists. "Then—well, for me—there was Great Russel coming at me, getting bigger and bigger, filling the whole world, just him and me in the world." Jordan's face paled and he closed his eyes. "That's the moment. Oh, oh, oh—that's the moment!" he said. He sighed, then looked at Craig solemnly. "I fired the pattern like it was somebody else, the way you just said. Three-sided and I *felt* it hit wide, but I picked it up with a spare."

Craig's heart thudded. He leaned forward.

"Were you scared then, even a least little bit?"

"You ain't scared then, because you're Great Russel himself." Jordan leaned forward too, whispering. "You feel your own shots hit you, Craig, and you know you can't never be scared again. It's like a holy dance you and Great Russel been practising for a million years.

After that, somewhere inside you, you never stop doing that dance until you die."

Jordan sighed again, leaned back and reached for his bottle.

"I dream about it lots," Craig said. He noticed his hands were shaking. "I wake up scared and sweating. Well, anyway, I mailed my application to the Hunt College by the ship you came here on."

"You'll gun through, Craig. Did you hear the Huntsman call you 'stout rifle'?"

"Yeah, like from a long way off." Craig grinned happily.

"Move your fat rump, Jordan!" a jovial voice shouted.

It was Joe Breen, the bald, squat lab man. He had six bottles clasped in his hairy arms. Sidis came behind him. Joe put down his bottles.

"This is Sidis, my Belconti seeing eye," he said.

"We know Sidis; he's an old ringwaller," Jordan said. "Hi, Sidis."

"Hello, Jordan, Roy," Sidis said. "Don't see you around much."

He and Joe sat down. Joe uncapped bottles.

"We're in the field most all the time now," Craig said.

"You'll be out more, soon's we pull the pure-line translocator seed," Joe said. "It's close. Sidis has kittens every day."

"You grow 'em, we'll plant 'em," Jordan said. "Sidis, why don't you get off Joe's neck and come ringwalling again?"

"Too much to learn here in the labs," Sidis said. "We're all going to make our reputations out of this, if Joe and his pals don't kill us before we can publish."

"Damn the labs. Give me the field," Jordan said. "Right, Craig?"

"Right. It's clean and good, out with the phytos," Craig said. "This resorption they got, does away with things being rotten and dead—"

"Well, arrow my guts!" Joe slammed down his bottle. "Beer must make you poetical, Blanky," he snorted. "What you really mean is, they eat their own dead and their own dung. Now make a poem out of that!"

Craig felt the familiar weak, helpless anger rise in him.

"With them everything is alive all the time without stopping," he said. "All you can say they eat is water and sunshine."

"They eat water and fart helium," Joe said. "Some old-time Belconti, name of Toyama, thought they could catalyse hydrogen fusion."

"They do," Sidis said. "They can grow at night and underground and in the winter. When you stop to think about it, they're pretty wonderful."

"You're a damned poet too," Joe said. "All you Belcontis are poets."

"We're not, but I wish we had more poets," Sidis said. "Roy, you haven't forgotten what I told you once?"

"I ain't a poet," Craig said. "I never rhymed two words in my life."

"Craig's all right. Barim called him 'stout rifle' on the range this afternoon," Jordan said. "Joe, that guy Toyama, he's still here, out on Burton Island. We got orders to move him in to Base Camp on our next field trip."

"Great Russel, he must've been here twenty years!" Joe said. "How's he ever stood it?"

"Got his wife along," Jordan said. "Craig here is going on three years. He's standing it."

"He's turning into a damned poet," Joe said. "Blanky, you better go home for sure on the next relief ship, while you're still a kind of a man."

Craig found Midori alone in her house. It looked bare. Her paintings lay strapped together besides crates of books and clothing. She smiled at him, but she looked tired and sad.

"It's hard, Roy. I don't want to leave here," she said. "I can't bear to think of what you're going to do to this island."

"I never think about what we do, except that it just has to be," he said. "Can I help you pack?"

"I'm finished. We've worked for days. And now Barim won't give us transportation for our cases of specimens." She was almost ready to cry. "Papa Toyama's heart is broken," she said.

Craig bit his lip. "Heck, we can carry fifty tons," he said. "We got the room. Why don't I ask Mr Wilde to take 'em anyway?"

She grasped his arms and looked up at him.

"Would you, Roy? I—don't want to ask him a favour. The cases are stacked outside the lab building."

Craig found his chance after supper at the Toyamas'. Wilde left off paying court to Midori and carried his wine bowl outside. Craig followed and asked him. Wilde was looking up at the sky. Both moons rode high in a clear field of stars.

"What's in the cases, did you say?" Wilde asked.

"Specimens, slides, and stuff. It's kind of like art to 'em."

"All ours now. I'm supposed to destroy it," Wilde said. "Oh hell! All right, if you want to strong-back the stuff aboard." He chuckled. "I about got Midori talked into taking one last walk down to that pool of hers. I'll tell her you're loading the cases." He nudged Craig. "Might help, hey?"

When he had the forty cases stowed and lashed, Craig lifted the flyer to a hundred feet to test his trim. Through his side window he saw Wilde and Midori come out of the Toyama house and disappear together down the gorge path. Wilde had his arm across her shoulders. Craig grounded and went back, but he couldn't rejoin the party. For an hour he paced outside in dull, aching anger. Then his crewmates came out, arguing noisily.

"Ho Craig! Where been, boy?" Jordan slapped his shoulder. "I just bet Cobb you could outgun him tomorrow, like you did me. We'll stick him for the beer."

"Like hell," Cobb said.

"Like shooting birds in a cage," Jordan said. "Come along, Craig. Get some sleep."

"I ain't sleepy," Craig said.

"Bet old Bork's shooting a cage bird about now," Cobb said.

They all laughed except Craig.

"Come along, Craig," Jordan said. "You got to be slept and rested for tomorrow. If you don't outgun Cobb, I'll disown you."

"All right, but I ain't sleepy," Craig said.

On the trip to Base Camp next morning Craig stayed at the controls and had no chance to speak to Midori. He wasn't sure he wanted a chance. Cobb outgunned him badly on the range and he drank himself sodden afterwards. He woke next morning to Jordan's insistent shaking.

"We're going out again right away," Jordan said. "Don't let Bork catch you sleeping in. Something went wrong for him last night over in Belconti quarters and he's mad as a split snake."

Four hours later Craig grounded the flyer again at the Burton Island station, with a cargo of pure-line translocator seed. The crew wore black pro-suits. Craig felt dizzy and sick. Wilde seemed very angry. He ordered his men to seed all the paths and open spaces around the buildings. Craig and Jordan seeded the gorge path and the area around the pool. When they finished, they rested briefly on the quartz boulder. For the first time, Craig let himself look around. Phytos danced piping above their heads. The stems marching up the slopes transmuted the golden sun glare to a strong, silvery moonlight that sparkled on the quartz ledge and the cascading water. He wondered if he'd ever see it again. Not like this, anyway.

"Say, it's pretty down here," Jordan said. "Kind of twangs your string, don't it? It'll make a nice hunting camp someday."

"Let's go up," Craig said. "They'll be waiting."

When he lifted out of the field, Craig looked down at the station from his side window. Midori's house looked small and forlorn and accusing.

Months of driving fieldwork followed. At Base Camp six men died of a mutant free-system before an immunizer could be synthesized. An escaped control virus wiped out a seed crop. The once jovial atmosphere turned glum and the Mordin lab men muttered about Belconti sabotage. On his first free day Craig checked out a sports flyer, found Midori in the Belconti quarters, and asked her to go riding. She came, wearing a white blouse and pearls and a blue-and-yellow flared skirt. She seemed sad, her small face half dreaming and her eyes unfocused. Craig forgot about being angry with her and wanted to cheer her. When he was a mile up and heading south, he tried.

"You look pretty in that dress, like a phyto," he said.

She smiled faintly. "My poor phytos. How I miss them," she said. "Where are we going, Roy?"

"Russel Island, down ahead there. I want you to see Great Russel."

"I want to see him," she said. A moment later she cried out and grasped his arm. "Look at that colour in the sky over to the right!"

It was a patch of softly twinkling, shifting colours far off and high in the otherwise cloudless sky.

"Migratory phytos," he said. "We see 'em all the time."

"I know," she said. "Let's go up close. Please, Roy."

He arrowed the flyer towards the green-golden cloud. It resolved into millions of phytos, each with its opalescent hydrogen sac inflated and drifting northwest in the trade wind.

"They stain the air with beauty," Midori said. She was almost crying, but her face was vividly awake and her eyes sparkled. "Go clear inside, please, Roy."

She used to look like that when she was painting in the gorge, Craig thought. It was the way he liked her best. He matched wind speed inside the cloud and lost all sense of motion. Vividly coloured phytos obscured land, sea and sky. Craig felt dizzily suspended in nowhere and moved closer to Midori. She slid open her window to let in the piping and the spicy perfume.

"It's so beautiful I can't bear it," she said. "They have no eyes, Roy. We must know for them how beautiful they are."

She began piping and trilling in her clear voice. A phyto patterned in scarlet and green and silver dropped to her outstretched hand and she sang to it. It deflated its balloon and quivered velvety wings. Craig shifted uneasily.

"It acts almost like it knows you," he said.

"It knows I love it."

He frowned. "Love, something so different, that ain't how I mean love."

She looked up. "How do you understand love, Roy?"

"Well, you want to protect people you love, do things for 'em," he said. He was blushing. "What can you do for a phyto?"

"Stop trying to exterminate them," she said softly.

"Please don't start that again," he said. "I don't like to think about it either, but I know it just has to be."

"It will never be," she said. "I know. Look at all the different colour patterns out there. Papa Toyama remembers when phytos were almost all green. They developed the new pigment patterns to make counter-substances against *Thanasis*." She lowered her voice. "All the colours and patterns are new thoughts in that strange, inconceivably powerful biochemical mind of theirs. This cloud is a message, from one part of it to another part of it. Doesn't it frighten you?"

"You do, I think." He moved slightly away from her. "I didn't know they been changing like that."

"Who stays here long enough to notice? Who looks around him to see?" Her lips trembled. "But just think of the agony and the changings, through all the long years men have been trying to kill this planet. What if something—somehow—suddenly *understands*?"

Craig felt the hair bristle on his neck and he shifted further away from her. He felt weird and alone, without time or place or motion in that piping, perfumed phyto cloud-world. He couldn't face Midori's eyes.

"Damn it, this planet belongs to Great Russel!" he said harshly. "We'll win yet. At least they'll never take back Base or Russel Islands. Their seeds can't walk on water."

She kept her eyes on his, judging or pleading or questioning, he couldn't tell. He couldn't bear them. He dropped his own eyes.

"Shake that thing off your hand!" he ordered. "Close your window. I'm getting out of here!"

Half an hour later Craig hovered the flyer over the wholesome green grass and honest oak trees of Russel Island. He found Great Russel and held him in the magniviewer and they watched him catch and kill a buffalo. Midori gasped.

"Ten feet high at the shoulder. Four tons, and light on his feet as a cat," Craig said proudly. "That long reddish hair is like wire. Them bluish bare spots are like armour plate."

"Aren't his great teeth enough to kill the cattle he eats?" she asked. "What enemies has he, to need those terrible horns and claws?"

"His own kind. And us," Craig said. "Our boys will hunt him here, here on this planet, and become men. Our men will hunt him here, to heal their souls."

"You love him, don't you, Roy? Did you know you were a poet?" She couldn't take her eyes off the screen. "He *is* beautiful, fierce and terrible, not what women call beauty."

"He's a planet-shaker, he is! It takes four perfect shots to bring him down," Craig said. "He jumps and roars like the world ending—oh, Midori, I'll have my day!"

"But you might be killed."

"The finest kind of death. In our lost-colony days, our old fathers fought with bow and arrow," Craig said. "Even now, sometimes, we form a sworn band and fight him to the death with spears and arrows."

"I've read of sworn bands. I suppose you can't help how you feel."

"I don't want to help it. A sworn band is the greatest honour that can come to a man," he said. "But thanks for trying to understand."

"I want to understand," she said. "I want to, Roy. Is it that you can't believe in your own courage until you face Great Russel?"

"That's just what women can't ever understand." He looked at her eyes again and that question or whatever was still in them. "Girls can't help turning into women, but a man has to make himself," he said. "It's like I don't have my man's courage until I get it from Great Russel. There's chants and stuff with salt and fire—afterwards the boy eats pieces of the heart—I shouldn't talk about that, you'll laugh."

"I feel more like crying," she said. "There are different kinds of courage, Roy." Her face worked strangely, but she kept her eyes on his. "You have more courage than you know, Roy. You must find your true courage in your own heart, not in Great Russel's."

"I can't." He clenched his fists and looked away from her eyes, "I'm just a nothing inside me, until I face Great Russel," he said.

"Take me home, Roy, I'm afraid I'm going to cry." She dropped her face to her folded hands. "I don't have much courage," she said.

They flew to Base Camp in silence. When Craig helped her down from the flyer, she was really crying. She bowed her head momentarily against his chest and the spicy phyto smell rose from her hair.

"Goodbye, Roy," she said.

He could barely hear her. Then she turned and ran.

Craig didn't see her again. Wilde's crew spent all its time in the field, blowing ringwalls and planting translocator seed. Craig was glad to be away. The atmosphere of Base Camp turned from glum to morose. Everywhere across North Continent new phyto growth in silver, green and scarlet spotted the dark green *Thanasis* areas. Other ringwall crews reported the same of Main and South continents. Wilde's temper became savage; Cobb cursed bitterly at trifles; even happy-go-lucky Jordan stopped joking. Half asleep one night in a field camp, Craig heard Wilde shouting incredulous questions at the communicator inside the flyer. He came out cursing to rouse the camp.

"Phytos are on Base Island," he said. "Stems popping up everywhere."

"Great Russel in the sky!" Jordan jerked full awake. "How come?"

"Belconti bastards planted 'em, that's how!" Wilde said. "Barim's got 'em all arrested under camp law."

Cobb began cursing in a steady, monotonous voice.

"That—cracks—the gunflint!" Jordan said.

"We can't turn loose *Thanasis* there," Whelan said. "What'll we do?"

"Kill 'em by hand," Wilde said grimly. "We'll sow the rest of our seed broadcast and go in to help."

Craig felt numb and unbelieving. Shortly after noon he grounded the flyer at Base Camp, in the foul area beyond the emergency rocket-launching frame. Wilde cleaned up at once and went to see Barim, while his crew decontaminated the flyer. When they came through the irradiation tunnel in clean denims, Wilde was waiting.

"Blanky, come with me!" he barked.

Craig followed him into the grey stone building at the field edge, Wilde pushed him roughly through a door, said "Here he is, Huntsman," and closed the door again.

Rifles, bows and spears decorated the stone walls. The burly Chief Huntsman, cold-eyed under his roached grey hair and the four red dots, sat facing the door from behind a wooden desk. He motioned Craig to sit down in one of the row of wooden chairs along the inner wall. Craig sat stiffly in the one nearest the door. His mouth was dry.

"Roy Craig, you are on your trial for life and honour under camp law," Barim said sternly. "Swear now to speak truth in the blood of Great Russel."

"I swear to speak truth in the blood of Great Russel." Craig's voice sounded squeaky and false to him. He began to sweat.

"What would you say of someone who deliberately betrayed our project to destroy the phytos?"

"He would be guilty of hunt treason, sir, and be outlawed."

"Very well." Barim clasped his hands and leaned forward, his grey eyes boring into Craig's eyes. "What did you tell Bork Wilde was in those cases you flew from Burton Island to Base Island?"

Craig felt his stomach knot up.

"Slides, specimens, science stuff, sir," he said.

Barim questioned him closely about the cases. Craig tried desperately to speak the truth without naming Midori. Barim forced her name from him, then questioned him on her attitudes. Craig sweated and squirmed and a terrible fear grew in him. He kept his eyes on Barim's eyes and spoke a tortured kind of truth, but he would not attaint Midori. Finally Barim broke their locked gazes and slapped his desk.

"Are you in *love* with Midori Blake, boy?" he roared.

Craig dropped his own glance. "I don't know," he said. How do you know when you're in love, he thought. You just know it, like you know you're alive. "Well—I like to be around her—I guess I never thought—" he said. If you have to think about it, it ain't love, it's just being friends, he thought. "I—don't think so, sir," he said finally.

"The phyto seeds came here in those cases," Barim said. "Who planted them?"

Craig avoided Barim's eyes. "They can walk and plant themselves, sir. Maybe they escaped," he said. His mouth was dry as powder.

"Would Midori Blake be morally capable of releasing them?"

Craig's face twisted. "Morally—I'm not clear on the word, sir—" Sweat dripped on his hands.

"I mean, would she have the guts to want to do it and to do it?"

Ice clamped Craig's heart. He looked Barim in the eye.

"No, sir!" he said. "I won't never believe that about Midori!"

Barim smiled grimly and slapped his desk again.

"Wilde!" he roared. "Bring them in!"

Midori, in white blouse and black skirt, came in first. Her face was pale but composed, and she smiled faintly at Craig. Mildred Ames followed, slender and thin-faced in white, then Wilde, scowling blackly. Wilde sat between Craig and Miss Ames, Midori on the end.

"Miss Blake, young Craig has clearly been your dupe, as you insist he has," Barim said. "Your confession ends your trial except for sentencing. Once more I beg you to say why you have done this."

"You wouldn't understand," Midori said. "Be content with what you know."

Her voice was low but firm. Craig felt sick with dismay.

"I can't understand without condoning," Barim said. "For your own sake, I must know your motive. You may be insane."

"You know I'm sane," Midori said. "You know that."

"Yes." Barim's wide shoulders sagged. "Invent a motive, then," he said. He seemed almost to plead. "Say you hate Mordin. Say you hate me."

"I hate no one. I'm sorry for you all."

"I'll give you a reason!" Miss Ames jumped to her feet, thin face burning. "Your reckless, irresponsible use of translocation endangers us all! Accept defeat and go home!"

She helped Barim recover his composure. He smiled.

"Please sit down, Miss Ames," he said calmly. "In three months your relief ship will take you to safety. But we neither accept defeat nor fear death. We will require no tears of you or anyone."

Miss Ames sat down, her whole posture shouting defiance. Barim swung his eyes back to Midori and his face turned to iron.

"Miss Blake, you are guilty of hunt treason. You have betrayed your own kind in a fight with an alien life form," he said. "Unless you admit to some recognizably *human* motive, I must conclude that you abjure your own humanity."

Midori said nothing. Craig stole a glance at her. She sat erect but undefiant, small feet together, small hands folded in her lap. Barim slapped his desk and stood up.

"Very well. Under camp law I sentence you, Midori Blake, to outlawry from your kind. You are a woman and not of Mordin; therefore I will remit the full severity. You will be set down, lacking everything made with hands, on Russel Island. There you may still be nourished by the roots and berries of the Earth-type life you have wilfully betrayed. If you survive until the Belconti relief ship comes, you will be sent home on it." He burned his glance at Midori. "Have you anything to say before I cause your sentence to be executed?"

The four red dots blazed against the sudden pallor of the Huntsman's forehead. Something snapped in Craig. He leaped up, shouting into the hush.

"You can't do it, sir! She's little and weak! She doesn't know our ways—"

"Down! Shut up, you whimpering fool!" Wilde slapped and wrestled Craig down to his chair. "Silence!" Barim thundered. Wilde sat down, breathing hard, and the room was hushed again.

"I understand your ways too well," Midori said. "Spare me your mercy. Put me down on Burton Island."

"Midori, no!" Miss Ames turned to her. "You'll starve! *Thanasis* will kill you!"

"You can't understand either, Mildred," Midori said. "Mr Barim, will you grant my request?"

Barim leaned forward, resting on his hands. "It is so ordered," he said huskily. "Midori Blake, almost you make me know again the taste of fear." He straightened and turned to Wilde, his voice suddenly flat and impersonal. "Carry out the sentence, Wilde."

Wilde stood up and pulled Craig to his feet. "Get the crew to the flyer. Wear pro-suits," he ordered. "*Run*, boy!"

Craig stumbled out into the twilight.

Craig drove the flyer northwest from Base Camp at full throttle, overtaking the sun, making it day again. Silence ached in the main cabin behind him. He leaned away from it, as if to push the flyer forward with his muscles. He refused to think at all, but he couldn't help feeling. He knew it had to be and still he couldn't bear it. It seemed an anguished forever before he grounded the flyer roughly beside the deserted buildings on Burton Island. They got out, the men in black pro-suits, Midori still in blouse and skirt. They stood apart quietly and looked towards her little house on the cliff edge. *Thanasis* thrust up dark green and knee high along all the paths.

"Break out ringwall kits. Blow all the buildings," Wilde ordered. "Blanky, you come with me."

At Midori's house Wilde ordered Craig to sink explosive pellets every three feet along the foundations. A single pellet would have been enough. Craig found his voice.

"The Huntsman didn't say to do this, Mr Wilde. Can't we at least leave her this house?"

"She won't need it," Wilde said. "*Thanasis* will kill her before morning."

"Let her have it to die in, then. She loved this little house."

Wilde grinned without mirth, baring his big horse teeth.

"She's *outlaw*, Blanky," he said. "You know the law: nothing made with hands."

Craig bowed his head, teeth clamped. Wilde whistled tunelessly as Craig set the pellets. They returned to the flyers and Jordan reported the other buildings ready to blow. His round, jolly face was grim. Midori had not moved. Craig wanted to speak to her, say he was sorry, say goodbye, but he knew if he tried he would find no words but a howl. Her strange little smile seemed already to remove her to another world, a million light-years from Roy Craig and his kind. Cobb looked at her, his rat face eager.

"We'll detonate from the air," Wilde said. "The blast will kill anyone standing here."

"We're supposed to take off all her clothes first," Cobb said. "You know the law, Bork. Nothing made with hands."

"That's right," Wilde said.

Midori took off her blouse. She looked straight at Wilde. Red mist clouded Craig's vision.

"Load the kits," Wilde said abruptly. "Into the flyer, all hands! *Jump*, you dogs!"

From his side window by the controls Craig saw Midori start down the gorge path. She walked as carelessly relaxed as if she were going down to paint. *Thanasis* brushed her bare legs and he thought he saw the angry red spring out. She did not flinch or look back. Craig felt the pain in his own skin. He lifted the flyer with a lurching roar and he did not look out when Wilde blew up the buildings.

Away from the sun, southeast towards Base Camp, wrapped in his own thought-vacant hell, Roy Craig raced to meet the night.

With flame, chemicals and grub hoes, the Mordinmen fought their losing battle for Base Island. Craig worked himself groggy with fatigue to keep from thinking. He felt a mingled sense of loss and grief and anger and satisfaction, and he wondered if he were losing his mind. The phyto stems radiated underground with incredible growth energy.

They thrust up redoubly each new day like hydra heads. Newly budded phytos, the size of thumbnails, coloured the air of Base Island in gaily dancing swirls. Once Craig saw Joe Breen, the squat lab man, cursing and hopping like a frog while he slashed at dancing phytos with an axe. It seemed to express the situation.

Barim made his grim decision to move camp to Russel Island and seed the home island with *Thanasis*. Craig was helping erect the new camp when he collapsed. He awoke in bed in a small, bare infirmary room at Base Camp. The Mordin doctor took blood samples and questioned him. Craig admitted to nausea and joint pains for several days past.

"I been half crazy, sir," he defended himself. "I didn't know I was sick."

"I've got twenty more do know it," the doctor grunted.

He went out, frowning. Craig slept, to flee in dream-terror from a woman's eyes. He half woke at intervals for medication and clinical tests, to sleep again and face repeatedly a Great Russel dinothere. It looked at him with a woman's inscrutable eyes. He roused into the morning of the second day to find another bed squeezed into the small room, by the window. Papa Toyama was in it. He smiled at Craig.

"Good morning, Roy," he said. "I would be happier to meet you in another place."

Many were down and at least ten had died, he told Craig. The Belconti staff was back in the labs, working frantically to identify agent and vector. Craig felt hollow and his head ached and he didn't much care. Dimly he saw Miss Ames in a white lab smock come around the foot of his bed to stand between him and Papa Toyama. She took the old man's hand.

"George, old friend, we've found it," she said.

"You do not smile, Mildred."

"I don't smile. All night I've been running a phase analysis of diffraction patterns," she said. "It's what we've feared—a spread of two full Ris units."

"So. Planet Froy again." Papa Toyama's voice was calm. "I would like to be with Helen now, for the little time we have."

"Surely," she said. "I'll see to it."

Quick, heavy footsteps sounded outside. A voice broke in.

"Ah. Here you are, Miss Ames."

Barim, in leather hunting clothes, bulked in the door. Miss Ames turned to face him across Craig's bed.

"I'm told you found the virus," Barim said.

"Yes." Miss Ames smiled thinly.

"Well, what countermeasures? Twelve are dead. What can I do?"

"You might shoot at it with a rifle, Mr Barim. It is a *Thanasis* free-system that has gotten two degrees of temporal freedom. Does that mean anything to you?"

His heavy jaw set like a trap. "No, but your manner does. It's the plague, isn't it?"

She nodded. "No suit can screen it. No cure is possible. We are all infected."

Barim chewed his lip and looked at her in silence.

"For your sake now, I wish we'd never come here," he said at last. "I'll put our emergency rocket in orbit to broadcast a warning message. That will save your relief ship, when it comes, and Belconti can warn the sector." A half smile softened his bluff, grim features. "Why don't you rub my nose in it? Say you told me so?"

"Need I?" Her chin up. "I pity you Mordinmen. You must all die now without dignity, crying out for water and your mothers. How you will loathe that!"

"Does that console you?" Barim still smiled. "Not so, Miss Ames. All night I thought it might come to this, and even now men are forging arrow points. We'll form a sworn band and all die fighting Great Russel." His voice deepened and his eyes blazed. "We'll stagger who can, crawl who must, carry our helpless, and all die fighting like men."

"Like savages! No! No!" Her hands flew up in shocked protest. "Forgive me for taunting you, Mr Barim. One never says Yes to death. I need your help, all of your men and transport, truly I do. Some of us may live, if we fight hard enough."

"How?" He growled it. "I thought on Planet Froy—"

"Our people on Planet Froy had only human resources," she said. "But here, I'm certain that somewhere already the phytos have synthesized the plague immunizer that seems forever impossible to human science." Her voice shook. "Please help us, Mr Barim. If we can find it, isolate enough to learn its structure—"

"No!" He cut her off bluntly. "Too long a gamble. One doesn't run squealing away from death, Miss Ames. My way's decent and sure."

Her chin came up again and her voice sharpened. "How dare you condemn your own men unconsulted? They might prefer a fight for life."

"Hah! You don't know them!" He bent to shake Craig's shoulder with rough affection. "You, lad," he said. "You'll get up and walk with a sworn band, won't you?"

"No," Craig said.

He struggled off his pillow, propped shakily on his arms. Miss Ames smiled and patted his cheek.

"You'll stay and help us fight to live, won't you?" she said.

"No," Craig said.

"Think what you say, lad!" Barim said tautly. "Great Russel can die of plague, too. We owe him a clean death."

Craig sat bolt upright. He stared straight ahead.

"I foul the blood of Great Russel," he said slowly and clearly. "I foul it with dung. I foul it with carrion. I foul it with—"

Barim's fist knocked Craig to the pillow and split his lip. The Huntsman's face paled under his tan.

"You're mad, boy!" he whispered. "Not even in madness may you say those words."

Craig struggled up again. "You're the crazy ones, not me," he said. He tongued his lip and blood dripped on his thin pyjama coat. "I'll die an outlaw, that's how I'll die," he said. "An outlaw, on Burton Island." He met Barim's unbelieving eyes. "I foul the blood—"

"Silence!" Barim roared. "Outlawry it is. I'll send a party for you, stranger."

He whirled and stamped out. Miss Ames followed him.

"You Mordinmen," she said, shaking her head.

Craig sat on the edge of his bed and pulled his sweat-soaked pyjamas straight. The room blurred and swam around him. Papa Toyama's smile was like a light.

"I'm ashamed. I'm ashamed. Please forgive us, Papa Toyama," Craig said. "All we know is to kill and kill and kill."

"We all do what we must," the old man said. "Death cancels all debts, Roy. It will be good to rest."

"Not my debts. I'll never rest again," Craig said. "All of a sudden I know—Great Russel, *how* I know—I know I loved Midori Blake."

"She was a strange girl," Papa Toyama said. "Helen and I thought she loved you, in the old days on our island." He bowed his head. "But our lives are only chips in a waterfall. Goodbye, Roy."

Jordan in a black pro-suit came shortly after. His face was bitter with contempt. He jerked his thumb at the door.

"On your feet, stranger! Get going!" he snapped.

In pyjamas and barefooted, Craig followed him. From somewhere in the infirmary he heard a voice screaming. It sounded like Cobb. They walked across the landing field. Everything seemed underwater. Men were rigging to fuel the emergency rocket. Craig sat apart from the others in the flyer. Cobb was missing. Wilde was flushed and shivering and his eyes glared with fever. Jordan took the controls. No one spoke. Craig dozed through coloured dream-scraps while the flyer outran the sun. He woke when it grounded in early dawn at Burton Island.

He climbed down and stood swaying beside the flyer. *Thanasis* straggled across the rubble heaps and bulked waist-high in the dim light along the paths. Phytos stirred on their stems and piped sleepily in the damp air. Craig's eyes searched for something, a memory, a presence, a completion and rest, he didn't know, searching with his eyes, but he felt it very near him. Then Wilde came behind him, shoving. Craig moved away.

"Stranger!" Wilde called.

Craig turned and looked into the fever-glaring eyes above the big horse teeth. The teeth gaped.

"I foul the blood of Midori Blake. I foul it with dung. I—"

Strength from nowhere exploded into the bone and muscle of Roy Craig. He sprang and felt the teeth break under his knuckles. Wilde fell. The others scrambled down from the flyer.

"Blood right! Blood right!" Craig shouted.

A bell note rang in this voice, as strange to him as the strength that flamed along his nerves. Jordan held back Rice and Whelan. Wilde rose, spitting blood, swinging big fists. Craig closed to meet him, berserk in fury. The world wheeled and tilted, shot with flashing colours, gasping with grunts and curses, but rock-steady in the centre of things, Wilde pressed the fight and Craig hurled it back on him. He felt the blows without pain, felt his ribs splinter, felt the good shock of his own blows all the way to his heels. Bruising falls on the rough slag, feet stamping, arms grappling, hands tearing, breath sobbing, both men on knees clubbing with fists and forearms. The scene cleared and Craig saw through one eye Wilde crumpled and inert before him. He rose unsteadily. He felt weightless and clean inside.

"Blood right, stranger," Jordan said, grim faced and waiting.

"Let it go," Craig said. "Great Russel go with you, stranger."

He turned down the gorge path, ignoring his chest pains, crashing through the rank *Thanasis*. *Home*! going *home*! going *home*! a bell tolled in his head. He did not look back.

Thanasis grew more sparsely in the shaded gorge. Craig heard the waterfall and old memories cascaded upon him. He rounded to view of it by the quartz boulder and his knees buckled and he knelt beside the boulder. She was very near him. He felt an overpowering sense of her presence. She was this place.

Dawn light shafted strongly into the gorge, sparkled on the quartz ledge, made fleeting rainbows in the spray above the pool. Phytos lifted from ghost-silver stems to twitter and dance their own rainbow in the air. Something rose in Craig's throat and choked him. Tears blurred his good eye.

"Midori," he said. "Midori."

The feeling overwhelmed him. His heart was bursting. He could find no words. He raised his arms and battered face to the sky and cried out incoherently. Then a blackness swept away his intolerable pain.

Titanic stirrings. Windy rushings. Sharp violences swarming.

Fittings-together in darkness. A trillion times a trillion a trillion patient searchings. Filtering broken lights, silver, green, golden, scarlet.

Bluntings. Smoothings. Transformings into otherness.

Flickering awareness, planet-vast and atom-tiny, no focus between. The proto-sensorium of a god yearning to know himself. Endless, patient agony in search for being.

Form and colour outfolding in middle focus. Flashings of terrible joy and love unspeakable. It looked. Listened. Felt. Smelled. Tasted.

Crystalline polar wastes. Wine of sweet. Warm sun glint on blue water. Perfumed wind caress. Thorn of bitter. Rain patter. Silver-green sweep of hill.

Storm roar and shaking. Sharp of salt. Sleeping mountains. Surf beat. Star patterns dusted on blackness. Clear of sour. Cool moons of night.

It knew and loved.

Ragged line of men gaunt under beard stubble. Green plain. High golden sun. Roar. Shaggy redness bounding. Bow twangs. Whispering arrow flights. Deep-chested shouts of men. Lances thrusting. Bodies ripped, thrown, horn-impaled and beating with fists. Great shape kneeling, threshing, streaming blood. Deep man-shouts dwindling to a silence.

It knew and sorrowed.

The woman bathing. Sunlight dappling rounded limbs. Black hair streaming. Grace beyond bearing. Beauty that was pain.

It shook terribly with love.

Ground firm beneath rested flesh, whole and unblemished forever. Bursting excitement. HOME! coming HOME! coming HOME!

It came home.

Roy Craig knew his body again and the solid frame of things around him. He lay on his back and a warm, aromatic breeze blew down the gorge and tossed the branches in graceful, silvery patterns against the blue sky. He heard the waterfall and the phytos and he felt rested and good. He groped for an old, lost grief and it was lost forever in Midori suddenly kneeling beside him, her face radiant and her fingers cool on his forehead. Except for clinging phytos, she was naked. He was naked too and he was not ashamed and not excited and he realized they were both dead. He sat up in fearful wonder.

"Midori," he said. "When you die—it's like this—how—what—"

He wanted to know a million things, but one came first.

"Can I ever lose you again, now?" he asked.

"Never again." She smiled. "We didn't die, Roy. We're more alive than we've ever been."

He took her hands. They were warm and solid.

"The plague killed everybody," he said.

"I know. You talked in your delirium. But we didn't die."

"What happened to us?"

"The phytos saved us," she said. "Somewhere in their infinite life-spectrum they matched up a band for humans. They mingled their substance with ours, cleansed us of *Thanasis* and gave us immunity." She smiled and squeezed his hands. "I know how you feel. I watched over you for two weeks while phytos came and went from you. Then I understood what had happened to me."

His hand discovered his beard and he nodded. "I have to believe you. But why, when we tried so long and hard to kill 'em? Why?"

"They couldn't know that. Here death and decay are only vital changings," she said. "This life never split apart, Roy, and in wholeness is nothing but love."

"I felt—dreamed that." He told her of his visions.

"It was no dream," she said. "You were diffused into the planetary consciousness. It happened to me, too."

"I'm afraid I'm dreaming right this minute," he said. "Can we still eat and drink and all?"

She laughed, jumped to her feet and pulled him upright.

"Foolish Roy. You still don't believe you're alive," she said. "Come, I want to show you something."

He ran hand in hand with her to the pool side. The gravel hurt his feet, but the scrubby *Thanasis* that brushed his ankles didn't hurt at all. Beside the pool, stems had fused ringwall fashion into a series of connecting rooms like hollow cones, clean, dry and silvery with shadows. He followed Midori through the rooms and outside again to where a grove of separate stems displayed brownish swellings. She tore away one covering like thin paper to reveal pearly, plum-sized nodules closely packed in a cavity. She held one to his lips and he ate it. It was cool and crisp, with a delightful, unfamiliar flavour. He realized he was very hungry. He ate another and looked at her with awe.

"There are hundreds of these vesicles," she said. "No two ever taste quite the same."

"Do they know us like people, then?" he asked. "Like I know you?"

"It knows us biochemically, as if we were giant molecules," she said. "Here's what I think, Roy. I think this life had infinite potentialities and mastered its environment using only the tiniest part of them. It never split up, to fight itself and evolve that way. So it lay dreaming and might have dreamed forever—"

She looked away across the pool to the stem clad slope and the dancing, rainbow clouds of phytos.

"Go on," he said. "You mean we came then, with *Thanasis*?"

"Yes. We forced changes, genetic recombinations, rises in temperatures and process speeds. Whatever happened at one point could be duplicated everywhere, because it's all one and a year is to it like a million years in the evolution of Earth-life. It raised itself to a new level of awareness. We awakened it." She brought her eyes back to Craig's eyes. "I feel it knows us and loves us for that."

"Loves us for *Thanasis*!"

"It loves *Thanasis* too. *Thanasis* is being fused into the planetary life, just as we are," she said. "It thinks us biochemically, Roy. Like each littlest phyto, we are thoughts now in that strange mind. I think we focus its new-found awareness somehow, serve it as a symbol system, a form-giver—" She lowered her voice and pressed closer to him and he felt her warmth and nearness. "We are its thoughts that also think themselves, the first it has ever had," she whispered. "It is a great and holy mystery, Roy. Only through us can it know its own beauty and wonder. It loves and needs us."

"I feel what you mean." He ran his hands down the smooth curve of her back and she shivered under his hands. "I feel what you mean.

I know what you mean." He clasped her to him and kissed her. "I love it, too. Through you, I love it."

"I give you back its love," she whispered into his shoulder.

"We're alive!" he said. "Midori, now I know we're alive!"

"We're alive. Do you realize that we'll never be ill, never grow old, never have to die?"

He pressed his face into her hair. "Never is a long time. But I want you for a long, long time, Midori."

"Our children will take up our duties," she said, still into his shoulder, and she was blushing now. "If we tire, we can be resorbed and diffuse through the planetary consciousness, as we did in our visions."

"Our children," he said. "Our children's children. Thousands and thousands. It's wonderful, Midori."

"It could be the same for any old or ill human being who might come to this planet, now," she said. "They could have youth and strength again forever."

"Yes." He looked up at the arching sky. "And there's a rocket up there in orbit with a warning message. Maybe they'll discover us someday. But for a long time yet they'll hunt shy of us like the plague they think we are."

"Yes. It's not fair they can't know—"

"That they are their own plague," he finished for her.

He kissed her tear-bright eyes and patted her head to rest again on his shoulder.

ADAM AND NO EVE

Alfred Bester

Alfred Bester (1913–1987) produced two of the immortal classics of science fiction in the 1950s, The Demolished Man *(serial, 1952) and* The Stars My Destination *(serial, 1956), also known as* Tiger! Tiger! *The first considered how a murder could be committed in a future where society is monitored by telepaths, whilst the second tells the kaleidoscopic quest for revenge of a transformed human. Bester's career in science fiction spanned over forty years, yet his output of novels and stories is slim because he spent much of the 1940s working in the comic-book field, the 1950s in television and the 1960s as a feature writer and senior editor at* Holiday *magazine. This makes his occasional trips into science fiction all the more special. His short fiction was collected in a variety of forms of which the most complete is the posthumous* Virtual Unrealities *(1997). One of the themes in Bester's works is of transcendence and rebirth and it is presented at its most potent in this story dating from 1941 which brings some hope to our fears for the planet's future.*

CRANE KNEW THIS MUST BE THE SEA-COAST. INSTINCT TOLD HIM; but more than instinct, the few shreds of knowledge that clung to his torn, feverish brain told him; the stars that had shown at night through the rare breaks in the clouds, and his compass that still pointed a trembling finger north. That was strangest of all, Crane thought. Though a welter of chaos, the Earth still retained its polarity.

It was no longer a coast; there was no longer any sea. Only the faint line of what had been a cliff, stretching north and south for endless miles. A line of grey ash. The same grey ash and cinders that lay behind him; the same grey ash that stretched before him. Fine silt, knee-deep, that swirled up at every motion and choked him. Cinders that scudded in dense mighty clouds when the mad winds blew. Cinders that were churned to viscous mud when the frequent rains fell.

The sky was jet overhead. The black clouds rode high and were pierced with shafts of sunlight that marched swiftly over the Earth. Where the light struck a cinder storm, it was filled with gusts of dancing, gleaming particles. Where it played through rain it brought the arches of rainbows into being. Rain fell; cinder-storms blew; light thrust down—together, alternately and continually in a jigsaw of black and white violence. So it had been for months. So it was over every mile of the broad Earth.

Crane passed the edge of the ashen cliffs and began crawling down the even slope that had once been the ocean bed. He had been travelling so long that all sense of pain had left him. He braced elbows and dragged his body forward. Then he brought his right knee under him and reached forward with elbows again. Elbows, knee, elbows, knee—He had forgotten what it was to walk.

Life, he thought dazedly, is wonderful. It adapts itself to anything. If it must crawl, it crawls. Callous forms on the elbows and knees. The neck and shoulders toughen. The nostrils learn to snort away the ashes before they inhale. The bad leg swells and festers. It numbs, and presently it will rot and fall off.

"I beg pardon," Crane said, "I didn't quite get that—"

He peered up at the tall figure before him and tried to understand the words. It was Hallmyer. He wore his stained lab jacket and his grey hair was awry. Hallmyer stood delicately on top of the ashes and Crane wondered why he could see the scudding cinder clouds through his body.

"How do you like your world, Stephen?" Hallmyer asked.

Crane shook his head miserably.

"Not very pretty, eh?" said Hallmyer. "Look around you. Dust, that's all; dust and ashes. Crawl, Stephen, crawl. You'll find nothing but dust and ashes—"

Hallmyer produced a goblet of water from nowhere. It was clear and cold. Crane could see the fine mist of dew on its surface and his mouth was suddenly coated with dry grit.

"Hallmyer!" he cried. He tried to get to his feet and reach for the water, but the jolt of pain in his right leg warned him. He crouched back.

Hallmyer sipped and then spat in his face. The water felt warm.

"Keep crawling," said Hallmyer bitterly. "Crawl round and round the face of the Earth. You'll find nothing but dust and ashes—" He emptied the goblet on the ground before Crane. "Keep crawling. How many miles? Figure it out for yourself. Pi-R-Square. The radius is eight thousand or so—"

He was gone, jacket and goblet. Crane realized that rain was falling again. He pressed his face into the warm sodden cinder mud, opened his mouth and tried to suck the moisture. He groaned and presently began crawling.

There was an instinct that drove him on. He had to get somewhere. It was associated, he knew, with the sea—with the edge of the sea. At the shore of the sea something waited for him. Something that would help him understand all this. He had to get to the sea—that is, if there were a sea any more.

The thundering rain beat his back like heavy planks. Crane paused and yanked the knapsack around to his side where he probed in it with one hand. It contained exactly three things. A pistol, a bar of chocolate and a can of peaches. All that was left of two months' supplies. The chocolate was pulpy and spoiled. Crane knew he had best eat it before all value rotted away. But in another day he would lack the strength to open the can. He pulled it out and attacked it with the opener. By the time he had pierced and pried away a flap of tin, the rain had passed.

As he munched the fruit and sipped the juice, he watched the wall of rain marching before him down the slope of the ocean bed. Torrents of water were gushing through the mud. Small channels had already been cut—channels that would be new rivers some day. A day he would never see. A day that no living thing would ever see. As he flipped the empty can aside, Crane thought: The last living thing on Earth eats its last meal. Metabolism plays its last act.

Wind would follow the rain. In the endless weeks that he had been crawling, he had learned that. Wind would come in a few minutes and flog him with its clouds of cinders and ashes. He crawled forward, bleary eyes searching the flat grey miles for cover.

Evelyn tapped his shoulder.

Crane knew it was she before he turned his head. She stood alongside, fresh and gay in her bright dress, but her lovely face was puckered with alarm.

"Stephen," she cried, "you've got to hurry!"

He could only admire the way her smooth honey hair waved to her shoulders.

"Oh darling!" she said, "you've been hurt!" Her quick gentle hands touched his legs and back. Crane nodded.

"Got it landing," he said. "I wasn't used to a parachute. I always thought you came down gently—like plumping onto a bed. But the grey earth came up at me like a fist—and Umber was fighting around in my arms. I couldn't let him drop, could I?"

"Of course not, dear—" Evelyn said.

"So I just held on to him and tried to get my legs under me," Crane said. "And then something smashed my legs and side—"

He paused, wondering how much she knew of what really had happened. He didn't want to frighten her.

"Evelyn, darling—" he said, trying to reach up his arms.

"No dear," she said. She looked back in fright. "You've got to hurry. You've got to watch out behind!"

"The cinder storms?" He grimaced. "I've been through them before."

"Not the storms!" Evelyn cried. "Something else. Oh, Stephen—"

Then she was gone, but Crane knew she had spoken the truth. There was something behind—something that had been following him all those weeks. Far in the back of his mind he had sensed the menace. It was closing in on him like a shroud. He shook his head. Somehow that was impossible. He was the last living thing on Earth. How could there be a menace?

The wind roared behind him, and an instant later came the heavy clouds of cinders and ashes. They lashed over him, biting his skin. With dimming eyes, he saw the way they coated the mud and covered it with a fine dry carpet. Crane drew his knees under him and covered his head with his arms. With the knapsack as a pillow, he prepared to wait out the storm. It would pass as quickly as the rain.

The storm whipped up a great bewilderment in his sick head. Like a child he pushed at the pieces of his memory, trying to fit them together. Why was Hallmyer so bitter toward him? It couldn't have been that argument, could it?

What argument?

Why, that one before all this happened.

Oh that!

Abruptly, the pieces fitted themselves together.

Crane stood alongside the sleek lines of his ship and admired it tremendously. The roof of the shed had been removed and the nose of the ship hoisted so that it rested on a cradle pointed toward the sky. A workman was carefully burnishing the inner surfaces of the rocket jets.

The muffled sounds of an argument came from within the ship and then a heavy clanking. Crane ran up the short iron ladder to the port and thrust his head inside. A few feet beneath him, two men were buckling the long tanks of ferrous solution into place.

"Easy there," Crane called. "Want to knock the ship apart?"

One looked up and grinned. Crane knew what he was thinking. That the ship would tear itself apart. Everyone said that. Everyone except Evelyn. She had faith in him. Hallmyer never said it either. But Hallmyer thought he was crazy in another way. As he descended the ladder, Crane saw Hallmyer come into the shed, lab jacket flying.

"Speak of the devil!" Crane muttered.

Hallmyer began shouting as soon as he saw Crane. "Now listen—"

"Not all over again," Crane said.

Hallmyer dug a sheaf of papers out of his pocket and waved it under Crane's nose.

"I've been up half the night," he said, "working it through again. I tell you I'm right. I'm absolutely right—"

Crane looked at the tight-written equations and then at Hallmyer's bloodshot eyes. The man was half mad with fear.

"For the last time," Hallmyer went on. "You're using your new catalyst on iron solution. All right. I grant that it's a miraculous discovery. I give you credit for that."

Miraculous was hardly the word for it. Crane knew that without conceit, for he realized he'd only stumbled on it. You had to stumble on a catalyst that would induce atomic disintegration of iron and give 10×10^{10} foot-pounds of energy for every gram of fuel. No man was smart enough to think all that up by himself.

"You don't think I'll make it?" Crane asked.

"To the Moon? Around the Moon? Maybe. You've got a fifty-fifty chance." Hallmyer ran fingers through his lank hair. "But for God's sake, Stephen, I'm not worried about you. If you want to kill yourself, that's your own affair. It's the Earth I'm worried about—"

"Nonsense. Go home and sleep it off."

"Look"—Hallmyer pointed to the sheets of paper with a shaky hand—"no matter how you work the feed and mixing system you can't get one hundred per cent efficiency in the mixing and discharge."

"That's what makes it a fifty-fifty chance," Crane said. "So what's bothering you?"

"The catalyst that will escape through the rocket tubes. Do you realize what it'll do if a drop hits the Earth? It'll start a chain of iron disintegrations that'll envelope the globe. It'll reach out to every iron atom—and there's iron everywhere. There won't be any Earth left for you to return to—"

"Listen," Crane said wearily, "we've been through all this before."

He took Hallmyer to the base of the rocket cradle. Beneath the iron framework was a two-hundred-foot pit, fifty feet wide and lined with firebrick.

"That's for the initial discharge flames. If any of the catalyst goes through, it'll be trapped in this pit and taken care of by the secondary reactions. Satisfied now?"

"But while you're in flight," Hallmyer persisted, "you'll be endangering the Earth until you're beyond Roche's limit. Every drop of non-activated catalyst will eventually sink back to the ground and—"

"For the very last time," Crane said grimly, "the flame of the rocket discharge takes care of that. It will envelop any escaped particles and destroy them. Now get out. I've got work to do."

As he pushed him to the door, Hallmyer screamed and waved his arms. "I won't let you do it!" he repeated over and over. "I'll find some way to stop you. I won't let you do it—"

Work? No, it was sheer intoxication to labour over the ship. It had the fine beauty of a well-made thing. The beauty of polished armour, of a balanced swept-hilt rapier, of a pair of matched guns. There was no thought of danger and death in Crane's mind as he wiped his hands with waste after the last touches were finished.

She lay in the cradle ready to pierce the skies. Fifty feet of slender steel, the rivet heads gleaming like jewels. Thirty feet were given over to fuel the catalyst. Most of the forward compartment contained the spring hammock Crane had devised to take up the initial acceleration shock. The ship's nose was a solid mass of natural quartz that stared upward like a cyclopian eye.

Crane thought: She'll die after this trip. She'll return to the Earth and smash in a blaze of fire and thunder, for there's no way yet of devising a safe landing for a rocket ship. But it's worth it. She'll have had her one great flight, and that's all any of us should want. One great beautiful flight into the unknown—

As he locked the workshop door, Crane heard Hallmyer shouting from the cottage across the fields. Through the evening gloom he could see him waving frantically. He trotted through the crisp stubble, breathing the sharp air deeply, grateful to be alive.

"It's Evelyn on the phone," Hallmyer said.

Crane stared at him. Hallmyer was acting peculiarly. He refused to meet his eyes.

"What's the idea?" Crane asked. "I thought we agreed that she wasn't to call—wasn't to get in touch with me until I was ready to start? You been putting ideas into her head? Is this the way you're going to stop me?"

Hallmyer said: "No—" and studiously examined the indigo horizon.

Crane went into his study and picked up the phone.

"Now listen, darling," he said without preamble, "there's no sense getting alarmed now. I explained everything very carefully. Just before the ship crashes, I take to a parachute and float down as happy and gentle as Winken, Blinken and Nod. I love you very much and I 'll see you Wednesday when I start. So long—"

"Goodbye, sweetheart," Evelyn's clear voice said, "and is that what you called me for?"

"Called you!"

A brown hulk disengaged itself from the hearth rug and lifted itself to strong legs. Umber, Crane's Great Dane, sniffed and cocked an ear. Then he whined.

"Did you say I called you?" Crane shouted.

Umber's throat suddenly poured forth a bellow. He reached Crane in a single bound, looked up into his face and whined and roared all at once.

"Shut up, you monster!" Crane said. He pushed Umber away with his foot.

"Give Umber a kick for me," Evelyn laughed. "Yes, dear. Someone called and said you wanted to speak to me."

"They did, eh? Look, honey, I'll call you back—"

Crane hung up. He arose doubtfully and watched Umber's uneasy actions. Through the windows, the late evening glow sent flickering shadows of orange light. Umber gazed at the light, sniffed and bellowed again. Suddenly struck, Crane leaped to the window.

Across the fields a solid mass of flame thrust high into the air, and within it was the fast-crumbling walls of the workshop. Silhouetted against the blaze, the figures of half a dozen men darted and ran.

"Good heavens!" Crane cried.

He shot out of the cottage and with Umber hard at his heels, sprinted toward the shed. As he ran he could see the graceful nose of the spaceship within the core of heat, still looking cool and untouched. If only he could reach it before the flames softened its metal and started the rivets.

The workmen trotted up to him, grimy and panting. Crane gaped at them in a mixture of fury and bewilderment.

"Hallmyer!" he shouted. "Hallmyer!"

Hallmyer pushed through the crowd. His eyes were wild and gleamed with triumph.

"Too bad," he said. "I'm sorry. Stephen—"

"You swine!" Crane shouted. "You frightened old man!" He grasped Hallmyer by the lapels and shook him just once. Then he dropped him and started into the shed.

Hallmyer cried something and an instant later a body hurtled against Crane's calves and spilled him to the ground. He lurched to his feet, fists swinging. Umber was alongside, growling over the roar of the flames. Crane smashed a man in the face, and saw him stagger back against a second. He lifted a knee in a vicious drive that sent the last man crumpling to the ground. Then he ducked his head and plunged into the shop.

The scorch felt cool at first, but when he reached the ladder and began mounting to the port, he screamed with the agony of his burns.

Umber was howling at the foot of the ladder, and Crane realized that the dog could never escape from the rocket blasts. He reached down and hauled Umber into the ship.

Crane was reeling as he closed and locked the port. He retained consciousness barely long enough to settle himself in the spring hammock. Then instinct alone prompted his hands to reach out toward the control board. Instinct and the frenzied refusal to let his beautiful ship waste itself in the flames. He would fail—yes. But he would fail, trying.

His fingers tripped the switches. The ship shuddered and roared. And blackness descended over him.

How long was he unconscious? There was no telling. Crane awoke with cold pressing against his face and body, and the sound of frightened yelps in his ears. Crane looked up and saw Umber tangled in the springs and straps of the hammock. His first impulse was to laugh; then suddenly he realized. He had looked *up!* He had looked up at the hammock.

He was lying curled in the cup of the quartz nose. The ship had risen high—perhaps almost to Roche's zone, to the limit of the Earth's gravitational attraction, but then without guiding hands at the controls to continue its flight, had turned and was dropping back toward Earth. Crane peered through the crystal and gasped.

Below him was the ball of the Earth. It looked three times the size of the Moon. And it was no longer his Earth. It was a globe of fire mottled with black clouds. At the northernmost pole there was a tiny patch of white, and even as Crane watched, it was suddenly blotted over with hazy tones of red, scarlet and crimson. Hallmyer had been right.

He lay frozen in the cup of the nose for hours as the ship descended, watching the flames gradually fade away to leave nothing but the dense blanket of black around the Earth. He lay numb with horror, unable to understand—unable to reckon up a billion people snuffed out, a green fair planet reduced to ashes and cinders. His family, home, friends, everything that was once dear and close to him—gone. He could not think of Evelyn.

Air, whistling outside awoke some instinct in him. The few shreds of reason left told him to go down with his ship and forget everything in the thunder and destruction, but the instinct of life forced him to his feet. He climbed up to the store chest and prepared for the landing. Parachute, a small oxygen tank—a knapsack of supplies. Only half aware of what he was doing he dressed for the descent, buckled on the 'chute and opened the port. Umber whined pathetically, and he took the heavy dog in his arms and stepped out into space.

But space hadn't been so clogged, the way it was now. Then it had been difficult to breathe. But that was because the air had been rare—not filled with dry clogging grit like now.

Every breath was a lungful of ground glass—or ashes—or cinders—

The pieces of memory sagged apart. Abruptly he was in the present again—a dense black present that hugged him with soft weight and made him fight for breath. Crane struggled in mad panic, and then relaxed.

It had happened before. A long time past he'd been buried deep under ashes when he'd stopped to remember. Weeks ago—or days—or months. Crane clawed with his hands, inching forward through the mound of cinders that the wind had thrown over him. Presently he emerged into the light again. The wind had died away. It was time to begin his crawl to the sea once more.

The vivid pictures of his memory scattered again before the grim vista that stretched out ahead. Crane scowled. He remembered too much, and too often. He had the vague hope that if he remembered hard enough, he might change one of the things he had done—just a very little thing—and then all this would become untrue. He thought: It might help if everyone remembered and wished at the same time—but there isn't any more everyone. I'm the only one. I'm the last memory on Earth. I'm the last life.

He crawled. Elbows, knee, elbows, knee—and then Hallmyer was crawling alongside and making a great game of it. He chortled and plunged in the cinders like a happy sea lion.

Crane said: "But why do we have to get to the sea?"

Hallmyer blew a spume of ashes.

"Ask her," he said, pointing to Crane's other side.

Evelyn was there, crawling seriously, intently; mimicking Crane's smallest action.

"It's because of our house," she said. "You remember our house, darling? High on the cliff. We were going to live there forever and ever, breathing the ozone and taking morning dips. I was there when you left. Now you're coming back to the house at the edge of the sea. Your beautiful flight is over, dear, and you're coming back to me. We'll live together, just we two, like Adam and Eve—"

Crane said: "That's nice."

Then Evelyn turned her head and screamed: "Oh, Stephen! Watch out!" and Crane felt the menace closing in on him again. Still crawling, he stared back at the vast grey plains of ash, and saw nothing. When he looked at Evelyn again he saw only his shadow, sharp and black. Presently, it, too, faded away as the marching shaft of sunlight passed.

But the dread remained. Evelyn had warned him twice, and she was always right. Crane stopped and turned, and settled himself to watch. If he was really being followed, he would see whatever it was, coming along his tracks.

There was a painful moment of lucidity. It cleaved through his fever and bewilderment, bringing with it the sharpness and strength of a knife.

I'm going mad, he thought. The corruption in my leg has spread to my brain. There is no Evelyn, no Hallmyer, no menace. In all this land there is no life but mine—and even ghosts and spirits of the underworld must have perished in the inferno that girdled the planet. No—there is nothing but me and my sickness. I'm dying—and when I perish, everything will perish. Only a mass of lifeless cinders will go on.

But there was a movement.

Instinct again. Crane dropped his head and played dead. Through slitted eyes he watched the ashen plains, wondering if death was playing tricks with his eyes. Another façade of rain was beating down toward him, and he hoped he could make sure before all vision was obliterated.

Yes. There.

A quarter mile back, a grey-brown shape was flitting along the grey surface. Despite the drone of the distant rain, Crane could hear the whisper of trodden cinders and see the little clouds kicking up. Stealthily he groped for the revolver in the knapsack as his mind reached feebly for explanations and recoiled from fear.

The thing approached, and suddenly Crane squinted and understood. He recalled Umber kicking with fear and springing away from him when the 'chute landed them on the ashen face of the Earth.

"Why it's Umber," he murmured. He raised himself. The dog halted. "Here boy!" Crane croaked gaily. "Here boy!"

He was overcome with joy. He realized that a miserable loneliness had hung over him, almost a horrible sensation of oneness in emptiness. Now his was not the only life. There was another. A friendly life that could offer love and companionship. Hope kindled again.

"Here boy!" he repeated. "Come on, boy—"

After a while he stopped trying to snap his fingers. The Great Dane hung back, showing fangs and a lolling tongue. The dog was emaciated to a skeleton and its eyes gleamed red and ugly in the dusk. As Crane called once more, mechanically, the dog snarled. Puffs of ash leaped beneath its nostrils.

He's hungry, Crane thought, that's all. He reached into the knapsack and at the gesture the dog snarled again. Crane withdrew the chocolate bar and laboriously peeled off the paper and silver foil. Weakly he tossed it toward Umber. It fell far short. After a minute of savage uncertainty, the dog advanced slowly and gobbled up the food. Ashes powdered its muzzle. It licked its chops ceaselessly and continued to advance on Crane.

Panic jerked within him. A voice persisted: This is no friend. He has no love or companionship for you. Love and companionship have vanished from the land along with life. Now there is nothing left but hunger.

"No—" Crane whispered. "That isn't right. We're the last of life on Earth. It isn't right that we should tear at each other and seek to devour—"

But Umber was advancing with a slinking sidle, and his teeth showed sharp and white. And even as Crane stared at him, the dog snarled and lunged.

Crane thrust up an arm under the dog's muzzle, but the weight of the charge carried him backward. He cried out in agony as his broken, swollen leg was struck by the weight of the dog. With his free right hand he struck weakly, again and again, scarcely feeling the grind of teeth gnawing his left arm. Then something metallic was pressed under him and he realized he was lying on the revolver he had let fall.

He groped for it and prayed the cinders had not clogged its mechanism. As Umber let go his arm and tore at his throat, Crane brought the gun up and jabbed the muzzle blindly against the dog's body. He pulled and pulled the trigger until the roars died away and only empty clicks sounded. Umber shuddered in the ashes before him, his body nearly shot in two. Thick scarlet stained the grey.

Evelyn and Hallmyer looked down sadly at the broken animal. Evelyn was crying, and Hallmyer reached nervous fingers through his hair in the same old gesture.

"This is the finish, Stephen," he said. "You've killed part of yourself. Oh—you'll go on living, but not all of you. You'd best bury that corpse, Stephen. It's the corpse of your soul."

"I can't," Crane said. "The wind will blow the ashes away."

"Then burn it—"

It seemed that they helped him thrust the dead dog into his knapsack. They helped him take off his clothes and pack them underneath. They cupped their hands around the matches until the cloth caught fire, and blew on the weak flame until it sputtered and burned limply. Crane crouched by the fire and nursed it until nothing was left but more grey ash. Then he turned and once again began crawling down the ocean bed. He was naked now. There was nothing left of what-had-been but his flickering little life.

He was too heavy with sorrow to notice the furious rain that slammed and buffeted him, or the searing pains that were shooting through his blackened leg and up his hip. He crawled. Elbows, knee, elbows, knee—woodenly, mechanically, apathetic to everything. To the latticed skies, the dreary ashen plains and even the dull glint of water that lay far ahead.

He knew it was the sea—what was left of the old, or a new one in the making. But it would be an empty, lifeless sea that some day would lap against a dry lifeless shore. This would be a planet of rock and stone, of metal and snow and ice and water, but that would be all. No more life. He, alone, was useless. He was Adam, but there was no Eve.

Evelyn waved gaily to him from the shore. She was standing alongside the white cottage with the wind snapping her dress to show the clean, slender lines of her figure. And when he came a little closer, she ran out to him and helped him. She said nothing—only placed her hands under his shoulders and helped him lift the weight of his heavy pain-ridden body. And so at last he reached the sea.

It was real. He understood that. For even after Evelyn and the cottage had vanished, he felt the cool waters bathe his face. Quietly—calmly—

Here's the sea, Crane thought, and here am I. Adam and no Eve. It's hopeless.

He rolled a little farther into the waters. They laved his torn body. Quietly—calmly—

He lay with face to the sky, peering at the high menacing heavens, and the bitterness within him welled up.

"It's not right!" he cried. "It's not right that all this should pass away. Life is too beautiful to perish at the mad act of one mad creature—"

Quietly the waters laved him. Quietly—calmly—

The sea rocked him gently, and even the agony that was reaching up toward his heart was no more than a gloved hand. Suddenly the skies split apart—for the first time in all those months—and Crane stared up at the stars.

Then he knew. This was not the end of life. There could never be an end to life. Within his body, within the rotting tissues that were rocking gently in the sea was the source of ten million-million lives. Cells—tissues—bacteria—endamœba—countless infinities of life that would take new root in the waters and live long after he was gone.

They would live on his rotting remains. They would feed on each other. They would adapt themselves to the new environment and feed on the minerals and sediments washed into this new sea. They would grow, burgeon, evolve. Life would reach out to the lands once more. It would begin again the same old re-repeated cycle that had begun perhaps with the rotting corpse of some last survivor of interstellar travel. It would happen over and over in the future ages.

And then he knew what had brought him back to the sea. There need be no Adam—no Eve. Only the sea, the great mother of life was needed. The sea had called him back to her depths that presently life might emerge once more, and he was content.

Quietly the waters rocked him. Quietly—calmly—the mother of life rocked the last-born of the old cycle who would become the firstborn of the new. And with glazing eyes Stephen Crane smiled up at the stars, stars that were sprinkled evenly across the sky. Stars that had not yet formed into the familiar constellations, nor would not for another hundred million centuries.

STORY SOURCES

The following gives the first publication details for each story and the sources used. They are listed in alphabetical order of author.

"The Man Who Hated Flies" by J. D. Beresford, first published in *The Meeting Place and Other Stories* (London: Faber & Faber, 1929). Passed into the public domain in 1998.

"Adam and No Eve" by Alfred Bester, first published in *Astounding Science Fiction*, September 1941 and first collected in *Starburst* (New York: New American Library, 1958).

"Survey Team" by Philip K. Dick, first published in *Fantastic Universe*, May 1954 and collected in *Second Variety* (Columbia, PA: Underwood-Miller, 1987).

"Shadow of Wings" by Elizabeth Sanxay Holding, first published in *Magazine of Fantasy & Science Fiction*, July 1954.

"The Man Who Awoke" by Laurence Manning, first published in *Wonder Stories*, March 1933 and collected in *The Man Who Awoke* (New York: Ballantine Books, 1975).

"Hunter, Come Home" by Richard McKenna, first published in *Magazine of Fantasy & Science Fiction*, March 1963 and collected in *Casey Agonistes* (New York: Harper & Row, 1973).

"The Sterile Planet" by Nathan Schachner, first published in *Astounding Stories*, July 1937.

"A Matter of Protocol" by Jack Sharkey, first published in *Galaxy Magazine*, August 1962.

"Drop Dead" by Clifford D. Simak, first published in *Galaxy Science Fiction*, July 1956 and collected in *All the Traps of Earth* (New York: Doubleday, 1962).

"The Gardener" by Margaret St Clair, first published in *Thrilling Wonder Stories*, October 1949 and collected in *The Best of Margaret St Clair* (Chicago: Academy Chicago, 1985).

"The Dust of Death" by Fred M. White, first published in *Pearson's Magazine*, April 1903. Passed into the public domain in 2006.

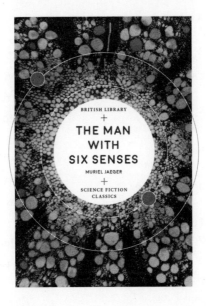

BRITISH LIBRARY SCIENCE FICTION CLASSICS

SHORT STORY ANTHOLOGIES
EDITED BY MIKE ASHLEY

Nature's Warnings
Classic Stories of Eco-Science Fiction

Lost Mars
The Golden Age of the Red Planet

Moonrise
The Golden Age of Lunar Adventures

Menace of the Machine
The Rise of AI in Classic Science Fiction

The End of the World and Other Catastrophes

Menace of the Monster
Classic Tales of Creatures from Beyond

Beyond Time
Classic Tales of Time Unwound

Born of the Sun
Adventures in Our Solar System

CLASSIC SCIENCE FICTION NOVELS

By William F. Temple

Shoot at the Moon

Four-Sided Triangle

By Charles Eric Maine

The Tide Went Out

The Darkest of Nights

By Ian Macpherson

Wild Harbour

By Muriel Jaeger

The Question Mark

The Man with Six Senses

We welcome any suggestions, corrections or feedback you may have, and will aim to respond to all items addressed to the following:

The Editor (Science Fiction Classics)
British Library Publishing
The British Library
96 Euston Road
London, NW1 2DB

We also welcome enquiries through our Twitter account, @BL_Publishing